Published by Cybermouse MultiMedia Ltd, 2013.
101 Cross Lane
Sheffield S10 1WN
Email: cybermousemm@gmail.com

All rights reserved. No part of this work may be reproduced or stored in an Information Retrieval System (other than for the purposes of review) without the express permission of the Publisher in writing.

1st. Edition November 2013

© copyright 2013 Ruth Valentine

The right of Ruth Valentine to be identified as the Author of this work has been asserted in accordance with the Copyright Designs and Patents Act 1988.

Cover Design by W. E. Allerton

© copyright 2013 Cybermouse MultiMedia Ltd.

THE JEWELLER'S SKIN

Ruth Valentine

*In memory of Catherine Müller, 1881 – 1918
and her daughter, Katherina, 1906 - ?
whose story this might have been, but wasn't*

Prologue

1915

Prologue - 1915

She woke with the sound of someone whimpering. The words like most English words were shapeless to her, like the gurgle of pigeons outside in the trees; then *No,* she heard, a complaining tone, *No John.* In the darkened ward it could be any of them, the voice transformed: perhaps the woman with the withered arm, or the girl who fought with the nurses. She could see nothing: or nothing beyond the grey blanket over her, which around her feet merged into the darkness.

There was some creaking, too: a bed perhaps? But the sound was wood, a bedside locker maybe, the door swinging on its hinges. Carefully Narcisa sat up in bed, not wanting to add to the betraying sounds for anyone else who was lying there awake. *No,* the voice whimpered, *No, it's not my fault.*

The air was cold: the stove would have gone out. There was the faint smell of damp coal, or ashes perhaps; and then another smell she breathed in, testing, a peppery, sour smell that after a while she realised was the odour of all their bodies, sleeping, sweating, days since the weekly bath. It came to her as if she could see them all, naked, with flesh in folds, or else thin across the ribs, their armpits and crotches and hair all giving off odours, their indecent closeness inescapable even in sleep.

She got down from the high bed slowly, her feet chilled,

and pulled the sleeves of her nightdress down over her hands. The blanket was scratchy but warm against her palms, the metal bed-frame icy. Her feet seemed to spread on the linoleum, seemed to stick to it, resisting moving on. At the end of the bed she paused, uncertain.

The ward was outlining itself in the dark around her. A foot stuck out beyond a tall white bedframe, as pale as bone, the toes half bent together. Something, perhaps a shift or a pair of drawers, had slipped off a chair and lay bunched on the floor.

She let go of her bedstead and walked on down the ward. By one bed there was the meaty smell of blood. Once she thought a woman might be awake, lying straight on her back with her hands outside the bedclothes; but there was no sign of attention as she passed. At the bend in the L-shaped room she stopped sharply: what if someone else was up beyond that corner? Her back felt cold under the flannel nightdress. She listened: nothing. And past the corner everything looked the same; she could have been entering her part of the ward again, with the lines of bedsteads, the grey blankets pulled up.

It seemed a long time before she reached the door. Where was it that the night attendant slept? She stopped herself reaching out for the china door-knob. Was it this end bed? She peered; but there was nothing to distinguish the grey mound, the sheet pulled up away from the foot of the bed, the hair blurred colourless against the pillow.

The door-knob was round and cold, and stiff to turn. She moved it slowly, slowly, hearing the quiet click, pulling the weight of the wooden door towards her. A half-light entered, a widening geometric shape that showed the linoleum as a dull blue-grey. *What..* a voice said from sleep and gave in again.

She slipped out through the gap and pulled the door closed again behind her.

Prologue - 1915

It was the long curve of the corridor. She had forgotten where the door would take her, the night world of the ward was so compelling, the sense of strangeness and risk filling each moment. Only two or three of the lights were on, the other brackets dull like broken branches. The opposite wall was blank, no doors, no windows, just the bulge towards her of the dado-rail and the brown wallpaper below it. On her side, on either side of her were doors, exactly like the one she was leaning against, panelled, with white china handles and finger-plates. And behind each of those doors there is a ward, with white bedframes lined up, and grey blankets; and upstairs above us exactly the same again; and beyond that door at the end of the corridor the men's wards, their different smells, what they say in their sleep.

Someone will come. I'll be punished in the morning.

She walked barefoot down the centre of the corridor, her hands stretched out a little towards the walls, till she came to an outside door, which was swaying, open.

The Jeweller's Skin

Part 1

1946

Part 1 - 1946

The men were carrying wire netting out to a van. Narcisa, on her way to the stores, rested the flour-bin on a brick ledge to watch them. The head gardener was there, and Wilf, the boy who'd recently come to help him: a heavy blond lad, clumsy in his walk, good-tempered. Then Colin the maintenance man with one of the porters. They manoeuvred the netting in its rusty frame down the path to the van. Colin saw her and nodded, one hand high on the frame, which seemed to have been cut through, sawn jaggedly across, the netting like blackened crochet fraying open: to make it moveable, she supposed. The men pushed the netting into the back of the van and rubbed their hands.

It must be the exercise yard they were taking down. The exercise yard will have to go, of course, one of the doctors had said. Of course. One evening years back there had been a ward sister, some gangling Scottish woman with a cross round her neck, explaining how humane it was, the courtyard with the high netting, back behind the workshop where it got hardly any sun: 'Otherwise their health would deteriorate, you know.' Why tell me? Narcisa had wondered, saying nothing. Not that the sister would have expected her to answer. Second cook, she must have been at that time; and known presumably for not talking. 'Let her alone,' she'd heard the cook, Mrs Olby, saying once. 'Nora Humphreys is all right, she's just not a talker.' By then she was almost used to being Nora.

She hefted the flour-bin onto her hip and entered the store-room. The air was mild and smelled slightly of grain. She opened the mouth of the sack in the corner, and began scooping out flour into the crock. The sack was almost empty, its depths tawny brown in the half-light. She leaned forward and scooped, stood to fill up the bin, enjoying the strong movement; like a farmer, she thought, like someone scything. It wasn't only the yard they were taking down; last week they had sawn away the bars on the ward windows. Well, they must think it's going to make a difference. She locked the store-room behind her. The late autumn sun was warm on the side of her face, the few steps till she was back in her kitchen. Doing the place up was a good thing. They were talking about painting the walls some pale colour, cream or light green, eau-de-nil someone said. So much paint! Just the long semi-circular corridor would need how many gallons? and several coats to cover the dark green. And then all the wards, the dining-rooms. Not that they'd notice, most of them: not the real patients. The others, the bombed-out civilians, still seemed to her intruders in the asylum, though they had been coming and going for six years, since almost the beginning of the war.

Not everyone felt as she did. She stopped again, though the van had gone, to feel the sun on her face, and rest the heavy earthenware crock on the ledge; after all the stew was on, she had a moment. Most of the staff, she knew, welcomed the sane ones, found them a relief; even though some had terrible injuries. 'You know how to get on with them,' that's what a porter had said. 'They don't scream and holler and tear off their clothes.'

She went in and closed the kitchen door behind her. Something was wrong, she felt at once. The thick mutton-stew steam hid what it was. 'June,' she called sharply, the girl thinned out and blurred in the fatty mist. 'What has happened?' They hated that she always knew, these young girls. They had left home and still there was someone who knew. Only she understood it was the best way to train them. 'You must not try to hide your mistakes,' she told them.

June, she found, stepping firmly into the steam so that after a moment it was no longer there, was at the sink, potatoes falling apart in the great colander. Narcisa took the handles and shook it hard. Another chunk of potato fell open; cloudy water dripped into the sink.

'What are you going to do?' she asked the girl.

'Mash?' The voice emerged high, upset rather than sullen.

Narcisa looked at the clock. 'Get the working patients to help. You know what to do?'

The girl set the colander on the side, and bent to the drawer to find a potato-ricer. Narcisa lifted the abandoned flour-bin onto its shelf. She never asked, she couldn't bring herself to ask, What were you doing? What were you thinking of? She'd had enough of that, in the past; it did no good. It made you resentful; made you not care. But these girls were used to being asked and so they told her, unnerved probably, feeling blamed by her silence. She knew they were always nervous of her. The only way.

June Ragless was not a bad girl. She wanted to learn, Narcisa thought; she minded that the food should be good enough, even for those poor things who scarcely noticed. June rammed the ricer down into the pan, and muttered, 'Sorry, Cook,' not looking at her. Hoping, Narcisa thought, I'll say it doesn't matter; but it does matter. 'I was cutting the beans.'

You were thinking about your young man, Narcisa thought. It was like that in the hospital; everyone knew. She couldn't have said how: June herself had never confided in her. June's young man, Donald, she thought he was called, had been working down here at something, the last year or so of the war. But why wasn't he fighting? What was wrong with him? He had gone back north, to Liverpool or Manchester. That was what happened with men. They were here, the sun shone or it snowed, something definite; and then they went, like a counter moved on a backgammon board, lifted and slapped down by some impervious hand, the army, the company; and never came back. Surely little June Ragless was too clever a one for that? Not one to stay moping about the kitchen, letting the potatoes disintegrate, the bread burn. That was what she quite liked in the girl: not a fool.

She lifted the lid off the stew and poked a piece of meat with a thin knife. Twenty minutes or so; she looked up at the clock. June was at the sink, with the second pan of potatoes. 'You have twenty minutes,' Narcisa said. June tipped the pan and steam rose through the kitchen.

*

In the evening she sat at the scrubbed-down table with her account books. The girls had gone. The smells of scouring-powder and cake and mutton stew had settled back into the heavy air. Narcisa raised her head briefly and sniffed. The kitchens had been built with not enough windows: just three, rather high, at either end, giving onto two of the closed-in courtyards. The smells never completely dissipated; as if they were stored on the high shelves, ready to be taken down next time they were needed. Sometimes at night she smelt them in her hair; she would be lying on one side, about to go to sleep, and smell greens or fried fish faintly on her pillow.

She opened the butcher's book. The meat he sent her was getting worse. The last order of bacon had been rank; she'd sent it back and he'd said there was no more, so she'd had to change the menu and give them gammon, eking it out, because in truth there wasn't enough. She must speak to Hartley the butcher yet again. An unpleasant man: he sneered at her accent. He stood, fat and blond, in his shop and looked at her, as if he knew something nasty from her past. Well, she thought, writing *Returned unfit* against bacon on the invoice, and folding it into the butcher's book; I've done it before. 'I can go to Gaffney's in Raynes Park,' she'd said, in the shop in front of his customers. 'They provide already for several hospitals.'

Perhaps soon she would get better vegetables again. It was true that the diet was not good enough. It had never been very good; she had no illusions. Coming back here, eleven years ago now, she'd been appalled. She had got used to a certain style of life. The food, anyway. With fruit: greengages and raspberries and plums from the garden; lots of eggs and cream. Working in a private house you could make good things. She added the butcher's account, leaving out the bacon. It was possible they had been late in paying him; that might be it. She would ask the accountant before she went to see him.

She sat back and stretched her arms above her head. Lately her back seemed to ache more often. It was standing; but her whole job was standing. She looked over at the cook in the picture tiles, next to the saucepans. A young woman, twenty years old perhaps, rolling out pastry. Not a real cook, she thought, as she always did. The hands on the rolling-pin were soft and flaccid; there was no effort in the arms or the thin shoulders. Behind this fake cook was a Welsh dresser with flowered plates; another young woman, with no cap on her dark hair, was carrying a pie straight from the oven. Narcisa stood up and looked for a cleaning-cloth, and wiped the sheen of grease off the tile picture. The colours shone; the late sun from the far window struck across them. Cobalt blue for the girls' uniforms, with white aprons; a rich dark green for the wall beside the dresser. He couldn't draw pastry though, she thought. The dough looked puffy; more like unironed muslin.

She turned to the greengrocer's book and began adding. It would be good to have more from the hospital farm again. She had never understood why so much had gone: the eggs she supposed sent off to make egg powder; and then the staffing, the farm workers called up, and fewer male patients to be working with them. Will they start that again? A lot of the men had liked farm work; it was outside, physical but not too exhausting; and probably the farm hands were kind to them. She remembered the men going out to the milking shed; and before that, years back, gangs of men in asylum uniform, being led out single file to the kitchen garden. The men at least were allowed to work outside.

I must have seen that out of the window some time.

The music pulled at her feet like flat waves. Narcisa almost looked down; as if a line of white foam might lap from under the row of wicker chairs, move forward up the nave of the little church. Insistent waves, demanding her attention. But there in her mind was the hospital; the new approach, all the changes they wanted, right down to her kitchen. And here at the concert there was Anthony Shearer, his flecked tweed sleeve all but touching her right arm. At the front of the church a shiny grand piano, a tall hunched woman. Stop fussing, she told herself, and closed her eyes.

The wave needed all its strength to lift, even so far. It fell, discouraged; began again. No longer pulling, she thought; had its own concerns. The piano testing itself, such concentration.

Her father, standing at the workbench, looking down. He turns a wheel, and gold is drawn through a steel plate to become wire; a fine line of light, stretched out from the plate and wound onto a drum. The ratchety sound of the wheel in the usual quiet.

The piano took up the gold wire and made it heavy. The music was bound round her in heavy loops. She held her breath. The music made her sit still; bound down her arms. For a moment she saw a canvas straitjacket, the flat tapes tied round and round; but no, it was wire.

It fell away from her body, the circles softening, the loops of gold light piling on the floor.

Leave me alone! she felt as it started again. She opened her eyes; Anthony Shearer's tweed arm was trembling to the rhythm. A navy-blue feather on a hat kept quivering. They'll let me out; who was it used to say that?

Clara. It was Clara, very thin, tubercular they found out later, in the shapeless blue asylum uniform, speaking slowly so Narcisa would understand. A high cracking voice, determined. Narcisa had never seen hair so fragile. 'They'll let me out, I swear it, they will have to.' In the ironing-room; steam from the sheets rising up to her pale face. So Clara coughed; laughed; put out a hand and stroked Narcisa's arm.

The piano had stopped. Someone murmured; the navy-blue feather leaned delicately to one side. Anthony Shearer turned and smiled at her. He thinks I'm not used to going to concerts. She nodded to him, and closed her eyes again.

But starting up the piano was now cheerful. This is not right! she thought, suddenly angered. Is this war-music? She had had enough forever of brass bands. Good for morale, one of the doctors had told her. She waited impatiently for the gold chains to return. Was that what he thought, the engineer Anthony Shearer: good for morale? They had not had a discussion about the war. For her it was young men crying on the wards; pamphlets instructing her on savings in the kitchen, when already she cooked on next to nothing. As for what happened beyond the hospital, beyond the English coast (she had seen it, arriving the first time on a ship at Dover) she knew nothing.

And yet she did know; she couldn't block out the chatter in the kitchen. 'All them against us, Italians, and everyone.' The grocery man, delivering his rant to her turned back. She was beating her pudding mixture with a long wooden spoon. Am I one of *us*, then?

Oh but this is too clever, she said, her eyes now open. The woman leaned jealously over the keyboard - pounced. Crash! The chord juddered through Narcisa. Such speed; she felt it rock her like anger. This woman wants to make us forget the opening. Narcisa tried to recall what that phrase was, the gold wire dropping in loops around her ankles. There was too much now, the jolting chords and the predatory runs. Her hands remembered that rush down the keyboard: glissando. You can't look back after all, she thought. Though once during the war Clara did come down, with her two grown children; the older boy a bit fat, taller than Clara. Who was still thin, with lines around her mouth. They had tea in the Copper Kettle. You can't look back. There was a pause - the woman's hands hovering - and please, Narcisa was saying to her, again.

What returns is never good enough, she thought, and moved dismissively on the wicker chair. The church was cold; she felt the draught on her ankles. The woman bent forward and let the music fall.

*

'Remarkable,' Anthony Shearer was saying, as they moved slowly between the rows of chairs, Narcisa pulling on her knitted gloves. Now he would want to talk about the music. A mistake to come to a concert with anyone. She had been to hopeful recitals in small-town theatres, and slipped out at the end, a small middle-aged woman in dull clothes, invisible. What was it people said to each other about music? They were all talking, the couples and the few old men and old women, shuffling out of the church; they were all saying something. Let him talk, she reassured herself; I can just listen. Or not listen; I know how to do that.

At the back of the church he bent towards her: 'Come and look at the font.' His hand rested briefly on her shoulder-blade, through the wool coat. The stone, he was saying. She stood docilely while Anthony Shearer the engineer crouched down, smoothing the worn carved figures with the flat of his hand.

'Well, Cook!' A young man's confident voice, blaring. The last people leaving the church turned round to look. 'How extraordinary to find you here!' It was the young bald doctor, Mr New Approach, in a good black winter coat, a girl with a pillbox hat smiling behind him.

Narcisa stood still.

'Mrs Humphreys,' she heard Anthony Shearer say with precision, 'might find it equally extraordinary to find you at a concert, Doctor.'

She watched the young man flush, laugh, point at the font. 'Wasn't it lovely?' the girlfriend said to Narcisa, peace-making. 'So intense.'

The three of them seemed to expect her to do something. The vicar strode cheerfully down the aisle towards them.

Narcisa walked past him into the air. She had almost forgotten it was afternoon. The tree at the gate was covered in red berries; down at her feet there were crab-apples, turning brown. They could be making crab-apple jelly, she thought.

*

Why did I do that? she asked herself ten minutes later, walking down the High Street. Anthony Shearer had invited her, and paid for the concert tickets. Didn't that mean some kind of obligation? I don't know how these things are handled, she thought; then shook herself, really shook her head so the blue hat almost came off. That's not the point.

She stood looking in at the chemist's window with the blue and red jars. Have I become that sort of person? Meaning: rude to people, ungracious. Perhaps I have.

She walked on, faster, past the Post Office and the George, where the month before Anthony Shearer had calmly escorted - that was the word, escorted her up to his room. That wouldn't happen again. She wondered if he had booked in at the George this time. Probably he had imagined taking her there, after the concert, or after dinner, perhaps. But he was the ill-mannered one, she thought, angry, hands in her coat pockets, waiting to cross the High Street. I have to work with Doctor What's-his-name; he doesn't.

Was that what men expected, she wondered later, sitting on her bed, a cup of tea warming both hands. To speak for you? Edwin had had to; she didn't speak any English. She could remember her mother-in-law's drawing-room; Edwin, careful as ever, sitting forward on the dark chintz chesterfield, explaining; first to his mother, then in French back to her. If she remembered him ever, that was what he was doing: explaining. How exhausting for him, she thought for the first time. What was he, twenty-four? Hard for a young man.

Still, there was no need of that with Anthony Shearer. Oh, men, she thought, like the women she worked with in the kitchen, like half the women she'd got to know here; oh, men. Which meant, she now realised, you have to forgive them.

But why? She put the cup and saucer down. It was dark already; an edge of cloud seemed to flap across the crescent moon. Because of what we did in bed together? Then it can't be worth it. She picked up her hairbrush and brushed hard at her hair, wishing it was long again so she could fight it, pulling out the tangles.

She was restless; she wanted to be moving. It was dark but

not late: six? And no more blackout. She took down her coat again, tugged it on as she closed the door to her room. The gate-porter would wonder what she was doing. Tomorrow it would be all through the hospital: Mrs Humphreys came back and went straight out again.

She took her bicycle out of the shed and checked the tyres. A few years back she'd have had to get permission. She rode slowly along the gravel paths, her front light flickering over a pruned rosebush, the bole of a tree. Already the motion was starting to pacify her. She rang her bell and the gate-porter opened: 'Off out again, Mrs H?' She rode into the lane.

This is who I am, she thought, feeling the damp air on her neck and cheek, the strength of her thighs as she pedalled up the slight slope. The poplars behind the hospital fence rustled. The phrase from the piano sonata came back to her, the gold chains loosening. If I'd been on my own I'd have remembered it sooner.

She rode down the alleys, past the backs of houses. A woman was unpegging pillow-slips from a line, her hands and the linen blue-white in the dark. A small dog yapped at her wheels as they clicked past him. There was a smell still lingering of Sunday dinners.

She remembered, abruptly, his hand on her hip, pressing. She had come back into town; she passed a pub where the lights were coming on. It must be nearly seven: opening time. A young woman, hugged close to her young man, turned to wave to her as she crossed the street.

Opposite the George Narcisa got off her bike, and stood wiping her face with her handkerchief. Her legs throbbed a little; not so young. She got her breath, felt the sweat on her back quickly cooling. Do I want to do this? Then she called to a child, and gave him a shilling to go in.

The train drew into a station: Ewell West. The young woman opposite Anthony stood up, fastened her cloak over her nurse's uniform. Already other people were in the corridor, waiting to come in. A tired-looking couple sat down, on either side of the door, a little boy babbling, letting himself sway between them. 'Sit down nicely, now, David,' the woman said.

Anthony looked out at the dark back gardens. What an extraordinary woman Nora was! But that was what the young doctor had said, that had made him so angry. *Cook* indeed! in a church full of Surrey house-owners: *cook!* As if she slaved for him in his own kitchen. So he had surprised himself, speaking out like that; and Nora had gone, had simply walked out of the church, to the town centre, and caught a bus back to the asylum. Not, as she'd told it, having a tantrum; not, he was quite sure, teasing him to run after; but because they were all there *expecting her to do something*. That was as far as he'd got her to explain. He had insisted, sitting in the rather worn lounge of the George; and Nora had shaken her head and said nothing, and kept on looking to see that her bicycle hadn't been stolen; and said in the end, 'You all expected me to do something.'

Another station; the whistle, the wave to the driver. The

little boy had fallen asleep against his mother, who leaned forward, hands held out in front of her, looking down, while the man was speaking. A striking woman: poor, obviously; tall, with thin arms, a rather old-fashioned hairstyle, all swept up; an interesting woman. But the astonishing thing, Anthony went on telling himself, was that Nora Humphreys had come back again. She had cycled in the dark back into town, and like some tragic Victorian heroine, someone in Wilkie Collins, or Conan Doyle even, she had bribed a child to come inside and find him. There *was* something Victorian about her; the stilted speech, some accent he'd never placed; and something that might have been a sense of duty, knowing her place, almost. And yet: he remembered vividly the other time, her naked body bearing down on him, sturdy, her skin-tone sepia in the darkened room. I might have been shaving, he thought, ridiculously. I might have gone out to meet someone. What had she wanted, coming back to him? It was flattering, he had to admit that, an attractive woman taking some kind of risk. It was a risk, certainly, even after the mad freedoms of wartime; to get a reputation, for a woman. More so, no doubt, in that shut-away institution. And she wasn't young.

So I'm flattered, he acknowledged. It was Wimbledon station; the family got out, the child carried sleeping against his father's shoulder. There seemed to be many people on the platform, but for some reason none came in to join him. He stretched his long legs and yawned. He was tired, a little; he'd worked a long day at the hospital; it was satisfying.

What had she wanted? Was it just to make peace? She was a fair-minded woman, he could see that: she wouldn't want to leave him confused over what had happened. But for that, a letter would do, surely? It was difficult for women, he thought: for an independent woman like Nora Humphreys.

For most women, his wife Mina for instance, it was not an issue. But for someone like Nora, with her professional correctness, her silence, her attractive foreign determination; she couldn't say, could she? if what she wanted was to make love again. A man could; he could say I had to come back to you, and the woman, Nora for instance, would understand.

Coming through Battersea, he closed his eyes, and imagined her in his room at the George, standing in her unfashionable light-blue hat and her plain coat, hands in her pockets, saying: Anthony, I had to come back to you. This is self-delusion, old man, he told himself, and smiled. He had not, this time, taken her to his room. They had sat as if they were visiting some respectable aunt, on flowery chairs set at right-angles, in the lounge. He had ordered tea, and watched her tasting - a professional, testing, almost - the hotel scones.

He could see the river: the Tate, that pretentious sugar-cube; then Millbank, the Houses of Parliament. The train slowed down behind St Thomas's, stopped. Was I kind enough to her? He was moved now: she had taken this risk, she had come out to find him. He wished he had hugged her - that at least; but even for that they would have had to go up to his room. In a small town. I did apologise about the doctor. But that wasn't enough; he was sure it wasn't enough. Next time I'm down there. There was nothing planned, so far; but no doubt the hospital would summon him soon. That's the nature of these affairs, he told himself: you have to be patient. He wished she had taken off the light-blue hat.

The train shuddered forwards again towards Waterloo. Anthony Shearer pulled down his suitcase from the rack. It was five to seven. Half an hour on the underground to Hendon; ten minutes' walk up the hill, and he'd be home. A pity the boys were away at school; he missed them. Mina would be in the drawing-room, probably sewing. And Renée was staying, Mina's elder sister, whose husband had died early on in the war; the two of them would be chatting away.

He swung down with his suitcase onto the platform, a tall man, rather thin, almost no grey in his toffee-brown hair.

The records were in a terrible state. That was what Howard Rathfelders saw, coming back to the asylum from the war, promoted from Assistant Clerk to Clerk, because Hume his irascible boss had been killed in action. Hume would have raged, seeing the gaps in the ledgers, the papers falling out of manila files. Hume would have stood still, hands in his pockets, the greying stubble sinister on his jaw, and defeated Howard with his sarcasm. 'Who did you think would sort this out? Stafford Cripps?'

Failing Cripps, Howard himself arrived at eight in the morning and left at seven, updating the patient records, locating minutes and pasting them into books, subtracting figures for bank reconciliations. 'You can't do everything,' his sister Lilian said, and he knew she meant: I miss you here at home. Somewhat nervously, he approached the Medical Superintendent, Dr Bosanquet; who glanced down casually at the black leather glove pinned over the blunt end of Howard's left arm, and said, 'Of course, of course, quite understand.' The result, the next Monday, was a Miss Carrington, pale and round-shouldered, as disappointing to Howard's suppressed sadness as he no doubt was to her, being both Jewish and maimed. For the first time he felt old Hume stir in him, the sarcasm that came he saw from humiliation. Fearing that impulse, he scarcely spoke to her. One day he saw her hurrying up the drive, a leather music case in her left hand. 'You play?' he asked awkwardly, as she took off her coat. She turned away from him to hang it up. 'Oh no,' she said, into the laden hat-stand. 'No, I sing. You know, in a choir.'

He remembered the madrigal group he'd joined at college, the strange lamenting harmonies of Dowland. 'What are you working on now?' he asked. But it was Mendelssohn: *Elijah*, of course, the stalwart of dull provincial churches. After that he imagined her in a white surplice; and once, in his startling dream, she took it off, and showed him unsuspectedly full breasts, with large dark nipples. He realised he scarcely heard her speak. Between them, without conversation, they filed and wrote in copperplate and added, and something a little like order crept back in; and in Libya the remains of his left hand, already fleshless in the heat, sank further under the dune and into fragments.

He was cold this morning, lingering in his hat and coat; thoroughly chilled by the long walk from the station. Before the war he had cycled every day, from Lilian's house in Kew and back again, an exertion that cleared his head and carried him through the heaviness of the asylum. Cycling was one more thing that was lost to him. He had tried, once, on the towpath by Kew Gardens, and nearly fell straight into the Thames, with neither grip nor balance. So he read the *News Chronicle* on the train, and walked through the back alleys of the town, to the wind off the fields and lawns of the asylum. It was cold; and he was worried about Lilian, whose husband Gibb was still fighting, stuck out in Burma, where the war wasn't over.

Miss Carrington had arrived before him, and opened the post. Howard warmed his hand on the radiator, then sighed and came to sit at his oak desk. Here were bills, a circular from the London County Council, instructions for transferring the war patients; and one of the small blue envelopes, hand-written, that would be a plea from some mother or brother for the discharge of an asylum patient.

Send them all out, he thought, nihilistic this morning. Why not? Why has Miss Carrington given me this to deal with?

Attached to the slit envelope with a paper-clip was a note in her small meticulous writing: *Are we permitted to release this information? MC.*

He held down the envelope with the weight of his arm, and took out the folded letter.

Dear Sir
I should be very grateful if you could assist me. My mother was a patient at Holywell in 1916..

Dear God, he thought, what happens to families? Thirty years. Didn't anyone keep in touch?

He stood up and went to the Admissions Registers. It took some time, working back from 1916, before he found the name given in the letter. Admitted just before the First World War. A small fear turned in his stomach, that the woman would still be here, on a back ward, aged and madder no doubt than the day she came in. His finger moved slowly across the line; but no, the final column was filled, in red ink: *Discharged cured, 7 April 1919.*

Cured, he thought. What optimists they were.

Not going to be much use to the letter-writer.

At lunch-time his assistant stood before his desk. He set himself once again to observe her voice, to find the tone or breadth it might have in her singing.

'Yes, Miss Carrington?' he asked, quite gently.

She was holding the letter.

'Is there something not clear in my note?' he asked.

It took her a long time to speak to him.

'No, Mr Rathfelders.' She never managed to say his name fluently. 'It's just that the person, the patient, is still here.'

He felt his impatience bubble. 'The register..'

'Yes, Mr Rathfelders, I know, I don't mean that. The patient, the former patient; well, at least there's someone of that name.'

When she had gone he tidied up his papers and walked briskly along the chilly corridors to the staff dining-room. Dr Bosanquet was already at the table, tucking in with enthusiasm to shepherd's pie and greens.

Well, I have to eat, Howard told himself, and sat down. Almost at once the plate was in front of him. He knew Bosanquet would watch how he ate with one hand.

At least today I have something to distract him.

Part 1 – 1946

The sun rose beyond the creosoted perimeter fence. The line of poplars that sheltered the female wing from the lane - or perhaps it was the other way - was shining, sun fractured through the small leaves and orderly branches. A squirrel ran head-first down the trunk of a horse-chestnut, and stopped alertly by the rose-border.

In E Ward, the nearest to the Medical Superintendent's house, Herbert Jennings tried not to be awake. His right hip was aching. He turned carefully onto his left side, hoping to rest it. But the mattress was terrible; he'd had no idea hospital beds would be so poor. The image came back, the same as every morning: waking in their big front bedroom in Haggerston, the daylight in slivers beside the curtains, Evie curled on her side in a pink nightgown. He put his hand flat on his hip-bone to draw the pain. The house was gone, the bed, the bedlinen - he didn't want to go over that list any more. And I'm stuck out here in the country with the loonies. At the far end of the ward somebody muttered gloomily in his sleep.

Kitty Bosanquet, the wife of the Medical Superintendent, sat in the drawing-room with a cup of tea. She preferred to be out of the way when her husband got up. Not that he was ill-tempered in the morning. Mrs Stewart had confided once that

Dr Stewart shouted at her in the mornings, which James would never do. Simply he needed his routine, his shaving water the right temperature, his breathing exercises at the window. She quite understood, with all his responsibilities, the massed grey-brick buildings of the hospital, all the people in it, that he needed to start the day with a routine. Only she could no longer bear to watch his thickened back in the blue pyjamas, as he stood at the open window and flung out his arms. She came down and made herself tea; got out of the way of the maid, Turner, a fat rather surly girl, and sat on the chesterfield. The white roses on the mantelpiece were starting to fall. She should ask James how he had enjoyed the concert. A pity she'd missed it; she would like some music. She looked out across the lawn where the grass was brightening, towards the men's wards with their dark windows.

In 12, the Women's Acute ward, Mary Godley sat crouched up on her pillow. The curtain edges were red like diluted blood. All the poor fools in the ward were still asleep, more than one of them snoring. They had no idea how important this time was. Time was what mattered. She no longer had a wrist-watch - it must have been stolen - but she always knew exactly what the time was. Now, with the curtains red, it was nearly six. Soon the nurses would come to wake them. The rest of them will complain or plead or pretend to be unwell, but not me. I know what I will have to do today. I will say nothing; if I say nothing, they cannot do anything. I have had that happen, being taken by surprise; I've learned my lesson.

In the milking-shed Alun Harris was half-way down the row already. The whitening sunlight poured in through the end door, and gleamed on the aisle which was already sleek with muck. The ten cows in their stalls stood beyond the slice of light. One near the door lifted her tail and pissed loudly. Alun stood and patted his current cow on her brown-and-white flank, then manoeuvred the full bucket out of the way of her hooves. She could be vindictive, this one. He lifted the bucket high and let the milk pour fast, foaming, into the churn. For a moment the smell of warm milk was stronger in his nostrils than the smells of cow-skin and dung and urine; then they blended again. He moved to sit by the old Friesian.

Noise spread from the farmyard up to the hospital buildings. Doors opened, curtains were swished back, water poured. The day gate-porter took over from the night gate-porter, talking about the film he'd seen last night. Win Dewhurst, who had overslept, ran downstairs to the laundry with her face unwashed. The skin on her cheeks felt thick as she crossed the yard. In one of the back wards a woman began to shout, short bursts like a dog yelping, on one note over and over. Nurses came and went in the long semi-circular corridor that linked the wards.

The hospital, cramped and neglected throughout the war, was starting up. The last of the civilian casualties - Herbert Jennings and a dozen others, slow-healing, recalcitrant - were to be transferred. The mentally ill would return. Those who all through the war had escaped diagnosis in the new sharp light were seen clearly again, their depression a silence amongst the festivities, the voices only they heard shouted down.

The wards were filling. The farm, all clanking and calling, was buying in livestock. The upholstery, the grocer's, the metalwork shop were staffed again.

In the locked wards and the open ones, in the needleroom and the greenhouses and the chapel, in the nurses' block and the offices, the long-past patients and their dead attendants watched as the routines settled back again. On the lawn near the mortuary George Thomas Hine, stout in his late Victorian hat and greatcoat, checked off the grey-brick buildings against his drawing. Of course they had lasted: this was his sixth asylum.

In the kitchen Narcisa watched porridge thicken in huge pans, air belching up through the surface like a geyser; boiling water being poured into gallon tea-pots; bread being cut; crimson jam being spooned onto flat dishes. For a moment there was a quite different taste in her mouth: apple. A long time since she'd had any such thing. What was the kind I liked at Edwin's? Laxton superb.

'Mrs Humphreys, I am disappointed in you.'

She flinched, and looked down. There was flour caked along the sides of her fingernails. She hadn't had time to scrub her hands properly, only rinse them under the tap, and take off her apron and overall, while the domestic sent to find her, a middle-aged woman with a broad incurious face, leaned against the doorframe, humming a tune.

Across the desk Dr Bosanquet was waiting. There must have been a complaint. Had somebody seen her at the George?

'You have worked for the hospital for a number of years, and on the whole your work has been satisfactory.'

On the whole! She stared at the side of his neck, where the collar dug in. I have worked hard, very hard, for how long is it? Nineteen thirty-five: eleven years. The injustice of it made her flushed and sullen.

His pale fat hands stretched out towards a letter on the desk in front of him: a small blue envelope, the address handwritten. Could it be the butcher, Hartley, aggrieved, trying to get her into trouble?

'I have reason to believe that you were once a patient at this asylum.'

All the force she'd summoned drained down through her body, till what was left was cold and motionless.

'Mrs Humphreys?'

She nodded.

She sat still while he went on berating her, in his rolling voice. She sat and felt herself switch off understanding, become again the solitary young woman around whom officials stated their decisions, in English she had no way of penetrating. Strange-sounding words came through to her: *false pretences.*

He was going to fire her. She would have to leave again, with just once suitcase, down the drive and out through the main gate, onto the lane and up the long empty road to the railway station, with no work and nowhere to live. Could she still stop him? When he paused for breath, leaning back in his chair, she managed, 'I am sorry. I did not think it was relevant.'

'Not relevant!' He leaned across the desk towards her, the lapel of his suit brushing the blue letter. 'Mrs Humphreys, this is a mental hospital. Our expertise is the nature of mental illness. The psychiatric history of our staff is of the utmost relevance. And in any event, as your employer..'

I will never find a job again, she thought. I did it before but I cannot do it now. Perhaps he is going to fire me on the spot. Not even let me go back to my kitchen. But who would they get to manage tonight's supper?

He turned the envelope over in his hands and took out a single sheet of paper. Someone must have told him. Can there be someone still working from that time? She watched as he unfolded the flimsy paper.

'This is from a person,' he said, and Narcisa's English returned reluctantly, 'who wishes to learn of your present whereabouts.'

'My.. ?'

He looked up, irritated, interrupted. 'Your whereabouts, Mrs Humphreys. Where you are living.' He spread the letter flat with his thick hand. 'She has written, ignorant of the fact that you now work here, enquiring because you were once, as she says, a patient. It was only the Assistant Clerk, a conscientious young woman, who brought it to our attention that there was in fact a person of that name.'

Clara, she thought, it must be from Clara. But no, Clara had come to see her, before the war, tall and thin as ever, with greying hair.

She waited. The Matron's voice sounded outside in the hall: 'Certainly not. What are you thinking of?'

'This person is claiming to be your daughter.'

*

She came out of Dr Bosanquet's office and walked the wrong way, across the tiled entrance hall and out of the front door of the asylum. Thin snow covered the grounds. The air was icy and almost still. One side of the giant cedar was mottled with white.

She walked tentatively down the steps into the cold. She had work to do. She needed to plan the menu for the week. Instead she turned right, along the path towards the gate.

Beyond the fence, across the road, were the milking sheds, the blacksmith's shop, the farm workers' cottages. She stood in the cold, her hands pushed inside her sleeves, the chill of the gravel path drawn up through her soles.

She remembered standing in the ironing-room, flat-iron in hand, turned towards the steam-covered window, a sound that could have been the workhouse cart diminishing outside on the drive. She had tried to keep it in hearing, straining towards it, and when it had gone she had put the iron down flat and run, calling her daughter, out of the room.

The smell of scorched linen.

She went on walking round the perimeter fence. A bus lumbered past between the hedges, tilting towards her as it turned the corner and went on up the lane towards the town. She caught sight of a boy in a flat cap, sitting upstairs.

Violeta. I wanted her so much. Her arms and her body ached, wrapped round a void. As soon as I got out, I wanted to have her with me. Even though Edwin said no. I did keep trying.

She remembered sitting on the piano stool, in the house in Pimlico; the image she kept having of Violeta running into the room, five or six years old, her thick dark hair in bunches.

Ahead of her eight or ten male patients, heads lowered against the cold, were walking back from the cabbage field, with Alun the farmhand sauntering behind them. Not wanting to speak, she stopped and stared out at the muddy road, till the men had turned down the path to the main building.

I wanted the best for her. I thought she would have a better life without me. Foster-parents, a nice house, an education. But when did I start to think that? I must have given up.

She turned back towards the asylum buildings. From here the chapel, long and low like a shed, half-blocked the view of the entrance porch and windows. The square brick tower was grey on the grey sky.

I betrayed her. In the end I did nothing.

A few hard snowflakes struck against her cheek.

'Cook!'

Someone was running down the path towards her. She gasped, looking up. But it was only young June Ragless, still in her apron, fair hair flying, her cheeks pink with the cold and the pleasure of coming outside on an errand.

*

A man was standing by the larder door, stocky and awkward in a rough brown jacket, a green knitted scarf loosened around his neck. She looked at him with fear, and then away, down at his wellingtons which were shiny with wet. There will be mud on the stone floor, she thought.

At the far end of the kitchen someone giggled. June leaned towards her. 'Please, Cook, he's off the farm.'

Not punishment, then. The new farm manager.

'Good morning, Mrs Humphreys. Sorry to disturb you.' His spectacles were blank with steam; he wiped them carefully on a blue handkerchief. The pale skin round his eyes made her feel queasy.

She was shivering suddenly, back in the warm kitchen, though outside she had hardly noticed the cold. She held onto her fore-arms to keep them still. There was another sound from the far end. Wrenching the words from somewhere lost in her, she said, 'You will please organise the working patients.'

She turned back with another effort to the man. 'There is a problem?'

'I'm sorry to say there is a bit of a problem. That's why I come down to have a word.' He went on; but she was already back in the office, Dr Bosanquet's fat hands on the blue letter. He would certainly fire her. Perhaps he had; perhaps he'd said it and she hadn't heard. *Down the drive*, that was that they called it: humiliated, the whole asylum knowing. Out past the porter's lodge without a greeting, without a goodbye, out into the lane and where? With all her things in a suitcase, just as she'd come here eleven years before; and who would give her a job once she'd been fired? Not at her age.

The man from the farm was waiting for an answer. What had he been saying? Something about the milk. She spoke weakly, her voice still rough and jerky, like someone's else: 'What do you suggest?'

He looked relieved; he cleaned his glasses again. The smell of strong stale tea reached her abruptly, and straight away the sound of water pouring, then June's high-pitched voice: 'No, what you do with the grouts..'

'We can see if East Hill have got some,' the man said. 'They might have, they've just bought some new Friesians. Otherwise it's the dairy down in Ewell. I'll get one of my lads to cycle over to East Hill straight away, if that suits.'

She tried to think. 'Yes, of course. Thank you.' But perhaps there was something she had not understood. 'You think this will be enough? From East Hill, or where you said, the dairy?'

'We'll manage between them, don't you worry, Mrs Humphreys.' He seemed more at ease now, offering reassurance. 'Can't have you short of milk for tea, now, can we? Now if you'll excuse me.'

Why had he come, she wondered, turning back to the busy kitchen. June and the round-shouldered girl who was her friend were dragging a sack of carrots to the sinks; the patients had washed up and were putting away. Had he been told she would be difficult? The sense she'd had, seeing him standing there in his brown jacket, stayed with her: that he was something to do with her disgrace; that he might be spying. Perhaps I would be difficult normally. Perhaps I should have been angry with him. It all seemed remote and trivial. If there was not enough milk they would use milk-powder. Dr Bosanquet, she thought, and saw him again, his round bald head, his wide shoulders in the good navy suit as he leaned forward. She had stood and stared across his desk at his tie, gold and red diagonal stripes that meant something, she was sure someone had told her they meant something. All the time he was berating her in his ponderous English, she'd watched the gold and red tie lifting and falling, as he breathed more air into his lungs; as if the simple answer, what his tie meant, would free her from all this, would be the answer she could give to him and stop him speaking at last, so that she could carry on as she had all this time, living here in the asylum, working.

'Excuse me, Cook,' the round-shouldered girl said. Peg, her name was Peg. 'Isn't it time to put the brisket on?'

She looked around. The kitchen, the line of giant cooking-pots, the sinks and dressers, the staff and working patients, all seemed poised to judge her. They know, she thought, and had to tell herself that it was nonsense. They will know when I'm fired. She turned to Peg, her neck and her spine aching. The girls looked down, hands wound in her apron.

'Very well,' she said, not knowing what would come out. 'You will see to the brisket, please. You have seen before how to do it?'

'Um, yes, Cook.'

'Ask two of the patients to work with you.' She looked to see what else there was to do. The week's menu was pinned up beside the dresser; she squinted slightly but couldn't make it out. The carrots lay gnarled and grubby in their sack. 'Today I will do the vegetables.' It was all she could do this morning, something simple, even if if turned out to be the last day in her kitchen. She was still there in her ordinary clothes. She put on her overall and apron, and went to the first sink, rolling up her sleeves. One of the patients by the larder whimpered. 'Enough,' she said, not looking, and there was quiet.

The cold water struck her hands with a kind of pain. For a minute or more that was all there was, her hands pale in the sink full of cold water, the effort to make them grip the scrubbing-brush and the large, lumpy carrots. The mud flaked off in pieces and then dissolved; the water turned milky brown. She scrubbed hard, one carrot after another, and tossed them into the bowl on the draining-board. As her hands got used to the cold, the fear returned. She should have said at the start that she'd been a patient. But no: she had come without references, having walked out of her job as housekeeper; she had had to lie, claiming she'd worked abroad. She tried to recall the interview, in the Matron's office some time in late autumn; but the figure of that Matron would not come clear, overlaid with the present stout form of Miss Atkinson, and the gaunt grey-haired woman from thirty years before.

At the next sink June Ragless had finished scrubbing, and was scooping potato peelings into the pig-bin.

None of this mattered, she understood suddenly, slicing the carrots in rounds, fast, rhythmically, the heavy knife bouncing up from the board. She would be fired; but that was not the point.

This person is claiming to be your daughter.

For a moment, standing in Dr Bosanquet's office, she had seen the young woman of her long imagination, slim and dark-haired, at an elegant writing-desk. If she had thought of Violeta at all, in these last years, it had been like this: calm and contented, stylish, educated; a spacious modern house with doors to a garden; the husband perhaps an officer in the Navy; two young sons. Then as he went on speaking it fell away, the image she now understood as her cowardice, her reluctance to wonder what had really happened. It collapsed like glass out of a broken window, and what was left was nothing, the blank of her knowledge of the past thirty years. Violeta could be anything, a teacher, a cook like herself, someone working long hours in bad light at a machine, always ill, always poor. She could be a married woman whose husband beat her; or even - she made herself think it - a prostitute, under a railway bridge with a drunk soldier. Narcisa bent over her work, tears in her eyes, the knife at rest in her hand. There was no knowing who her daughter was, except that she had lived all her life without her mother.

She straightened, and blinked, and went on cutting carrots. Now the hard orange roots seemed to resist her; she was aware of needing the strength of her hands, bringing the blade down again and again. How had it happened that thirty years had gone, and her daughter had lived them somewhere unknown to her, unhappy perhaps, unloved; and she had simply stopped wondering about her? She tipped the board, and the slices of carrot splashed into the pan; she began again.

I have not fought for her. I told myself I always wanted her back, but it wasn't true. I thought about it, but I never made it happen.

The knife skeetered; she pulled her finger away just in time. I abandoned her: that's what she must feel. She must want revenge. The thought seemed to hollow her out with fear. She will come and shout, 'How could you?' and she will be right.

June Ragless lit the gas under a pan. The smell of braising meat had filled the kitchen, rich and fatty. I must work, I must work, she thought; and with a great effort became what she had been for a long time, nothing more than a cook in an asylum kitchen, making sure that lunch would be ready for fifteen hundred.

Part 2

1911 - 1917

In my father's workshop there was order. Gold is a soft, biddable metal, and makes no screechings or crashes while being tooled. My father liked to work without conversation. His friends, fellow goldsmiths from our small community, knew when they called in to stand quiet, watching my father's very long light-brown hands, nodding and murmuring in their throats when he achieved some detail that impressed them.

Many days of my childhood I spent like this, lifted onto a stool beside the work-bench, the light flowing in, men and women passing in the narrow street. When I was very young I wanted to play with the flexible bright toy; but I learned never to touch it, only to watch. Once I jumped up eagerly and upset the leather apron fixed under the bench. The shavings of gold scattered onto the floor, catching the sunlight. Out of necessity, my father spoke. Then he knelt on the stone floor, took the hare's-foot brush and the small dust-pan, and poured the sweepings into a wire sieve. When he had picked out some fluff, and one of my wavy black hairs, he tapped the gold crumbs into a square wooden box, and closed the lid. I tried not to weep.

After that I sat tidily on my high stool, hands in my lap, watching him turn a fat slice of gold into a circle, and fit it over the ring triblet, a kind of tapering stick; or drilling holes in the wire frame of a bracelet and setting green stones in it one by one. When I reached ten or twelve, and spent less time with him, my favourite was the filigree-work, fine glinting wire that he curled into its minuscule frame, a fraction at a time, the pincers steady in his hand. Later, I longed for a filigree bracelet made by him, all his concentration and wordlessness wound into intricacies to grace my wrist, to show the little city I mattered to him. By then I had little patience to watch in silence; I wanted to speak, to understand everything, to be out on the street, past the low stone domes of the ancient hammam, walking down to the river, my long skirt rustling around my ankles.

1911

It was only six weeks until her wedding. Her father was spending long days in his workshop, while the sun sneaked into the narrow streets of Prizren, and groups of elderly men in their white hats were worrying about the Turkish government. She knew this because Edwin had been to a meeting, invited by some man he did business with. They thought he as a foreigner would know something.

The sun ate its way in through the narrow windows, under the doors, into the houses with the thick stone walls. With her sister and Edwin, she walked along the river, swishing her skirt, knowing the women were all looking at him, her Englishman whom the elders wished to consult. She showed him the places she loved in the small city, the ancient bridge, the hillside rising behind it. He had seen them before and still he listened to her.

And all the time she longed to be with her father. He would not let her into his workshop any more. At the beginning once she had taken Edwin in, to let him see the alchemical process, the transformation of raw gold into beauty. Edwin watched in silence as she had told him, the sunlight slanting in on his pale-gold hair. She stood still, willing him to understand, to be transformed as she was by what he saw.

She was going across all of Europe with this man, and Prizren might soon be viciously attacked, and her silent father closed his door to her. She wanted to sit on the high stool again, not to talk nor to ask him questions but to be there, the intent observer of his intricate craft, the one who loved what he could do with his hands. Soon no-one would watch him, and he would step back farther, into his place of silence and manual skill, like a monk illuminating a manuscript that would be taken out of the monastery and sung over by distant unheeding choirs.

The week before the wedding he called her in. He had made her a necklace, a looping chain that lay flat on her collar-bones, the glint of the gold reflecting on her cheek; a bracelet that would cover her strong wrist and make it seem as supple as a snake; and a pair of wide reddish-gold wedding-rings.

As a bride she would be the goldsmith's beloved daughter. She would wear these pieces and feel his work in them, when she was at home in distant London.

She would have her English husband for company.

She woke in the night, wanting to collect the morsels of gold off the jeweller's skin, the leather apron fixed under the bench, that caught the fragments left over from his work, and take them with her, hidden in her luggage.

Only once, early in the morning as she was washing, she thought she should stay here in her father's workshop and make his coffee and keep his house for him.

*

A bell, outside in the dark, the sound trailing away, going up the scale, no longer metallic but a woodwind shriek. She could almost see it, a circle of white light pulled out in the wake of the train like the tail of a comet.

Above her, Edwin murmured in his sleep, and turned, the high bed creaking under him. The sleeper smelt of leather, and the coffee they'd had the night before at Zagreb, little cups handed up to them through the window, and a train to Prague stood at the next platform. Handing back her cup she had split some of the dregs on the carriage floor, and the warmth, she imagined, brought the smell out, a smell of home, her father and his friends around the low table, talking.

And the smell of their bodies, hers and Edwin's. She stretched out contentedly under the starched sheet. Already the pleasure of what they could do with their bodies was part of her, as if they had been doing all these things for years. Late last night, after the Austrian border, the sleeping-car attendant had come to advise them to lock their door and hang the ladder across it, in case of thieves. Then Edwin had taken out all her hairpins, so her hair sprang out, freed, down past her shoulders, and brushed it with the silver-backed brush with her initials, her new initials NH, which had been part of his mother's wedding present. She had stood in front of him on the rocking train, looking out of the window under the edge of the drawn blind while he brushed her hair, with long even strokes that seemed each time to wake her and put her half to sleep. 'You do it very well,' she said, amazed. 'I used to watch the maid do my mother's hair, when I was little,' he said, and she saw how strange his life was, how strange hers would be, a bedroom of a shape she couldn't see, and Edwin's mother, tall and fair like him, letting her maid plait her hair. So she turned, and took the brush out of his hand, and kissed him, pressed against him in her shift.

They had made love here, in her bottom bunk, while the train growled and clattered over the tracks, somewhere in

Austria she had thought once, briefly, her hand on the top of his head as he reached into her body with his tongue. Then he had come back up to kiss her mouth, and she could taste her own body as he had. The narrow bed tilted and rattled under them. At one point he had sat up, astride her, and banged his head on the upper bunk, and sworn in English and laughed. 'What if the thieves came in now?' she'd said.

The sheet was still damp, cold in one patch by her thigh. She turned on her side, By breakfast they would be in Germany. 'You'll miss seeing the mountains,' he'd said and it had mattered, the last sight of a landscape she knew from home.

She knelt on the bunk to peer out of the window, holding the blind an inch or so to the side, so as not to wake Edwin. A little station sped out of her view. Otherwise there was nothing, no houses, no fields or hillsides, a great blackness. The train sounds changed abruptly, a muted roaring, a change in the air and they were in a tunnel, compressed, the train a slick instrument caving its way under great invisible mountains.

She got back under the covers and closed her eyes. In less than two days they would be in London. She wondered if Edwin's family would come to meet them. Her father, her sister Alma and Aunt Apolonija had come as far as Belgrade, stayed in the hotel and had breakfast with them, and stood on the platform as the train pulled away, Alma waving, her father with his hands in his pockets, sturdy. 'It's so far,' she's said the night before, in Alma's hotel room just before dinner. Alma and Altin were going to come and stay, perhaps next year if his business was doing well. As for her father: it would happen that he'd come, it would have to happen. Prizren, all of Albania was in danger, they all knew that, the old men asking Edwin's opinion as a foreigner, her father's friends around the *sofra*. And Aunt Apolonija had said it, trying to be cheerful about her wedding: 'At least you'll be safe over there.'

She tugged the pillow down and held it against her, hard, as she thought of her father, alone in his workshop, working all the time, eating with Aunt Apolonija in the evenings. She rocked slightly in the bunk. Her father would miss her. She had Edwin now, but he had no-one. Still, Edwin's work might take him back to Prizren. It would, she was sure, and she would go with him, and take her father all sorts of gifts from London, some cloth perhaps for an English suit. Or they could make it up in London, if they had the measurements? No, it was better to buy cloth and send it to him, tweed like Edwin's nicest jacket perhaps, and he could find the best tailor to make it up.

The train stopped suddenly, with a rush of steam and a grinding noise. The compartment rocked forward and then settled. She heard Edwin breathe out slowly. So what would her new family be like? There was his mother and two younger sisters; like her he had only one parent, though he'd been twelve when his father died in his sleep. 'Tell me about your mother,' she had said, and he'd looked sad, solemn almost, perhaps because she couldn't come to the wedding.

'My mother has very high standards.'

'What do you mean?' They were out walking along the river with Alma and Altin; she'd stopped in front of him, laughing, confident, and a bird had risen slowly from the bank and veered up over the hillside towards the mountains. 'Will I meet her standards?'

'She will think you are the most beautiful girl she's ever seen.'

Men could say these things easily, she knew that. Alma had told her: men say all sorts of things, you have to keep your head. But Edwin was so unlike the men in Prizren. His looks of course, tall, slim, fair-skinned, with that soft straight hair. But more than that: compared to the men she'd seen, young men she'd talked to like Alma's Altin and her cousins, he was quiet, subtle. He listened to her; when they were walking along, he would bend down carefully to catch what she said, and think about it all and ask her questions. That was the first thing to take her by surprise. Her father had brought him home to dinner, and he had asked her about her piano lessons: 'Tell me, Mademoiselle, what do you most like playing?' She had been awkward, like a little girl, stupid; but she'd managed to say there was a piece by Mozart, and he had known it and said it was delightful.

The train started again, juddering first, then getting up speed, the now familiar rhythm and clattering. She should sleep; she wanted to be fully awake tomorrow, to see Munich and the other cities they'd go through. She settled down under the white sheet. His mother didn't speak French; that was a problem. But she would learn English very soon; already she knew a few words, and his mother would be impressed and charmed. She imagined the older woman at the station, tall and elegant, with a fashionable hat, kissing her on the cheek and saying welcome. 'Welcome to your new family, Narcisa,' she would say in English, and Edwin would translate. And she would say – what would she say in return? 'Thank you, belle-mère. I am so excited to be here.'

1912

In three hours' time Edwin would be home. She stood up and went over to the window; but the street looked much as it had half an hour before. A boy in a cap ran down the opposite pavement, waving a large white envelope, and ran back empty-handed a moment later. A man with a walking-stick stopped to lean on a gate. The sky was an even grey; there were no shadows. The long first-floor windows, which should have made her drawing-room bright and open, instead seemed to leave the air a greyish blur. She sat down again with the English book.

Tomorrow I shall go to the theatre.

She repeated the line to herself under her breath. At first she had said the new words out loud; but once the maid had heard and gone out giggling.

Tomorrow he will go to the opera. Would Edwin take her to the opera? She had an image of a great domed theatre; lights all along the balconies; beautiful women leaning from the boxes, in low-cut dresses of the last century. Probably it wasn't that at all; she must have read it in some French novel. *Tomorrow you will go...* Oh, all these tomorrows, she thought, and dropped the book onto the Turkish rug. I'll do it later.

A knock: the maid came in with a tray, and unloaded it onto the side-table: teapot, hot water, sugar, cup and saucer, milk. She had given up saying that she didn't take milk; they didn't believe her, or they didn't care. 'Thank you,' she said, careful with the *th,* which could betray her. The maid was called Hammond; but hating to call a young woman by her surname, Narcisa ended up using no name at all, and no doubt seemed rude. The girl was younger than she was, fifteen maybe, with a bustling walk and a smirking, knowing air. Narcisa had tried early on to talk to her. 'That will be all,' she said, like her mother-in-law, who managed to make it definite and dismissive.

Perhaps Edwin would bring the newspaper. He bought it every morning, and, she supposed, read it on the train or over lunch; but often he forgot to bring it home. Once or twice there had been news of the Balkan War. 'So what about Prizren?' she'd asked, urgent; but he'd said he was sure nothing would happen there. How could he know? she wondered, but didn't ask.

It was five months since she had had news from home. Five months: the last letter from Alma, with a note at the end from her father, was dated May, and had reached her in early June. Alma had written about the new baby, Ljuljeta, and Aunt Apolonija's cooking: silly things, that they might have laughed over on a warm May night. Her father as ever asked after all the Humphreys, who he'd never met but regarded as family, and ended *I'm glad you are happy and safe there.* She had all this time, while Edwin was at work, when she was 'running the household,' whatever that meant, and learning English and playing the piano, to worry about what might have happened to them, and write more letters that still got no answer. 'We must go there,' she'd said one night to Edwin, as they were going to bed; and he said, 'Where?' and then apologized, and sat down with her, on the satin counterpane. 'It's not the time to be travelling, you know; it's really not safe;' but that had made it worse. She'd burst into tears, and he had held her hand, and been kind, but repeated, 'No, really, too dangerous.' He'd promised he'd find out what was happening, he'd ask his old contacts at the Foreign Office; but if he had, she'd never heard the answer. Sometimes she wondered if there had been letters, and he'd not told her, because the news was bad. But I'm upset anyway, she thought, and felt guilty, having doubted his honesty; in any case, he can't read Albanian.

She had let the tea stew too long; she poured half a cup, and topped it up with hot water. Edwin's mother would frown if she saw that, and murmur. It does you no good, worrying about them all: that was what Edwin said. But I have to worry. Still, it was true she needed to do something. She bent down and picked up the English book again.

The grandfather clock on the landing struck half past four. An hour and a half until Edwin came in. He was at his desk; she'd been to his office once, when they'd first arrived. Perhaps he'd be starting to put his papers away. Perhaps he'd be thinking of her already. Then at five o'clock he'd come out onto Cheapside, and walk through the streets, past the cathedral to Ludgate Hill station. There would be people waiting on the platform, men in their dark suits and stiff black hats, some in winter coats for the damp November evening. Perhaps on the train he'd talk to some of them. He'd get off the train at Camberwell; and by then she'd have done her hair, and changed into the lilac dress he liked, and be standing here in the drawing-room by the fire when he opened the front door and called up to her.

1913

Along the street where Edwin's mother lived, the cherry trees were in flower again. Last year she had jumped up to catch at a branch, and broken off a spray for a corsage; and Edwin had looked at her, delighted and shocked at once. She could see the expression now, as if his face – his real face, she thought – had become detached from him, and walked along bodiless next to the new Edwin, who never looked delighted at anything. Today the blossom was like a low roof, or a raincloud that might burst over all of them, and soak them through in their elegant spring clothes.

In very bad French Edwin's sister said, 'This is going to be such fun.'

Where was it they were going? His mother had announced it, addressing Edwin, and when at last she had stopped talking to him, Edwin had turned and spoken to Narcisa in French. She hadn't listened; it made no difference, she knew already; his mother planned things for them all to do, and wherever they went, his mother and Edwin talked, and Narcisa was left with Eleanor, the sister, who spoke little French and didn't know what to say.

Who was saying now, 'You'll see, it's beautiful. It's right by the river. There's…' but Eleanor didn't know the word. She looked hopefully, sweetly, at Narcisa, wanting help. But it was too much, to turn towards Eleanor with her large grey eyes and her girlish, giggling manner; to work out what Eleanor wanted to say to her, and find the word in French and say it twice, three times till Eleanor had grasped it.

She said nothing.

'Enfin,' said Eleanor in her English accent. Eleanor was to be married in the autumn. Her fiancé, Gerald, looked very like Edwin, but with red hair instead of fair, and even whiter skin. Then Eleanor too would stay alone in her house – they were to live in Streatham, close to the mother – and have to work out how to make the servants respect her, and wait for Gerard to come home from the office. Perhaps then Eleanor would understand.

Edwin's mother and Edwin had stopped at the street corner. His mother was looking at Narcisa and saying something; perhaps that they were too slow, keeping her waiting. Increasingly it seemed to Narcisa that they, the three Humphreys, talked about her, openly, knowing she wouldn't understand them. It was true that she understood less than she had a year, even six months ago. It was too much effort.

The park was a big one, with strange tall trees, and an old house on the edge, and greenhouses. They walked till they came to a shaded place with lots of blue flowers. 'Voilà!' Eleanor said. It was clear that Narcisa was meant to be impressed. She managed to say, 'Very pretty.'

There was more walking. Now something seemed to have been agreed. Edwin and Eleanor went on ahead, and Edwin's mother came and took her arm. The old hand on her sleeve looked like a piece of wood stripped of bark by the river. She stared down at it.

Her mother-in-law spoke stiffly, slowly, in English. 'Narcisa, I wish to speak to you.'

Something surfaced in her and chose to know the words.

'You are a married woman. You understand me?'

She looked down in assent.

'You have a responsibility. You are responsible. For Edwin. For...' but the next word was strange to her. 'You must make an effort.'

Something hot glowed through the thick layer of wood-ash that was her feelings. She looked up at the bony, pitiless face.

'I effort. Now. I effort.' It was unjust; but her mother-in-law would not listen.

'You are letting things go.' What did that mean, letting go? What was going? I should go, she thought. I should go back to Prizren. For a year she had not heard from Alma or her father. Perhaps Edwin was keeping their letters from her.

She made herself concentrate on the strong cold words.

'The servants. They must...'

Respect me. Yes yes, that was what Edwin said. How can I make them respect me, she wanted to cry, when they don't understand what I say?

They came to a gate. Edwin turned and called something to his mother, who nodded, and the four of them went out onto a footpath. A river, the Thames, was it? lay greyish and full beside them. A boat with two men passed, their oars entering the water like kitchen knives.

'Look, said Edwin. 'That is Sion House. Do you see the statue of the lion on the roof?'

A dull stone English lion. She nodded.

'When we were children we would walk along here all the way to Richmond.' He smiled at her anxiously. He gives me his childhood, she thought, to make me love him. But I do love him, only...

His mother said something. Edwin turned awkwardly back to Eleanor.

There was a call behind them. A heavy brown horse was

plodding along the bank, head down. There was a smell now of horse-dung and coal-dust. Attached by two ropes, a green-painted barge trailed steadily in the water. A man in a black hat stood on the front. I could join him, she thought dully. I could jump onto the barge and be taken away.

The three Humphreys stood back from the bank. Edwin's mother was frowning.

The man shouted again. The horse was close to her. She could see its domed brown eyes, expressionless, and smell its sweat. The ropes were taut, at an angle to the harness.

'Narcisa!' Edwin shouted, and moved forward. The man on the barge waved his arms. The water looked thick enough to carry her. She waited.

The cab went through a wide gate and up a path. There were flower-beds with pruned roses on either side, and a huddle of buildings. The cab stopped at a square porch. Edwin got out and came round to open her door. She leaned on his outstretched hand as she stepped down; but almost at once he moved away again, and rang the bell.

The hallway was very bare, the floor highly polished. A dark painting of cows and trees hung by the door.

A tall woman came towards them, not smiling. 'Mr Humphreys?' she asked, and Edwin went with her over to the window. She had thick grey hair pulled back in a bun, and a white scar along the side of her jaw. She was listening gravely while Edwin spoke to her. At one point he took out a handkerchief – she could see the blue *EH* she had embroidered – and blew his nose with a soft regretful sound.

A door at the back of the hallway opened; a young woman in white came through, carrying a bundle. The tall woman caught sight of her and shook her head; the young one retreated. Is it because we're here? Narcisa wondered.

She felt tired. As soon as she moved, Edwin turned quickly round, and watched till she had sat down on the far window-seat. She looked out idly at the flower-borders.

There were a few yellow roses almost open, and by the porch a bed with red tulips.

Edwin came over. 'It's all arranged,' he said in French to her. 'This lady will make sure you are comfortable.'

'But why?' she asked him again. 'Why do you want me to be here?'

She stood up; he led her over to the woman. He said something in English and the woman reached forward, Narcisa thought at first to shake her hand; but no, to touch the collar of her dress. She flinched.

1915

Someone was singing in the long corridor. At the end of the silent file towards the chapel, Narcisa turned, pulled into the narrow force-field of the music. A peasant song, she thought, if they had any here: a four-line melody with a rise and dip, each verse sounding to end in disappointment.

'Get a move on, you back there!' an attendant called; but just before she caught up with the line, Narcisa glimpsed a woman on hands and knees, her broad strong bottom in blue cloth pushing at the air, the worn soles of her shoes turned to the light, head lifted a moment as she shuffled backwards, bright yellow hair curling up round her cap. '*Oh slowly, slowly;*' so much Narcisa understood, and then the words fell into the tune again, a line that lifted hopefully and dropped.

When they turned off from the main corridor, a heavy door stopping the woman's voice, Narcisa played the tune through in her head, to fix it, to give herself a fragment of music to come back to. She followed the file out along the path. A fine rain blew across the lawns towards them; she hunched, but her sleeve clung wet to her arm.

The chapel was cold. A woman was labouring over an air from Bach. Some key in the upper register was silent; the melody limped over the gap like a man on crutches. *Oh slowly, slowly,* Narcisa sang to herself, to block out the uneven counterpoint. Every week this thudding music, the piano as they filed in and at the end; and the simple tedious tunes of the English hymns, sung loudly off-key by the staff and a few patients. Not music, she thought, surprised that she still remembered. Then the chaplain arrived, pale in his off-white vestments; and the chapel creaked with the give of dark hassocks.

It was back on the ward that the tune came back to her. *Oh slowly, slowly,* she sang under her breath, and filled up the rest of the verse in her own language: a stream, a man on a horse, a tall castle. She was sewing two buttons back on her overall. The rain thrashed against the long windows. The lines of the ballad circled in her head.

'Here,' said the attendant dramatically: 'What's this? '

She was standing directly in Narcisa's light.

'You hear that?' the woman said, to anyone who might enjoy listening, diverting attention from their own misdemeanours. 'The Boche here is singing. Trying to, any road.'

Boche was clear enough, and not the first time. Narcisa laid the overall on her lap. Her shoulders were cold in the ill-fitting petticoat.

'Come on, Boche,' the woman called, her narrow eyes glistening, her arms akimbo in the grey uniform. 'Let's have another chorus. How'd it go?' She sang a few bars in a squeaking comic voice. The red-haired woman from the ironing-room tittered.

'How does a Boche know an English song, eh? Perhaps she's a Boche spy, eh? What do you reckon?'

Narcisa sat still. She understood enough. The attendant began again: *In Scarlet Town, where I was born.* Her voice cracked on *Town.* 'Don't you know the words yet, Boche? Suppose we teach her.'

Her face was pink; her breasts pushed against her apron. She leaned forward and pulled the sewing off Narcisa's lap; the needle caught against the palm of her hand. Two or three drops of blood fell on the fabric. 'You wicked girl,' she said, 'you've spoiled your uniform. Now they're going to have to scrub it out.' She leant forward and rubbed the cloth on Narcisa's cheek.

The patients watched. Narcisa's back tensed with the effort of sitting still. 'Go on then, sing,' the attendant said. 'I'm ordering you.' She sang a verse through herself in her high harsh voice.

An old woman caught Narcisa's eye and nodded. Did she mean it was better to give in? But silence was always better, that was what she had learned: you said nothing, and hoped they got bored with you.

She remembered the woman scrubbing the corridor, on her hands and knees, singing to please herself. What were the words? Something about love, no doubt.

The attendant was standing too near, leering down at her. Why was she staring? There had been another attendant who did that - no, she would not remember what had happened. She pushed her chair back suddenly and stood, so the woman was off-balance and teetered backwards.

She began to sing, the first thing that came to her.
'Du holde Kunst..'

The strength of her voice surprised her; it reached to the far end of the ward, where she saw a woman sit up in bed, and another, limping, stop and turn round. Now they will be certain I'm German, she thought grimly. In the crowded ward no-one spoke, just for that moment; the attendant was leaning against the window-sill; someone up by the door was nodding to the rhythm. I must make this last, she thought, singing in German about a better world, *eine bess're Welt,* putting all her force into it, anger perhaps though the tune was slow and sweet. They waited for the second verse to start. She could all but hear the piano accompaniment, her Aunt Apolonija who had taught it to her; she paused for the few bars. Her voice was not good any more, how could it be? Oh god I am going to be punished for this, she thought, carried up with the swell: *'ich danke dir dafür..'*

The attendant slapped her hard across the face.

She heard herself make a sound, loudly, as if the song had clotted in her throat. 'Shame', the woman by the door muttered, but the attendant glared and she was quickly silent. Narcisa put her hand up to her cheek. Now it will start, she thought.

The woman grabbed Narcisa's arm and dragged it down to her side again. The words she said were vicious and flowed together. Narcisa's chest was still full from the singing. For a second she thought: I could just start again.

The attendant must have called for help; someone else came, sour-faced, stooping, and grabbed her by the shoulder. 'No!' she shouted, but it was still in German.

The first attendant wound her hand in Narcisa's hair. They dragged her down the middle of the ward. Light from the windows slashed across her face. The patients moved clumsily out of the way; Narcisa saw the red-haired woman jeering. Her right arm was being twisted behind her back; she felt the fingers bruising her meagre flesh. The two attendants were still berating her, or maybe talking about her to each other. Let it be only the strait-jacket, she thought. It was a long time since she had been restrained. The fear leapt in her. The strong dress or the strait-jacket: both were terrible. She had felt mutilated, her arms cut off for her sins. But then they'll leave me. Was it true? Oh, I should never have sung to them. I should have stayed quiet.

They stopped outside the door of a padded cell. Before they were in there she remembered the smell: old leather and urine. She gagged.

The attendant had not stopped shouting. She put both hands to Narcisa's petticoat, and tore it down from the neck. Her knuckles bumped over Narcisa's breasts. I will not cry, Narcisa thought, I will not speak.

If she does any more it will be the other thing. She could not make herself know what that was. Please, only the strong dress or the strait-jacket.

The sour-faced attendant waved a rubber hose. Narcisa stood rigid. The first one looked at her watch and shook her head.

She let her arms be put in the strong-dress sleeves, the hard canvas wrapped round and tied with tapes. Then they pushed her, so she fell into the corner, unable to steady herself with her hands tied down.

One of them laughed before they closed the door.

1916

A week after Narcisa's daughter was born, they brought the French interpreter again. She was a small, stylish woman with crimped black hair, who kept her gloves on all through the questioning. They were blue kid, reaching half-way to her elbow, and while she was listening to the Medical Superintendent she kept stroking them down over the backs of her hands.

Nobody had told Narcisa they were coming. She was in the infirmary, still exhausted and in some pain from the long labour. They brought her the baby to feed every so often, it seemed at the simple whim of the nurse on duty. Sometimes she didn't have enough milk, and the child went on wailing. She was sturdy, although so small, with a slick of black hair. The sound she made, crying Narcisa supposed from hunger, spread out from the bed into the whole ward. Then a nurse would come and carry her away, and Narcisa would hear cries fading down the ward, till a door closed and it was quiet again.

That morning she was sitting up in bed, trying to knit a bonnet for the baby. It was July, sunny, and the ward was stuffy; her hands sweated onto the white knitting. One of the attendants had taught her to knit, soon after they discovered she was pregnant. The baby-clothes she made were plain and misshapen, but she kept on knitting because the child needed clothes, and it seemed to be her duty to provide them. By now at least she worked less awkwardly. The thin wool pulled taut across her fingers, the wooden needles clicked more or less rhythmically. The narrow fringe of fabric grew very slowly. At the end of each row she stopped and stretched it out.

The little fat nurse called Wendle came hurrying in. 'Come on, Humphreys,' she said, and more that Narcisa didn't understand. She took the knitting out of her hands. 'Doctor coming,' she said impatiently. She pushed her forward and straightened up the pillows, then yanked her back by the shoulder to sit against them. The movement pulled at the torn place between her legs, and she cried out.

'Big doctor,' she said, pulling the sheet flat. 'Oh, can't you understand? Medical Superintendent. Dr Gross.'

They came down the ward: Dr Gross with his light-coloured beard; the Matron; and Madame Taté, the interpreter. They had brought her in only once before.

They stood round the bed, these three important people and the nurse. Narcisa thought they must be talking about her, but couldn't make out what it was they were saying. She felt blood seeping heavily out of her, onto the pad of rags under her nightgown.

She crossed her arms to cover her swollen breasts. Dr Gross smiled and spoke to Madame Taté.

'Monsieur the Medical Superintendent says there is no need for you to be embarrassed.' She spoke flatly.

'I am cold,' she said to defend herself.

The nurse found a shawl and put it round her shoulders. She drew the corners down over her chest.

They pulled up chairs, the Medical Superintendent and Madame Taté on one side, the Matron and Nurse Wendle on the other. Dr Gross cleared his throat and began to speak.

His cheeks in the gap of the beard were smooth and rounded; his lips seemed too red under the fair moustache. Madame Taté stroked her gloves and listened.

'Monsieur the Medical Superintendent says that now your child is born the asylum has to consider arrangements for its welfare. In order for the legal position to be established you will have to provide full information as to the circumstances of its conception.'

She said nothing. Dr Gross sat straighter in his chair.

'He remembers that you refused to speak at the time you were first questioned, but he thought that now your child has been born you would be concerned for her welfare.'

'What has this got to do with her welfare?' She heard her own tone, sullen. She was frightened.

Further down the ward a woman cried out twice, as if in pain. Narcisa turned and saw her try to sit up in bed, her long hair hanging lank over her face. Nurse Wendle murmured something and went to her.

'Her father should be obliged to contribute to her upkeep.' Madame Taté turned back to listen to Dr Gross. 'Also you will be able to retrieve your reputation, if a man has taken advantage of your situation here.'

She watched Nurse Wendle take a brown bottle from the cupboard, and pour from it into a spoon, which she held out. The sick woman took it and lay down again. Nurse Wendle pulled up the covers, and patted the woman's shoulder.

Dr Gross was looking at her almost kindly.

'I was not raped.' For a moment she remembered lying in the grass, and holding the boy's head against her shoulder.

'You must not be ashamed to tell Monsieur the Medical Superintendent if you were forced in any way to consent. He understands that you were in a vulnerable position.' Madame Taté said all this completely without expression, looking down all the time at her blue gloves.

'I was not forced.'

Dr Gross' voice rose a little louder. Madame Taté said in the same neutral tone, 'Then you must give us the name of the man concerned.'

She said nothing.

Dr Gross and the Matron stood up and moved away. She was a bony, grey-haired woman who rarely spoke. Now she stood with her head slightly bowed in the white cap. Every so often she said something that sounded cautious. Dr Gross shook his head.

Nurse Wendle went back to the sick woman along the ward. Madame Taté turned to Narcisa. 'Listen,' she said quietly, 'you are making it worse. Can't you understand, they don't know what to do. You don't have to say who he is. Just tell them something.'

She was still sitting perfectly upright in her chair. Dr Gross and the Matron came back to the bed. Before he could speak, Narcisa said to Madame Taté, 'Tell them it was the day that I escaped.'

She nodded slightly and turned to Dr Gross. His shoulders slumped a little as he listened.

'So the incident took place outside the asylum?' Madame Taté's voice was toneless again.

'Yes,' I said.

'And you are not willing to reveal his name?'

'No.'

Dr Gross spoke at length. At the end of the ward, a patient in overalls started mopping the floor. The smell of bleach made her gag. Matron spoke to Nurse Wendle, who shooed the patient away.

'Monsieur the Medical Superintendent says you are being very foolish, but that clearly he cannot oblige you to give the name. They will consider how this should be handled.'

They got up to go. 'What will happen?' she asked.

'They will tell you when the arrangements have been made.'

The others were already walking towards the door. She reached out and touched Madame Taté's arm. 'What does that mean?'

'It means they will send the baby away out of here, after three months, six months? I don't know.'

'Thank you,' she said, but the interpreter was already catching up with the doctor and matron.

1917

She woke and a woman was sitting on her bed. She was wearing patient's uniform, a too-large dress. Her hair was pulled back in a thick fair plait. There was a birthmark high on her left cheek, a raised stain.

'Look,' she said, and held up a baby's white wool dress. Narcisa reached out and felt it.

She could not stop crying. Her lungs and shoulders ached with it. The woman moved to go, but she grasped her arm. Awkwardly, the woman patted her once on the shoulder.

She wailed as her daughter had, in desolation.

The woman felt in her pocket and produced a handkerchief. 'You poor thing,' she said.

Narcisa stared at her.

'Do you understand?' She was speaking slowly, whispering not to be heard. 'I'm sorry about your baby.'

She cried again.

'What's your name?' the woman asked. 'I'm Esther.'

She nodded.

'I think it's awful, what they do,' Esther said. 'I've got a little boy, you see.' Then she spoke more quickly, and Narcisa couldn't follow. She lay listening to the quiet hoarse voice. At one point tears were running down the woman's cheeks. One spread out across the crimson birthmark.

The woman wiped her eyes with the flat of her hands. 'Listen,' she said, speaking slowly again. 'They want to move you. Do you know what I'm saying? To the locked ward.'

'Locked?' she asked, frightened. 'Me? Locked ward?'

'They think you're bad. You know' – she was searching for kinder words – 'having a bad time now. Ill. Nurse Holmes said.'

'No locked. No. No, I can not.'

'Can you get up?' the woman asked. 'Put your clothes on?'

She nodded.

To avoid the locked ward she would have to be quiet. She thought of her daughter screaming out to her, carried by Matron out of the long ward. 'Baby,' she said, but couldn't explain in English. She rocked on the bed, as she had with the child in her arms.

'Try,' Esther said, and stood up, as the attendant Parsons came bustling towards them.

*

The thought of returning to the locked upstairs ward sent her back to the security of sleep. She dreamed of Edwin at the first-floor window of the Camberwell house, making signs to her as she stood across the street. He repeated the few gestures again and again, and she spread her arms wide in incomprehension, until a policeman came to bring her back. Then she was inside the house, in some room she had never found before, alone. She was still pregnant, and her daughter's kicks were making a noise inside her like kettle-drums.

When she woke she remembered the threat. It was daytime: the ward was washed with a pale grey light. Someone a few beds away was mumbling. There were the usual smells, disinfectant and unwashed female bodies and urine.

She sat up. She must get dressed. There were no clothes on the chair beside her bed; the last that she'd worn must have been sent to the laundry. She got out of bed and looked for an attendant.

There was no-one around, apart from the old woman talking to herself, and a young girl down near the door, bedclothes thrown off, her hand under her nightdress, masturbating. As Narcisa passed she raised herself on one elbow and spat.

She opened the door onto the corridor. A porter, a big man with a bald head, was pushing a trolley stacked high with brown parcels. 'Hello, darling,' he said. 'You looking for someone?'

Her nightdress felt very thin and clinging. She wanted to shrink away and close the door. Instead she said, shivering, 'Attendant.'

'You need an attendant? Fine, love. Leave it with me.' He winked and went on pushing the heavy trolley. She watched his broad back in the sepia cotton coat. At a bend in the corridor he spoke to someone.

The attendant Parsons came towards her, half-running.

'Oh, it's you, Humphreys.' She pushed her back into the ward, holding her elbow. 'What are you doing?'

'Better,' she said, and pointed to her chest. The English words she'd known came back piecemeal. 'Dress.'

'Oh, you're better, are you?' She laughed. She was a cheerful woman, with a smooth face, and large firm breasts under her uniform. 'Has the doctor seen you?'

She knew she had to be clever to defeat them. 'No doctor. Better. Work now. Work.'

'Well,' she said, 'not many patients ask to work, do they? I don't know.'

'Bath?' she asked. Her skin felt heavy with lint off the sheets and grease .

'You can't have a bath, it's Wednesday, isn't it?'

'Please, bath,' she said. 'Bath - dress - work.' She could feel the panic expanding in her stomach. She longed to be back under the rough blankets, wordless.

'I don't know,' Parsons said again. 'I should wait and ask Sister. I'll tell you what, you have a wash and take your time.'

Narcisa looked at her, helpless.

'Oh Lord. You wash' - she spoke loudly, and the young woman in bed swore - 'You wash' - she mimed it - 'all over - no hurry. All right?'

She stood naked at the stone basin, and washed herself quickly with a worn face-cloth. There was no hot water, and the wash-room was icy. It should have been luxury to wash alone; but she was anxious, planning the next steps, to get herself sent to work and avoid attention. She soaped her breasts, and the memory of feeding the baby made her dizzy. She leaned on the basin. As she straightened again, she thought she saw her mother, in the doorway to one of the bathrooms. She called out, but her mother had already gone.

'You all right, Humphreys?' the attendant called. She came in and leant against the wall, watching idly. Narcisa stopped herself shouting *go away*, the words so close to her tongue they made her cough. Instead she finished as quickly as she could, and rubbed herself hard with the little towel, for warmth.

Back on the ward, she put on the clothes Parsons had found her. The dress must have shrunk in the wash: it was too tight over her chest and the upper part of her arms. 'Work?' she asked.

'Oh, you can't work until Sister has seen you. Come on, I'll brush your hair. You've got nice hair.'

Narcisa stood in front of the woman. She was rough,

pulling the hair out straight with the brush, almost beating at it to tug out the tangles. Narcisa's head jerked back with the strokes; her scalp was painful. She remembered her Aunt Apolonija doing the same, how she would wriggle and cry out when the brushing hurt her. There were tears in her eyes, maybe from the pain; but she felt the panic release in her a little. Then she was cautious, afraid of being outwitted.

Parsons plaited Narcisa's hair and looked round for something to tie it. There was a length of pink tape on someone's night table, so she stole it calmly and made it into a bow. 'There,' she said, standing back and patting her shoulder. 'You look quite nice.'

'What I do?' Narcisa asked. She couldn't sit in the day-room, doing nothing.

Parsons thought for a moment.

'I'll tell you what,' she said. 'You can clean my room. But you mustn't tell, we're not meant to. Promise?'

Narcisa followed her out to the curving corridor. Parsons looked to either side, then grabbed Narcisa's wrist, and pulled her along. They went like this along a side corridor and up some stairs.

The room was narrow, and full of heavy scents. Narcisa stood when the woman had closed the door, and breathed in smells she'd forgotten, talc and face-cream and some kind of florid perfume.

'All right,' Parsons said, sullen. 'I know it's a mess. You don't know what it's like..' Narcisa lost the rest, a complaint perhaps.

A petticoat drooped from the seat of a chair, towards a pair of drawers collapsed on the floor. The bed was a bundle of sheets and counterpane, with a red flannel nightdress thrown over the pillow. A bright-covered book lay open face down on the night-stand, next to a hairbrush and two or three letters.

'Now what you do,' she said, cheerful again. 'Make the bed for me, and dust - I'll find you a duster. And sweep the floor. The clothes go in here' - she pointed to the chest of drawers. 'And the pot..' she considered. 'You can empty it, down the end of the corridor, only wait till there's nobody around. Do you understand?'

She went out, and came back with a broom and a duster. 'You've got to be quiet,' she said. 'It's really important. Trouble - bad trouble. For both of us. I'll come and get you in an hour or so.'

Narcisa sat on the bed, wondering how to manage. The sultry smells of the room were like a trap. She could fall asleep in them, in this woman's sheets, a child waiting for her mother to return. She closed her eyes, bracing her arms not to fall sideways. There were more layers to the smell: rosewater, and stale urine from the pot under the bed.

She was supposed to empty the chamber-pot.

She opened her eyes. There was a man's black comb on the night-table.

She stood suddenly, full of energy and revulsion. She wanted to shout: I am not your maid. I am not used to having to clean rooms. She wanted to pick up the pot and empty it, over the woman's bed and her red flannel nightdress, and run away back through the hospital.

In Camberwell there had been a pink satin bedspread. She could see it superimposed on this narrow bed, folded back, slipping off because they had been making love; and herself lying back, supple and soft-skinned, her legs wide open, in satisfaction.

Stop.

She made herself stand, and lift the flannel nightdress up to fold it. It smelt intimately of sweat and lavender water.

She drew the curtains, undressed, and put it on. The smell of the other woman's skin was disturbing. The cloth was soft and comforting on her shoulders.

She looked in the mirror. With her hair in a plait, she could have been any young woman, going to bed in the plain single room.

It is my room, she told herself. I am allowed to come and go in it. These are my letters, from my family. My lover came in late and spent the night here.

She made the bed, smoothing the sheets with care, tucking in the corners as she'd been shown. She pulled up the blue cotton counterpane. There, she thought, they'll never know he was here. Then she took off the nightdress, and laid it, carefully folded, at the head. The red was fierce against the dark blue.

She put on the white drawers and petticoat. They were much too big, but the cotton felt pleasantly crisp still from the laundry. Dressed in the woman's underclothes, she took the duster, and wiped the top of the chest of drawers, the back of the upright chair, the night-table. In the back of her mind the young married woman she'd been was indignant at having to learn such menial work. I am not Narcisa, she told this person: I am Florence Parsons. She opened the window and flapped the rug outside, singing an old song under her breath, pretending that the words were in English.

Her mother joined in. She didn't see her at first, but heard her voice, sweetened and amplified in the narrow room. When she turned from dusting the mirror her mother was there, in the armchair, very pale in her grey turn-of-the-century dress.

She began to weep. 'I thought you'd gone,' she said.

Her mother went on singing.

'I'm not that woman,' Narcisa said, and took off the clothes. 'Look,' she begged, naked. 'You can see I'm Narcisa.'

Her mother looked steadily at her breasts and the stretch marks on her belly.

'I know,' she said, 'I know, but I couldn't help it.'

Her mother stood up and Narcisa rushed forward to hug her. She fell onto the empty chair, and howled, over and over, beating her forehead on the upholstered seat.

Then the door opened. There were hands gripping her arms, and shouting voices.

Part 3

**1946
-
1947**

The Jeweller's Skin

The snow had stopped. On the pavements the morning's covering had been scuffed to slush. The roadway was already clear, with a black sheen that might soon turn to ice. Most of the roofs on the High Street were patterned in white with the outline of the slates; only the pub, where the upstairs room must be warmed, and Johnson's the draper's were dark, with little slicks of white snow at the edges.

The town was not unattractive like this, Anthony thought, looking out from the window of the Warming Pan Tearoom. The clock-tower outlined in snow was rather fun. The street was wide: he seemed to remember a market. Still, you would never think it was so near London. A country town; narrow, he supposed, conservative, in the way of such places. And burdened with the asylums - five, were there? What on earth had possessed the LCC to build so many?

'You wouldn't like a pot of tea while you wait, sir?' The waitress was middle-aged - his age, he supposed - with dyed black hair and that dry, lined skin that women seemed to have when they smoked a lot.

'Perhaps I will; that's a good idea, thank you.' He watched while she fussed with the crockery. She was bored, he supposed. And then men didn't come in on their own, did they? It was a women's place, for chatting in; no doubt she thought he would be feeling awkward.

'A bit better this afternoon,' she said, bringing the tray.

'You know, I rather like it like this,' he said. She unloaded the tea-things and arranged them in front of him. 'Makes me feel like skiving off and tobogganing.'

She straightened and laughed, a hoarse guttural laugh, incredulous.

'Didn't you ever do that when you were a child?' He was being personal, but he knew she would like it: a tough woman nobody asked about her childhood.

She put the tray down on the next table. 'Oh, I'm not from round here,' she said. 'I'm a Londoner. Borough, I grew up, right near the market.'

'Not far from the river,' he began to say; but from the corner of his eye he saw Narcisa, leaning her bicycle against the lamp-post. 'Here's your friend, then,' the waitress said in her professional voice, as the door opened. She stood by the table to take Narcisa's coat.

'This lady comes from London, from the Borough,' he said, wanting to bring the two of them together. But of course the Borough meant nothing to Narcisa.

Was there something wrong? he wondered as they sat down. Certainly she wasn't quite as he'd remembered. She seemed smaller, her shoulders a little rounded, more grey in her hair. Perhaps she was tired: they worked her too hard at the asylum, that he'd seen.

'I am a little late,' she said, seeing his cup. 'I am sorry; there was someone I had to see. Nothing serious; only about the butter.' She smiled quickly, putting it aside.

'What would you like?' he asked. 'This is Ceylon, but they have Earl Grey, too, if you like that?'

'Earl Grey?' she said. 'Oh yes. No, I will have what you are drinking.'

He topped up the pot with hot water, and poured her tea. 'What about something to eat? They have teacakes? Or scones?'

This was what he always felt, now he remembered. He wanted to pour tea and butter scones for her; and if they weren't in public, he'd feed them to her, a piece at a time, from his hand. And yet she wasn't thin and under-nourished. A strong body, he recalled, with small dark breasts, and heavy thighs. 'How have you been?' he asked.

She considered, while the waitress took their order. Toasted teacakes, he had decided, since she seemed so unwilling to make a choice. He turned back from the waitress for her answer.

She refolded and smoothed the napkin by her plate.

'Is there something wrong? Nora, has something happened?'

'My name is not Nora.' Her voice was very flat. 'They have always called me Nora but my name is Narcisa.'

He remembered her walking out after the concert, and put his hand over hers, as if to keep her. 'I do apologise, I didn't know. Narcisa? Is that how you say it? It's a pretty name.'

She looked down. She didn't seem to be angry with him.

'If there's anything I can help with.' He was caught, concerned, knowing he was connected to her. He had looked forward to an easy afternoon; but after all, people were more than that.

He buttered a teacake and handed her the plate. She ate attentively, as if it were something she'd never tasted. Her hands seemed very large and capable.

He waited. The teacakes were perhaps a little stale. It was rationing; no doubt they did their best. And the place was empty, apart from himself and Narcisa.

When she had finished she wiped her mouth on her

napkin, then the tips of her fingers. She sat back in the wheelback chair, and looked at him.

'I am thinking about giving in my notice.'

She seemed calm now; as if she really had only been hungry. Still he felt he needed to be cautious.

'How long have you worked at Holywell?' he asked.

'Ten - no, I think it is eleven years.' He was hearing the accent in her voice, the vowels drawn out.

'It's a long time. Are you just ready for a change?'

She shrugged. He poured them both some more tea.

'Do you know what you want to do? Have you something in mind?'

'No,' she said simply. 'I have no idea. And perhaps it's impossible. But I have done this before, when I was younger.'

'Well,' he said, considering, 'I'm sure you can. I assume you don't want just to go to another hospital?'

She spread her hands. 'I don't know. I have been a housekeeper; perhaps I could do that again.'

He hated the thought at once: Nora in service, at the beck and call of some ignorant rich couple. He hoped the war had done away with all that. 'You should come up to London,' he said. 'Get out of here. You would find more people you could get on with.'

'Shall we go?' she said abruptly. He gestured to the waitress, and paid the bill.

Outside on the slush-brown pavement he said, 'Shall we go for a walk?'

She collected her bicycle and walked beside him.

'I should hire one of those,' he said. 'We could go out into the country. Up on the Downs.' He looked around the High Street for a cycle shop.

'Is it the George where you are staying again?'

He was startled.

'I want to go back there with you. To your room.'

He stopped, and bent down to kiss her on the mouth. Then he took her bicycle from her, and wheeled it along, walking very close to her, not quite touching.

*

I'm rattled, he thought, hanging his jacket on the back of the chair. Nora - but he must call her Narcisa now - had gone off down the corridor to the bathroom, a small, determined figure, head down, overpowered he'd thought by the hotel corridor, the brown embossed wallpaper and flowered carpet. He'd stood at the door and wanted to call out.

He pulled at the knot of his tie. Wasn't this what he had wanted, after all? But it wasn't just that she had pre-empted him. She had cut through all the delicious civilities, that was true, the things that you did together to pass the time, when you both knew really you wanted to go to bed. But that wasn't enough to have left him shaken. He thought back to the tearoom. It was Nora: that revelation of her name. Why now, after the months that he'd had it wrong? And this sudden idea that she'd leave, go off into service.

She knocked at the door and he went swiftly to open. 'I hope it was clean,' he began to say, but stopped, bending down to wrap her in his arms and crush her against him. He felt her breathe out, with something like a sigh. Then he leaned back a little to take hold of her face. The roof of her mouth against his tongue made him dizzy.

I am out of control, he thought as he took off his shirt. He had undressed her already, impatiently; she was lying in bed, the sheet pulled up over her breasts. I am not like this. He got into bed and made himself hold back, watching her dark face for what she wanted. Her eyes with the deep shadows disturbed him again.

He moved his hands carefully over her body. Everything about her seemed smaller today, her breasts in the swabbed light through the green curtains, the bones of her hips. He became absorbed, as if testing for a response, finding her hard to reach in her sombre state. A tremor went through her and she sheltered against him. Then she lay back and put one arm over her eyes.

'What is it?' he asked.

She reached down to the floor beside the bed, then turned back to him with something in her hand.

'Your stockings? Do you want.. ?' He was nervous, alive with dread.

She reached out and grasped the bedpost, the stocking trailing still out of her fingers. He saw she couldn't say the words to him.

He took the stocking gently out of her hand and tied it in a knot round her wrist, then to the bedpost. Her arm was stretched out, the inside pale in the underwater light.

'Please,' she said, and he moved naked around the bed to find the other stocking, then, seeing he needed more, his red scarf. She watched him in silence, her eyes almost black. He looked round for something to tie her other ankle. In anticipation she stretched her right leg out, spread-eagled.

Doubtful, he lifted his leather belt to show her. She nodded.

What have I done? he thought as he tightened it above her ankle-bone, and clicked the buckle. He leaned over and covered her black pubic hair with his hand. Then he climbed back on the high bed and left his thoughts, as her body rose to his against the restraints.

*

She left her bike in its place at the far end of the shed. The racks were full: everyone else it seemed had stayed back here, on duty, or playing cards in the staff canteen, or gossiping in their rooms. She felt the weight of the habitation of the place, the hundreds of patients and nurses, ground-staff and domestics. And probably she knew all of them by sight; in her mind there were people for each of these bicycles, every uniform that went through the laundry, every spoonful of mashed potato that she cooked. She flexed her shoulders. The warmth of cycling was already leaving her; she felt stiff. All of these people who knew her, and didn't know. Not for the first time, she wondered if word had got around, if the new Assistant Clerk had talked. But even if they knew, would she find out? Would she be able to tell from the way they looked?

Up in her room, she shook her coat and put it on a hanger behind the door, then took off her shoes. The snow had seeped in at the toe of the right one; the stocking was damp. She unclipped the suspenders and peeled it off. Her skin seemed sallow under the central light. She ran both hands down her calf. Just above the ankle there was still a mark, where Anthony's brown belt had been pulled tight.

I wanted that. It came to her as a hollow feeling, as if she had learned she had some hidden illness: malaria, perhaps; or TB, like Clara. The idea had come to her suddenly; and then she couldn't have gone through anything else; her body was aching to stretch out against the knots. Never before; she'd never even thought of it.

There was more; she knew there was more of it inside her. As Anthony was doing what she'd asked, as she closed her eyes and fought against the bonds, she had seen something else, another familiar image, and shaken her head, hard, so the hair fell into her eyes.

I wanted..

She leaned forward and covered her face with her hands. The smell of her room surrounded her, talc and polish and the subtle smell of her own skin from the sheets. Her leg began to feel chill, without the stocking.

So I am still the same asylum patient. But this was worse; it was not just remembering. This is how they keep you, she thought, with a new bitterness. Thirty years later you're begging for what they did.

She stood up, and looked for a dry pair of stockings in the drawer. On top of the chest was the sewing she'd left from last night, an ochre dress she was making into a blouse. She picked it up; pins fell onto the floor. The cotton between her hands was soft with wear.

No, I can't sit here sewing all evening, she thought, and knelt down to pick the pins off the rug. She looked round the room. It was neat as ever, clean, the varnished oak of the chest of drawers almost black, the flat panel at the foot of the tall narrow bed.

She put on the stockings and dry shoes, and brushed her hair, and went out into the corridor. The sounds of other people were seeping out under the closed doors, and mixing up in the cold green-painted space: the high-pitched laugh of a young woman, amongst other voices; the low murmur of a man's voice, forbidden here in the women's block; music. She stopped to listen. It was jazz, a radio she supposed or a gramophone; a sinuous plaintive sound, was it a sax? and a woman's nasal, plaintive voice: *Ain't these tears in my eyes telling you?*

The slow emphatic line stayed in her mind as she went down the stairs. *Ain't these tears.* That's what I want, music, she told herself. She was becoming someone else, erratic and restless, fallen outside the nest of work and order. *Ain't these tears in my eyes.* But she wasn't sad. She walked through the corridors.

There had been the concert with Anthony: the pianist hunched over the keyboard in her black dress, the melody that seemed to fall in gold chains.

I want a piano.

It was years since she'd played; not since Felix, the piano teacher, way back before she'd come to work at the asylum. Still she knew now that that was what she needed, the pads of her fingers on the yellowed keys, her whole body filled with the music in her head that she had to press out through her fingertips, a kind of violence that flowed up her spine.

A piano? Here? You are mad, she was saying to herself, even as she went through doors and along hallways towards the housekeeper's office at the centre. And if Miss Fleming is in there? Or it's locked?

She knocked at the door. Miss Fleming had stuck something against the glass, a chart perhaps. She knocked again, then tried the china handle.

The door opened. There was a wide desk, like her own, and cupboards and filing-cabinets, and in a jar on the desk chrysanthemums, little bright-yellow flowers they called button chrysanths. The smell - it was like allspice, she recognised - reached her as she was closing the door behind her.

No time to stand in the middle of the floor, wondering about the bony Miss Fleming, who frequently reduced domestics to tears with her sarcasm, and nevertheless had flowers in her office. Narcisa felt clear-headed and light. Beside the desk there was the key-cupboard, its wooden door slightly greasy with finger-marks; then the rows of the keys and the numbered list at the side.

She peered at it in the dim light from the window. There: *36 Chapel.*

She lifted the long key off its hook, and closed the cupboard. Suppose at this moment Miss Fleming came in? Or Dr Bosanquet in the corridor?

They won't.

It was snowing again as she went out to the chapel. She ran along the gravel path and huddled against the door as she unlocked it, the iron key turning readily in her hand.

Inside she felt around for a light switch. A pale grey snow-light was filtering through the windows, picking out the polished ends of the pews. All this is going to be visible, she realised; as soon as I put on the light, they will all see it, everyone in the rooms at the front, and the nurses' homes.

She gave up on the switch and walked slowly on the checkered black and white tiles towards the altar. The piano was pushed to one side, a dusty green cloth thrown over it.

She folded the cloth and laid it on a pew. As she sat down and opened the lid her hands were trembling.

She played a tentative scale with her right hand. The sound was not good, dull and a little tinny.

Never mind.

It seemed for a moment that there was no music in her, nothing to make her lifted hands come down and search out inflections amongst the keys that were blurred to grey in the half-light of the chapel. Then something came back, not a title, a sensation, an impetus of sound, and she let it lift just as she remembered, up along her spine and through her shoulders and down the length of her arms. The music unfurled itself steadily in her mind, just at the second when her hands were making it; there was no delay and yet she could make a choice, slow now and solemn, holding it back -

Her hand stumbled. Stopped.

Is that all I can do? *No,* she told herself, and stretched her arms to the side and began again, the start of the phrase just before she had faltered: *no,* as it happened again and she made herself open her hand and find the fingering in the right, *no, again,* like an insistent teacher, so the sound, louder now, repeated, opened out in the cold chapel with its smell of bleach and wax, her anger riding up through her into the phrasing till her hand would work and she started to play again, breathing out, leaning back.

After a while she stood up and stamped her feet. I should have brought my coat and scarf, she thought. She buffeted herself to get warm, to make sure the blood kept flowing into her fingers, the joints didn't stiffen. Then she sat down again.

Hold back here, soften it, she told herself, and the tone the piano offered her was kind, the notes fell through the air one at a time like snowflakes. *Now:* and she leaned into it, her foot on the pedal, the sound expanding out all around her, *now.* But then it sounded wrong, and she stopped again, upbraiding herself, telling herself she could do it, like a jockey in a long race, up in the stirrups, shouting and beating the horse at the same time. Nothing for many years had mattered so much. *Now:* and the chords crashed, she was an orchestra, occupying the air, jostling the people with noise, pushing at the lit windows of the main asylum buildings across the grass, a sound that was travelling over the grounds and flooding out the gate onto the lane, where one October day she had escaped, and pulled the young gardener down with her onto the leaf-mould, under the tree, and smoothed his worried face with the flat of her hand, saying to him in her own language, 'Thank you. Thank you.'

But the work still had to be done. There were new patients arriving every week, and new staff; and they all had to eat, breakfast and elevenses and lunch and supper, cooked food and coffee and tea and bread from the bakery and milk from the farm. There were menus to plan and meat and fish to order and discussions about potatoes and kale and carrots. The snow melted off the lawns and the trees, the paths glistened wet. A little brown slush remained under the hedges, along the perimeter fence where it stayed dark, between the isolation huts and the dank brambles. Then a few days later it was all white again.

A new Assistant Cook arrived, a tall broad-shouldered woman with short grey hair. She opened the door of the kitchen at six o'clock on Monday morning, and held out her hand. 'Rosaleen Shaw,' she said. 'From Australia.' But what did that mean about her? Narcisa wondered. 'Later,' she said to the woman. 'We will speak later'; and left her standing, to go back to June Ragless who was mixing up egg-powder. Behind her the woman whistled under her breath. But later, there she was, in cap and apron, placing slices of bread flat on the grill with large reddish hands.

Once the breakfast was served and the girls were clearing up, Narcisa led Rosaleen Shaw through to the office. The woman had already been hired; there was no point in questions. 'I don't mind,' she said, as the woman opened her handbag and took a certificate out of an envelope. 'You will work, we will see.' She felt her English stripping itself bare, down to the simple verbs she had first learned. The certificate lay awkwardly across the table. Dear god, she thought, I had better be civil to her. She managed to smile. 'Tell me where you worked before.'

'Well, in fact, the place was very similar,' the woman said, and went on, though Narcisa wasn't listening. The voice was nasal; it went up and down at unexpected times, as if the statements all turned into questions. She had pale blue eyes beneath thick eyebrows. She told her story with enthusiasm, half there still in her Australian hospital, feeling her competence appreciated. She won't see that anything's wrong, Narcisa thought. She'll gossip, this woman, but she's not observant. Still the threat of being gossiped about made her shiver.

The voice had stopped. 'Very good,' Narcisa said. What did you do if you had an Assistant Cook? It was so long now since she'd had anyone: Theda Marshall, who'd gone to join the Wrens. 'This week,' she said, making it up hastily, because if not she would have to talk to the woman, tell her something about herself: 'This week you work with me. Then we will divide, what I do and what you do.'

'That will be fine.' The woman sounded relieved.

It was like having someone there to stop her thinking. She woke in the night and found herself in panic, imagining Violeta looking for her, walking up the path to the main door. In her cold room, huddled under the blankets, she would see her daughter, tall and strong with long black hair, enraged with her, lifting a hand to hit her. I couldn't help it, Narcisa told herself, trying to stave off a kind of fear she had thought belonged only on the wards, on the far side of the curved corridor. What else could I have done? She made herself lie flat on her back, arms by her sides, willing heaviness into her feet, her legs, her torso; then found herself anyway whimpering again, curled up on her side on the cold stretch of sheet. It was a release when five o'clock came and she had to dress.

In the kitchen there was the woman, Rosaleen Shaw, with her large impassive face and powerful arms, waiting to be told, watching. Narcisa soon could see she was capable. She watched respectfully and asked a few questions; and the next day she was saying 'May I do that?' organising tea and biscuits for mid-morning, even suggesting one or two minor changes, a way to cook sprouts that made sure the stems weren't hard. I can leave things to her, Narcisa thought, and thawed a little. Still she had some sense that the woman might break out, and laugh raucously one morning, or dance perhaps.

Rosaleen was there all day long in the kitchen, and though she made few demands, her presence made it impossible to daydream. I have left my daughter upstairs in my room, Narcisa thought one morning as she unlocked the kitchen; and imagined the young woman she had never met, at a first floor window, leaning both hands on the window-frame, locked in. She shook her head and entered her safe domain, the earthenware crocks lined up on the shelf, the pans hanging. Almost at once Rosaleen Shaw came in, her skin shiny, her powerful voice suppressed to a courteous murmur. She has become the guard of my sanity, Narcisa thought, and focussed with relief on the question of lard.

She had done nothing. It was three weeks since Dr Bosanquet had told her, and she had neither replied to the letter nor asked him to. It seemed to her that there was no point in action; that just as the endless eggs and roasts had to be prepared for the hungry asylum, so this other thing would roll on, the search that had started already somewhere in London and would end with her, unable to forestall it, standing face to face with her thirty-year-old daughter. By day, in the brief times that she was alone, the horror came back to her, that she had done nothing to find her child and claim her. When she finds me I will have nothing to say. I have no defence. In the kitchens, working, she suddenly felt old, her shoulders aching, her body heavy beneath the overall and apron. By the end of the working day she was exhausted, a dull throbbing ache behind her eyes; but still she sat on till late in her office, planning the menu or adding up the accounts. Back in her room was the image of Violeta, abandoned again.

*

The letter came, in a thick white envelope without a stamp, along with the outside post. She was too busy that morning to be curious, June and one of the working patients off sick. A letter from the other butcher, in Raynes Park, to inform her of their competitive prices, and that East Hill and St Botolph's were more than satisfied. Instructions from the London County Council about nutrition and the need for vegetables. A hand-written note from the bakery; she'd come back to it. She stood up, ready to get back to the kitchens, thinking already how she would change the rota to get everything done, and slit the white envelope open with her thumb.

It was on the hospital's good headed paper.

He is dismissing me after all.

She leaned back against her desk and made herself read it. The type was fuzzy with too much ink. The paper smelled she thought of hospital soap.

Dear Mrs Humphreys
Further to our discussion of 3rd December,
Further to: what does that mean? These stupid phrases.
I am writing to confirm my strong disapproval of your conduct heretofore in the matter discussed.

She looked up at the office door, her eyes smarting. He has told me already how much he disapproves. Of course it was not only her lying, as he saw it, nor that she had been mad and might be again; it was the disgrace, the illegitimate child. She wondered if he had looked up the hospital records. He would think her immoral, an unsuitable influence.

As I emphasised, an employer has the right, not only morally but in English law, to expect the honesty of his staff at all times. The fact that the act of deception took place some years ago is of no relevance.

Yes, yes, she thought, hearing him pronounce the clumsy English words in his throaty voice. He breathed thickly, she remembered, between sentences. She skimmed down, impatient to know his verdict.

...I think it important to put this in writing to you..
...should there be any further instances, at any level at all, of dishonest conduct...

Dishonest! she thought indignantly, and put the letter behind her on the desk. Dishonest! I have been responsible for hundreds, thousands of pounds-worth of supplies. I could have stolen enough to keep a whole family, and no-one would have known. He has no idea.

She picked up the letter.

...of dishonest conduct brought to my attention, I shall have no alternative but to recommend to the Committee your immediate dismissal.

She sat down and pushed both hands up through her hair. The weight of the words, their ponderous contempt, made her feel heavy herself, and middle-aged.

So if anybody chooses to go to him. If one of the kitchen assistants turns against me. Or the baker, if I complain about the bread.

She read through to the end of the letter, but there was nothing more that seemed important.

I would rather be dismissed outright than this. To be spied on; to wait for something to happen.

She looked at the clock. Twenty past ten, and the morning tea to do.

I told Anthony I might leave. Perhaps I should. Dr Bosanquet waiting for me to make a mistake. And then Violeta.

I cannot think about her, while this goes on.

She swept the letter into her desk drawer.

*

The snow lay thick against the trunks of trees, across the expanse of grass, banked up in the lane beneath dull brown hedgerows. The paths across the grounds were swept clear every morning by a work-gang of male patients, but iced over quickly, so that nurses running to be in time for the afternoon shift squealed together and staggered. The sky was grey and low, the air raw-cold. Narcisa began to long for her bicycle, to ride again down the alleys into Epsom, leaning into the wind, feeling strength in her thighs. Or somewhere further than Epsom, she thought, and wondered why she had never ridden far; on the the Downs, say, where the race-horses were exercised. She had seen them once, silhouetted on the horizon. A long time ago, when she was a housekeeper.

The roads had not been gritted: that was the talk. Well, she thought suddenly, coming back to her room with the afternoon free; I can still go on foot. There must be something I need. She looked round, but the room was plain and diffident as ever. Some knitting-wool perhaps; she could make new gloves.

The lane was slippery, but her boots gripped well enough. She walked quickly, along the edge where the snow was clean. A car passed, wide of her, and hooted: perhaps someone she knew. The damp cold air seemed to scrape at her cheekbones, her wrists when she took her hands out of her pockets. Another car; she had to step back sharply, towards the hedge; her coat caught in the brambles. Never mind, she told herself; better to be outdoors, moving.

Johnson's the draper's shop was almost empty. The assistant, an elderly woman with a black built-up shoe, remembered her and seemed to want to chat. 'You still working over there, dear?' A leery fascination on the powdered and lipsticked face. Town people kept away; they didn't want to know about the asylums. And if I told her I was once a patient? She looked at the older woman, curious; but there was no hint of compassion in the face. 'Double knitting, I think, for this weather,' she said, pleasantly enough, and bought a skein of scarlet, and a set of double-pointed needles to do the fingers.

Here in the town centre more of the snow had melted, or turned to light-brown slush in the gutters and doorways. It was still only three o'clock. By four it would be getting dark; she should start back then. She could go now; there was nothing else she needed. Still there was some sense of adventure in being out, away from the hospital on this icy day. She looked around. There was Hartley the butcher's shop; the ironmonger's; the elaborate white facade of the car showroom; and there across the road the little tea-room where she had met Anthony. A sign she'd never noticed, on the first floor between the narrow windows, offered CYCLISTS' TEAS.

The waitress seemed to remember her, was friendly. She ordered a scone and a pot of tea: 'The other kind, very scented, what do you call it?' The room was warm, a coal fire in the corner. Left alone, she sat back and took off her gloves. She was by the window; people passed, hunched and hurried, on the street. She had a sense of shelter, privilege.

'Patricia,' a woman's voice, pinched and offended. 'Patricia, I have told you, you mustn't take so much jam all to yourself. Put some of it back now.'

A clatter of cutlery. Narcisa smiled, half-listening. She had been feeling strange in the past week, aware that she should be worried and unable to think, even most of the time remember what it was.

'That's better. No, she's doing terribly well, she was top of her class last term, weren't you, Patricia?'

But work had become straightforward again. That was the relief, to go back to the competence she was used to, to manage the staff as she always did, a little severe perhaps, but fair, they knew she was fair.

The waitress brought a tray, and unloaded a teapot, milk-jug, hot water jug, glass dishes of jam and butter, a small blue-rimmed plate with two scones. The table was crowded. It's the ritual, she told herself, suppressing astonishment. This is how the rich have afternoon tea. Not only the rich; anyone with a little money. Or time. Miss Grey and Miss Ainsworth, and I made the scones and jam. Anthony and his wife, sitting at home.

'We're really lucky, Patricia loves school, don't you? She's a clever girl.'

A mutter, presumably from the child.

'Another piece? Well, let's see if Aunt Lizzie wants one first.'

Narcisa shifted slightly so as to see them. The woman

speaking had a black pillbox hat on marcelled hair; her friend, or perhaps it was her sister, was taller, with a pearl necklace and blue silk scarf. The little girl, Patricia, sat between them, in a grey school uniform blazer and a white blouse, and played with her cake-fork.

She made herself look away, and poured more tea. It was hard to relax. It was true that she had been waiting for something to happen; and though it now seemed nothing would, she was cautious still. As if I might see Violeta here, she thought, and looked abruptly at the child's mother, so that the woman coughed and looked away. How could I tell, that woman or anyone?

The little girl had left her table and come to the window, to watch a coal-lorry parked across the street, a man unloading, lifting the grey sacks one at a time on his shoulder and walking half-stooped along an alley. The second time he vanished, the child turned back towards Narcisa and stared.

'Hello,' Narcisa said, feeling uncertain. The child was eight or nine, a little plump.

'I've got bronchitis.' She said it importantly, and waited.

'Goodness,' said Narcisa. 'Isn't it too cold for you, if you are ill?'

'The doctor says I'm much better. Our doctor's called Dr Meadowcroft, do you know him? He says I can go out but I can't go back to school yet.'

She considered. 'Is that good, then, not to go back to school? So you can come and have tea here instead?'

'It's all right.' She came closer to Narcisa's table. 'What I really like is playing with my friend. She's called Veronica but I call her Ronnie. Why do you talk like that? You know, funny?'

'Because I'm not English.' She smiled, awkward. It was a long time since anyone had reminded her of her accent.

The child looked at her intently. 'Are you a German?'

'No, I'm not German.' But what could she say, that would make sense to a child? 'I come from another country, a long way away.'

'I thought you were a German spy.' She stared at the teapot. 'Were you on our side during the war?'

The doubt again. 'I have lived in this country a very long time.'

The child began to play with the tablecloth, pleating the starched edge between her fingers. 'You could always go to elocution,' she said helpfully. 'I'm going to elocution next term. And Ronnie is, if her Daddy will let her.'

'Elocution?' She was puzzled.

'They teach you how to speak nicely. Usually it's children but I expect grown-ups can go too.'

'Thank you,' she began to say; but at once in spite of her there were tears in the back of her throat, and behind her eyes. If I start to cry I'll frighten her, she thought, and reached in her handbag for a handkerchief. The child watched, curious, as she blew her nose. 'Well,' she said, after what seemed a long time. 'It has been good to talk to you, but I must go. It will be dark soon and I am walking.' She turned and signalled to the waitress. The little girl shrugged, and went back to her table. As she closed the door, Narcisa heard the mother saying, '..and you mustn't bother people.' She hurried away, the tears already running down her cheeks, making ice-cold tracks that the wind then chilled further, in the half-dark of the alleys out of town.

*

I am going mad again.

She was sitting up in bed in the cold room, in the dark, an old cardigan round her shoulders, the bedclothes pulled up to her collar-bones. A faint light bled in through the gap in the curtains. The washbasin had a dull bluish sheen against the dark wall, next to the unlit mass that was the wardrobe.

I am losing my mind. This is how it happens.

She had wept all the way back, in the bitter cold, with no idea why. That was how it had been before. That was how it had started, when she was young, with Edwin: days of crying, unable to stop or explain. But was that what had happened? So many years ago: thirty-three, thirty-four. She was hardly the same person. It was different, she told herself, hunched under the bedclothes. He was out at work and I was all alone. He was the only one who spoke any language that I could understand. The tears came back but she rubbed them away: self-pity.

She went back over the time since she'd had the news. The first day it was shock, understandable. But I was useless all day, she told herself; I had to make that girl take charge of lunch. Was that more than shock? Then Anthony, what she had made him do to her. I have never wanted that before, never, she thought. He had not objected, no; but would he object? I am not his wife, she thought bitterly, only his mistress. And in any case, men have different ideas, what is acceptable. Even Anthony.

But that is not the point, she told herself, leaning forward under the covers to warm her feet in her hands. It's not whether other women do these things, but if I am suddenly behaving differently. The thing she hadn't told him came back, the vivid image that had come to her mind as he entered her: herself, in a white linen straitjacket, her arms tied down, her body open to him. She bent her head to her knees and sobbed once, in shame.

I can't be mad. I will have to control myself. There was a high-pitched yelp out in the grounds; she started, turning towards the curtained window. Not human: some animal, out in the woodland. Today I thought I was in control, she went on; as if winning the argument with her fearful self, her mad self, would mean she could stay sane. Today I felt better and then look what happened.

It was the child; she supposed it was the child. A plump little English girl with pale fine hair. Nothing like Violeta. Who anyway is thirty, not a child. It was the child, asking about my accent. More honest than adults, who think it but don't remind you. But why should I burst into tears when a sulky child says I sound peculiar? I must be already in a dangerous state. The old phrase came back to her from the time as a patient: *in a dangerous state. In need of medication.* And of course it is worse since Dr Bosanquet's letter.

Then what do I do, if I am in that kind of state? She got out of bed and stood in front of the window, holding the curtains apart with both hands. Her flannel nightdress flapped slightly in the draught. Cold seeped into her feet from the polished boards. How happy Dr Bosanquet would be, proved right: no more former patients on the staff. I could go to his office and tell him I'm mad again. Totally honest: that's what he said he wanted. She laughed in silence, a small desolate laugh. They'd send me away, East Hill or even further. There was that young nurse who started hearing voices; they sent her over to Hanwell, on principle. Though what was the principle? That patients must not know that staff can be ill?

I'm avoiding the issue, she told herself severely. That fact was that it was too terrible to imagine; to remember at all how she had felt before, her five years as a patient. She'd decided, long ago, to cancel the memories. Otherwise how could I have worked here for so long? Now for the first time it seemed to her terrible, that she'd come back, years after being discharged, to work in the same place where she'd been detained.

Perhaps I always knew I'd go mad again.

She shook her head, and went to the chest of drawers for some knitted bedsocks. Who could I tell? Not Matron, Miss Atkinson. One of the ward sisters? She pictured them lined up in the corridor, a dozen brisk unimaginative competent women. No, none of them. They would panic, or else try to reassure her; or go to Matron.

She got back into bed and lay down stiffly, on her back on the now cold sheet. What help do I want from them anyway? she wondered. Drugs, or electric shock, or insulin? The straitjacket? Back in the padded room? She lay still and waited till her body warmth spread out a little and warmed the thin bedclothes. I will have to be careful. It was all she could think of. I will have to watch, and see if it gets worse. And then I suppose I will just pack up and leave.

And then of course Violeta will never find me.

It was almost comfort; but not enough for sleep. The animal, a fox perhaps, barked again. She thought she heard a car rattling down the lane, but it could have been a milk-float, or something older, a horse and cart out of her memory, driving away, what she had once most feared.

'Go on, Cook,' June Ragless was saying, speaking over her shoulder, leaning to scour inside a great black saucepan. 'Give yourself a night off for once. It'll do you good.' Then a deep-pink flush spread up over her neck, and she turned back to work at the pan.

Rosaleen Shaw stood calmly by the table. The patient, Esme, was at the draining-board, with a tall pile of white plates against her apron.

'Very well. You do not have to stop working,' Narcisa said. Esme moved carefully over to the crockery cupboard, holding the top plate in place with her chin.

'I only thought you might like to consider,' Rosaleen Shaw said at last, when they'd watched the plates safely restored to their shelf. 'The meal is quite straightforward, don't you think?'

The girl whose name Narcisa could never remember came back from the bins, and stood beside June Ragless, who whispered to her.

Do they all think I need a rest? Narcisa wondered. She sat down at the table and looked over at the young cook in the picture tiles, kneading improbable pastry with slender hands. Don't be stupid, she told herself. More likely the Shaw woman wants to prove herself. She looked up at the Assistant

Cook, large and capable, her white apron stretched tight over her stomach. Perhaps she was reporting to Dr Bosanquet. But what can she report? That I am tired?

'If you feel you are ready,' she said, with some effort.

'I reckon I can do it,' the woman said; and Narcisa felt a familiar disquiet, the faint note of triumph in the careful voice. 'June here and Peg will put me right if needs be. You go out and have yourself a good time.'

She is patronising me, Narcisa thought. 'What I will do does not matter. It will be good practice for you, that is true. We will see how you manage. Now please go on working, all of you.'

The clatter restarted. Rosaleen Shaw, avoiding Narcisa's eye, sat down at the far end of the table with pencil and paper. June Ragless rinsed out the pot and upended it to drain. The patient Esme slid another pile of plates onto the dresser, and tucked a strand of colourless hair into her cap. 'I'll tell you what, Cook,' she said, in a high tense voice. 'If you don't want a night out, I'll go for you.' She giggled, but there was something else in her lashless eyes.

*

Outside she started walking towards the bike-shed, but changed her mind and headed for the main gate. Four or five nurses were going out, laughing and leaning against each other. Narcisa passed them just before the gate-house. 'Good afternoon, Cook,' one of them called; and another one, daring, 'Going for a night on the town?' She walked on, hearing the suppressed laughter behind her.

What would it have been like, she wondered, walking fast along the lane to keep warm, the dark already spreading across the fields: to go out giggling with other young women? She hadn't, not in Prizren. Young women didn't go out alone.

And when she came here there was always Edwin. She wondered if Violeta had had that, a group of friends to go out with after work. Though perhaps it was only working-class girls who did?

She passed the parade of shops and came to the station. A poster showed a family staring at Big Ben. Yes, that's what I want, she thought, and waited at the window to buy a ticket.

A cold wind off the Downs swept along the high platform. A man in uniform came towards her. 'A good quarter of an hour yet, the Victoria train,' he said. 'You'd best be waiting inside.'

She followed him, and he opened a door with *Ladies' Waiting Room* engraved in the glass. An iron stove with a great black pipestack was pushing heat into the bleak room. A young woman sat in a corner reading a book.

Narcisa went up to the stove, and held her gloved hands close to the stack for heat. Was it true that her daughter wasn't working-class? She had wanted to think that Violeta had been fostered by people with money and education. But suppose she hadn't been fostered at all? Now she allowed the idea it was obvious. Did all the workhouse children get boarded out? That was what it was called, Clara had told her: boarded out. Why had she been so sure Violeta would be?

She sat on a bench, away from the woman reading. Or she could have been fostered by someone quite ordinary. Someone like Clara. A feeling of shame drained the warmth down out of her. Clara is a good woman, she told herself. She thought of the thin girl ironing opposite, taking on the ironing-room bully for her. Clara was so poor. When she left Holywell she had gone to live with her sister and brother-in-law, and shared a bed with the two children. I wanted my daughter to have more. More than I had, or Clara. A proper school, and music, and an easy life.

I was too afraid to think anything else.

The man in uniform leaned in at the door. 'Five minutes,' he said. 'It's just left Sutton.' The young woman opposite folded down the corner of a page, then closed her book. She was tall and thin, a little like Clara, with a red scarf. Like the one Anthony had tied her up with. She saw the hotel room, the wallpaper, Anthony bending over to fasten her ankle.

The woman went out onto the platform, limping slightly. As the train pulled in a man leant out of a window, and the young woman ran along, limping, waving to him.

Narcisa got in and found a seat by the window. There was one other person in the compartment, a plump elderly woman, sitting in the centre of the bench-seat opposite. 'I hope you don't mind,' the woman said at once. 'I have to travel facing, or I get queasy.'

Narcisa nodded.

'I was so relieved,' the woman continued. 'Sometimes at Epsom the most unpleasant people get on. When my poor husband was alive it was all right, of course. But what can I do? I'm not going to stop getting the train.'

She had a pale-green hat, tilted forward, and a coat a few shades darker, with a fox tippet. All of the details seemed sharp and real to Narcisa, the carefully waved white hair beneath the hat, the plump feet pushed into court-shoes with brown leather bows.

'You make this journey often?'

'Every Thursday I go and see my sister in Wimbledon. She's a widow, too, now, her poor dear husband passed away in June. A sweet-natured man he was, nothing too much trouble, you know?' She sighed. 'Do you have sisters?'

Narcisa hesitated.

'Like that, is it?' the woman said. 'Such a shame. My sister Ellie and I, we've always stayed close. Even when they were living up near Blackpool, we always wrote.'

'My sister is far away,' Narcisa said, with some effort, because who knew whether Alma was still alive, even. 'It must be very good to have your sister near. Now you are both alone.'

'She says she doesn't know how she'd have managed,' the woman said, with a smile. 'So every Thursday we have our tea in the Marlborough Tearooms. Do you know it? It's very nice. Sometimes we do some shopping, or have a little walk, and back to her house. Nothing very exciting but it suits us.'

The train slowed down and drew in to a station. 'Where are we?' the woman asked, suddenly anxious. 'There I've been talking to you, I don't want to miss my stop.' She leaned forward ineffectually over a round stomach.

Narcisa went out to the corridor to look. 'Raynes Park,' she said, coming back and closing the door. 'It is all right.'

'Thank you, dear,' the woman said, and took out a little hand-mirror with a carved handle. 'Well, I suppose I'll do,' she added, and pushed the hat a little to one side. 'No, but you know, I don't move as fast as I did. Now, where were we?'

'Do you have any children?' Narcisa asked. The woman seemed so certain, her life so ordered.

There was a pause. 'I have one son,' the woman said; but it seemed as if she was making her voice sound bright. 'Maurice. He's forty now, would you believe? He's a good boy, he comes to see me whenever he can. He has a very responsible job, in shipping.'

'You must be proud of him,' Narcisa said.

'Oh I am. He was always the quiet one. No trouble, ever, Maurice, since he was born.' She paused. 'Well, I'll tell you, I did have another son, Teddie, he was my youngest, but he was killed in the war.' She sat upright and smiled at Narcisa.

'That is terrible.' Narcisa was shaken. 'Terrible.'

'In Italy. They did say he was a good soldier, he was very brave. Well, he always was, he was fearless, my Ted.'

The train slowed again. 'Here I am,' the woman said. 'See that spire over there?' She buttoned her coat and pulled on brown fur gloves. 'It's been very nice talking to you,' she said brightly. 'Perhaps we'll meet again?'

'Wimbledon, this is Wimbledon,' a man's voice called.

The woman stood up. 'Would you mind reaching my stick down? Thank you, dear. - Wait a minute, guard,' she called from the carriage door, and Narcisa saw the guard hurry to help her down to the platform, where another plump elderly woman, dressed in pastel blue, was waiting.

*

At Victoria there was a crowd pressed up close to the barrier, men in dark coats and bowler hats, a few women. She looked around, bewildered, for an exit. The people were streaming onto the station, walking fast, determined. Rather than venturing through to where they came from, she set off to her right, a narrow gap between station offices. It came out onto a side street. But I know this, she realised after a moment, and walked more firmly. It was almost dark, the streets with their corner pubs and tall houses glowing dully like cinders under the lamps. If I turn left here. There were signs of a street-market, empty stalls, a box with browning cauliflowers on the edge of the pavement. Then this is the road that goes towards the river.

Who have I ever mourned for? she asked herself, remembering the woman on the train, in her carefully chosen clothes and her doubtful smile. Violeta, of course; but was that the same? This woman had had the news of her son's death, and gone on, getting up in the morning on her own in the house, having tea with her sister, whatever you did if you were seventy, say, and living alone. Have I ever done that?

On the embankment she turned her back to the water, and scanned, distracted, for the house she'd lived in. People had died, of course, at the asylum. Patients died, and if they had no family were buried in the field across the lane. She remembered a plain little gathering, too awkward to be a procession: the chaplain, one of the doctors, two farmhands pushing the coffin on some sort of barrow. You knew that it happened; sometimes even the details found their way into the kitchen, in patients' gossip. TB, of course; and once there was a girl, seventeen or so, who'd managed to hang herself. Theda, her assistant at the time, full of shock and excitement, telling them.

Perhaps it was the street ahead of her. She roused herself and crossed over the road. It was hard to tell. The houses were dark now with soot. What was the number; was it seventeen? A small boy slammed a brown front door behind him, and ran off down the street ahead of her. There had been a shop, there where he went in, and the house was diagonally opposite. Not number seventeen then: twenty or twenty-two.

She paused across the road from the two houses and stared; but there was nothing to recognise. At number eighteen an upstairs sash window was pushed open with a creak, and a big woman with glasses leaned out and glared at her. Did I know my neighbours? she wondered, moving on, as the woman shouted towards another window. And if I did, or if they remembered. After all this time. Oh you were that tart - the word came to her out of the kitchen gossip - you were the tart with the fancy visitor.

She walked slowly, past the corner shop, a pub, a man carrying a heavy cardboard box. Did I feel like a tart? I didn't know what to think. How to live my life. She was sitting in an office in the City - Mr Stokeley's, her husband's solicitor - and he was explaining. Edwin would continue to pay her rent, as he had for the past six months, and the allowance; but only as long as she did not reclaim the child, 'Who is not his, and he does not recognise.' The voice expressionless, infuriating. 'Your husband believes that as he has been told the child is in the care of the authorities, this condition will be a formality, and should not cause you any difficulty.'

In French; all this had gone on in French. She turned at the top of the street and walked back. By the shop the small boy made a face at her. In French, or she would not have understood, not been able to answer. She had stood up; shouted. 'Then he is wrong.' The pain was so terrible, so unexpected, she had to shout or she would have fallen down. 'He is English and so he has no idea. She has a name. Violeta. She is my daughter.' He stayed in his seat, leaning forward, listening. 'If my husband will not support me, very well. On these conditions I will not accept his money. I am not a spoilt English lady. I have learned to work, in the asylum where he sent me.'

He had listened, and offered her lunch. The next week he wrote, to say that a client of his had a small house, and wanted a respectable tenant. 'You will not have to concern yourself with the rent.'

She was back at the river. The water was dark, the tide low. I used to come down here and stare at the water. Once or twice with Claud Stokeley. We walked along, and he showed me the house where the Archbishop lived, a big brick house behind a high wall; but he'd said that area was one of the poorest in London. 'They hardly have the money to be buried.' That was what he had said, and she had somehow remembered.

But what did I do about finding Violeta? She watched a barge go past, low in the water, tarpaulins tied across a heaped cargo. I remember how good it was, to be on my own. I sat in the drawing-room and played the piano. The housekeeper, Mrs Rubinstein, brought me tea. And then I persuaded her to teach me cooking.

She shook her head, and moved away from the railings. A bus was turning the corner from the bridge. On impulse she ran across the road, and jumped on as the bus slowed behind a taxi. 'Careful now,' the conductress said, as she steadied herself again and went upstairs, into the stale smoke.

*

The bus lurched sharply around a corner, and stopped. She looked out. There were naked walls, with blue and cream wallpaper and black fireplaces, teetering over a crater of stone and weeds. She stared down horrified at the rubble of buildings, the blackened beams sticking up at an angle, the piles of unidentifiable matter. The bus started up and she turned in her seat to keep the wall in sight, the delicate blue of the chimney-breast almost the colour of the winter sky. They passed a square church-tower in dark stone, but again when she looked down there was no chancel, only half-fallen walls and an empty window. On the other side, vast and oblivious, was St Paul's.

So this was what people had talked about: the bombing. No-one else on the bus looked at the bomb-sites. A man in the front was reading an evening paper, one arm leaning on the back of his seat. A woman was talking disapprovingly to her children. Perhaps they had lived here all through the war. There was a reproach to her in all this. It seemed a specially brutal demolition, that left the wallpaper someone had chosen, the fire he or she had sat by, and made them irrelevant, demolishing floorboards and carpets and chairs. And people too, she understood, a second later. Beneath that rubble would be the bones of people. So many people had been killed like this, in their own homes, at night; or injured, like the war casualties at the asylum. And then there were the ones killed abroad, like the son of the woman on the train: Teddie, she'd called him.

Didn't I ever think that Violeta.. ?

She got up hastily and went down the stairs of the bus, just as it turned a corner, wrenching her arm as she gripped onto the rail. The conductress grinned. 'It's the lights,' she called, but Narcisa leapt away, onto the pavement.

She headed up a side street, walking quickly. There were as she remembered the pompous buildings, banks she supposed, with great carved doorways and elaborate window-frames, and men in black with umbrellas entering. She turned a corner and found another church, intact this time, and a walled graveyard with white box tombs. Then she crossed a street and another bomb-site loomed, a spindly tree growing out of the debris, and two small boys clambering over the stones. She watched till one of them saw her and called something.

She sat down on a low wall. All these years I thought I was longing for her, and I never even worried she might be dead. In a bombing raid; or illness, like anyone.

For a while she watched the people passing. A young men ran down a flight of steps, his arms full of parcels. A van stopped and a boy threw out newspapers, tied in a bundle, into the doorway of a little shop. The woman on the train: she must have been worried all the time, about both her sons; the other one would have been in the forces too. And then how did she hear? A telegram? It was beyond imagining, the ordinary woman with all that grief. How she lived with the grief, and still was able now to get on a train and enjoy afternoon tea with her sister; and still of course the pain would be always there.

But I do know about the grief, she thought, and stood up, cold. All the time after they took Violeta. Crying at night in the ward, screaming. And even when I came out again. She had walked at Twickenham, along the tow-path for miles, hugging herself because of the aching space where the three-year-old child who lived god knew where would never press against her.

She went on walking, here through the city streets that were glittering cold under the street-lamps, with tears in her eyes that wouldn't fall.

*

'Victoria Station,' the bus conductor called. 'Who was it wanted Victoria? Was it you, darling?'

Narcisa stood up hastily, then waited in the aisle of the bus while a man in a worn coat hauled a vast suitcase out from under the stairs. The conductor watched cheerfully, one hand on the bell. 'Oh, come *on,*' someone muttered, standing behind Narcisa.

On the pavement she looked around, disoriented. The bus sped on, past dingy stuccoed hotels. The man with the suitcase was waiting to cross the road. She followed him, towards a row of half-glazed wooden doors, in a low building set back from the road. As she crossed, a taxi drew up, and a family emerged, calling to each other and laughing: two young boys, an elegant woman with a veil on her hat, a girl of eighteen or so with bobbed hair.

Was this the station? *Paris Brussels Geneva* said one of the signs. A man with a neat grey beard got out of the taxi, and the family headed towards a door marked *Golden Arrow,* a porter following with a pile of leather cases on a barrow.

At last she found the passage through to the station. People were hurrying towards a centre platform. Two men passed her, one either side, arguing in French: 'Tout à fait idiot, tu comprends pas?' An elderly woman was asking anxious questions of a very tall man in uniform. A small boy waved to Narcisa from his father's shoulder.

She stood, at the edge of all this excitement, looking along the platform. People opened carriage doors and pushed their luggage up before them, or leaned down from windows to talk to those on the platform. At the barrier a man was checking tickets and passports.

'Paris, madam?' someone asked beside her. It was the very tall man with the peaked cap.

She looked at him.

'Excuse me, madam. Are you for the night train to Paris?'

'Am I.. ? Oh, no, no.'

He began to move away. She was aware of the sour taste of the smoke. 'It goes to Paris?' she asked quickly, to keep him.

'That's the Golden Arrow, madam,' he said, proudly. 'It leaves here at eleven pm, and at Dover they load it into the hold of the ship - yes, onto the ship; and then at Calais they change the gauge, the breadth of the wheels, because they have a different track over there. And the passengers, they don't know nothing about it, they just wake up as it comes into Paris at nine o'clock tomorrow morning.'

'They stay on the train?' She stared at a woman in a travelling coat. The journey seemed some kind of modern magic, that only people in London would understand.

'That's the beauty of it,' the man said. 'They can have a night-cap tonight, and go to sleep, and wake up in time for breakfast and there they are, Paris. Excuse me, madam,' and he turned to examine a ticket in a young woman's hand.

Narcisa wandered away across the station. So simple, she thought. I have been living in this little town, when all I had to do was come up to London, and get on a train. The continent had swung back into view, Paris, the Swiss Alps, Milan, Venice, the shining parallel lines laid in one long straight path across the countries, the way she had come before the First World War.

She walked through the arch to the second part of the station. The board showed platform eight for Epsom, at five past ten. She looked round for the station clock; it was quarter to. I didn't even check the last train, she thought. I could have missed it and been stuck in London.

She found her ticket, and stood close to the barrier to wait. The station had cleared since the afternoon; the flower stall had gone, the chemist's and the bookshop were closed. A rattling sound made her turn, in time to see the metal shutter pulled down over the Left Luggage office. A woman came out of the Ladies' Waiting Room, pulling on her gloves.

A train drew in, the steam hissing and spreading out against the roof. A few people got off and walked slowly towards the barrier. She turned to watch two young women in high heels cross the concourse briskly to the tube.

A little group of men was heading towards her. There were two policemen, pale-faced and solemn under their helmets, walking one either side; and two strong-looking men in heavy coats, holding a thin young man by the elbows. The young man seemed scarcely to walk, as if his two companions were lifting him. He looked down, away from the few people watching idly as they waited for their trains. She thought he looked exhausted, and defeated.

'Evening, Mrs H.' She recognised one of the men just as

he spoke: it was Jim Morris, one of the male nurses, back a few months ago after the war. The group of men stopped as he addressed her, the policemen bored, the young man thin and unhappy between them.

'You been having a night on the town, then?'

She smiled. The other nurse looked curiously at her.

'This young man,' Jim went on cheerfully, 'had an idea of seeing the sights of London. Didn't you, lad? So me and Mike here had to come up and get him.'

The young man flushed and looked over Narcisa's shoulder. She wanted to say something comforting to him; but even her presence was a humiliation.

There was a silence. Eventually she said, 'Perhaps you should get on. You will need to find a compartment to yourselves.'

She watched while they walked along the length of the train, then found herself one of the little half-compartments, one bench and a blank partition, and sat looking out of the window onto the tracks.

She had to remind herself where the registry was, right at the end of the front corridor, past Dr Bosanquet's and Matron's rooms. She stood outside, then walked away again, out of the front door and down the steps. The wind was so cold it made her nostrils hurt. At least there was sun, the sky such a pale blue it was almost white, the shadows thin like smoke on the crisp lawn. She walked along the front of the building to the corner. Through the last tall window she could see a desk, and rows of ledgers on dark book-shelves. Someone, Mr Rathfelders she supposed, moved across the window towards the fire.

She went back inside and knocked on the registry door.

She had forgotten about his missing hand. He greeted her courteously, walked round his desk to pull up a chair for her: a good-looking young man, with a thin, intense face and hooded eyes. The awareness of his injury swept into her, how his life must have changed; have stopped, she thought; he had become someone else. She remembered him on his bike, before the war, slim and graceful, waving as he passed her on the lane.

'Well, what can I do for you, Mrs Humphreys?' He was waiting; but there was that strained note in his voice. Of course, he knows about me; he's embarrassed.

She settled more firmly on the upright chair.

'I believe you have seen the letter that came for me?'

'The letter: yes. Yes, I have it here.' He bent to open a low drawer in his desk. For a few moments, all she could see was his back, the navy-blue jacket of his suit. Then he sat up, the little blue envelope in his hand.

She stopped herself trembling.

'I am afraid I cannot give it to you,' he said, a little curtly. 'Since it was addressed to the hospital. But if you would like to read it?'

Her hand wanted to reach up and grab the paper.

Her eyes were hurting. Not in front of him.

'Thank you, but no. That is not what I wanted.' She made her voice harden. 'Mr Rathfelders, can I ask you: have you answered the letter? I am sorry, but you see, I need to know.'

She watched while he fidgeted the paper out of the envelope with his one hand, and flattened it out on the blotter in front of him. If she leaned forward, she would be able to read it all.

There were so few lines.

She sat back, and looked away, towards the fireplace. A few small flames flickered over large coals.

'I understood that Dr Bosanquet had informed you. I am sorry, I had assumed you would reply.' He seemed perturbed. 'Normally of course we answer letters within a few days. Perhaps I misunderstood?'

'No, Mr Rathfelders, please, it is my fault.' She rubbed at the swollen joint at the base of her thumb. There was a silence. She started reading the spines of the red ledgers: *Farm income. Needleroom supplies. Staff wages 1906 - 1910.*

He said, 'It must have been a surprise.'

She looked quickly at him. He was sitting very straight in his leather chair, the useless arm at his side. She had a sudden, illicit picture, herself in tears, the Clerk beside her with his one hand on her shoulder.

'Thank you,' she said steadily. 'I am afraid I also have not replied.' How could she explain this? He would think any mother would long to hear from her daughter. 'Mr Rathfelders,' she went on. 'Please, I want to ask you a favour.'

'Whatever I can do.' He looked puzzled.

'Please, will you write to - to the person who wrote the letter. And tell her..' What did she want him to say? 'Tell her you have not yet found..' But that was lying; she couldn't ask him to lie.

A car engine stuttered and stopped, out on the drive.

'Would you like me to tell her that we are making enquiries?'

She considered. 'Yes, that will be very good. Please. You are still making enquiries, and..'

He looked down at the blue letter again. 'I think I should say that we have found your name - the name she gives. It seems only..'

'Yes, yes,' she said, drenched with relief. 'What you think best. Only not that you know I am working here.' She looked at him again, the hooded brown eyes. 'I need more time, that is all.' She was making excuses.

'I quite understand, Mrs Humphreys,' he said, and stood, the empty cuff of his left sleeve swaying slightly.

*

She entered the kitchen and could sense something. There was a faint smell of stewing tea. Two of the patients were loading cups onto a heavy trolley, ready to wheel through to the dining-room; someone else was lifting down a stack of saucers. June Ragless was intently slicing bread, and the untidy girl, Peg, was buttering.

Perhaps the bakery had not sent enough cake again. Narcisa was about to ask 'What's wrong?' but the tall, bulky figure of Rosaleen Shaw, drying her hands by the draining board, discouraged her. 'This is all very good,' she said awkwardly.

She thought she saw the Assistant Cook raise her eyebrows.

June put down her bread-knife. 'Please, Cook, there's been trouble with one of the patients.'

'I thought we agreed,' Rosaleen Shaw said sharply, and June flinched. 'It's all in hand, Cook, nothing to worry about.'

So this is it, Narcisa thought, as though she had been waiting for weather to break. She will tell Dr Bosanquet. 'Thank you,' she said, the effort already becoming familiar, 'but I like to know what happens in my kitchen.' She turned to the patients, two thin, greasy-haired women. 'You can take that trolley through and lay the tables.' She watched as they steered it reluctantly though the door.

'It's just routine,' Rosaleen Shaw said, though her lifting accent seemed to contradict her. 'One of the patients arrived unfit to work. It seems like the nurses had problems with her too. I sent her to the infirmary and back to the ward.'

'Unfit?'

'Her wrist was swollen; I would say sprained. Well, she wouldn't be much use to us like that. The left wrist too, and unfortunately she's left-handed.'

June was evidently desperate to speak.

'Very well,' Narcisa said. 'I will see what has happened. Thank you. Now we must serve the tea, or they will be complaining.'

After the meal June Ragless busied herself, wiping down the trolleys, cleaning drips of jam off the kilner jars, till the others had finished and Narcisa, doing the books, had let them go. June washed out the dish-cloth and put it to dry over the side of the sink. Then she stood by the table, looking urgently at Narcisa.

'All right, June. Sit down.'

The girl sat forward, fidgeting with her fingers. She was pretty: blue eyes with maybe a smudge of last night's make-up, not allowed while working, and a clear, pale skin.

'You want to tell me something about the patient?'

She watched the flush spread up across June's throat. 'You won't tell *her?*'

So June Ragless is afraid of that woman. Narcisa felt her own anger surge again.

'Never mind Miss Shaw. I am still the Cook, I think.' She shouldn't have said that: not professional. 'I want to understand what has happened. I do not even know which patient it is.'

'Esme something, you know, the youngest one? A bit round-shouldered.'

'She was working this morning. She was well then?'

'She was OK, she was telling me about all her brothers and sisters, there's ten of them. It's all right, Cook, we were getting on with the work, I just thought it didn't do any harm.'

'But this afternoon?'

'She came back and her face was all puffy, you know? And she was holding onto her wrist, like this.' June demonstrated. 'So I said what's wrong and she didn't want to tell me. Only I made her show me, and it was all swollen, and it hurt when I touched it. You weren't in yet, so I said: We'd better tell Shaw. Sorry, Cook, Miss Shaw. She was right about one thing, Miss Shaw: Esme couldn't have worked with her hand like that. But Esme didn't want to tell. She said..'

June stopped and picked at the side of her nail.

'What did Esme say?'

A small tear made a smudge of the black make-up. 'She said one of the nurses did it. She said this nurse wanted her to do something, something stupid, and Esme wouldn't do it, and the nurse got hold of her and banged her arm up hard against the wall. And then she said Esme wasn't to tell. Cook..'

Narcisa sat still. The young cook in the picture tiles opposite made her pastry as if nothing was going on.

People are like that, she wanted to tell June; people have a little power and they use it. Instead she asked, 'So what did you do?'

'Well, I said to Esme something should be done. And then Miss Shaw came up and I said to Esme she had to tell her. So she did, she didn't want to and she just said a nurse did it, but not how. But, Cook, she - Miss Shaw - she just said Esme must have got out of hand, and as a punishment she wasn't to work today. And it was only because I said she should have it seen to..'

Narcisa looked away, over June's shoulder, at the dresser shelves. A saucer had been put on the wrong pile, on top of the tea-plates.

'The thing is, I'm worried I've got her into more trouble. It'll come out that she told, and then the nurse..'

'Let us hope Esme is sensible and will lie.'

June Ragless opened her mouth and closed it again. After a moment she asked, 'What are you going to do?'

*

The infirmary nurse was sitting at her desk, making notes in a ledger.

'Hello, Cook. What brings you up here?'

It was still a shock to her to be recognised. Still there was something about those broad cheek-bones.

'I remember you,' Narcisa said cautiously. 'Before the war, yes? You were working here?'

'May Gemmell,' the nurse said flatly. 'I left to get married, but he was killed. I started back last October. You might have known my husband too, he worked in the metal shop. Harold Bunce?'

It came back to her: shortly after she'd started, two young people and an older man, standing smoking one night outside the back door, the young man offering her a cigarette. 'I am sorry,' she said awkwardly. 'He was fighting?'

May Gemmell was visibly older, her face drawn, her hair under the cap a duller brown. 'That was what was so stupid,' she said, as if exhausted. 'He'd been in Egypt. Lots of his mates got killed and he didn't have a scratch. No, he was on leave, visiting his mum. An air raid.'

There was always something she'd liked about this woman. Though the night of the cigarette they'd been taunting her; or the husband had.

'You came down once to find me in the kitchen?' It was not quite a memory: an odd sense of excitement, with May, tall and supple, leaning in the doorway.

'Maybe. I can't remember. To be honest, I'm not that thrilled to be back here. But I've got two kids, you've got to do something, haven't you? Anyway' - she folded the ledger shut - 'nice to see you again. Did you want something?'

She wanted to ask May Gemmell about leaving, what life was like outside here; or perhaps, she thought, how you start your life again. Her shoulders ached a little; she flexed them. 'One of the patients who works in the kitchen: Esme Washbrook.'

'Oh yes, the sprained wrist. I strapped it up. She probably shouldn't use it for a day or so; after that, if you can find her something light to do.'

She could see the nurse was wanting to get on. 'Did she tell you how it happened?'

'I asked, but she just said an accident.'

'She told one of the girls that a nurse banged it on the wall, to punish her.'

There was a silence. I am taking a risk, Narcisa thought. She is a nurse too; she may think it's nothing. Or that I'm making trouble. She looked round for a chair, but there wasn't one. 'I know her, she has worked nearly a year in the kitchen.'

'You believe her?'

'I have not seen her; I was not there. But I do not think she would lie.'

'Oh Lord.' May Gemmell leaned her elbows on the desk, and pushed her fingers into her hair beneath the cap. Then she stopped suddenly and looked at her hands. 'I shouldn't be doing that.'

She opened the ledger again and ran her finger down the day's entries. 'Washbrook: she's on D Ward. That's Sister Healy. I suppose you could talk to her.'

'What will she say?'

'Look, to be honest, Cook - what's your name? Nora isn't it? I don't know, Nora. Some of them I could tell you, yes, they'd do something, the nurse would be up on a disciplinary. Healy - maybe. You know how it is.'

Do I? Narcisa asked herself. It seemed as if she had managed not to know. 'Very well,' she said. 'I shall have to think.'

'If it was worse,' May Gemmell said. 'I mean, heaven forbid, but if it was more obvious. A sprain, well, she could have fallen. She looked up at Narcisa. 'Don't get me wrong,' she said. 'I think there's a fair chance she's telling the truth. But I'm saying, to get them to do anything about it. Unless you're in with Bosanquet, that is?'

She remembered his fat hands holding Violeta's letter, and shook her head.

May Gemmell stood up to go and wash her hands.

*

She woke in the night. The curtains were rippling out into the room; the window rattled. She pulled the blankets up over her shoulders. She had had a dream; but nothing was left of it, except the image of a high dark wall, and a dull feeling of dread.

She turned on her side, and shifted the pillow down, to keep out the draught. There was June Ragless, her mascara smudged, saying, 'I'm worried I've got her into trouble.' 'All right,' Narcisa said, 'I'll find out; I'll make sure the nurse who did it is disciplined.' But that wasn't what she had said. She lay on her back again and closed her eyes; but soon the whole scene started up again, Rosaleen Shaw warning June, 'I thought we'd agreed,' herself responding sharply; June waiting to see her.

She gave in, and sat up, leaning against the pillow. She could hear the wind swishing through the trees. The bed in the next room creaked briefly. It's true, she thought, I ought to do something. I'll go and see Sister Healy in the morning. Which one was Healy? There was a small, plump woman, always making jokes; was that her? But surely it was the Ward Sister's job to tell her, if a patient couldn't work. Except that the Shaw woman was the one who'd decided.

The side of her neck was starting to ache with the cold. This is stupid, she told herself. All I have to do is talk to the Sister. But it wasn't so simple: June was right, it might get Esme into more trouble. So I will just have to be careful what I say.

She sat with her eyes closed, listening to the sounds of the wind outside, with the same dread that the vanished dream had left her. It would be safer if she said nothing. It might count against her if Dr Bosanquet got to hear. It was never wise to speak out, she'd learned that. These things happened. How did she know Esme wasn't exaggerating? Perhaps she had been getting out of control, and the nurse had restrained her.

She got out of bed and put a cardigan round her shoulders. The curtain billowed and she pushed it aside, and stood looking out at the grounds in the dark. The trees dipped and swayed in the wind. Further along the block, light from a window lay in a yellowish streak across the gravel.

I have no reason to be afraid, she told herself. It's normal to raise concerns with the Ward Sister. I have done it before. But it didn't feel normal, or safe. She watched a branch sway in the wind, and thought she heard it crack.

*

'Well now,' said Sister Healy, still arranging bottles in the medicine cupboard. 'That's quite an accusation your girl is making.'

The cupboard smelled sweetish and powdery. Narcisa tried to read the names on the bottles, but there was nothing there that she had heard of.

Sister Healy glanced at her, over her shoulder. 'She didn't say which nurse it was, by any chance?'

You see: something in Narcisa was vindicated. She doesn't want to take it seriously. It's too much bother.

A patient in a washed-out dressing-gown shuffled behind them. Narcisa waited till she was out of hearing.

'I have told you what I know. It will be for you to find out what has happened.'

Sister Healy locked the cupboard and turned round. 'I'm two auxiliaries short this week with the flu. Admissions is full so I've got three of theirs down here. One of them keeps trying to cut herself with broken glass. You see what I mean?'

She made herself stay there. 'I can see you are busy. But if a nurse has assaulted a patient..'

'Assault! I can tell you don't get on the wards much, Cook. Assault, indeed! Where I worked before, they had an investigation - '

She had to stop herself shivering. 'Sister Healy,' she said again, 'It is for you to decide. I have told you that there is' - but what was the word? - 'there has been an allegation.' She turned and walked out of the ward, though she could hear Sister Healy's voice following her. A domestic was mopping the floor between the beds; Narcisa stepped carefully across the wet patches.

The ward looked much the same as in her own time.

Part 4

**1918
-
1919**

To make fine filigree wire you need rubies; but the rubies themselves must have been mined and cut, a hole drilled through the centre of the stone, the thing then set in a thick plate of brass; so that what the ruby is, its individual way of drawing in light and letting it seep out like blood from a cut finger, the faceted surfaces that look like movement, all these are ignored, are made invisible, the uncopiable stone put into service, the brass plate mounted on a wooden bench with a chain, a hand-wheel, heavy machinery, the engineering processes through which men drive their determination that the world must be re-formed as they wish it to be. A ruby then is only an inner surface.

The gold wire has been softened on the flames; but that's not enough. Here is the workbench, the ruby plate: a machine such as you see in early paintings, a serf set to his work turning a wheel that will draw out the guts of some misguided Christian who believed he was all soul. The gold wire has been filed smooth, the tip pointed, the great labour of pulling out fine begins. If the wire won't go through, it is annealed again. If it survives the first drawing-out - but it must survive; if it breaks it will only be sent back for rolling, and return reshaped to the wooden bench, the smell of sweat on the man turning the wheel, the screech of the coarse machinery. So it's squeezed as through the eye of a fine needle, into the orifice of the first ruby; then again, burnt up and cooled once more, through the tighter second; then when it is hardly recognisable, through the third which is like the hole made by a bee-sting.

Only now is the goldsmith satisfied. The ruby is cleaned, ready for the next time. The wire is now available for working into something beautiful, whatever beauty it already owned crushed and drawn thin in the strong grip of the draw-tongs.

She was working on a pile of petticoats. This one had thickened darns in several places, and a square patch near the hem. The cloth was thin and yellowing under the arms. She sprinkled more water onto the patch. It was put on badly, the cloth underneath pulled slantwise. With the point of the iron she pushed towards the corners. The steam rose to her eyes.

She folded the petticoat and ironed it flat, then laid it on the pile on the shelf behind her. Across the room a bony red-haired woman was talking loudly to the woman next to her, who was pressing shirts dispiritedly and nodding. The red-haired woman made an impatient gesture, the iron in her hand. Somebody ducked out of her way and swore.

The windows were already netted in steam. She paused at the shelves, trying to see out. The sky was pale blue. At the far edge of the grounds there was a chestnut-tree, and every day she tried to catch sight of it; for no reason, for something green when it was green, something tall and beyond the order of the asylum. Through the misted window she could see it was bright brown.

She worked on, smoothing out the thin white cotton, the anonymous petticoats one after another, so mostly she didn't think of them as garments, something she herself might have worn the day before, but as puzzles, to make a shoulder-strap lie flat, a flounced hem hang properly without creasing. She liked the energy needed to press down, the strength in her arm as she did it; the precision. And then there was the feel of fabrics under her hand, the sturdy linen of bedclothes, the fine cotton under-things, the men's shirts: evidence of another universe, closed to the women in the ironing-room, with a locked door on the semi-circular corridor; a place where men stood doing up shirt-buttons, contemplating the day. She had no curiosity about them, no need that could pull her towards the male wards or the ground staff; not any more. Better to arrive in the ironing-room at eight-thirty, after breakfast, and work through, with breaks, till four, and then be tired.

And now it was better not to be on the ward; or only to sleep. The illness was spreading; she had seen it. The old woman, Amelia, had died of it. Amelia who shouted out at everyone, the doctors, the other patients; she had been on the ward when Narcisa was first moved there, a strong old woman with grey hair she had cut short herself with scissors, so she looked like a farmhand. She shouted out, and sometimes people laughed, and she raised her arm, threatening them. Narcisa had never known what it was she said. She had woken one morning, in the bed at the end of the room, and shouted out but this time clearly with pain, and fallen down on her way to the wash-basins, fallen and stayed lying on the floor, curled up like a child and moaning all the time. - *Please,* Narcisa had said to the attendant, and grabbed her arm: *Please. Amelia.* The attendant, a fat young woman, had laughed at first, and shaken free of Narcisa's hand; reluctantly she had wheeled round, calling *Come on!* ; but when she touched Amelia's sallow arm, the attendant's expression had changed, and she'd gone, half-running, calling: *Oh my lord!*

Narcisa pressed the last of the petticoats, and added it to the pile. Someone, the laundry-maid probably, had wiped a patch on the window clear. Drops ran down it. She could see the chestnut-tree, half in sunlight, and a scattering of rich brown leaves on the grass. 'You finished them, Humphreys?' the laundry-maid called out. Narcisa nodded. 'Take them pillow-slips down at the end there.'

She spread out the first of the pillow-slips and started; but her iron was cooling. She took it back to the stove at the end of the room, and picked up another to test on the ironing-sheet. The cloth was luke-warm against the palm of her hand. She put back the iron and tried another one.

'Here,' called the red-haired woman, close to her, but looking out at the others: 'What's wrong with her? Too la-di-da to spit like the rest of us?'

Somebody sniggered.

Not again.

She couldn't grasp the words but the tone was enough, and the one word *spit* that she could guess from the sound. She stood tense, next to the stove, the weight of the iron dragging at her hand.

Across the table someone called out something. There was a laugh. The laundry-maid looked up from sorting linen.

'Well,' said the red-haired woman, flapping a sheet out in front of her: 'Ain't you got nothing to say for yourself, then?'

Again the words meant nothing. She felt herself flush. What little English she knew had all left her. She thought in her own language: *You stupid ignorant woman, what does it matter whether I spit or not?*

She moved to go back to her place at the ironing-table.

'You! I'm talking to you!' the woman said, and brandished her iron close to Narcisa's arm. 'Watch out now Fairbairn,' the laundry-maid said flatly.

She must not speak. Her accent, her bad English would make it worse. It had all happened before, it was terrible and at the same time tedious. *You are not worth speaking to,* she said in silence. She made herself move away, back to her place.

'Did you see that?' the woman began, but the thin girl opposite Narcisa interrupted. 'Come on Bet, you know yourself she don't speak English.' The tone was relaxed; Narcisa looked up sharply. The girl made a slight move of her head towards her.

'Well she bleeding should. What's she doing in here if she don't speak English? My boys are off fighting the likes of her.'

The girl laughed, still folding and pressing handkerchiefs, more swiftly than Narcisa had ever seen. 'You think it's so good in here it should be rationed? She's here cos she's mad, just like the rest of us.'

The others chuckled; the red-haired woman subsided. Narcisa wondered what the girl had said. The dinner-bell rang. She held back, finishing a pillow-slip, till the others had put back their irons and got into file. The thin girl was just in front of her. She turned and grinned, and walked beside her towards the dining-hall.

She was taller than Narcisa, with an easy walk, that seemed only half-constrained by the double-file moving sedately along the corridor. Her hair was pale, and very fine, wisps of it escaping the untidy bun and drifting across her face.

When she was sure they would not be overheard, Narcisa said, 'Thank you.'

'Oh,' said the girl, and grinned: 'so you do speak English!'

Narcisa shook her head: 'Little.' She demonstrated, her fingers an inch apart. She searched for what she needed to say: 'You help. In ironing-room.' The girl was bending towards her, listening. 'I understand little, I can not say. There. Cannot say to her.' She was frustrated, needing for the first time in years to explain something.

'Not worth it,' the girl said, laughing. Narcisa shook her head. 'She' - the girl pointed ahead to the red-haired woman: 'stupid. You understand? Better to keep quiet.' She laughed again. 'Here, what's your name?'

'Narcisa.' The girl stopped and looked at her. 'Come along, you two,' the laundry-maid called over her shoulder.

'Say it again? I didn't get it. Nar..?'

'Narcisa.' She said it slowly this time; but the girl shook her head. 'Too difficult for me. I'll call you Nora.' Then she must have seen Narcisa's expression, for she took her arm: 'Look, I'm sorry. It's me. Not very bright.' Narcisa was still perplexed. 'Me - school - only three years.' She looked crestfallen. 'Can I call you Nora instead? My name's Clara.'

'Clara, 'said Narcisa, and smiled back. She had said her name for the first time in so long, she realised now; she had hoped to be called by her name, a sharp, sudden hope, but it would not happen. She would be Nora; but still it would be worth it. To be called anything at all except Edwin's name, she thought. They reached the dining-hall and went in in silence.

The asylum is ill. When it breathes it is in pain. The attendants hurry along the great corridor. There are fewer and fewer of them, and more to do. Outside in the grounds the grass has not been cut. A broken branch hangs down next to the gatehouse, and no-one snaps it off to chop for firewood, though it bangs impatiently on the gatehouse roof as if it too were desperate to escape. The kitchen garden is wavy with loose tendrils, potato plants hoping to attract attention, runner beans climbing their poles to see the giant.

It may be that god is against the asylum. For the first time, on Sunday there was no communion, the chaplain being too ill to leave his bed; being (though this is not said) in such a fever, he calls out more than once for his grandmother, who when he was small and sick used to read him stories. Though whether the illness is the punishment, or the cause of divine wrath, no-one in the chaplain's absence can explain.

The asylum aches all over: shoulders, hips, thigh-muscles, back, head. It is too weak to move. In the laundry they are forever boiling linen, and bleaching out the stains that seep out of illness, for who wants to be reminded of what happened to the last mouth to press on this pillow-slip? The sheets flap on the line and are unpegged damp, and carried through into the ironing-room, where those patients that are still able press order into them, before they must be put to use again.

The Medical Superintendent himself is ill, or so it is whispered in the staff quarters. He paces between the wards in a heavy coat, sweat shimmering on his forehead. Spreading the illness further, someone murmurs; ungrateful perhaps; but then everyone is frightened.

At the best of times the asylum is in poor health. It flushes; shivers. More than the shouts and whimpers of the insane, the brisk order of the matron and the doctors, the usual sound of the asylum is a cough, a wretched, exhausted cough that can never reach the resolution it's looking for.

First the war, people are saying, all those men gone, look at the ones left you can get to work. The patients sent from the neighbouring asylum, where they have wounded soldiers instead (is that easier?). And TB up, what with the overcrowding. And now when the war might be coming to an end (but can you believe them?) this, the influenza.

Morgan Redpath, farmhand. Went to a dance in Esher, and danced all evening with a lively girl, whose laugh he specially liked. The next day headaches, he thought from all the beer; then pains, intolerable; and then dead.

Ella Winthrop, laundry-maid, aged just eighteen. Started work two weeks ago. Her friend Lydia caught it, and then she did. No time to inform her parents back in Sheffield.

Also handymen, porters, attendants, needlewomen. The assistant matron, the doctor who came out of retirement. As for the patients. The beds are crammed close together in the wards, the symptoms are not recognised fast enough; or not by the nurses, who are overworked and frightened, and stay away from the wards as much as they can. In any case there is little to be done. The infirmary never has an empty bed.

Insanity no protection against the germs. Though a doctor

somewhere else had tried to prove it, before he and his patients provided the evidence against.

The asylum shudders; with fever, up to a hundred and five at times, and fear. Of death, of having to watch the others dying, drowning, a high tide with breakers crashing inside them, red sea-spray marking their lips. Is this the Old Testament you are living in? You lie in your bed and you listen for people dying. And because it is not only here, the outside world, always absent-minded about asylums, seems to have forgotten. Flour doesn't come these days, or fish from Grimsby. So few left eating, you'd think they might have plenty, for once; but no, it is less than the usual ration. The cook refuses to be ill, but her assistants are pale, and their mothers want them home.

The asylum may not recover, and who will notice?

It was still light. The curtains were closed, but still the subversive brightness crept back in, through the worn loose weave, or at gaps where someone had tugged them roughly together. A bird sang madly somewhere out in the grounds. The gravel crunched at a foot's pace; a man's voice chuckled.

Narcisa's neighbour got carefully out of bed, and walked silently to the far end of the ward, a tall broad figure in a cloak of hair. In a little while there were gasps and moans. A hoarse voice complained, 'You two, leave it out.'

Somebody snored, a steady complex rhythm. Somebody coughed.

The curtain opposite billowed out, then subsided.

Narcisa slept, not for long it seemed. The light seeping into the ward was cooler, perhaps moonlight.

The cough again, muffled, a rasp, persistent.

She lay on her back, watching the curtain moving.

'Nora?'

The curtain swelled sideways and stayed a moment.

'Nora, you awake?' It was the coughing voice, husky: Clara's voice.

I must be Nora. 'Yes.'

Someone turned over, mumbling in her sleep.

'Come and talk to me.'

Narcisa leaned on her elbows and looked round. The chair where the night attendant sat was empty. It was the epidemic: not enough staff.

'Where you are?' In the dusk the beds were smudges of grey muslin.

'Here.'

A hand waved, on her side, half-way down.

The small cough guided her along the row. Clara's face on the pillow was full of shadows.

Narcisa stood awkwardly. 'Ill?' she whispered.

'I've got this cough, it's worse at night. And I'm hot - feel.' She reached and pulled Narcisa's hand to her forehead. 'Have I got a fever?'

The skin was dry, smooth and very warm. 'I think,' said Narcisa. She wanted to keep her hand there on Clara's forehead, the fine pale hair wisping across her fingers. Instead she let go. 'You say nurses?'

'What are they going to do?' She wriggled across and held up the bed-covers. 'Do you want to get in? It's all right' - seeing Narcisa hesitate – 'not like them two.' She laughed, but the sound turned into a cough. 'Oh damn it.'

Narcisa was trembling.

'You afraid you'll catch it?' sadly.

'No afraid,' said Narcisa, though it wasn't true.

Under the sheet, with Clara's arm round her, Clara's thin body relaxed next to her own, the heat of Clara's illness pressing through cotton, she had to tense up her face to stop herself crying.

'You never done this, all the time you been here?' The lost seductive whisper of confidences, herself and Alma after their mother died.

'Here, I no speak. No know someone.' She heard her own voice breaking as she said it. She will hate me, she thought; she will think I'm self-pitying.

'When I was a kid,' Clara said, story-telling, 'there was four of us. Me, two sisters and my little brother, we all slept in the one bed. That was all there was. Till my mum thought Robert was getting too big.' She giggled. 'Coming here was the first I ever slept on my own. Hey, do I talk too fast? Do you understand?'

She understood the warmth against her skin, Clara's voice, humorous, wistful, out of breath. A burst of Clara's coughing shook both of them.

'Course,' the voice went on, 'it was different with my boyfriend. Clarence he was called. How's that for a name? Clara and Clarence.'

She didn't know what to ask first. 'Still boyfriend? Clarence?'

The arm tightened round her shoulder. She let herself relax in the narrow space, and turned her face towards Clara's on the pillow.

'He's alive in any case. He lost his right leg: you know, in one of the battles, I can never remember all those foreign names. When he came back he was, I don't know, moody. Who wouldn't be?'

Narcisa was struggling. 'His leg? Cut?' She made a sawing motion with one hand above the bedclothes.

'More like boom. I ain't seen him since I been here.' She lay back. A strand of fine hair drifted over Narcisa's face.

Narcisa ventured a touch on Clara's shoulder.

'Oh it's all right. Well, it's not all right, but you know. He was nice, but he wasn't the love of my life, exactly.' She turned to smile: 'Still, he was nice in bed. Very cuddly' - she hugged Narcisa to demonstrate. 'I like that. Liked making me happy.'

So it was possible to speak these things. And if you can't say them in the asylum, where? she wondered.

'What about you?' Clara asked. 'You're married, ain't you? What's he like?'

What was there she could say to explain Edwin? It was too long since she'd had to say anything.

'English,' she said, by fits and starts. 'He English. In my country. He work. My father know him. He English, not like men in my country.'

But that was only the half of it, she thought.

'So you came here? Was he nice to you, then?'

She turned and hid her face on Clara's shoulder. A hand stroked her hair. She breathed in the acrid smell of Clara's sweat.

'You got any children?'

She felt her shoulders shrink from Clara's arm. Oh let me not be here. It is too dangerous.

'Oh Lord,' Clara whispered. 'Here's me making it worse. Here, I'm sorry.' She hugged Narcisa close and rocked her a little. 'You should shut me up. I ask too many questions.'

Someone wailed at the end of the ward, a drawn-out sound, high like a trumpet; then stopped. Narcisa held her breath. The wailing started again, on the same high note. There were steps, a slap, loud in the dark like a pistol. The wail drew back into whimpering.

A long pause. Only the simmering sounds of breathing.

'What do you say we go to sleep?'

In the bed opposite someone farted and groaned. The bird sang again from the tree outside.

She woke pressed up against Clara's back, her own nightdress clinging with the heat and damp, Clara's breathing rasping in and out like old leather bellows. It was light already. She got out of bed and tucked the covers back over Clara's shoulder. 'Another one at it,' a voice muttered as she passed the ends of the beds. Her tall neighbour was back, asleep and snoring.

She lay between the cool unused sheets. Her flesh felt different, soft around her bones. There seemed to be handprints, one on her left shoulder, one on her hair.

I must not show this, she thought. I must be careful. She lay awake till the attendant came, and listened out for the sound of Clara's coughing.

That night, though it was light till late, and the trumpet wailing started up again, she made herself sleep straight away, out of fear.

*

She waited to go to the wash-basins the next morning, restless, standing at the foot of her bed, while other women muttered or combed their hair. The washed-out nightdresses were bright with deep blue creases in the sunlight.

The attendant, a short dark woman with a bad limp, was scolding someone further down the ward. Someone laughed; the wailing started up, then stopped.

She saw that Clara was still in bed, the covers drawn up, her pale fine hair glinting on the pillow.

She will get into trouble.

The attendant leaned forward to grab the bedclothes. Clara was speaking, her light hoarse voice half-audible from where Narcisa stood. Then coughing took over, dry, unrelieving. The attendant pressed her hand on Clara's forehead. Then she left the ward, with her deep lurching limp, and came back with a nurse who hurried on before her.

She is going to die, Narcisa thought in the wash-room, rinsing the soap off her face with tepid water. She thought of Amelia, the old woman, falling down in the corridor and moaning. She moved aside to let the next person in. Something seemed to be draining out of her like fluid, down through her bare feet on the stone floor. She stood until someone jostled her out of the way.

When they filed back, Clara seemed to be asleep.

Narcisa worked steadily, all day, in the ironing room, keeping her concentration on the worn fabrics, the creases she chased out with her weight on the black iron. It was as if the room had fallen silent, or she was deaf. Once or twice in the day, as she went for the mid-day meal, or waited for another batch of washing, she thought again: Clara is going to die. Already the message seemed to be losing meaning. Only the draining feeling, as if there were nothing left under her skin.

By evening, exhausted, she thought: I should never have known her. Then slowly the shock of thinking it came through, the smell of Clara's skin as she turned her head, the warmth of her body as they fell asleep.

I can't cope with this. I will go mad again.

*

After supper she found two women standing by Clara's bed. She recognised them from the ironing-room, a small, thin woman with grey hair in a bun, who complained a lot, and Bet, the red-haired woman who had taunted her. She walked past quickly, and then heard Clara call 'Nora!' in a small, breathless voice, so painful she pretended not to have heard. She walked past her own bed to the bay window, and stood looking out at a blackbird pecking at something in the lawn. After a while it jerked out a long pink worm, that dangled from either side of the yellow beak like string.

When she turned back the two women were gone. She wanted to go straight away to Clara, but was stopped by shame. Instead she stood holding a fold of the curtain, till Clara turned towards her and waved a hand.

But then the words in English refused to come. She looked down, puzzled, at Clara's thin face, the hair darkened with sweat, the blue eyes deep in their sockets of mauve shadows.

'I had a day in bed. Ain't I lucky, then?'

She nodded, not knowing how to understand. 'Very ill?'

'I don't know about very.' Clara coughed. 'I didn't think I could do the ironing-room.'

'Hot?'

'Yes, I'm still hot. Here' - she smoothed the grey blanket – 'Sit down. It's not the influenza, that's one thing.'

'No influenza?' She felt her body slacken.

'That's what they say. I was worried, I thought I'd given it you.'

'You think...?'

'Sorry, I'm going too fast, ain't I? I thought - if I had influenza - you'd catch it. The other night. Well, you still might get whatever it is, but it's not that.'

She stopped trying to understand; the relief was what mattered. 'Today I think' - but she couldn't say I thought you were going to die. 'Infirmary?' She stammered over the word.

The attendant limped purposefully towards them. 'Come on now, Humphreys, leave the patient alone.'

Clara said something she didn't understand. She sat on the edge of the bed, looking down, not trying to interpret the words that went between them. A spider scuttled across the floorboards by her feet.

'Did you hear that, Humphreys?' The attendant gripped her shoulder. 'Fifteen minutes, no more. She needs her rest.'

'I hear.'

'Well, do it then.' The hard fingers released her. She watched as the woman went towards the door with her lurching walk, the weight thrown heavily onto the left foot, the right hip jutting and the leg dragging.

'Don't worry about her,' Clara said. 'She's not too bad. I told her you cheered me up - made me feel better.'

'I make you better?' She looked in astonishment.

'Course you do. I've been bored stiff all day on my own. Come on Nora, talk to me, tell me something.'

She looked down at the floor by her feet, where the spider had been. There was a groove of dust between the boards. She had nothing to tell, only ironing, the tasteless food. She spread her hands, helpless.

'Like the other night.'

The smell of Clara's skin. Sleeping curled beside her.

She took a breath. 'English. Difficult.' But she had to say it. Clara might still die and there would be no-one. She realised she had been preparing this.

'Two years. Before two years. I have baby.' She watched Clara's expression. 'No Edwin, you understand? No my husband.' She was speaking as low as she could. A woman pushed past her to the next-door night table. Narcisa paused till she was out of hearing.

'Here, that was bad luck. Was that why they sent you here?'

She shook her head. 'No, no sent.' She struggled for words. 'I here. Escape, one day only. Then baby.'

'Blimey.' Clara pushed damp hair out of her eyes. 'Who was the man, then?'

'Does not matter.' She remembered briefly his head on her shoulder. 'Clara, you hear. Baby' - she covered her face a moment. When she looked up Clara took her hand.

'What happened to the baby?' she whispered. 'Did it die? '

'No' - she was vigorous, refusing. 'No die. Baby here - I have here - six month. Then they take. One day, take away. Out of asylum.' She could hear the cart clattering down the snow-thick lane.

Clara lay back, stroking Narcisa's hand. After a while she asked: 'Boy or a girl?'

'Girl. Violeta. I call Violeta.' But now she wondered why she had wanted to tell. It was easier to forget when no-one knew.

'Vee - say it again? I'm not much good on foreign names, remember?'

'Violeta.' She said it slowly, and nodded as Clara managed.

The boards creaked under the attendant's uneven walk. Narcisa looked hopelessly down at the thin face.

'Time's up,' the attendant called, a few yards away. Narcisa stood; but Clara pulled at her hand till she bent down.

'Do you want her back?'

Did she?

'All right, Humphreys, back to your bed, it's time.'

'We'll think of something,' Clara whispered. 'There must be something.' Then she coughed, long and painfully, the attendant helping her to sit up, while Narcisa walked back along the ward.

Jessie Pilgrim had William home with a sore throat. Perhaps she should have sent him to school with the others? 'He's just pretending,' Izzy had said; but no, she'd decided not to take the risk. William was wrapped in a rug beside the fire, trying to read Fred's book about explorers. Every now and then, while she got the dinner, she looked in to see how he was. He was very good, William; he didn't make a fuss. After dinner she'd go and read to him.

I am too soft with him, probably, she thought. Would Frederick have made him go to school? It was hard to know. At the beginning she'd been always consulting him, it had seemed so awful to make up her mind alone. Then after a while the pretence was worse than the loss; sitting by the fire late in the evening, wanting to think he was in the other chair – but he's not! she'd almost cried out. It's all me having to decide, he's doing nothing!

Certainly he wouldn't have had the idea of taking a lodger. There isn't enough, she'd admitted, guiltily, not wanting to blame him for not providing: how could he have known there would be a war? I could take in sewing. He'd have hated it. She remembered sitting back abruptly in his wing-chair, and looking up, up through the bedrooms with the children sleeping, up to the top of the house, where the maid slept, a pale little thing, only just left home; but she was a help and it was all Jessie could afford; and there, she saw, was the front attic empty, or it could be with some work, bringing down the trunks, moving the second bed out of Izzy's room, since there wouldn't now be another daughter. She'd stood up, just as if Frederick were there, as if she would have to argue it out with him.

Of course it had had to be a woman. That had made it harder; it was men mainly who lived away from home; but there was no question. She'd heard of women like her, widowed, who took in lodgers; and the next thing they were married again, or worse.

She drained the beans and started serving up. It was true she had hoped the lodger could become a friend; though Frederick might have been cautious about that: business and pleasure, too complicated, he said. She'd imagined her lodger coming down in the evening when the children had gone to bed: someone to talk to. Someone to tell about Frederick, she supposed. Perhaps one day she'd talk about something else.

'William, I'm just taking the tray upstairs,' she called. It was simpler, really, the woman not speaking English; and then for so long she'd just stayed up there in her room, Jessie had wondered if she was ill perhaps: so thin, those dark brown eyes with shadows all round them. She could have had the influenza last year, and lived; they did say it took months before you were well.

Jessie knocked at the door. 'Here's your dinner,' she said clearly, when the woman opened. 'I hope you enjoy it.'

The woman took the tray and stood like a statue. Perhaps she was wanting to announce something. Jessie waited, though her own meal was on the table, and William would be squirming in his chair.

'Mrs Pilgrim,' the woman said, though *Pilgrim* certainly didn't come out right. She seemed to be hunting for the next words. Oh get on with it, she wanted to say, shocked at herself. She's your paying guest, Jessie Pilgrim. At least she's trying.

'Your boy,' the woman said at last. '*Little* boy.' She showed her hand at hip-height. 'No... school?' He accent was bad; a good many people would never understand her. But it was kind, Jessie thought, and found herself blinking.

'William,' she said, and the woman repeated, 'William.' 'Oh, he's just got a bad throat.' She pointed to her own throat, and coughed a little.

'Bad?' the woman asked, looking concerned.

'No, no, not bad.' She gestured wrapping up. 'He'll be fine tomorrow.' She looked to check the woman understood. 'Do you have children?'

There was a pause again, the thin woman standing holding the tray, with the cutlet getting cold. And she couldn't be that old, Jessie thought suddenly, a few years younger than she was, only she looked... Then a few sounds, you couldn't say it was words: 'I... no... can no...' and then as she stood herself, gawping no doubt, 'Thank you thank you,' the tray held to one side, the door pushed back towards her, the woman shaking her head, and all that piled-up black hair shuddering, almost like some foreign animal.

*

She sits still.

The rocking-chair tilts her gently back, then forward. She sets her feet firmly on the pink and blue rug. The chair stops, in mid movement: just there.

Now the only movement is her lungs, steadying; the blood flowing past the pulse-points in her wrists.

She sits still in her rocking-chair, in her rented rooms; in her landlady's house, in what is now her street. Although she was brought here, not knowing where it was, it seems that now she has chosen all this: the bright sunlight slanting down from the dormer window, the two attic rooms with their sloping ceilings, the smell from downstairs where her landlady is cooking, the front garden, the suburb. She sits like a stone dropped in a pond, and feels the concentric circles spread around her.

I hope I will not fall to the bottom.

Outside on the street some children are playing a game. She can hear their heavy jumps, between ragged pauses, their voices calling out words she doesn't understand. A bicycle judders over the cobbles. A woman calls to someone. A dog squeals.

Nobody here will ask her to do anything, except pay five shillings to Mrs Pilgrim the landlady on Fridays. At first Mrs Pilgrim seemed to hope she would talk; but she shakes her head. Later she will start to put English words to things. Thank you, she says when the tray is brought to her door.

If she goes out of the house she will start to say Good morning. So far she does not want to leave the house.

So far I do not have the strength to leave it.

I can choose not to do what I say I have no strength for.

The rocking-chair is made of dark varnished wood, and upholstered in worn brocade. The smooth wood cools the spread palms of her hands. The rug at her feet is faded pinks and blues, knitted from soft rags. In the bedroom there is a patchwork counterpane.

She thinks: no-one else has just this bedspread, made by a woman, Mrs Pilgrim perhaps, from old summer dresses. It will not return from the wash and be allocated to another patient.

I am not a patient.

The light pours in with a torrent of bright dust. The room smells of dust and lavender-bags. When she has eaten, the smell of boiled potatoes and casseroled meat will fade from the air slowly.

She sits here waiting to find who she has become. Though she thinks to find out she will have to get to her feet, pushing the rocking-chair forwards; go out of the door and down the two flights of stairs. When the front door latches behind her, she will be a person, in a street with children and dogs and bicycles, a city where there are men apart from doctors. There she will be one particular person, in the way that the pieces of dress have become a quilt.

While I sit here I do not need to be anyone.

*

She wakes to some sensation from the asylum, a sneering shout, an intrusion on her body; by the time she wakes, she no longer knows what it was. She lies rigid till the fear moves away a little, when she can feel the touch on her hands of these lighter sheets, and see the slopes of the steep attic ceiling. These are not memories, in the dreams she can't remember, but facts that she only knows like this, when no-one, not even she, can challenge them. But she wakes and cannot bear to be awake; what she thought she had learned from the asylum, to wash and dress, is not enough to take her into the day.

Someone knocks at her door to bring her breakfast. She pulls the blanket up over her mouth. The knock again; the maid Libby's high-pitched voice: 'Mrs Humphreys.' She lies still with her eyes closed. Another try, and she hears the tray put down, Libby running downstairs.

She is not Mrs Humphreys. Mrs Humphreys must be the

wife of an Englishman, and live with him on Camberwell New Road, in a house with long windows.

Nor is she Narcisa Gashi, daughter of a goldsmith in the ancient city of Prizren. Narcisa was a young woman with long black hair, who loved music and wanted to know about politics. She can see her questioning the Englishman her father has brought to the house, about the world.

Then I can only be the mad woman.

She curls up in bed but her mind will not let her sleep. She longs for one of the day attendants to wrench the bedclothes out of her weak grasp, and pull her by the shoulder out of bed. If she could, she would use that violence on herself, the fingers digging into her flesh and leaving bruises, the tearing of muscles. She wants to be walking to the ironing-room, at the end of the silent ramshackle file of women; and stand at the table with a heavy iron, pressing sheets and folding them and pressing again, hours when the push down through her right arm and the whole of her body as she leans over the sheet is the only thing she knows, another sheet done and laid on the pile behind her, so that even the breaks for tea or lunch are a distraction, a requirement to be aware of people round her.

She turns in her bed but nothing is comfortable. Her nightdress is soaked cold with her sweat, and caught round her thighs. She makes her hands stroke the pieces of patchwork, the colours dulled in the half-light of the room.

Out here people speak and she understands nothing. It would be better if they shouted at her, since then she would grasp something from the tone. There are too many lives, people talking, making meals, bringing milk on a horse-drawn cart. Even Mrs Pilgrim with her widow's grief has a substance to her life, and it bangs at Narcisa's door, it forces itself into her till all there is inside her is the noise of all these people, their incomprehensible words and expectations; and she has nothing, not even a pile of ironing to put between them and the mad woman.

Part 4 – 1918-1919

Napoleon Road: so easy to remember; with the sounds and the great thunderclouds of steam when a train went through behind the short streets. It was not like anywhere she had been before, it was all strange but it could be anywhere, fifty yards from the asylum or the other end of the country, with English people, not very well-off, in little anonymous houses.

She had changed trains, waiting on a high station platform, rain blowing along the tracks, with the thin young man, Mr Noones he was called. Who had bought the tickets, and carried her trunk, and knocked on the half-glazed door in Napoleon Road, and handed her over to Mrs Pilgrim. So she had thought of it: being handed over. By Edwin, in the end, for the second time: the young man worked for Edwin's solicitors. He had tried to explain why this house, this woman; but she hadn't made the effort to understand. It was a room; and safe; and not the asylum.

It was when she went outside that amazement took her.

Whichever way she walked, there was the river. I am on an island, the thought, the second time she headed away from the house and came to water. Had the train crossed over a bridge? She couldn't remember. It seemed suddenly to be a special place, a town; was it a town or a suburb? With a name, a life, the way Prizren had those things (but she could not manage just yet to think of Prizren).

The first time, she had put on her coat and hat, her boots and gloves: so elaborate it seemed, such armour she needed to go out onto the street, for when had she last gone out all on her own? Once from the asylum; but that too couldn't be thought. Before that, Camberwell, and Edwin even then had not much liked it, her being out on her own, while he was out at his work in the City of London. So she had her armour; she had the key Mrs Pilgrim had given her; and still, standing outside the door she had felt giddy, leant her gloved hand hard on the door of her room, hearing the milk-cart rattle down the street, the horse stand still, head down, the milkman call and the maids run out with their jugs. She had seen all that from the window, the first days that she'd been here: the young girls clustered and chatting, the man flirting, the milk poured out into heavy earthenware, jugs clasped as the girls went regretfully in. She waited, waited, till she heard the cart rattle out of the cul-de-sac; then went down.

But that time she had gone almost no distance. Out of the street onto the main road, where there were horse-drawn carts and a motor-bus, and people walking rather fast by the shops, and up to the station where she had first arrived, with its wooden canopy, its sign *St Margaret's*. It was what? a month back? And she had hardly seen it then; but the entrance, the ticket-windows were reassuring. She sat on a bench, and people hurried back and forth around her; a train came in, a man with two small boys ran fast too catch it, someone in uniform received a parcel. Then the station cleared again and she sat still, not thinking of anything. After a while a man with a white moustache, in uniform, stood in front of her and said something. Fear leapt up through her; words in English drained away. He spoke again, looking into her face. There was train-noise, and a group of children chattering. All she could think was: I must escape from here. She managed to stand up, not looking at him.

A younger man arrived, holding a glass of water. The old man took it and held it out to her.

Perhaps after all she had done nothing wrong?

She drank a little and handed the glass back: 'Thank you.' There, she had spoken, it was possible. She breathed in, drawing her strength together, while the two men watched her. Perhaps they would not make her do anything. 'I go,' she said, and took a step forward.

If she hadn't been shaken, she might have run all the way to her room.

Two days later, determined to shift her fear, she went out a second time, in the other direction. At the main road there was a busy junction, with carriages, carts, even one or two motor-cars; but eventually she steeled herself to cross. On the other side were high brick walls. She couldn't think what would be behind them, unless another asylum; but the walls looked old, the brick soft-coloured and blurred with lichen. She headed down a quiet street, the high walls on either side, a few low trees. There was a cool tinge in the air, the day fine but this street smelling of damp. She came to a footpath, and the wide river.

It was mud-coloured and bluish, and flowing fast. The water seemed low; there was a holding wall, with vivid green marks, still wet. There was a post with a sign, but she couldn't read it, except for the word *Thames*. She stood and looked down. A worn piece of wood was carried hurriedly past, twisting and turning. A black-and-white duck upended itself abruptly, and came up yards away, a long time later.

She walked slowly along the path in the mild sunshine. From here she could see what the high walls were protecting:

large houses with elaborate gardens. The lawns sloped down towards her; elegant trees and clipped hedges divided them. There were long ground-floor windows and white stone walls. Who lives in a house like this? she wondered. Someone like Edwin's mother perhaps: a tall thin woman, severe, lofty in manner.

I don't think I will go in a house like that again.

She sat on a bench and watched the busy river. A blue-painted boat chugged down, with a smear of smoke; a man poled a raft across with three women, who each took his hand to jump onto the bank. What she'd wanted at the station: to sit and observe. I was stupid that morning, she told herself. I only need to learn the rules out here.

If she had enough English, the landlady would help her. She seemed not unfriendly; she might answer questions. No need for her to explain; being foreign was reason enough not to know things.

Yes, but the language? She leaned forward and watched the water moving past, folding over on itself, pushed into fine pleats like some think smooth fabric, bucking over some obstacle, a rock? something thrown in and settled on the bottom? It was viscous, heavy, anything dropped in would disappear. She looked for something to test this with; picked up a light-brown pebble and tossed it in.

The water gulped it down in half a second. It was flowing too fast to leave even a ring. The black-and-white duck paddled busily to the place, and let itself drift a little before diving.

I will learn the same way I learned in the asylum: listening to people. I managed to talk to Clara, after all.

A boy bumped along the path on a bicycle, calling out to her as he passed. She tensed, corrected herself: I must understand. She thought through the sounds; had he said *afternoon?* She wanted to call him back, but the heavy bike was far down the path already. I think he must have said *Good afternoon.*

She said it over to herself: *Good afternoon.* I do know some English. It's the same language I started to learn when I lived with Edwin.

Still, on the way back when an old woman spoke to her, she could only smile, and nod; her mouth wouldn't open.

Part 5

1947

Part 5 - 1947

It was a long time since he'd driven any distance. During the war, he supposed, going along the coast, talking to councillors about sea-defences. And a stupid lot they had been, on the whole; middle-aged men afraid of their ignorance.

No, that was unfair: a good few had been thoughtful and straightforward; and one, Miss Wishart, a thin elderly woman with scraped grey hair, had a better understanding than many of his colleagues.

There was little traffic, so early on Saturday morning. The sky was grey but with that faint shimmer, that might mean it would brighten up quite soon. And the car handled nicely; he settled into his seat. He'd looked pretty hard at the motor, before he'd bought it; had detailed discussions with the Morris salesman, an agreeable chap with a good grasp of mechanics. He'd tried it, out along the Edgware Road, rounding Marble Arch with a light touch on the steering, on Bayswater Road a little sleet splashing the windscreen. It was a luxury, after all, a big purchase. But Mina had been surprisingly keen as well: *We can go up and take the boys out more often.* He'd wondered for a moment if they'd be pleased, if seeing their parents during the term was difficult; but he'd said nothing.

At Swiss Cottage a milk-float was in front of him. He

slowed down, and began to notice people. A waitress opened the door of a dark café, and a bulky, round-shouldered man went straight in past her, as if he'd been waiting outside on the pavement.

Well, Mina could have whatever she wanted, he thought, overtaking the milk-float, accelerating towards St John's Wood. He saw her as she'd been sitting last night, in her high-backed chair, the firelight red-gold on the side of her face. Those cheekbones he'd fallen in love with, and the grey eyes: she had kept her looks, the way fine-boned women did. Less fiery, now, though, a lot more measured.

She hadn't said, 'You're taking that woman, aren't you?' No, that wasn't what she would have said; she would make sure she had the name correctly, a specific person. You're taking Narcisa. That was what they had agreed, ten days ago, after a long night of talking, with no tears, ending with tender love-making: he would not tell her when he was seeing Narcisa, and Mina would not ask. But she is amazing, he thought, as he passed Lords, the ground closed up behind its high fences. This summer there should be a full season's cricket. He would go to the Lords test, take a few days off. Mina is an exceptional woman, he thought again. She could have insisted; after all, most women would. She could have said: Give her up, or I divorce you. He had taken a great risk, telling her, he realised. Except that he'd never really believed she'd do that: give him an ultimatum. A clever woman; no doubt she manages me. The thought was surprisingly comforting.

On Baker Street there was a slight delay, a broken down bus, the bonnet open, the passengers standing listlessly on the pavement. A ray of sun came through and lit up the scarlet hat of a small round woman. A young man in a flat cap stood in the road, directing the few cars needlessly round the obstruction.

Through central London he drove without reflecting, enjoying the familiarity of the streets, Selfridges with its ornate window-frames, the bow-fronted Regency houses on Park Lane. A tune came into his head and he started singing: *You saw me standing alone.*

Vauxhall Bridge? or Battersea perhaps. There was plenty of time; he'd said he'd pick Narcisa up at ten. Then through Pimlico and along the embankment. Now there were people coming out on the street: a woman with an empty wicker basket; a group of young boys, evidently bored, throwing stones at a cat which whisked itself out of sight; two girls playing hopscotch.

It wasn't till Esher that he started to think of the weekend. How would she be, taken out of the hospital? As if she were a patient, he thought, and shuddered. It was what he had wanted, to get her out of there; it was sordid, after all, the afternoons - there had only been two - up in his hotel room. Not what they had done; he was clear that that wasn't sordid. In some ways he was proud she had trusted him. It had been unlike anything he had known, though he'd had adventures with prostitutes in his time. But it wasn't like that with someone you cared about. It had made him realise he did care about her. And the sense of everything she hadn't told him; how small she'd looked in the tea-room beforehand. Her name.

A Daimler overtook him and hooted twice. 'Fine, fine,' he said aloud, 'so your car's bigger'. He watched the road-signs. It was different, coming down by car; he didn't know it.

Then suddenly he was in the High Street, and Narcisa in her dark coat and that ridiculous hat was outside the George; and he was full of excitement, seeing her.

*

As they came over the crest of the North Downs she breathed out, as though she had been waiting for this plain with its brick houses and dark green hedges. Anthony looked sideways at her and smiled.

'Look,' he said. 'It's like a Bible painting.' The cloud over to their right had split apart, and a widening shaft of sunlight was pointing down at a cluster of buildings and a few bare trees.

She said nothing.

'Maybe you didn't have them,' he went on cheerfully. 'When I was a child there were these biblical scenes, and God was always making his will known, pointing out of the sky at you like that. Or maybe it was the Holy Ghost.'

She studied the houses, their gable-ends lit up. 'You believe in God?'

'Not since I learned about the first war,' he said. 'The Great War, so they called it. My older brother was in the trenches. He survived, thank god' - he laughed - 'maybe I do - but once he told me what it was like, God didn't have a chance. I was called up myself, but it ended just in time.'

And I was in the asylum then, she thought.

'What about you?'

It took a moment for her to grasp what he meant. 'I stopped believing at that time as well. Though perhaps I did not believe so strongly anyway. Even when I was a child, I mean.'

'Your family? Were your mother and father religious? Mine were.'

He asks questions, she thought, and wasn't sure she liked it. Well, I am here in his car, I can hardly get out. Anyway, this is not what's difficult. 'We were Catholic. But my mother was against the church, that's why she gave me a name that is not a saint's. My father I think never went to church, or maybe once a year, because you are meant to. After my mother died I think he was not interested any more. My aunt took my sister and me to church.'

It felt strange, to be talking about her childhood; embarrassing. Probably he would find it all trivial.

After a while he asked, 'Your mother died?'

'When I was four,' she said, evenly. 'Now I think she must have had cancer. They didn't say. - Ah, it was a long time ago,' she added, with a rush of energy, sitting forward in her seat, as they passed through some town with neat squat houses. She looked at him. 'I do not know if I am really the same human being. Even the clothes we wore, I cannot imagine.'

He pulled in to the side of the road, by a row of shops. She stopped speaking. 'I am sorry,' he said, 'I'm interrupting. But I thought we might buy ourselves some lunch, and picnic. Unless you would rather have a meal in a pub?'

She considered, 'No, no pub, I do not feel..' She couldn't say what it was that seemed too hard. 'But we need ration books, I don't have one.'

'We'll manage,' he said, and turned off the engine. She got out and stood bewildered on the pavement. 'Of course,' he said gaily. 'You don't shop for yourself. Well, come on, this can be a treat. Anything you fancy, as long as they've got it.' He opened the shop door and let his hand rest lightly on her shoulder as she went in.

They came out with a bottle of ginger beer, a thick slice of Caerphilly cheese, a small loaf and a pound of slightly wrinkled russet apples. 'What was wrong with the cold meat?' he asked.

'The tongue was going off, you didn't see? Very dark. The

ham, I don't know.' She looked across at him as he opened the car door. 'Did you want ham? Probably it is all right - only..'

He got in. 'No, no, it's fine, we've got a feast. I forget that you are an expert on these things. I thought we might eat up on the South Downs - on the hills - if you can wait that long?'

She began to relax in the car as they drove on. He talked about the places they were passing, famous people she hadn't heard of who had lived there, distant relatives he'd visited with his children. He made no attempt to avoid talk of his family, and she liked that, his matter-of-factness saying his wife's name. It made her wonder for the first time about his life, whether he had had other women before her, if his marriage was happy. He spoke about the two boys with amused pleasure. 'Ah, they're terrific, we don't see enough of them,' he said laughing, at the end of a long story.

'You don't see.. ?' She was puzzled.

'They're at boarding-school, in Norfolk. In four weeks' time they'll be down for Easter. Maybe we'll collect them, in this' - he tapped the dashboard - 'One up on their friends, a father with a flash car.'

How can he love them and send them away? she wondered. 'My husband was sent to boarding-school,' she said.

He will ask me if I have children. Her stomach caved. I will have to lie to him.

The fields on either side were sodden, light glinting on narrow channels cut through the turf at regular intervals. 'Look,' Anthony said. 'That's Amberley. Can you see the castle?'

She peered ahead. Before them a there was a steep hillside, with reddish houses between trees, and a dark, jagged wall. 'There?'

'That's it. It's still lived in, I think: some minor nobility.' He laughed. 'I don't have much time for our ruling class. With any luck the war will have shifted some.'

What does he mean? she wondered. The King of England? It was so many years since she'd talked like this: not since Felix, the German music-teacher. Perhaps she would get back into this world. She was aware of his hands on the steering-wheel, capable hands that had also touched her skin.

The road wove along the bank of a wide river. The reeds were pale gold in the fitful light. Two swans drifted close to the bank; one stepped out and opened its wings, raucous and ugly. 'This is a bit out of the way,' he said. 'But it's good for a picnic. In the car, I mean.'

He reached into the glove compartment for a penknife, and cut the fresh white bread into thick slices, and broke a lump off the cheese to give to her. It was sharp and pungent, crumbling onto her lap as she ate. 'Don't worry,' he said. 'We'll clear up later.'

He opened the ginger beer and she drank from the bottle, the glass stopper tapping against her chin. As she passed it back, he said, 'You know, I'm sorry but I've never known where you're from. Which country.'

She wiped her mouth, and smiled. 'It depends when you are asking.'

He raised his eyebrows.

'When I was born it was part of the Ottoman empire. Then it became the Kingdom of Serbs, Croats and Slovenes. Not that we were any of those, you understand. Well, no, my mother was from Croatia. Now it is Yugoslavia. I suppose it is still Yugoslavia, since the war?'

He considered, making a thick sandwich with his cheese.

'Of course,' she said, 'it seems strange, when you live on an island. And you have been the country conquering.' She drank some more. 'But you see I have lived here much longer than there. I am not English, but I am not Yugoslav either.' I do not know what has happened to my family, she thought of saying, but couldn't face the concern it would raise in him.

*

The village was on the far side of the Downs, across a flat plain with farmland. 'Look,' he said, 'the light, you can tell we're near the sea.' Had she known they were coming to the sea? Soon there was an inlet on one side, and on the other embankment trees, bushes. She glimpsed an expanse of water hidden behind them. A goose rose up calling and wheeled away.

They drove through the village, past a grey stone church; then Anthony stopped and called out to a woman passing. She pointed them down a side road, nodding. What does she think? Narcisa wondered. That we are married? Two middle-aged people, what else would she imagine? It made her feel not guilty but distant, as if her life were too strange to be understood.

The road came to a pond with one duck, and a wide green. He parked the car and they went up a grass slope. Anthony strode before her to the top. 'Come here, look,' he said, turning towards her, his hair blowing. He reached down to help her up the slope, and held onto her hand once she stood beside him.

The tide was in; the sea was still, at the foot of a bank of shingle. Fishing-boats bobbed up and down at anchor, a green-painted one very close to them, two or three more farther out. The sky was pale grey, with a thin line of blue far out over the water. The air smelled of salt; she could feel it sticky against her face, and tangling her hair as the wind caught it.

'What are these?' she asked. There were round black baskets, domed, with a narrow opening, in a line in the lee of the sea-wall.

He looked down quickly. 'They must be lobster-pots. That's what they catch here, crab and lobster, it's known for it. Have you ever had lobster?'

A restaurant in the City, white damask cloths, Claud Stokeley choosing wine in consultation with the waiter. 'Perhaps,' she said. 'When I was very young.'

'It's delicious; one of the best foods. I don't know, maybe we could get one, if it's the season. Come on, let's see if we can find this house.'

She had almost forgotten there was a house to look at. He had explained in the car, and she had half-listened, gazing out of the window: a house made from the carriage of a train; had she misunderstood? A friend of his, someone he'd known in the war, had bought this train-house and wanted Anthony to see it.

They walked along the sea-wall, the wind in their faces, the sea down to their left hissing softly on the stones. She would have liked to sit still, anywhere here, and stare out at the sea, and not have to speak for a long time.

'There,' he said; and it was true, there were railway-carriages, three of them, each on its concrete base, lined up along the edge of the beach, with succulent plants growing out of the shingle in front of them. She put her hands up to her mouth in shock. Someone opened the door - an ordinary train door - in the centre of the far one, and shook out a duster.

She began to laugh, surprised at herself, unable to stop and half-ashamed of it. After a moment Anthony came back and put an arm round her, smiling. 'You like the idea, then?'

She swallowed, trying to calm herself. Eventually she said,

'To live in it? Your friend wants to live here?'

'For the summer. He's thinking about it. He wants me to tell him if it's secure.'

She laughed again, silently, rocking where she stood. 'I am sorry. He wants to know - the train will not start?'

'Come on,' he said, and drew her along to the first carriage. There was a little wooden verandah at the front. They stood on it as he rummaged for the key. 'Or sail out to sea,' he added, and she giggled again. 'Well, that's one thing,' he said. 'First time I've seen you laughing.'

*

She closed her eyes and pictured the great waves surging up the shingle only yards away, lifting high up and crashing and sucking down. That was the sound, the pebbles being sucked back and thrown again as the next wave broke. In the dark the sea would be invisible, except for this edge, like the head of some animal drawn back before it strikes, a white crest and the sleek blackness of the throat. The noise filled the narrow room of the railway carriage. Beneath it, close to her, was Anthony's breathing, a faint regular sigh. She turned her head. He was asleep on his back, the blanket thrown off his right shoulder, his other arm flung straight out beneath her neck.

She sat up a little and pulled the blanket over him, then arranged the other corner across her breasts. It was all the bedding they had, a tartan rug he'd pulled from the boot of the car. She thought it had the sweetish smell of a dog. Under her back the mattress ticking was cool and harsh.

The sea pounded and swished; it was high tide. Farther away there was a lowing sound, like a cow in distress. They had heard it earlier, in the afternoon, a long low hooter out over the sea, which someone had told them came from a lightship. The lowing and the sea sound were like one thing, one creature beyond the frail walls of the carriage, something dangerous that was still at bay. She closed her eyes again. And the lifeboat, she thought, having just today learned about it; the men would take the lifeboat out on the rough sea, and search for anyone whose boat was missing, pull them on board and turn back towards the village. She wondered if the fishing-boats were out, and if the sea was rougher than usual.

But there is this, she thought, and moved her head to lie on the flat of Anthony's shoulder. He made some sound and wrapped his arm around her. Simply: he seemed to make everything simple. Their picnic by the river; the afternoon wandering, exploring the village. And sex: they had made love twice, the first time urgently, as soon as they arrived, standing just inside the little sitting room, the glass of the carriage door cold against her back; and again late at night. Though he has never mentioned the other time, she thought.

His body next to her was warm and lean. Perhaps I should tell him about Violeta. The thought brought with it a surge of longing. Perhaps he will make that simple for me too. He wouldn't be shocked; he doesn't think like that. But was that true? She lay in the dark, looking up at nothing. He would say: Of course you must live together. To make up for lost time: that was the phrase. Perhaps the whole thing was simple after all.

She was almost asleep. She had left the asylum. Violeta was already living with her, here by the sea, if not in a railway carriage then one of the black and white bungalows close by, with a dazzling garden. On weekends Anthony drove down to be with them. The three of them walked along the sea-wall, in the summer, Violeta slim in a flowered cotton dress, the full skirt flapping around her legs. Violeta and Anthony were laughing together. She hurried forward to catch up with them, wanting a glimpse at last of her daughter's face.

'It was Stan made me do it,' Clara was saying. 'Not that I didn't want to see you, I did. But you know how bad I am about writing. Stan said, Go on, she'll be pleased to see you.'

'I am very pleased,' Narcisa said, and looked across the kitchen table at this middle-aged woman, rangy, the unbelievably fine hair now henna'd russet, the thin cheeks as lined as worn leather gloves. 'It is good you came. Only in the afternoon I have not much time.'

'That woman's face.' Clara began to laugh. 'When you said you can go now! Hey, she's not going to get you into trouble, is she? You're the boss, right?'

'I am the boss. I don't know - well, I will talk to you later about it, perhaps.' She was still astonished, feeling something trembling inside her, as if Clara's presence removed a covering. 'Clara, I did not understand, tell me again. Your husband - ?'

'Stan's got an old aunt in Leatherhead, and he thought he'd better get down and see her. And David, my youngest, he's home for a week, and the old lady always liked him. So we came down in the van and had lunch with her, and Stan dropped me off on the way back. David and him will have gone to the pub in Epsom, and jolly glad not to have me with them. You know men. Sorry, Nora, am I going too fast for you?'

She shook her head. Clara, her husband Stan, David and what was the other one called? Dennis; and Stan's aunt. Clara's life seemed extraordinary, peopled, full of events and choices and sudden journeys. But this is how people live, she told herself. If I had had Violeta living with me. No, not even then.

She sat back. 'Clara, I am sorry, we are in my kitchen and I have not offered you tea.'

She busied herself, lighting the gas under the giant kettle, lifting down cups and a teapot that wasn't chipped. 'There is cake,' she said, a little doubtful. 'It is from the bakery, fresh. Of course it is for the patients..'

'Go on,' Clara said. 'We're patients, at least we used to be.' She sat back in her chair and watched as Narcisa cut four slices of coffee cake. 'I'll tell you, it took some nerve for me to come in. When Stan dropped me at the gatehouse, I nearly did a bolt. Looking up the drive at all them gloomy old buildings.'

Narcisa brought the tray over with the tea-things, and laid a hand awkwardly on Clara's shoulder. Clara patted her fingers and went on. 'I said to myself, they can't do anything to you now. But still, Nora,' she said, as Narcisa sat down and poured milk into the cups. 'I don't know how you stand it. I know you've been back here a long time and all that, but still.'

There was a pause. Narcisa pushed the cake-plate towards Clara, who took a slice and then broke some off and ate it delicately, with a hand to catch the crumbs. Always these elegant gestures, Narcisa thought.

'I am used to it, of course,' she said slowly. The shame of Dr Bosanquet's letter threatened. 'But now I am thinking about leaving. Only what work can I get? I don't know. I have only worked here, and as a housekeeper, you remember?'

'Your two old ladies. I don't know, Nora, but there must be something.' She looked around the kitchen with its stacked green-painted shelves and huge ovens. 'I reckon if you can run this you can run most things.'

'What about you? You are still working?'

'I'm still at the laundry.' She laughed. 'I'm as bad as you. I went there when I got out of here, and I've stayed ever since, except for a few years when the boys were little. It don't pay much, but it suits me, to be honest. Stan says I could stop, but I don't know that I want to. I don't see you there, though, Nora, you're cleverer. Though you were pretty nifty in the ironing-room. Do you know, Nora, it's nearly thirty years? Can you believe it?'

They drank tea, both of them, Narcisa in her white apron and overall, Clara with her long elegant limbs, her pink blouse. Soon she will have to go, Narcisa thought. Perhaps it is better not to start to tell her. Still she felt Clara would know what to do; or better, she would know what to feel about it.

'I'll tell you what,' Clara said. 'If you like I'll ask Stan to keep an eye out. For a job, I mean. You know, he's got his own business, he's a builder. He does get to hear of things sometimes. What is it, though; has it started to get to you?'

Narcisa spread her hands. 'Oh, it is - I don't know. Many things.' *Tell her,* she ordered herself, but it seemed too much. She looked quickly over at the kitchen clock. 'Well,' she said, 'Clara, I will tell you. You are my friend, you know what has happened.'

'I should think so,' Clara started, then stopped herself, leaning forward, elbows on the big scrubbed table, her long hands pressed to either side of her face.

'It is Violeta. My daughter. She has written.'

'Violeta's written to you? Nora, you're kidding!'

You see, some part of Narcisa reprimanded; most women would be excited. 'She wrote to the asylum. She said I was a patient in 1916 and did they know where I was. And of course they did.'

'Oh Lord. Did she get you into trouble?'

'Perhaps.' She thought of Dr Bosanquet, his plump hands fingering the blue envelope; his own accusing letter. 'Certainly this makes me think, do I want to work here? Before I have never wondered. But Clara, it is not that.' She held onto the teacup with both hands, trying to explain.

'So what have you said?'

She looked up. 'Clara, you will think I am a stupid woman' - a bad mother, she wanted to say, but couldn't - 'I have not written. I do not know what to say.'

The door opened; June Ragless' blonde head appeared. 'All right, June,' Narcisa said. 'Five minutes.' The two women waited while the door creaked back.

'I thought it was what you always wanted.'

So Clara knew that. 'It was, wasn't it?' But not enough, she wanted to cry out. 'But she is not a child now. She is thirty.'

'Nora, you've got to write to her,' Clara said, and held Narcisa's wrist. Above her wedding ring was a little delicate one, with a blue stone. 'Honestly. You'd never forgive yourself.'

'Perhaps,' she said, and brushed the cake crumbs into the palm of her hand. 'Clara, I do not know what to think. If she was a child, yes, but a grown woman?' She took the crumbs over to the bin, and came back to her chair. 'I cannot imagine it, meeting her. What will happen.'

'Well, I don't know either.' Clara smiled for a moment. 'I always wanted a daughter myself, and look what I get, them two ruffians.' She looked out into the expanse of the kitchen.

'I don't know. Family's family, after all. I mean, she's not just anyone. Even if.. Anyway, she's your kid, Nora, she's bound to be lovely, ain't she?'

She could hardly say it. 'But if she is angry? Really angry with me?'

'Come on, Nora, she's not going to all this trouble just to tell you you're a nasty old cow, is she? Maybe she'd be a bit upset, but you'd explain.'

'I do not know why she goes to all this trouble.' But there she had shocked her friend; she had gone too far. She laid her hand over Clara's for a moment. Then she moved to stand up.

'Have you got to go?' Clara asked wistfully. 'I know, I should have warned you. Then maybe you could have made a bit more time.'

'Clara, tell me..' but what exactly was the question? 'You have been happy? With Stan?'

Clara stood, and looked round for her coat. 'Well,' she said finally. 'What can you do? He's a good man. If I hadn't been in here - you never know, do you?'

She came round the table, in her smart red coat, with the belt and the fur collar. 'D'you like it?' she asked, and twirled on the spot. 'Stan bought it for me for Christmas. Black market, of course. So you see.' She stepped forward and hugged Narcisa. The fur brushed against Narcisa's nose. 'Next time,' Clara said, 'we'll do it properly.'

They walked to the door. 'Go on, do it,' Clara said. 'And let me know. Promise?'

Rosaleen Shaw was out in the corridor, looking stern. 'Thank you so much, Mrs Humphreys,' Clara said suddenly in a loud, strained voice. 'You've been most helpful.' Then she winked at Narcisa and strode off towards the entrance.

She had cycled into town, to the draper's shop. It was a long time since she'd done any sewing; it would be good for her to start again, she'd thought, looking at Clara's pleated skirt. Perhaps it would calm her.

The assistant waited impatiently for her order. She was a young woman, with marcelled hair, thin in her navy-blue uniform. 'No,' Narcisa said, 'that is not the colour. Will you show me a darker blue, please? I think it is called ultramarine.'

Reluctantly, the girl opened the drawer, and took out another card of bias binding. Narcisa held it against the swatch of fabric. 'Yes, that will be fine. Now I need some cotton, the same.'

She was edgy, she thought, coming out of the shop. Perhaps it was the unfriendly shop assistant. She usually enjoyed shopping for sewing things. She was putting her purchases in the bicycle basket, when someone came half-running across the square towards her: a tall woman, gawky, holding on to her hat.

Of course it was Shaw.

'Oh, Cook.' She was out of breath. 'I'm so glad I caught you.'

Narcisa forced herself to be polite. 'Miss Shaw, good morning. Is there something wrong?'

'No, no, nothing like that.' She rested a hand on the handlebars; Narcisa flinched. 'I just wanted to tell you. It's about that patient, Washbrook, wasn't it? There's going to be an enquiry. Young June and I have been asked to give evidence.'

So Sister Healy had acted after all. 'Good morning, Mrs Humphreys,' a man's voice said beside her on the pavement. She turned and nodded, but whoever it was had moved on.

'Well,' she said eventually, 'it is a good thing that they take it seriously.'

'Absolutely. Though of course, you know my opinion. Still, I suppose it will show the others. I just hope June doesn't get it out of proportion. You know these young girls, how excitable they can get.'

But you're excited too, Narcisa thought. She straightened the bike, so the woman had to let go. 'Thank you for telling me. Do you know when this will happen?'

'I think it's Thursday morning. We may miss coffee duty, I'm afraid.'

'That is quite all right. It is important for you to take part.' And I've disappointed her again, she thought, getting into the saddle and waiting for Rosaleen Shaw to move away before she could start.

*

Back in her room, she sat down on the bed, still with her coat on, and put her head in her hands. It was Clara, she thought. Clara is a good kind woman; but that is the problem. She cannot imagine why I have not written. What did she say? 'You'd never forgive yourself.'

She stood up slowly and hung up her hat and coat. There was something else that came back to her. 'She's your daughter, she will be a nice woman.' Something like that. And she means it, she thought, wandering through her room, from the door to the long window and back again. She believes I am good like her, and Violeta will be.

From the next room, she heard the creak of floor-boards. Her neighbour, the laundry-mistress, must be off sick. Then there was the sharp sound of water.

Anger rose in her throat like nausea. I cannot bear it, she thought, and almost shouted. I cannot bear it. To be living listening to some stranger pissing.

My daughter will be like me: that's what Clara thinks.

Perhaps Violeta is mad already. A patient in an asylum. Or has been. Perhaps she's become like me, a bad person. A woman able to abandon her own children.

Clara, she thought, longing for comfort; but Clara was more distant than before.

I cannot meet her. It is too much. I will choose not to see her, and get on with my life. I have lived without her; I do not need her now.

She stared out of the window, restless, angry. From the farm she could just hear a cow mooing, on one long note, like a patient howling.

'I've got some nice spring lamb,' Hartley the butcher said, standing in her kitchen, a large male presence, smelling of soap and animal blood, disrupting. 'I just thought I'd come up and give you the opportunity. Do you a good price.' He looked critically at the row of steel deep-fryers.

He knows we can't afford it, Narcisa thought. He's come to snoop. 'Thank you,' she said, 'but we will have the mutton, as usual.'

Was there a look, from the butcher to Rosaleen Shaw? The woman was standing with her hands on her hips, her pale blue eyes almost hidden beneath the eyebrows. 'Personally, I think you should consider it, Cook,' she said. 'You might find neck of spring lamb is just as good value. Well, scrag end, at least. Like Mr Hartley says, it's a special offer.'

She could see June and Peg, peeling carrots at the sink, listening intently with bowed heads.

'And spring lamb would be a real treat, don't you think?'

She remembered from her days as a housekeeper, the lacework of fine white fat over the meat, the taste of the juices. 'I am afraid we cannot afford it,' she said to Mr Hartley. 'Your mutton will do very well, thank you. Also some oxtail please; to add to the order. You will see from the book how much I ordered last time.'

She showed him out and came back to the table, where Rosaleen Shaw was standing, a little flushed, waiting to speak. Narcisa felt dizzy with sudden anger. 'Come to my office, please.'

Behind the desk she made herself speak clearly. 'You have made an agreement with the butcher?'

'Not an agreement.' The woman's voice, the defensive tone and the querulous intonation, jarred on her like the sound of a knife being sharpened. 'I happened to meet Mr Hartley in the street, and he suggested the spring lamb, at a good price; in fact I bargained him down a bit. But I said, of course it's up to Mrs Humphreys.'

She could see them, sneering about her in Epsom market. Was Rosaleen Shaw getting something from the deal?

'If I may say so,' the nasal voice continued. 'You never even asked him how much. I reckon he would have brought it down even more. He said to me, he's got a good supplier.'

'Then it will be black market. We cannot have anything to do with that.' She was speaking too loudly. 'The ordering is my responsibility; please remember.'

The rough skin was flushed, the eyes glittering blue and narrow, the thick grey eyebrows like some kind of challenge. 'I must say,' the woman said, and Narcisa felt herself trembling with hatred. 'I have to say, Cook, I think you are most unfair. I do not feel you are giving me appropriate responsibility here. I am an experienced cook myself, as I have told you. I think you could delegate more to me. I mean, you could make better use of my skills. There may be things..'

Things that you believe you could do better, Narcisa thought. It was a speech; it had been prepared before this morning.

'Well, I mean, on menu planning, for instance. I myself

learned with a very professional cook, back in Melbourne. You can plan your week so that nothing ever gets wasted. And what I see here' - she stopped herself, red in the face, a visible effort. 'And the way the kitchen assistants are managed. I have to say, I would be much stricter with them. I'm sorry if I'm speaking out of turn.. '

Narcisa was standing now, leaning both hands on the desk, her whole body shaking, not knowing what it was she was going to say. 'You are not sorry. You do this to give yourself some power. You think that because I am a foreigner..'

The woman's face seemed distorted, pale and bloated and too far away. She might have flinched. Narcisa made herself stand up straight. Her pen fell off the desk and clattered away across the brown lino.

Rosaleen Shaw looked down at her apron.

The words kept forming themselves in Narcisa's mind, how stupid and sly this woman was, how callous. She stared in loathing at the thick eyebrows, the broken veins on the cheeks, the scrawny neck. Her hands felt full of blood, ready to strike.

She closed her eyes. 'You may go.'

On her feet, very tall and angular, Rosaleen Shaw said, 'I hope you will think about what I told you, Cook.'

'Please go back to the kitchen.' Narcisa watched the woman's big haunches as she turned away.

Alone, she sat in her chair, still trembling. The woman must be scheming to undermine her. And Hartley, after her argument with him; he would be only too happy to have someone to side with him, and someone British at that, or as good as British. To do it all in front of the kitchen staff. It must be deliberate.

She rubbed both hands over her face. Then the horror moved up through her like cold water. She had lost her temper, shouted at the woman. She had never shouted at a member of staff, never. And what had she said? Something about power. About herself - it was terrible, shameful. Rosaleen Shaw would know, even if she had been frightened - but it was hard to think of her being frightened - she would know she had won, because Narcisa had lost control. Perhaps she would even report it, make a complaint. It was enough for Dr Bosanquet to fire her.

Outside in the corridor there were sounds of sweeping, the broom hitting the skirting-board over and over. Narcisa sat tense in her office chair. No, probably Shaw would not make a complaint, because her deal with the butcher might be uncovered. But still she would know that she had won something. I will have to be very careful with her, Narcisa thought.

She ought to get back now, to supervise the lunch. But it was dreadful: not Rosaleen Shaw, but the fact that she, Narcisa, could be provoked so quickly, and not know what she was saying. She provoked me deliberately, she told herself; but it was no excuse. Really he will have to fire me after this. She stood, with a sigh, and bent to pick up the pen that had rolled towards the waste-paper basket by her desk. The movement made a dull ache in her hip. Then she locked the office, and went back in a kind of dread to her kitchen.

*

It was true, she thought as they prepared the lunch, watching Rosaleen Shaw organise the working patients to drain the greens. The woman was more professional than she was. She moved authoritatively, without hesitation; she knew by heart the order of doing things. So do I, Narcisa tried to remind herself: I have been working here for more than ten years. Still the certainty that she was an amateur came back to her as she saw the Australian woman, large and competent in her uniform, checking the meat, making sure there was enough water to steam the puddings. She is putting on a show, trying to impress me, Narcisa told herself, but it made little difference. At one point, just as the food was being taken in, she found herself face to face with June Ragless, who was waiting impatiently for an explanation or order. 'Ask Miss Shaw,' she told June hastily, and went back to the larder to check the supply of suet.

I should be learning from her, she thought, in the long cool larder, amongst the earthenware jars. The idea filled her with resentment. Anyway, what is it I have to learn? Mrs Olby taught me; and then I have been cooking for how many years? She remembered again the house in Pimlico: the housekeeper, Mrs Rubinstein, from the East End, with a husband shell-shocked from the first world war. Teach me to cook, she had said, and spent half of every day in the kitchen, watching, or given tasks to do. Mixing fat with flour, that was the first, the texture as it crumbled between her fingers. I must have known, she thought, that it wouldn't last. That I would have to earn a living on my own. Or was it just that I wanted something to do, between the times that Claud would come and visit?

She made a note: suet, caster sugar, tapioca. No, it was because I would have to live alone, with nothing from Edwin, as soon as I had Violeta. She had gone out one evening, and leaned over the river, breathing in the sweet stale smell, and made herself know it. Edwin's money will stop; and Claud will not want me with a three-year-old daughter. To get her back, I will have to be independent. And the next day she had gone to the housekeeper.

It was all Violeta.

She left the larder and closed the door behind her.

Then she was at the far end of the kitchen, taking off her apron; and one of the patients was swabbing the stone floor; and Rosaleen Shaw was looking strangely at her, as if waiting too long for an answer; and the clock said ten past three; and what had happened in the hours since she closed the door, she had no idea.

The spring was arriving. The trees round the perimeter fence began to shine with a haze of little leaf-buds. Beyond the grounds, the snowdrops along the lane had given way to untidy daffodils. Nurses, coming back at night just before time, lingered with their boyfriends outside the gate, and then sauntered up the drive, turning back once or twice, out of sight of the lodge. A group of male patients, trusted to keep calm, was taken out to give a hand with the lambing.

It was light when Narcisa came down in the mornings. Once or twice, with a few minutes to spare, she went outside and stood in the dawn wind, at the back of the hospital, looking at the trees, which were black and close against a deep blue sky.

Wards were re-opened. The last of the war casualties were transferred, to the London Chest Hospital and the Orthopaedic in Stanmore. More and more mental patients kept arriving. Two, an elderly man and a youngish woman, were Polish and refused milk in their tea. A Polish welfare worker with red lipstick visited them. A new Deputy Medical Superintendent started: Dr Whitchurch, young and athletic, with intent eyes. He was said to have new ideas, though no-one knew precisely what these were. The younger nurses hoped to be noticed by him. One of them wore her new court shoes to work, and was disciplined.

Esme, the patient who'd been working in the kitchens, had a relapse and was moved to another ward, so the investigation was postponed.

Another blue letter came to the Clerk's office. Howard Rathfelders put it aside to show Narcisa, and then forgot.

They had put on the puddings to boil. The basins rattled in the great boiling-pans. The steam smelling of suet and sugar spread up along the ceiling and out across the kitchen. One of the working patients began to cough, till Peg, looking anxious, mimed covering her mouth with her hand.

'Please Cook,' June said, lifting a mixing-bowl into the sink. 'Isn't that someone at the door?'

The woman who had been coughing scurried to open. A thin young girl, no more than seventeen, stood in the doorway, frowning.

Cold air from the corridors began to reach them. 'Born in a barn,' the coughing woman muttered, and pulled the girl by the arm.

The girl took off her glasses and polished them; but almost at once they steamed up again. Like the farm manager, Narcisa thought, with a shiver. 'Yes?' she asked, quite gently. 'You have a message?'

The girl peered around, her glasses in her hand. Rosaleen Shaw had turned to her from the stove.

'Are you the Cook?' A surprising loud voice, casual and confident.

Rosaleen Shaw bowed her head, smiling. 'I am the Cook,' Narcisa said firmly. The girl looked round at her steadily, unembarrassed, assessing.

Middle class, Narcisa thought. She is used to servants. 'You have a message for me?' she asked again.

'It's from the Medical Superintendent,' the girl announced. The attention in the steam-filled kitchen quickened. 'He wants the Cook to come and see him at once.'

So now it is happening.

A pudding-basin began to clatter loudly. 'June,' Narcisa said, 'will you turn that down? Thank you. Peg, did you find enough custard powder?'

Peg nodded.

'Very well.' Narcisa turned back to the girl. 'What is your name?'

The girl tried her glasses again before answering. 'Stevenson,' she said. 'Priscilla Stevenson.'

'Priscilla.' She managed to pronounce it; well enough, anyway. 'Please tell Dr Bosanquet I will be ten minutes.'

'He said..' Priscilla began, and stopped. At the same time Rosaleen Shaw said, 'Really, Cook, I..'

'I'm sure Dr Bosanquet doesn't want the lunch to spoil,' she said, smiling.

*

It was theatre, a show; but she didn't mind. She was very calm. She went on confirming the tasks for lunch, though Rosaleen Shaw was standing too close to her, on the point of speaking. Then she took off her apron and hung it behind the door.

Should she get rid of the overall as well? she wondered. But no: Dr Bosanquet should see her like this, in working clothes. He should understand he had interrupted her.

She was very calm, walking towards his room; almost as if she had wanted this interview. At least it will be over, she told herself, though the words didn't seem to match what she was feeling. She knocked, and heard his heavy voice call out.

There was another man, a big man with fading blond hair, standing close to the fire. She steadied herself as he came forward to shake her hand.

'Sir Timothy..' but she didn't catch the surname. 'Sir Timothy is the Chairman of our Committee.'

So Dr Bosanquet had told the Committee already; they agreed with him. She had thought he would warn her first; but it didn't matter.

'Mrs Humphreys. Do sit down.' Sir Timothy's voice was light, like a young man's. He waved towards a chair, and waited till she settled before sitting himself, next to Dr Bosanquet behind the table.

'Now Mrs Humphreys.' She could see he wanted to be friendly. The thought made a small surge of anger start up in her chest. She grasped her hands together, not to allow it.

'I'm afraid we have a problem. There has been a complaint.'

I don't want to know what it is, she thought, impatient, dreading the drawn-out questioning that would follow. It doesn't matter.

'The family - the father, I believe - of one of the war casualties. The normal patients. It seems his son is unhappy with his treatment. More particularly, with the diet here. The father has taken the matter up with his MP, who raised the matter with me. Quite rightly, of course.'

He looked at her as if expecting something, a defence, a confession perhaps. She said nothing.

'Right,' he said. 'Well. Now this is a serious matter, Mrs Humphreys, as I'm sure you understand. These war patients, they're healthy young men and women. Or they were, rather. They've come to us so that we can build them up. They need a good nutritious diet. Simple, but nourishing. You understand?'

And the mental patients don't? she thought, indignant. She said carefully, 'There is a particular meal he did not think good enough? Or all of them?'

'Mrs Humphreys,' Dr Bosanquet said, like a warning, but the Chairman interrupted. 'No, no, James, perfectly reasonable question.' He looked down at a sheet of paper on the table. 'My feeling is, it's a general complaint, but one day in particular, if you see what I mean. Something to do with gammon, as I remember.' He smiled, as if gammon were something strange.

She was thinking very clearly now. 'Thank you. You would like me to explain the problem with the gammon?' At least, she thought, I'll have defended myself.

'Excuse me, Sir Timothy.' Dr Bosanquet was leaning forward at his desk. 'That will not be necessary, Mrs Humphreys. Sir Timothy needs to be assured that the culinary standards are of the highest.'

He knows about the problems with supplies, she thought. He's defending himself. She let them wait while she thought how to respond. Then deliberately she turned back to the Chairman.

'Before the war I had pork from the farm. Bacon, sausages, ham: I often boiled ham. Also potatoes, cabbages, runner beans.'

He nodded, as if he knew about farming.

'Now there is much I have to buy. It's true, I have had a problem with the butcher. One day he sent me bacon that was unfit. I had to make do with gammon, but there was not enough. I understand why someone is unhappy. The war patients, they are used to better.'

'Right,' he said again. 'Eh, Bosanquet?' He seemed unsure

what he could say next. She went on, a little hastily, 'I am very..' Conscientious, she wanted to say, but couldn't pronounce it well enough for him. 'Very responsible as Cook. I would like to give the patients, all the patients, better. However there is not enough money. Fruit, for example.'

'Quite so,' he said. She could see it was finished, for him. 'Well, fruit, we all wish, eh Bosanquet? So what shall I write to this man, Mrs Humphreys? What do you think?'

'Perhaps you will like to say - ' she saw Dr Bosanquet wince. 'Perhaps you will say that there has been a problem, with one supplier. But I am dealing with it.'

Dr Bosanquet sat, still frowning, 'And that you will pay particular attention to the war patients. Otherwise, I need hardly stress, Mrs Humphreys..'

She flinched. Of course he had not given up his campaign against her, even if Sir Timothy was more lenient. And what he wanted was impossible; he knew that all the patients ate together. She stood. Sir Timothy came round the table.

'So glad we've got that one sorted out, eh Mrs Humphreys?' He held out his hand.

'You are staying for lunch?' she asked.

He looked down. 'What a pity - good of you. No, no, I'm afraid I have to be in town.'

Already as the door was closing she could hear Dr Bosanquet's voice rise in complaint.

*

There was a smell of hot tin as she entered the kitchen. 'One of the pans has boiled dry,' she said sharply. 'Peg, put more water, but carefully, it will steam.'

As she put on her apron she heard the hiss of steam behind her, and Rosaleen Shaw's voice muttering. You should have noticed, she thought, with satisfaction, and went to the table to look at the menu again. June was already slicing cold roast meat.

As the girls were serving up, Rosaleen Shaw came and stood beside her. 'Anything I should know?'

She pretended ignorance.

'The Medical Superintendent.. I just wondered.'

'It was the Chairman as well.' She watched the woman gape. 'Sir Timothy. But I have dealt with it.' She was boasting; but her victory merited boasting. 'Somebody has complained, a war patient. But I have explained to Sir Timothy. There is no problem.'

'We should learn from complaints.' The voice was insincere. 'Can I ask what it was?'

'Before you arrived. You see you need not worry.' But that was rude. I have lost my temper with her once; I need to be careful. 'A problem with a supplier. One day we were short of food.' Your friend Mr Hartley, she thought, but moved away.

So I am not so bad, she told herself. Today I had something difficult, a crisis - Rosaleen Shaw would see it as a crisis - and I did well. And perhaps I made it harder for them to fire me. She surveyed the row of puddings, rounded, unblemished, waiting to be taken through to the dining-room; and the white custard jugs on the next trolley. I can do this. I can make all this happen.

'Good,' she said, and Peg pushed open the doors.

She had been dreaming of Howard Rathfelders. She woke with this in her mind, an image of him silhouetted against the long bay window, both arms outstretched, the left one ending abruptly above the wrist. She pulled the covers up over her shoulder and lay in the half-light, trying to piece the improbable dream together. There was something he had said: something that in the dream had made her flinch and run away, out of the main gate, but he had caught up with her in the lane. Then later she had been standing in a field, leaning her back against a tree-trunk.

That was how it was with dreams, she thought, warm, still relaxed, her hand slipping down between her legs and finding the place wet. But the truth was that for years she had rarely dreamed. These days she would wake with a sense of something, a taste, a voice calling out some important phrase; and for the first half-hour, until she unlocked the door of the kitchen, it would stay with her, as if she were missing someone. This one at least had left her with an image.

She closed her eyes and let the sensation flow out along her body. He was not bad-looking, Howard Rathfelders: a dark, intense young man. She remembered again how he had been before the war, on his bike, taking a bend in the lane, fast, standing on the pedals, the bicycle frame tilted out to one side.

What would he look like without the brown suit? He was still slim, she supposed; the rib-cage would be outlined under sallow skin, the hip-bones looking fragile as porcelain.

He was standing naked in front of the bay window, in silhouette, giving instructions to her, in a calm commanding voice. She stood as he ordered and he came over to her. The figure of Howard become half-anonymous, his one hand touching her roughly as she stood; or perhaps it was the other, the missing hand, that had the power to make her want his anger?

*

It was as she was dressing that the memory came back, as if she had not quite understood it before. She had woken up - that was the only way to put it - she had woken in the kitchen, with the Shaw woman staring at her. Someone had said, 'Cook, are you all right?' And she'd sat down, not ill, only terrified. Someone had poured her a cup of tea, and she'd sipped it, though it was much too sweet, because it was safer to do what she was told. Of course she couldn't tell them what it was. June Ragless had said, 'I thought she was going to faint,' and she'd let them believe it. All the time the knowledge, that she had lost four hours, became hard inside her, like a bone she'd swallowed, that stuck in her stomach and couldn't be absorbed. In those four hours, she realised, sitting still, she could have done anything, said anything: she could have lost her temper again with Rosaleen Shaw, or hit a patient, even; there was no way of knowing. Shaw had hustled the others back to work, and she had sat there, drinking the tea as slowly as she could, because when it was finished she'd have to do something. More time had gone, fifteen minutes perhaps? but she had known about it, every minute, with Rosaleen Shaw keeping her in sight, and the girls whispering, and one of the patients starting to whimper, till Peg took her aside. And then, because there was nothing else to do, she'd stood up, and said, as firmly as she could manage, 'Thank you. I am better. We will continue.'

But it was frightening, to have lost time. Pulling on her stockings, fastening the suspenders, she tried to think what it meant. Was it something like epilepsy, a kind of seizure? There was a type where you didn't have convulsions; someone, Mrs Olby she thought it was, had worked at the epileptic colony down the road, and told her about it. People felt strange afterwards, she remembered that.

She stood in front of the window and brushed her hair. But surely it wouldn't come on in your fifties? If it wasn't epilepsy, it might be something else that affected the brain. A tumour? Or they said that the new kind of therapy they used, with electricity, made you lose your memory.

You're avoiding the issue, she told herself, leaning both hands on the dressing-table to stare in the mirror at this frowning person, with shadows beneath her eyes, who behaved so strangely. It wasn't physical, she was sure of it. She ran both hands down over her face. It had never happened before; or she thought it hadn't; but if back then, in her first year as a patient, or after Violeta was taken, she'd lost some time - she didn't know how else to describe what had happened - no-one would have noticed. Not even me, perhaps, she thought, and flinched.

Perhaps she really was going mad again. Dealing with the complaint about the gammon, she had dismissed the idea; but it might be true. After all, I can't remember the time before Edwin had me admitted; or not much of it. Perhaps it is true that you're never really cured. These last weeks I've been angry all the time. And then with Anthony..

She turned away from the mirror, and took a clean overall

out of the wardrobe. There was nothing she could do about it, nothing. Just watch herself, and be ready to tell someone if it got too bad.

And the dream about Howard Rathfelders; did that mean anything? Was that mad, or only strange? She looked round the room, as if for a secret message, then made some movement to pull her wayward body into form, and went out to the landing and locked the door.

*

When breakfast was cleared she went again to the main block. The door was open; she could hear Mr Rathfelders speaking to someone. 'And the discharge records, please.' She knocked, and a young woman in a dark-green wool suit came from the far corner and looked at her.

'I have come to speak to Mr Rathfelders. If it is a convenient time. I am Mrs Humphreys.'

'Oh.' The woman blushed and turned away. She knows about the letter, Narcisa thought.

'Good morning,' he said, coming out from behind his desk. 'This is Miss Carrington, Assistant Clerk.'

The young woman blushed again and held out her hand.

'We will go over the discharge records later,' he said. Miss Carrington ducked her head and walked away, into the next room.

'I am not disturbing you?' She felt awkward now, as if her dream had in some way damaged him.

'Of course not.' He gestured for her to sit down. It seemed for a moment as if she were starting again, as if their first meeting was yet to happen.

She made herself speak.

'Mr Rathfelders, I have waited very long.' She wanted to tell him why; but was there a reason? 'Now I think I must reply to the letter. To my daughter.'

'Very well,' he began to say; but then sat up, eyes wide, his hand covering his mouth for a moment. 'Oh my g..' - he stopped himself. 'Mrs Humphreys, I must apologise. How terrible. There is another letter - I meant to tell you. Now where is it?'

He pulled open the drawer of his desk. His face was pale. Poor young man, she thought, as though it were nothing to do with her. Then he put the letter before him on the desk, another blue envelope, just like the first.

She found herself trembling.

'Please,' he said, and pushed the letter towards her. 'You will want to read it?'

She reached out and took the envelope in both hands. The writing was large, the letters carefully formed.

'I am sorry,' she said at length. 'Please read it to me.'

Again she watched him weigh down the envelope with his maimed arm, and fumble to take out the folded letter. He looked it over. 'It is very short,' he said, and began reading. *'Dear Mr Rathfelders. Thank you for your letter of 7 March.* - That was when I wrote, as we agreed,' he said, looking up. 'To say we were still making enquiries.' He went on. *'I do not wish to cause the hospital any trouble. If it is easier I will carry out any* - I'm sorry, I can't read this - *any enquiries myself, if you will send me details. I look forward to hearing from you. Yours sincerely.'*

'Is that all?'

'That's all.'

She sat still for a moment. Then she asked, 'What is the name? The signature.'

He looked down at the page again. 'Miss Violet - no, I am sorry, it is not Violet; Violeta Humphreys.'

She sighed. It felt almost peaceful to sit in the leather armchair, in the Clerk's office. Outside she could see small acid-green buds on one of the trees. The sky had cleared slightly; it hadn't rained.

Mr Rathfelders moved his blotter an inch to the left.

'Well,' she said. 'I have decided. I will have to tell her.' Then the fear rose in her throat, and she looked down again. A typewriter clattered in the room where the woman had gone.

'You intend to write to her?'

How formal he is, she thought. Is that because of his job, or does he hide himself? There were those deep-set brown eyes, hooded, careful, and a small scar high up on his right cheekbone. She wondered if that too was from the war.

Something about him forced her to be honest. She spread her hands. 'Mr Rathfelders, you will think I am a barbarian, but I have never written a letter in English. Not in many years. Or only to the butcher, the fishmonger.'

He fiddled with his pen, considering. 'Of course,' he said. 'If you wish I can reply. The letter is addressed to me, after all. But you might want..'

'I do not know what I want,' she said, and laughed.

They sat together in the chill high-ceilinged room. The typewriter stopped and started behind the wall.

'If I may,' he said. 'It strikes me.. I mean, you could write just a short letter. To say you are here. That this is your address.'

She hadn't thought what she might say in the letter. 'Not explain, you mean?'

He looked away, at the grate, where the coals hadn't caught.

'Please,' she said. 'I do not know what I should do. If you have any idea, please tell me.'

'Well,' he said slowly. 'I just thought: I mean, I assume you haven't seen her? For a long time?'

Since she was six months old, she wanted to say, but couldn't.

'Well, you don't know - forgive me, Mrs Humphreys, but you don't know what sort of person she is. Of course,' he said hastily, 'she is your daughter, and I imagine.. But perhaps it is better to wait until you meet her, before you tell her very much.' He ran his hand through his straight dark hair. 'But of course I don't know.'

How kind he is, she thought. He is not judging. She breathed out slowly. 'Thank you,' she said. 'I think perhaps you are right. I will have to think.'

The blue letter lay on the blotter between them. 'May I?' she asked, and picked it up. 'Of course I will return it to you afterwards.'

When he shook her hand she could have held on much longer.

*

In Epsom she had bought daffodils for her room. But then she had nothing to put them in: she stood in the middle of the floor, the edge of the bedspread just touching her shin, and gripped the stems, looking round at the wardrobe, the wash-basin, the dressing-table. In the end she laid them carefully in the basin, and went down to the kitchen. Half an hour before the staff would return. Some almost-memory made her climb on a chair to rummage in the back of the jug cupboard. That was it: a white milk-jug without a handle. She locked up after her and carried it guiltily up the stairs to her room.

When she came off duty, three were already out, big double-daffs with frilled, yolk-coloured trumpets. The rest were fat buds, a chink of yellow pushing out through the sepals. They might have been all day soaking up the sunlight.

She took off her overall and found a cardigan.

I have been putting it off, she thought. After supper she had been busy around the kitchen, supervising the girls as they cleaned up, planning to drain the fish-fryers in the morning. She sat, and opened the dressing-table drawer. There were the writing-pad and envelopes she had bought that morning, square-cut, white.

Well, she said to herself, and let out a long sighing breath. The paper was very smooth, cool like marble under her hands. And not only today I've been putting off writing.

She looked round. The curtain fluttered a little in the draught. A windy night; it had been blowy all day. She had cycled hard, into a head-wind, enjoying the effort. So I still have some strength in this ageing body.

She pulled one of the daffodils towards her. How delicate it was: she could see her fingers through the open petals. Why am I so reluctant to write to her? It was the first time she had asked herself. Most women - Clara for instance - would have been overjoyed; would have got the address from Dr Bosanquet and written at once, or gone straight to the house: *Here I am, your mother.* And the truth is, when I was younger so would I. If a young Violeta had come to Miss Grey and Miss Ainsworth's, knocked at the door and announced herself, I would have run to hug her, and never mind what those two old women thought. Even if I'd lost my job, and I might well have.

But is that true? she wondered, and leaned on the dressing-table. The scent of the flowers reached her faintly, like a doubt.

She stood up and pulled back one of the curtains. The draught from the ill-fitting window touched her ear. The grounds were dark. A tree became clear, the still-bare branches dipping in the wind; then the side wall of C Villa, with one lit window. What could I have done? Come back to the asylum, and asked to see their records? She shivered. I could have found out what happened in such cases. There would be a procedure.

Something moved on the grass. She watched a fox, running across the lawn, low to the ground, tail streaming out behind him. I suppose he is heading towards the farm. To attack the chickens; could he get into the run? Should I tell someone?

She let the curtain fall back, and sat down again. Perhaps after all it would be good to meet Violeta. She let herself drift into a wordless scene, the young woman tall, sweet-faced, forgiving her. I want her to pity me. She was ashamed.

And what about her? Will I feel pity for her? Will I need to? I have tried not to think what life she has had without me, she reminded herself, severe, because she needed to know all of her failings, before her daughter could come and face her with them. At least if I am still sane by the time we meet.

She unscrewed the top of the bottle of blue-black ink, and studied the pen. The new nib looked too fine to write with, scratchy. She dipped and touched it against the neck of the bottle, then wrote on the cover of the writing-pad: *Violeta*.

It could have been the first day she had learned to write. How foreign my handwriting still is, she thought.

She opened the pad, and straightened the line-guide under the first sheet.

Holywell Hospital. They don't call it asylum any more.
Dashwood Lane
Epsom
Surrey.
Is that how I wrote to Edwin when I was in here?

She sat back and contemplated the four short lines, in her flowing writing, the ink all but black. Do I write her address? To find it she would have to look at the letter again.

Mr Rathfelders had said not to explain. But he was cautious: suspicious of Violeta.

I could tell her everything, now, in this one letter. For a long time she sat and thought what it would mean: her marriage to Edwin, the house in Camberwell, the asylum, her escape, the housekeeping job, Felix. Coming back. The fear of going mad again.

Poor young woman, she thought, amused, with tears in her eyes; I would terrify her.

27th March 1947
Dear Violeta,

Part 6

**1922
-
1935**

My father is very patient, and I am not. He is going to make a brooch in filigree-work, for the wife of a Dubrovnik businessman. I have looked at the drawing; I think it will be the most beautiful brooch anyone has ever seen. So I sit on my high stool, trying not to squirm, waiting for him to take the wire [like embroidery thread; I could embroider him a handkerchief] in his narrow tongs, and twist it, oh, terribly slowly into place. But he is not ready.

He is starting what I call cooking, and he calls annealing. This is a process out of a fairy-tale, something a bewitched prince might use to dispel a curse. If I were not so impatient I would let myself be enchanted, even though I have seen it many times. I have to stay still, stiller than usual on my stool by the bench, because of the fire. The charcoal is already red, and sputters, though quietly, hushed by the rules of my father's workshop.

My father is holding a skein of fine gold wire on the palm of his hand. He picks up a length of ordinary wire, iron, to tie the gold down. I hate this iron wire, which is dull-toned, and stops the gold from springing out on the heat.

With his right hand he scoops sawdust out of a sack, and scatters it over the floor of a wide pan. The bright ring of wire with its iron shackle lies flat - how carefully he places it - in the centre of the pan; then another handful of sawdust to disguise it. In spite of myself I have forgotten the brooch. There is a lovely roasting smell as the sawdust catches, brightens as if infected by the gold. He pulls back the pan; takes it off the burner and settles it on a trivet. Little flames flicker around the disguised mass.

For once, my father looks over at me, and smiles. I am helping him cook the wire, I tell myself. I want the sawdust to burn for a long time.

It flops; there is a heap of soft ash. My father leans down to the pan and blows gently. The ash flies up, and falls like snowflakes towards the floor.

This is the magical part. The wire is no longer gold, but burning red. My father leans close to check it is red all over. If even a fraction of the wire coil isn't cooked through, it will break when he works it: just there, at the cool part.

I sit high up, some feet away from the pan, leaning forward, holding onto the sides of the stool with both hands, watching the red-hot wire blanch back to gold.

1922

But there were changes. So many men had come back from the war - so many had not come back, which was part of it - shaking, afraid of nightmares; and had been, still were, housed in asylums, many originally built by George Thomas Hine. The men, or their families, trekking out to visit, had reported back: the diet, tuberculosis, the sudden access of brittle bones among otherwise fit but unruly patients; so that even the gentlemen of the House of Commons, eight miles from the nearest asylum, were forced to consider. They produced an Act. If the desperate and the deluded, after all, were not afflicted by moral degeneracy, since some had been moral enough to fight for their country, then their condition must be conceded to be an illness, and their places of care hospitals, not asylums. What was more (and here the gentlemen recognised human frailty; even called hospitals, asylums were far away, and good staff hard to retain) the Committees visiting them should be critical. They should take care that patients were not only nourished, but provided with food to tempt the appetite. 'What?' said Mrs Olby at Holywell when she heard, from the ponderous Matron, 'and on the same money?' But her voice didn't carry; and the House by now was musing on other things.

Staff were a problem. It was the War, again: women had worked in all kinds of occupations, many unsuitable, but what could you do? And now the men had taken over from them (but not entirely: so many young men lost), the women turned out to have new ideas. Carrying a chamber-pot down all the back stairs, five flights, of the Midland Hotel at St Pancras, or a full coal-scuttle up in the other direction, was not a new idea. So the Midland Hotel, that Florentine palazzo, that great terracotta station front with imported French tiles and stencilled walls and mythic mosaic ceilings, and the trains behind it steaming in from Sheffield, was closing, for want of chambermaids. Young Dr Bosanquet, setting out to walk in the Peak District in the months before his marriage, found it very trying, arriving with his bags from Russell Square, instead of breakfasting above the station.

So much change. Miss Grey and Miss Ainsworth found the girls they'd taught quite frivolous, these days, when small groups came to visit; quite exhausting; they were relieved to have retired. Although two, it seemed, would go to Bedford College, where thank heavens they would be allowed to graduate, unlike Oxford and Cambridge, still full of foolish men. 'As long as they don't become bores,' Miss Ainsworth said, 'like those young men with their ridiculous decadence.' Though of course the war… It was more likely, Miss Grey pointed out sadly, they would marry before they had finished their degrees. Ah well.

As for what happened far off, in the Kingdom of Serbs, Croats and Slovenes: who knew? Not Edwin Humphreys; his former though unsaid trade, finding out that very thing and reporting back, to a room on the third floor of the Foreign Office, was not needed. The death of King Peter was not after all important; the Regent seemed to have sufficient grip. Or it was important, but Edwin was superfluous. So he travelled simply, from Camberwell to the Bank, by way of the Waterloo and City Line, and thence to the office, where the wool trade, pretext for his exciting life in Prizren, had become the reality. There had been enough excitement.

'Just a plain vegetable soup,' Miss Ainsworth said. 'You don't have time to do anything fancy.'

Narcisa's back was still turned, her hands in the deep white sink, with the knives and colander.

'Do you understand, Humphreys?' The voice-tone went up, as if scrabbling on a scree slope for a footing. From behind, Narcisa's nod was invisible. Miss Ainsworth spoke to Miss Grey in the corridor. 'I suppose she's going to be ready in time. You might as well be talking to a rock.'

The japonica tapped against the kitchen window. 'We make *this* from *this*,' Miss Grey had said, opening the pot a little reluctantly, offering a bead of pale red on the end of a spoon. They were outside, in the kitchen garden, a row of bright lettuces beside Narcisa's foot. Disbelieving, she jerked her head at the straggling bush reaching across grey brick with a few pink flowers. Miss Grey tightened the jam-jar lid: 'I will teach you.' It was two nights before Narcisa, dawdling after the ladies had gone to bed, dared enter the larder and find the pot again, with its looped script label. She lifted out no more than Miss Grey had given: it was true, the taste she'd remembered: quince. She stood still in the larder and almost smiled.

Japonica, she told herself now in silence, drying her hands. *Did* she understand them? She couldn't have said how. They spoke, sometimes loudly, sometimes laboriously; and out of the breakers and streams of sound something, maybe not the words, splashed up and soaked her. So it seemed: each sentence an assault, a drenching. This was not new; it had been like that for years. Only here in the house there were only the four of them with the maid, plus Spencer who came once a week to do the garden; and so the splashing and buffeting happened more often. I will have to get used to it, she told herself, drying the knives, taking the lid of the soup-pot so the steam rose in her face. She prodded a piece of carrot; another few minutes.

Back at the window, with nothing more to do till the soup was ready, she wiped her face with her apron. A blackbird stopped between the lettuces, jabbed at the earth. At the asylum it was all extreme; people wailed, they shouted, they stared at you in disgust and gave you orders. What had struck her most, coming to this house, was the cushioned quiet. Miss Grey and Miss Ainsworth raised their voices only when they couldn't get through to her. Everything they addressed to her was practical: *No, the other plates; just a plain vegetable soup; half past eleven.* Their talk together, as far as she understood, carrying in cakes and tea to the drawing-room, was much the same: *Did you speak to Spencer? What time is the dressmaker?* But over the weeks, less worried about mistakes, getting used to their voices, she had started to read deeper. Just now, for instance, the *plain vegetable soup;* Miss Ainsworth was saying, *For goodness' sake, woman, don't make me spell it out: it's not worth much trouble.*

She warmed the billy-can, and began ladling. If I were poor I would not want to be given this. She tasted it off the spoon; it was thin and sweetish. What else could she put in?

The stock itself was weak, that was the trouble. She stood at the larder door and scanned the shelves. They used so little seasoning; no herbs, apart from bay-leaf, which she'd used in the soup, and mint; spices they seemed to think were just for baking. As for wine... In the end she opened a bottle of Worcester sauce, tasted a drop on her finger: that might do it.

Perhaps the poor family liked watery soup too. If you are poor, no-one asks you what you like. She clipped the lid onto the billy-can, and wrapped it round with a tea-towel. Would the woman have some way of re-heating it? What sort of kitchen did you have if you were poor?

She walked behind them down the steep street, past the row of tall grey houses, each on its own, with a dark tree in most of the front gardens. Miss Grey and Miss Ainsworth nodded to an old man with a walking-stick. The basket weighed heavy with the soup and the loaf; she changed hands again. I am not going into the house. I will not do that. The determination had gradually grown inside her. I have made the soup, that's enough. I do not want to be there.

They crossed the road, Miss Grey turning to see she was following. How would she do it? They would want her in there, she was quite certain; they would want her to see them giving the food to this woman. When we get to the door I will hand over the basket. Miss Grey will take it. Then I will shake my head, and turn away.

A woman with a small dog was speaking to them. She walked more slowly, not wanting to catch up. The problem of staying outside was worrying her. I could not bear it. They will think I'm running away to do something. I will show them I'm not. I will find somewhere to sit and wait for them.

The sun was hot on her head through the dark-blue hat. She looked up. It was good after all to be outside, to have the sun on her face and to be moving. She let herself feel the strength of her legs, walking. Beyond the wide street, the spire over to her right, the heavy green tops of trees that might be a park, she could see the bare flat line of a hill-top. A horse, tiny and intricate in silhouette, walked daintily along the grass line, led by a small figure, a boy or man. After a little while another followed.

*

The upstairs maid was a fair, plump girl called Nutting.

Narcisa had looked blank at the introduction. 'Oh, she works upstairs,' Miss Ainsworth said, impatient. 'Not in the kitchen with you, you understand? She knows what to do, in any case. She's a good girl, mostly.'

When Miss Ainsworth had gone, Narcisa asked, 'Your name?'

'Nutting, please, Cook.'

Narcisa shook her head. '*Your* name.'

The girl stared. Then, eyes wide, as if it were an extraordinary question: 'Oh, *Christian* name, you mean. Oh, sorry, Cook. Emmie.'

From which Narcisa understood she would have to call the girl by her surname, as the women called her Humphreys; at least when they could hear.

Emmie was slow and careful, completing each task solemnly and (to Narcisa's relief) in silence. She came in from her parents' house early in the morning, and left after lunch. 'As much as we need,' Miss Ainsworth said, as if Narcisa might be expected to complain. 'Don't believe in all that fuss, you know.' At lunch-time Emmie came down to the kitchen, and Narcisa prepared something from leftovers, or a plate of cold meat and cheese, for the two of them. She thought Emmie wanted something more from her, gossip perhaps, or, even worse, guidance; but it was as much as she could do to offer food, and smile, and once or twice manage to ask a question.

In spite of this, Emmie seemed to want to help. 'Ssh, give it here,' she whispered one morning, as Narcisa was preparing a tray to be taken in. 'It's the vicar, he has to have the best china,' and she pointed to the tea-set with the roses, high in the end cupboard. 'Look, it's bone,' she said, and held up a cup to the light, her fingers showing through as shadows. Then she laid the tray and carried it to the drawing-room, pushing the door open with her wide bottom. Narcisa, grateful, kept back a couple of scones; which Emmie ate at a rush, as though someone might come in and grab them off her plate.

It was Emmie who arrived with a letter for her.

Narcisa stood still, her hands in the mixing-bowl, her heart beating. 'I'll just put it here on the side,' Emmie said.

Narcisa leaned over to look. The stamp was English.

My dear Nora, Clara had written.

At lunch-time she was at the cleared kitchen table, reading.

I hope you are well and settled in your new life. They sound as if they could be difficult, your two ladies! But it's good you have a position, don't you think?

She pushed the bread-board over to Emmie, who cut four thick slices, and gave her one on the point of the knife.

I am still with my sister Flora, and brother-in-law, but as I have told you it's very small, and I may take a room with another girl. I wish you were here to share with me, but there we are! The laundry is a good job, and very –

She couldn't make it out. Clara, she knew, found it hard work to write.

'Emmie,' she said urgently, 'what is this?' She pointed to the word. Emmie came round the table, to see better. '*Is a good job and very* – oh, friendly *–is a good job and very friendly.*' She might have wanted to ask more, but Narcisa was reading again, so she sat down. Narcisa pointed to the bowl of apples.

The doctor thinks the TB is more or less gone. What we put up with there, Nora! But I do feel stronger.
As for you –

She waited while Emmie took off her apron and fetched her coat from the closet,

– As for you I am sure you will think about your little girl, and hope to have her with you very soon. Never mind what your husband said, men don't know anything. Save all the wages you can. I am sure you will find a way, if you have some money! Like everything.
Remembering you fondly,
Your loving friend,
Clara.

When Emmie had gone, Narcisa read the letter over again. She was not sure she had understood it all; but Clara was there, her low, hoarse voice, her thin face, the secret grin that had seemed the thing that saved them.

She says she's better. Is the TB really gone?

Clara decides to have hope, Narcisa thought. *I am sure you will find a way:* how can she be sure?

It is this country, she thought, remembering Edwin; they believe whatever it suits them to believe. They do not give you any time to despair. For the first time Clara seemed strange and remote to her.

She ran upstairs, and tucked the letter under her nightdress on the bed. It was still true that Clara had made this effort to write to her. She could see her, tall, leaning over the table, thinking each phrase and laboriously writing. *Your loving friend:* it was true, that was what she was.

As she came downstairs, the board showed that the morning-room bell was ringing.

*

She was out in the yard with the mangle, feeding the wet sheets through, cranking the handle. The flattened sheets folded themselves over and then fell; she caught them, tightened the screw, and put them through the rollers once again. Water splashed grudgingly into the tin bath.

Her fingers were cold right through, with the wet linen, and the sharp breeze on her skin. When she carried the basket over to the line, the pale sunshine made a bright triangle on the washing. She took dolly-pegs from her apron pocket, and hung out the pillow-slips side by side, then the sheets, and hoisted the line on the cleft of the worn pole. The washing lifted and beat against the wind; the sun shone through it.

She wiped her hands on her apron, and stood a moment. A lock of hair was whisked across her face.

There were firm footsteps. Narcisa turned quickly, tucking her hair back. A man stood just by the corner of the house, at the edge of the yard.

'Do excuse me, Miss,' he said. 'Or is it Madam? I did knock at the back door, but there was no reply, so I ventured to look.'

She shook her head.

'Of course,' he said, 'you're the foreign housekeeper. They said about you down the road.' He was short and strongly built, with brown hair curling up around his cap.

'The kitchen,' she said, and walked past him to the back door. He stood back, looking her up and down.

Indoors, she said, business-like: 'You sell something?'

'Ah yes,' he said cheerfully, 'I definitely sell something. Or at least I hope to.' He was speaking more slowly, needing her to understand. He lifted his leather box onto the table. 'Have a guess?' he asked, hands on the brass clasps.

She didn't move.

'Dusters!' he announced, as the lid flew open. She was smiling, she couldn't help it: all the drama, and here he was with a yellow duster in each hand, as if he'd made them appear out of the air. 'Now you may laugh,' he said; but she could see it was all he could do not to laugh himself. 'But that just shows you have not been at this house long. Isn't that true? You are new to this position?'

She nodded, reluctant, but pleased at the same time.

'Ah well, you see. Now just feel that,' he said, and put a yellow duster straight in her hand. 'How about that? Is that not the softest duster you've ever seen?'

She managed to say, 'But I am not *wearing* it.'

He looked at her sharply over the leather box. 'A beautiful lady like you ' - he took up the patter again, though just for a second she had taken him aback – 'should be wearing silks and satins. And believe me, if I had those silks and satins…'

She stepped back, without meaning to. 'Quite right,' he said, 'I am letting myself be distracted. But these dusters, you see, will pick up any dust which an ordinary cloth' – he swept it over the table – 'though of course in *your* kitchen… You ask your maid here,' for Emmie had come in at just that moment. 'Here, young lady, you know all about dusters. Feel that one, eh? You tell the lady here.'

Emmie, she could see, could not resist being consulted. 'They are a bit worn, all ours,' she said to Narcisa, but softly, as if he shouldn't hear.

'Good! Fine!' Narcisa said suddenly, as if the words had been waiting to burst out of her, since before today even. She threw the duster in her hand to Emmie. The salesman looked startled. 'We take!' she said happily. 'Emmie, how many we take?'

'A dozen?' But the man had already lifted out a tied bundle. 'That will be four shillings the dozen,' he said. 'And for you two beautiful ladies, the two in your hands I will give you for free.'

Narcisa took the purse from the dresser drawer, and looked at Emmie, who nodded. 'That's right!' said the man, who seemed to miss nothing; but she thought he looked tired now; perhaps a four-shilling sale was a lot to him. 'She can tell they're value! Now, a receipt for your books, of course.'

She told Emmie to make him tea, and went back out to the washing, feeling herself walking more lightly than usual. She paused in the open air, a streak of sunlight touching the side of her face. Then suddenly the rare gaiety he had opened closed down again. A door-to-door salesman; and she was flattered he wanted to flirt with her! She put the towels through the mangle angrily, turning the handle as fast as she could manage, keeping the rollers tight so it was hard.

What do you expect when you're a housekeeper? No more English gentlemen like Edwin Humphreys, sitting correctly on the edge of his chair, listening deferentially to your father. Not with your history.

She waited till she'd heard the back gate shut, then went indoors and sat down, pushing the bundle of dusters away with her elbow. So am I going to marry a man like that? She made herself consider the idea, without flinching. He was attractive; she would not be enduring a man who repelled her. He was lively, and most likely would be kind, and grateful to have a woman concerned for him. No doubt he would enjoy being a father. Am I just thinking of status, after all? You have no status here, Narcisa Humphreys; or only that of a cook-housekeeper, and even there you still have to prove yourself.

She stood up; she had a pie to make, and the grocer's man would be coming with the order. But music, she thought; discussion. There came back, perhaps for the first time since before the asylum, the sense of what she'd been missing. The piano; concerts; people discussing politics. I am sure the salesman would buy you a piano, she told herself drily. But it was not one single thing, to say, oh no, I couldn't like without *that*. She measured flour onto the scales; how cooking helped one think, it was so ordered. She had lived without everything, or so it had seemed at times. I am a strong person; I have had to be. Before the asylum I would never have known that.

I don't mind working; it isn't that. Making pies seemed no worse than embroidering cushions. It was simply that her future was terrible. Clara's wrong, she thought, it will take more than money. She mixed the dough, feeling the texture of the fat and flour combining, adding the milk a little at a time. I will spend the rest of my life without a husband, because I could not live with a good man like that, and the men that I might want will never see me.

It was better to be saying this; to make herself hear it. She concentrated on the pie for some time. The stewing-beef was not good; she would have to work out how to make her complaint to the butcher. It will be tender enough, I suppose, cooked slowly. And they will not starve. Miss Grey's and Miss Ainsworth's opinions seemed not to matter, in view of the rest of her life. Well, that was something.

It was her afternoon off. She walked and walked, up past the house where they took the soup she made, onto the hill-top where the horses were exercised. The race-track was down far to her left, misty in the cold light. Out of breath at the top, rubbing her gloved hands on her cheeks for warmth, she recognised what it was she was still not facing. It is too terrible, she thought, standing up straight, letting the tears fall and not wiping them. I have to go on living in this country, with its cruel politeness and charitable works. There seemed in the future she was at last looking at – the low English hills blurred in the weak light, houses with red roofs spreading up the slopes – no time, no rooms, in which she could have her daughter to live with her. But I do not know that for sure. There may be something.

Walking back down the steep streets, with their dull evergreens and their pruned-back roses, she realised she could tell no-one what she'd just learned, not even Clara.

1930

Miss Ainsworth stood up, and turned off the radio. 'I suppose he knows what he's in for there,' she said.

'The PM? Oh, I'm sure he'll have thought about it a great deal.'

'Mm, well, let's hope so.' She looked round the room as if something might be missing. It was getting colder; there was a draught from the door. Miss Grey leaned over the sewing-box, unwound a yard or so of rose-pink thread and snipped it. 'Just one more seam,' she said. 'Just this sleeve.'

'You'll ruin your eyes.' Miss Ainsworth was putting Shakespeare back on the bookshelf. It was her school prize copy, fat, with a tooled binding, the plays printed in two columns on india-paper. 'I could have sworn it was *Twelfth Night*,' she said. 'There we are. Do you remember in Brighton…?'

'That ghastly Malvolio with his cross-garters?' Miss Grey looked up, laughing. Her eyes were still the same blue, Miss Ainsworth thought. Well, perhaps slightly faded. She shuffled the books together, and pushed the bookend hard against the end one, *Ivanhoe*. 'Met the new vicar again this afternoon.'

'You're quite right, Leah, I can't see to do this. It'll have to wait till the morning.' Miss Grey folded the sewing. She was making a dress for a little girl, the daughter of the fruit-and-veg woman. Not the child's fault about her mother's habits. Another one on the way, she wouldn't wonder. 'What did he say to you? The vicar, I mean?'

There was the sound of rain on the French windows. Miss Ainsworth raked at the fire, till the ash fell into the pan, and the coals brightened and settled lower. A spark flew out towards Miss Grey's feet. 'Sorry. Oh, he's a poor thing, if you ask me. Long neck, great Adam's-apple like a turkey.'

'And after poor Mr Chadwick. Oh dear.'

'Come on, Lettie, you're taking an awful time.'

They tidied the room; Miss Ainsworth put up the fireguard, Miss Grey turned off the wall-lights, and put her sewing things back in the side cupboard. 'Did you check the French windows? You still haven't told me what the vicar *said*.'

'Oh, he was worried about the Christmas crib. I told him, the ladies in this parish have always managed, no doubt we still will. I know he's a man of God, but he should have a little more sense by now. And respect. Oh, and then he said,' – she went into a rather anxious high male voice – '*Christmas is Christmas for the servants too, we must remember.*'

'Really, what a…' Miss Grey struggled with piety. 'I hope you put him right.'

'I said, I'm afraid you won't see our cook-housekeeper in church. And I knew he was thinking we wouldn't let her because of the dinner. So I let him, just for a minute, and then I said, She's RC, you know.'

Miss Grey leaned on the newel-post on the landing. Her back was aching: lumbago, she supposed. She hoped Leah hadn't gone too far.

'He looked quite shocked, but I said, Yes, I know, but in our considered view she's a good Christian, and a good housekeeper too. And there I left it.' She put up her hands to begin removing hairpins. The straight grey hair uncoiled, in a long tail. 'By the way, what *is* Humphreys doing for Christmas dinner?'

'Oh, I said to her, nothing fancy: a joint of veal, perhaps, or a leg of lamb. And pudding, of course; she's already done the puddings. They were good last year, weren't they?'

They might have been tasting the brandy butter.

'I expect he will need all our support,' Miss Grey said. She looked round suddenly. 'Is Humphreys…?'

'Up in her room, of course; where else do you want her to be at this hour? She can't hear from up there. I didn't say she doesn't go to the RC church either. Do you think I should have?'

They stood pondering a moment. 'He can always decide to come and visit her,' Miss Grey said in the end. 'He'll know what to do. After all, if Mr Chadwick never managed. I doubt if he'll get any joy. Well, good night, Leah.'

'Night, Let.'

They went, Miss Ainsworth reluctantly, to their rooms.

Only the sleet stopped her going away again. The sleet was wheeling along the village street – was it a village, in the endless stretch of suburbs? If she gave up, she'd have to walk back to the station, into the wind, the sleet blown in her eyes. She hunched further into her coat collar, lifted one hand from her pocket, knocked at the door.

The knocker seemed too substantial for the house: a stone cottage, right onto the street, with no front garden. The footsteps came too soon to the door, to open.

'Mrs Humphreys?'

Then she was inside the small parlour, the room looking out on the street, with thin net curtains – would she be visible? – and the reason she'd come right opposite the window. The piano.

'It is only an upright,' the piano teacher was saying. She'd thought he would be an older man, a plain, balding man, like Schubert in the engraving, only much older. 'However, you will find it is quite good. It is *overstrung,*' – he said the word solidly, as if he had just learnt it in English; she knew the tone. 'It is not mine,' he adds, 'but belongs to an English colleague.'

She wanted to warm her hands at it, like a fire. She took off her hat and coat, and put them somewhere. She went to sit on the piano stool, but stopped herself quickly, and looked at him. 'Please, please,' he said.

She stretched her hands out over the keyboard; but they had forgotten. Everything. She let them fall to her thighs. The cold from outside seeped from them, through her skirt.

She wanted him to understand, but of course he didn't. He nodded helpfully. A broad, pleasant face, and russety hair.

The sleet slapped at the window behind them. 'I am sorry,' he said. 'I am being very forgetful. You see it is not my house. Would you like a cup of tea? You must be cold.'

She shook her head. 'It is too long ago,' she said. 'I do not remember.'

'Of course,' he said cheerfully. 'In your letter you wrote that it has been a long time. But I would like to know what you used to play, even though naturally it will not be fluent. Perhaps we can find…' She stood up from the piano stool, and he brought out handfuls of sheet music, which he piled on the sideboard, on top of a lace runner.

The paper was heavy, the covers creased, with elaborate engravings. One worn fat volume, the Beethoven sonatas, was so known that she lifted it, closed, and sniffed in the smell; then smiled, embarrassed, and laid it aside. No, Chopin.

She settled her weight on the piano stool, and leaned forward to flatten the music with both palms. Sat up straight, and breathed out, as Madame had taught her.

Her left hand felt stiff and mechanical; she struggled to achieve any sense of flow. Then the melody in the right started to come, the feeling of searching, like walking up a mountain she used to think, a bit higher, a bit higher, the view still hidden. Her body leaned into the rhythm: not good enough, not right – there, too slow, she was losing the shape of it – but the piece had gathered her in like a dancing-partner. Until – Oh no, wrong – painful – she stopped.

'I can see you lack practice,' he said, solemn. Ah. She must have been terrible; must have caused him pain; he was a musician, and had to endure this. 'But do not despair! This can be remedied!'

He was very young. Only recently she had begun to see people as young. When did anyone ever say to her *Do not despair?*

'I cannot practise.'

'Ah, of course. I am sorry! You said this in your letter. You have no piano at home?'

'Herr Untermeyer.' He looked a little startled. That was his name? 'I am a servant. A housekeeper.'

'Of course. Forgive me. But the family has…?' She was shaking her head already; he was young, he was only a musician; what did he know of the disentitlements of service?

'Can you teach a pupil who will not practise?' She was almost kindly, almost teasing him.

'Of course,' he said again, and looked at her, this impossible pupil – so she thought he saw her – this shabby woman who will never learn. But he was young; he believed in the future. 'You will simply have to work very hard when you are here. Now, the opening…'

So it started.

'Miss Grey,' asked Narcisa, having rehearsed herself *(I am reliable. It will not change the routine)*. 'I like to change my afternoon off. I like to have Thursday, instead of Tuesday.'

'I *should* like, Humphreys,' Miss Grey corrected her. 'Well, I will have to see what Miss Ainsworth thinks.'

'I don't think she'll take advantage,' Miss Grey told Miss Ainsworth, hoping she'd agree. Better to give in to minor requests, she thought; keeps them good-tempered.

That was one thing arranged. Felix Untermeyer, of course, had nothing to arrange. Thursday was already his free afternoon, when the boys at the school played rugby, or read in Tacitus about tortoise-formations, or did anything except music and German. As for Alfred Michaels, the English master, whose home it was: it was his idea that Felix should give lessons: 'Don't play it enough. Better get it tuned before you start.'

During the lessons Ita Michaels sat upstairs, not doing the things Alfred set out for her – 'Perhaps you'd like to try some watercolours' – in tones of increasing perplexity and concern. Ita listened as the woman pupil (she had looked surreptitiously out of the bedroom window) attempted again and again the lifting phrase. Oh, she'll never get there, Ita thought, enraged. Sometimes, shocked at herself, she hated the pupil; perhaps for her hour of Felix Untermeyer's attention. I should have married a musician, Ita thought: someone passionate, who would understand my moods, and enter with me – but what they might enter together she couldn't quite say. The parlour door sighed open, then the front. 'Thank you,' she heard the woman pupil say; an older woman, rather dowdy, Ita thought, and smoothed the skirt of her new linen dress.

It must be Thursday, Elias Smith concluded, walking back slowly from the library, Lamb's essays and the history of the Stuarts under his left arm. His right hand grasped the head of his walking-stick, as if it were some moral principle: the staff of faith, perhaps. On Thursdays someone endeavoured to learn Schubert. No, no, he wanted to say, pausing on the pavement outside the house, to get his breath as much as anything. That's far too slow; why doesn't the teacher tell him? He imagined the pupil a boy, twelve or thirteen, the age when they want to be doing something else. But the boy was progressing, he'd grant him that, as the C flat major impromptu started again and flowed on, expressively, he would admit, as far as where – but Elias lost patience; he was getting cold (it was early March by now, the wind still biting). He prodded the pavement dismissively with his stick.

So it continued. On the train back, and up the hill from the station, Narcisa carried the music as long as she could, in her chest, she thought, or her now stilled gloved hands. This is my way of practising, she told herself later, wiping over the cleared shelves of the larder, her right hand wanting to start on the first theme. But the music left her too soon, driven out of her head by arithmetic – the tradesmen's books – or the two women's orders. I shall never get there, she thought, lying awake, the night after Elias Smith had stopped to listen. This is foolish; I am deluding myself. A housekeeper cannot learn to play the piano. I will go and tell him. Probably he'll be relieved. But when she went there, the next Thursday, the sun was shining, an almond tree was in flower in a front garden. 'I like – I *should* like,' she corrected herself, 'to learn a piece that is modern. That I did not know as a girl.' 'Good! Excellent!' said Herr Untermeyer, and produced, not from the piano-stool but his music-case, some crisp sheet music.

They began working on a piece by Bartok. It gave her no comfort; it was angular, she thought: more suited, perhaps, to an odd pupil like her. 'Ah, Herr Untermeyer,' she said, in the fourth week (how expansive she was becoming in this room!) 'I am not a real pianist. It is difficult for you?' She looked up; there was the sound of driving rain. She found herself suddenly anxious about his judgment. And would he think she was flirting? She was serious; she had forgotten years ago how to flirt.

He opened his eyes wide (light brown, she saw, the colour of caramel) and began to laugh. 'Of course!' he said, 'when you play it as if it were Mozart! Now, please, a little more *nervousness*, Mrs Humphreys.'

On the step, the shower having passed, the tarmac bright, a baker's boy cycling past, one split-tin loaf left in the front basket, he kept her talking, first about harpsichords, then by some train of thought Vermeer. He had to say it more than once for her. 'Yes, yes! But I have seen only - ' she searched for the word.

'Engravings? Then you must see the paintings. You cannot respond to Vermeer in black and white.' Then in a little rush he said he would see to it, if she liked; they could go one Sunday, if she could take the time, to some house in North London. 'It is essential that you see this painting.' 'Essential?' she asked, 'for my playing?' But she would do it.

*

She had thought she was paying for the pleasure of learning music. A good deal out of her wages; but what else could she spend it on? She hadn't thought about getting male company; he was meant to be old and strict, as she'd now told him.

When had she last had a conversation with a man? She was at the sink, scouring the Yorkshire pudding pan. There was jasmine tapping at the kitchen window. A bee tried to get in, and bounced back. - Apart from the functional talk: coalman, greengrocer; once, reluctantly, the doctor: bronchitis, but Miss Grey had worried about TB. *I have seen tuberculosis,* she could have said: *many people, all round me;* but it would hardly have been reassuring.

She emptied the sink, rinsed and wiped it round, dried her hands. The previous vicar, once; but she'd had so little English. Which indeed had helped her, in that case.

The fact was, she thought, taking down Mrs Beeton, for the Sussex pond pudding they liked so much, which she never remembered properly; the fact was, she didn't have conversations. This struck her as both astonishing and obvious. *And the people I've been around, ever since Edwin, they have been just women.* At the asylum, at Mrs Pilgrim's and after, when Edwin had paid for her lodgings and she'd learned all this, kitchen stuff, from one or other woman; and now, here. At the asylum the only men who came to the women's section were the doctors. And then not often, she thought, remembering Clara coughing up blood, and they had told the attendants, even the Matron, and how long before they did anything for her? It was a miracle that Clara had lived, and that she'd not had tuberculosis herself. *I must have been fit even then,* she thought, and stretched her arms, there in front of the window.

What would Clara say about Herr Untermeyer? *You got an eye on him?* That was her phrase. *You got your eye on him, Nora?* Though Clara surely would have men as friends, men she liked talking to, who weren't her husband. Or would the husband disapprove of that? Stan, he was called: *He's a good man,* she'd written, *though a bit fat! Still with my history I think I'm lucky.* Would Edwin have disapproved of her talking to men?

She brought the ingredients together on the table: lemons, suet (she must order more suet), flour, sugar. Baking-powder. Four eggs. The sun made its way through the kitchen window, and lit up the paring-knife and the two lemons.

Her hands smelled of rosemary.

She reached back over her head to clutch something. The soft spokes pressed themselves prickling into her palms, the roots and tough stems resisted, as she'd wanted. The sky was bluer than seemed possible; or perhaps more southern, through her half-closed eyelids.

When she let go the plant to cover her face, there was the sweet, pungent smell, strong enough to make her eyes water, if she'd not already been weeping. The smell stayed close to her face for a long time. Then she felt sorry for him, and opened her eyes.

He was sitting up, perplexed. As if a phrase in Schubert would not come right, however he sang it and she felt it in her hands. She pulled off a twig of rosemary, and held it out to him. Still the grief held her closely, like a sheet.

She had no words, let alone in English. His shirt was open. She put her hand flat on his chest. His body-heat seeped slowly back into her.

'Can you tell me...?' he began, but she shook her head, and pulled him down onto her, so that he couldn't watch her any more. He kissed her forehead; that was good, as if he were giving her her father's blessing. Her body sobbed again, once, but she stopped: enough.

When they were dressed and the twigs and earth brushed off, as they walked towards streets and buses and work, she took his hand tentatively, and said, 'Felix, you must know, I am glad.' Then she laughed and made him smell the herb on his hands.

'I do not want that you regret,' he said. So his language had slipped out of place, too. She was pleased or perturbed that it had mattered for him.

They walked hand in hand, their two shadows leaning along the grass, 'Well,' she said, 'I am a *domestic servant,* and now I have done this as the servant girls do, in the open air.' She pulled him to run down the slope of the open field, before he could protest about *domestic servant.* At the bottom, just before the hawthorn hedge, he brought them to a stop, swinging her round into his embrace. 'Nora,' he said, into her thick bobbed hair.

'Narcisa.' She tasted her name, strangely, saying it out loud for the first time, ever perhaps. 'Narcisa, my name is Narcisa, say it, Narcisa.' She made him practise, before they climbed over the gate, till he could say it with almost no accent.

*

'Humphreys,' Miss Ainsworth said, as Narcisa raked ash from the kitchen boiler. 'Your young man may call to collect you from the house, you know.'

Her scraped-back hair looked especially like iron.

They had been observed. Debated: the two old women by the fire, when she had brought them the coals, making their judgment. She wanted to say *He is my music teacher,* but knew it would sound ridiculous, from a servant. And in any case, who knew what had been seen?

Not the afternoon with the rosemary, or she would have been straight out of the door.

'Thank you, she said. 'It is not necessary.'

They would have to go farther. 'Brighton,' he suggested, 'the Pavilion. But you will think only about the servants.' It was his complaint: at Kenwood, after Rembrandt and Vermeer, she'd wondered how many maids were needed to do the floors.

'Of course,' she said, teasing, 'you look at the harpsichords, and I look at the kitchen range, if they let us see it.' Nevertheless he was uncomfortable, she knew: that she could not put aside her occupation, and be the woman that she might have been.

In any event, they did not go to Brighton. So few Sunday afternoons.

July: almost the end of the school year. The boys, he said, were restless, squirming in class, anxious about re-entering their families. To distract them he taught them German drinking songs: 'Both my subjects at once.' The headmaster asked questions, but was pacified.

His mother expected him home in Königswinter. For the summer; perhaps forever. His contract was renewed for another year. Narcisa knew now that he had had ambitions, to break into the London music scene. She imagined him climbing in through a smashed window. The windows had been too high, or too far away.

Perhaps he had spent too much time with her, instead of with the daughters of opera-goers.

His mother, she supposed, would learn about her. He was asleep, on the grass on Wimbledon Common; she was sitting up in the sun, making daisy-chains, as Edwin's younger sister had once taught her. He had showed her a photo of his parents, the father tall and stooping, with a moustache; the mother big-breasted, with curly hair: 'the same colour as mine,' he had said. She knew, as he must too, surely, that a woman eight years older, who had once been married and perhaps still was, working as cook-housekeeper, would not be welcomed. *Let alone* the rest, she thought, in new English.

His father's party believed in the superiority of Germans. Felix was indignant; she was not. 'All people believe this about themselves,' she said. 'Certainly the English.' 'And yours?' he'd demanded, standing by the piano. 'I am a goldsmith by race,' her father had once claimed. She laughed: 'No, it was difficult even for us to believe. Though some did, I am sure. I was too young.'

She arranged the daisy-chain on his face, like a beard. He opened his eyes and closed them again. A small girl in pink ribbons stared, dragging at her father's hand.

I am younger with him than I have been for many years. Sometimes, at her stolid tasks in the house, polishing silver, or washing yellowing sheets, she felt amazed that she could be both people: an efficient woman of no age and with no choices, and this irresponsible girl who played Schubert. Though not so irresponsible, perhaps. 'I do not want to *fall pregnant*,' she'd told him, at the music lesson after that first time, using the phrase she remembered Clara using.

She lay back beside him, head resting on her handbag, looking up. There were heavy green branches, the chestnut tree behind them; and a mid-blue sky, with a few rags of white cloud. Some men were playing football not far off; she could hear their cries to each other, though not the words.

Suppose he wanted me to marry him? Is it possible? This is not a Catholic country; perhaps it is. Perhaps I am already divorced from Edwin. Or to live with him without marrying? I would not mind that, but I think he would.

She imagined them in the Michaels' cottage, he setting off for the school on his bicycle, she making the fire, then sitting at the piano. Or a maid, even: the fire already lit when she came downstairs. It seemed a luxury quite unreachable.

He stirred. She put her hand on his forehead, to keep him lying there while she considered; but he rolled onto his side, and leaned to kiss her.

1935

There is a ticking sound like a great slowed cricket. The field in front of her is oak-brown, the tractor making a dark border of turned earth. The slope of the field is flexed, like a stopped wave.

She stands on the footpath opposite, just out of range in case it should crash down.

To the left of the ploughed field the grass is thin, chalk showing through like the webbing of a carpet. There are sheep, small and almost motionless, fat and creamy in the slanting sunshine.

From beyond them the sea breeze streams between the downs. She sits with her back against the trunk of a tree. Little pieces of twig, broken leaf and beech-mast are scattered around her on the dry brown earth.

She has not come far. It was simple. Her blue leather case is at Victoria, in the left luggage. Miss Grey and Miss Ainsworth, back from doing the church flowers, will have found a steak pie ready and her note. She imagines they won't be surprised that it doesn't say much.

She has been in this country more than twenty years, and did not know there was anything like this.

She took the train yesterday to Newhaven, not even knowing why she had heard of it. It came through suburbs she knew and others she might have: redbrick, back gardens. She thought: there is nothing more than this, anywhere. The land heaved up steeply but the buildings clung on. Then there was more space, flat, and a line of bare hills.

At Newhaven she watched a ferry docking. Spray blew sideways off the tops of waves, and made rainbows briefly. There just out of sight was France, and beyond it Switzerland, then Italy, then at the far end of Yugoslavia, Prizren. She leaned on a railing, a freed lock of hair beating in the sea wind against her hat; but the little half-pictures of Prizren stayed separate: the stone bridge, the low domes of the hammam, the steep street. Stone the mind could imagine, but not people. She had no idea even what clothes they'd be wearing. She walked back through the town, and watched by the side of the road as the flat bridge opened and a cargo-boat went slowly up the river.

Beyond the warehouses there was a tow-path, and reed-beds, and up ahead the line of the tall downs. The water was thick and mildew-green. She crossed over a painted footbridge. The light was going, the bright copper leaves in the woodland in front of her blurring.

She went into a pub, as if she were used to it, and sat in the window with a glass of beer. It tasted like dried fruit, dates or prunes. After an hour or so she asked for a room.

*

The man driving the tractor is out of hearing, and in any case absorbed. His rectangular journeys, up the left-hand slope, along the top, black against the pale sky, then down the steep right-hand edge, seem to Narcisa a kind of ceremony; but perhaps he is worrying how to pay the doctor. In any event they are not forced to speak. A while ago a woman came with a small dog along the path, and said Good morning.

At the pub they are courteous, and ask nothing except, 'What would you like for your breakfast?' She sits in the empty bar, and food is served her.

How long is she staying? 'You'll be staying on tonight,' the fair-haired woman asked, or maybe stated. There is nowhere she would rather be than this.

She woke last night in her attic bed in the pub, at about three, and thought: Am I having a breakdown? Her mind and her feelings seemed to her quite clear. Perhaps that poor soul she'd seen in the street in Epsom, bare-legged, in a patched frock, felt the same, wailing outside the grocer's, 'I want to go home.'

At least she knows she does not want to go home, wherever that is.

The sheep have moved closer together, up at the top of the field. Where they are is still in sunlight; most of the rough grass is already dulled. The dark ploughed border encroaches slowly onto the oak-brown.

Part 7

1947

Part 7 - 1947

The rain had stopped. The clouds were still low, but massive and whitish-grey, moving steadily across a soft blue sky. Anthony looked up, as a light wind passed across the nape of his neck.

The bad-egg smell of the drains lifted heavily into the three men's faces. Dr Whitchurch stepped back from the trench. 'Is there anything else we need to look at out here?'

He was new, Anthony thought; wanted to make things happen. No doubt he thought the hospital very old-fashioned. He watched the younger man struggle with nausea, standing small and strong, the breeze riffling through his fair hair. Well, and a good thing if he starts to change it; god knows the place needs modernising. Good to have someone young and keen to tackle it.

Mischievously, though, Anthony made him wait, squatting down at the edge of the newly-dug trench and prodding at the cracked pipe with his slide-rule. Beside him the overalled knees of Colin Allen, the Works Manager, were broad and immoveable, just in his line of vision.

'You can bodge it,' he told the Deputy MS. 'But you'll be calling me back again in less than a year.' His thighs started to cramp, and he stood up. 'What do you think, Allen?'

There was a pause. He could feel the doctor's impatience

from across the trench. Colin Allen would need to assemble his thoughts, like the parts of a motor, before he spoke. A tractor rumbled up the lane behind them.

'To be honest, Mr Shearer, I think these drains have always been rotten. As long as I can remember, they've blocked up; and that's getting on thirty years. I don't think it's just wear, I think it's how they were laid.' He looked from Anthony to Dr Whitchurch, square-shouldered, stubborn; a good man, Anthony thought, with a rush of warmth.

'And you, Mr Shearer, do you agree with that?'

'I agree with Allen,' Anthony said calmly. 'It's poor quality piping, and probably always was. The builder cutting corners. Plus it's not laid with a sufficient incline. If you really want to solve the problem, you need to dig the whole lot up and re-lay them. That means closing the place, for maybe three months.' He watched Dr Whitchurch, who didn't blench. 'Not easy, I appreciate. The alternative is you have regular blockages, and leaks like this.' He pointed down. 'Of course there is also the public health question.'

'I've said that.' Colin Allen was emphatic. 'I've been saying for years, all these upset stomachs and so on, I thought it had to do with the drains. But the MS, I'm sorry to say, he wouldn't have it. Said it must be the cooking.'

Narcisa, Anthony thought, and felt something hollowed out under his ribs. So the old bastard Bosanquet was blaming her. He looked away from the two men, towards the brightening chestnut-trees by the gate-house.

'Can you give us an estimate for replacing the drains?'

'Certainly,' he said, regaining his calm. 'In the meantime' - he turned to Colin Allen - 'you know how to patch up that crack, don't you?'

'I've done it often enough before.'

'Then thank you, gentlemen,' Dr Whitchurch said. The

courtly words hovered awkwardly above the trench. A cloud spread upwards and dulled the light on the flattened grass and the pile of clay-ey earth. 'Heading back to London, Mr Shearer?'

'No, no, I have to be at St Botolph's in the morning.' He was going to say more, something chatty about the country inn where he was staying. Instead he shook hands hastily with the two men, before walking with mud-caked shoes back to his car.

*

It was still early: ten to five. The sky had cleared slightly; the black bonnet of the car reflected the top of a tree in the mild sunlight. Twenty minutes till he picked up Narcisa outside the church. He drove slowly out of the grounds onto the lane, waving thank you to the gate-porter, a thin bald man whose name he could never remember. His hands on the wheel and the gear-lever tingled slightly.

Did she know that Bosanquet blamed her for the health problems? He was indignant again on her behalf. He wouldn't tell her. Though it was quite possible that she did know. She was so stoical; he could imagine her hearing the insult and swallowing it, letting it stay inside her, like a pill to be taken, along with everything else. Though what everything else was he had little idea. Her mother had died when Narcisa was quite small; well, that was hard. Enough to make you a stoic, he supposed.

A van overtook him on the bend of the lane, the words *Hartley Purveyors* in red script flashing past. Fool, he thought mildly as the van sped on, having survived the blind curve, towards the town. He wondered if he'd handled the meeting badly. He wasn't too bad, the new Deputy MS. A bit conscious of his position; but that could be nerves. Still, they wouldn't re-lay the drains, that was obvious. What have I ever done that they've used? he asked himself.

At that moment he caught sight of Narcisa, tramping along the road, hands in her pockets; and the pleasure and fear threatened to overwhelm him, as he pressed the horn, and drew in just beyond her.

*

'You were looking sad,' he said as he drove off, through the market square and out towards the Downs.

'Sad?' She considered and then smiled. 'No, I was thinking there is a hole in my shoe' - she raised her left foot and pointed down - 'and I must find someone to repair it. Before the war there was a shoemaker's shop in the hospital, but they have not opened it again.'

He was silent a moment, looking for the turning. 'Right, here we are.' It was a lane like a tunnel, beneath lime-trees not yet in leaf. The sunlight came and went across the windscreen. 'You used to have everything there in the hospital.'

'Everything. It is only now' - she hesitated. Did she mean with him, he wondered - 'now I see how different it is from the rest of the world. My clothes are washed, my room is cleaned, I am in charge of the food but when I sit down to eat it is what we all eat. Now they say even they will have a cinema, show films for us. If my bicycle needs repair, I take it to the metalwork shop. You see?'

He thought about it, manoeuvring the car on the muddy road, past farm buildings with corrugated roofs, and up the steep slope. Perhaps it was part of her strangeness, to have lived and worked so long in that closed place. He smiled and laid his hand lingeringly on her knee. 'At least for some things you have to come out of there.' Though of course she could have had affairs with her colleagues. He winced.

'Here we are,' he said, and pulled in on the grass beside a whitewashed building, the hanging sign swaying in the wind.

She got out and stretched, and looked around. 'You are staying here?'

'I thought it would make a change. And with the car, it is so much easier.' He took his suitcase out of the boot and slammed it shut. She was moving towards the front door, holding her hat on with one hand against the wind, but he called her back. 'When we sign in. I think you had better use my name, you know.'

She turned to face him, her eyes blank, the lines of her face suddenly dark. 'I must sign in? But I cannot stay. I am working in the morning.'

I will drive you back in time, he wanted to say, but it wasn't the moment. He had not told her all of what he'd planned. 'You will be with me for the evening, I trust?' But she didn't smile. 'Of course, if you would rather not sign, I can probably do it for both of us. You know what these places are like.' But she doesn't, fool, he told himself.

'You will write Mr and Mrs Shearer?' The front of her coat flapped twice in the wind.

'Come on,' he said, afraid she would go, walk back down the lane holding her hat like this. His voice was hoarse. He took her elbow and to his relief and surprise she let him guide her in through the thick oak door, into the warm bar that smelled of beer and smoke, and leave her standing while he spoke to the manager.

*

Before supper they sat in the back bar, not far from the fire. She said, 'I remember a pub near Newhaven.' She seemed to him to have withdrawn somewhere. Her green knitted jumper showed the shape of her small breasts.

'When were you in Newhaven?' he asked, but she didn't answer. I've played this wrong, he thought. She's still offended.

A black labrador lumbered past them towards the fire. He held out his hand; the dog sniffed it once and moved on. He said, 'This afternoon I was wondering whether the work I do at Holywell is worth it.'

She was sitting quite still on the high-backed bench, holding her beer-mug in one hand. He wasn't sure if she was listening.

'They called me in to look at the drains, and I told them, if you want to deal with it you should replace the lot. So they ask me nicely to send an estimate; but it's hardly worth the effort, they won't do it. They'll go on having sewage leaking into the soil beneath the buildings. I'm sorry' - he interrupted himself, awkward. 'Not the thing to talk about before dinner.'

She turned a little towards him. 'They will do nothing?'

'Oh, they'll mend the drain - patch it up. Then it will leak somewhere else again. I've had this conversation before, not with this guy but one or other of them. And really I don't know why I mind. They pay me enough. Professional pride, I suppose.' He could hear his voice, a little high-pitched, strained.

She took a drink of beer and put the mug down. The firelight glowed in the facets of the glass.

'I do not think I understand,' she said. 'You were hoping this time they would change their minds?'

'Narcisa, I didn't have you down as a cynic.'

'Cynic? No, no, I am not.' She was looking away, at the dog asleep by the fire. After a while she said, 'I suppose in other places they are different. Where you work, I mean. If you have a choice, probably it is better not to work here.'

He managed to make a joke of it: 'Wouldn't you miss me?' But she didn't say what he'd hoped for. She looked as if she'd only just noticed him, frowning, her eyes deep-set and very dark. 'Probably I will leave too. Or I will be fired.'

A man in worn dungarees came round, picking up glasses from the other tables. The acrid smell of his clothes reached over to them.

'Fired?' He turned to her and held her shoulder. The bones felt angular, hard, through the green jumper. 'Narcisa, you're not really worried about being fired?' But there was Bosanquet, blaming her for the drains.

She shrugged, and the movement made him take away his hand. The man with the dungarees came back and threw a fat, bark-covered log on the fire. The wood hissed; a thin line of steam rose from one end.

She seemed to decide something. 'I do not think I am very professional any more.' She smiled. 'Certainly the Assistant Cook thinks so; and as she tells me, she is very experienced.'

'Is she after your job?'

'Probably.' She considered. 'Of course she is. Perhaps she should have it.'

'You said - '

'I said I wanted to leave there. Yes, I know. Only it is better to leave than be fired, don't you think?'

He slid along the bench and put his arm round her shoulders. 'Why so sad this evening?'

'Am I sad? I don't know. Perhaps I am.' She sat and looked into the fire, very small and distant. He waited till she seemed to bring herself back. 'But really, Anthony, why should I stay here now?'

For me, he wanted to say, and felt ashamed.

'Anthony,' she said in a little while. 'Have you ever met again someone you have not seen for many years?'

He looked at her, puzzled. 'I don't know; let me think. Well, an uncle of mine, my father's elder brother, came back from Canada just before the war. I suppose I hadn't seen him for ten, fifteen years. Why?'

She drank down the last of the beer, and sat quiet, so that he wondered if she'd heard the question. He was aware of the great tracts of her life that he'd never seen. He was still for a minute, watching her, in case she wanted to tell him what it was. The taste of the beer was strong in his mouth, like molasses.

Slowly she turned back to him and smiled. 'Another half?' he suggested awkwardly.

'I can finish it with the supper? Yes, why not?'

Then the fat landlady waddled over with their meal, the steam rising from the two green plates on the tray, the knives and forks clanking together as she walked.

*

In bed Narcisa lay on her back, docile, her eyes on something he couldn't see. After a little while anger rose in him. He held her wrists together above her head, and came into her grimly, watching her face. He lifted almost free of her and plunged again, and felt triumphant as her body lifted up not to lose him. Then he let go her wrists and thrust deep into her, and felt himself dissolve into despair.

She laid one hand on his head till he stopped sobbing.

There was a new patient to work with them, a woman in her forties, very fat, with downcast light-blue eyes and a sly expression. Or perhaps she was just sleepy, starting work at six, Narcisa thought. Her own lack of sleep made her feel empty, floating.

June and Peg were giggling, making tea. Rosaleen Shaw had asked for the day off. 'Though of course if you need me to help with the new patient?' she added, deferential; and Narcisa swallowed back her irritation.

The woman walked slowly, stiff-legged, with a great lurching motion of her hips. Narcisa took her round the kitchen, opening cupboard doors on mixing-bowls, roasting-tins, tureens, and naming each pile, perhaps unnecessarily. 'You will soon remember it all,' she said, though the woman had given no sign of being awed. There was a faint smell about her of diarrhoea. Dear god, I hope she's clean, Narcisa thought. She would talk to the Ward Sister later. 'This is where you wash your hands,' she said, perhaps too loudly, since June Ragless looked up. 'You must not wash at the sink, it is not hygienic. You wash your hands here when you come on duty.' She stood back to let the woman get to the basin.

The woman muttered.

'I did not hear what you said?'

'I done it already.'

'Still you must do it again. It is the rule.' She took the soap and lathered and rinsed her hands, then dried them on the roller-towel beside her. The woman copied her, hastily, not bothering to pull dry towel towards her.

She will be an ally for Rosaleen Shaw, Narcisa thought. There was something about her sullen half-compliance, the way that she stood blocking space with her body. Well, I must get her on my side first, she thought; and felt tired at the effort that would mean.

'What is your name?' she asked, trying to sound gentle.

'Dunlop.'

'Here we use first names, not surnames. What is your first name?'

'My *Christian* name?' The woman said it sullenly; it was an attack. I suppose she thinks I am heathen, Narcisa thought.

'Yes, your Christian name.'

'Betty.'

'Well, Betty, I hope you will like working here.' But why should she like it? The glib phrase seemed hypocritical. It was work. Bad enough to be in the asylum, without having to work.

'It can be satisfying,' she went on. 'We feed all the patients and all the staff. It is a lot to do, and we manage it every day, three meals, and tea in the morning and afternoon.'

The woman shifted about, as if embarrassed. Her feet were small, the flesh at her ankles puffy and overflowing.

'June will show you what to do,' Narcisa said, giving up. 'If there is anything you don't understand, please ask.'

June tried to catch her eye as she led the woman Betty away, towards the great jars of marmalade, by the trolleys.

Certainly this one would be difficult. She would resent being managed, that was clear. She would need supervising:

she might try to steal, food probably, maybe other things. At the start of the war there had been that other woman, a little skinny thing, subservient, who turned out to have taken four serving-dishes. Am I being unjust to this one? she asked herself. It was the woman's physical presence that disturbed her; something she read as stubborn and ignorant. But she was a patient; she had learned to survive there. Narcisa watched as the woman spooned out marmalade onto white dishes. Her movements were jerky, in spite of the short fat arms; as if with each spoonful she were saying: So there.

Narcisa sat down to go over the lunch plan. She was tired. She had stayed after all at the inn with Anthony. She had not had permission to be out overnight. Mullins the gate-porter might well report her. And here I am telling this woman about the rules.

Lunch at least was straightforward, no long preparations: steamed cod, green beans, potatoes, then tapioca. Was this the last of the salted-down beans, or was there another crock in the back of the larder? She made a note.

She had woken and found Anthony looking down at her, serious. 'I'm afraid it's time to get up,' he had whispered. Now it seemed to her extraordinary, that he had remembered and got up for her, driven her over to Epsom in the dark.

Then why this time hadn't she enjoyed being with him? She had sat in the bar and struggled to concentrate. He had seemed so remote from her, a professional man who could come and go, criticise Dr Bosanquet or whoever he'd met. She thought with some dread: perhaps feeling this is the same as losing time?

There was a clatter, Peg dropping a pan. 'Sorry, Cook.' It had been a relief, his aggression in bed with her. Before that nothing he did had roused her body; she had felt solid as wood, unreachable. She remembered from the previous time his belt tightened round her ankle. I am becoming someone different. I was rude to him; and I wanted him to hurt me.

She sat still, the noise of the kitchen rising round her, kettles boiling, smells of tea and scouring-powder. I should go to the office, she thought, but didn't move.

Betty Dunlop was muttering to another patient. And why is she in here? Narcisa wondered. She seemed so ordinary, with her shifty manner, her evident contempt for authority. Not depressed, or manic, or deluded. What catastrophe in her life had brought her here? It seemed suddenly, oddly, important to find out. If Betty Dunlop with her immoveable bulk, her cunning could still find herself in here…

But I was a patient. I could be again. She smoothed open the pages of the meal-plan in front of her. It wasn't that she had ever forgotten. She had never pretended that it hadn't happened, even if she'd chosen not to tell Dr Bosanquet, or Miss Gray and Miss Ainsworth before him. Or Anthony.

I can't do this now, she told herself abruptly, not even knowing what it was she had to do. She stood up and walked slowly through the kitchen. The patients had taken the trolleys through. June and Peg were relaxing, leaning against the sink, June telling some story that was making Peg look shocked. They caught sight of her and turned back to the draining-board.

*

Miss Fleming, the housekeeper, had asked for a meeting. In her office beforehand Narcisa combed her hair and pulled her skirt straight. She felt bloodless from lack of sleep. Later, she told herself, I'll think later. Betty Dunlop's sweetish unclean smell stayed in her nostrils.

'Is Miss Shaw not joining us?' Miss Fleming seemed taller, her grey hair more metallic.

There were white chrysanthemums in the vase on her table.

'Miss Shaw is needed to supervise the lunch.'

Someone else came in, a younger woman with colourless hair in earphones, and a doubtful manner. 'Miss McNab, my assistant; Mrs Humphreys.' Miss McNab stood leaning against the bookcase. The little key-cupboard was just above her shoulder.

'It is about your kitchen assistants.'

The smell of the chrysanthemums reached her, almost like cumin.

'The kitchen assistants?'

'Ragless, is one of them called? And her friend.'

'June Ragless and Peggy Skinner? There is something wrong?'

'My girls tell me that they are behaving, well, not properly. Not how you'd expect of Holywell staff.'

She felt indignation rising. 'I do not understand. Please explain, Miss Fleming.'

'Behaving.' Miss Fleming was irritated. She opened the stapler on her desk, and closed it again. 'Unsuitably. That's what my girls tell me.' She put the stapler down. 'Perhaps it would be better if Miss Shaw - '

It was sex, of course; nothing else would make this woman so tongue-tied. No doubt they had talked to the Shaw woman already.

'You have some evidence?'

Miss McNab came to stand beside Miss Fleming. 'Well, not evidence, Mrs Humphreys, you wouldn't expect it. It's just that the girls felt it was rather disturbing.'

'You mean they have gossiped.' She stood up. 'You have encouraged the domestic staff to spy on other staff and report to you.'

'Mrs Humphreys. This is quite unsuitable language. Your staff...'

'My staff work very well. I have no complaints about them. You are telling me, what? That they have boyfriends?'

'Not boyfriends,' Miss McNab said, her accent sad and insinuating. 'No, Mrs Humphreys, not boyfriends. That is the point.'

And I am meant to be shocked. She turned back to the housekeeper. 'Well, Miss Fleming, it is not the first.. ' She stopped herself with some effort. 'What my staff do in private I am not interested.'

A vein in her neck was throbbing as she went back to her office. Miss Fleming and her girls! What had she wanted: Narcisa to discipline June and Peg? To fire them? She wanted to prove she knew something I didn't. Perhaps it is true, she thought, remembering the two young women working together. It is not important. And are the domestics spying on me too? Is that it, that she knows I was out all night?

She close the door of the office and went to the window. It was raining, a dark puddle on the asphalt marked with grey rings that spread and were replaced. I am questioning everything now, she thought. This place expects to know everything about you. Probably I am supposed to ask June and Peg if it is true. Miss Fleming might tell Dr Bosanquet that she's told me.

I am angry with everyone, she thought. Have I never seen these things before? It is Anthony; he has shown me how people live.

She warmed her hands on the big grey radiator.

And if they knew that I had an illegitimate daughter? That I made love in the open air with one of the gardeners?

She crossed the room on the threadbare pink carpet, and

back to the radiator, and warmed her hands again.

I should show them. I should bring Violeta here and introduce her. Oh, didn't you know? I was a patient here. After all, she thought, I have nothing more to lose.

She could see Violeta, tall and confident. 'Of course,' she said, facing the housekeeper down. 'She's my mother. I am very proud of her. Illegitimate? How old-fashioned you are.'

Stupid, she told herself, and sat at her desk. Still the imagined victory made her smile.

She hasn't answered. Perhaps she is ashamed, because I work here.

Perhaps she is simply away. Or very busy.

I wonder how it will be, to get an answer.

The clock on the library wall clicked and whispered. At the long oak table an old man turned a page of the *News Chronicle*, with a rustle like the wings of a beetle opening.

The dust of dried leather and newsprint and human skin held still in the daylight through the leaded windows. Miss Cowden, the new young librarian, slotted white cards into an index box, the crowded contents squeezing the tips of her fingers.

A small boy stood on tiptoe to reach a book, afraid he would fall forward onto the shelves, and be shelved himself, unnoticed, under CHILDREN. He pulled at the top of the spine and heard it tear. With the book in both hands he stood right in the corner, as invisible as he could be against the dust-jackets. The words like a paperchain turned into a story as fast as his narrow blue eyes could read them.

Alone at a table in the reference section, Narcisa sat with a pile of newspapers, and three heavy volumes lettered in gold on the spines. In front of her another book lay open, thin, with smudgy black print and foxed paper. On the right-hand page, the first paragraph began: *In Prizren.* Her navy hat was pushed back on her head, her coat unbuttoned. The skin on her hands felt dry with ink and dust.

She had been sitting reading for three hours. The English

was hard, the sentences in the books long and obscure. The newspapers all referred to events she knew nothing of. There were leaders' names, and places that had some significance, and dates: *since the assassination* and *before the defeat*. None of this print connected in her mind with the full, fast river, or the low stone bridge where as a child she had stood with her sister Alma, looking up at the hills, or the orchards outside the city, or the icy winters.

Perhaps it was that, she thought in desolation, staring ahead at the encyclopaedias. That it was so hard to believe she had once lived there, in this place that even a two-day-old newspaper chose to report from: *Yesterday, Marshall Tito and his forces*. While all the time her father, Alma, her aunts, Alma's husband and children were living there, were eating and working and speaking and getting older. Or dying there. Her father if he had survived would be eighty. What killed people was not only war, but illnesses, accidents, heart attacks, malnutrition.

So much had happened. So many events, kings created and dying, one she had never heard of assassinated, in his car in the South of France; there was a photo. Poor harvests and new economic policies. The imprisonment and release of political figures. Alliances, within the country and with other countries, the Croats with one, Slovenes or Serbs with another. Reported all of it in passionless English, in a tone she knew from the asylum itself: that scientific contempt for human beings. And now, at the end of her long reading bout, she could not have told what had happened first, why anything had happened, not even where, amongst the fragile collection of small nations. Not even, she thought, and stared down at the book, what might have reached the lives of her family there.

In Prizren, meanwhile, the paragraph began. But it was no

use. Her ability to read sentence after sentence in this language, more unforgiving than ever, had been worn through. I can come back, she thought as she closed the yellow-covered book, but knew that she would not.

She stood, the chair scraping on the parquet floor. A greyhaired woman looked up and frowned at her. I do not want to be here, she thought, exhausted, not knowing what *here* was. She did up her coat.

Outside the air was soft against her cheek. She turned her bike and rode back out of the town, along the back alleys and out into the lane, where the chestnut trees of the asylum were in bud, and the asylum cows looked up from the grass to assess her.

*

She felt the stillness come over the room, at once, like snuffing a candle. They were all facing towards her, Rosaleen Shaw, June and Peg, and three, no four of the working patients. For a moment she thought she had caught them out at something.

'Oh, Cook,' the Shaw woman said, too loudly, so that one of the patients started to shake. 'Thank heavens. Are you all right? We were so worried.'

'Thank you,' she began, not understanding, though the woman's tone was sickly, menacing. Then suddenly it was clear, the used white plates stacked on the trolley, the massive teapots ranged next to the sink. She stopped herself reaching out to hold onto something, the dresser it would have been. Her feet in her old shoes were heavy on the stone floor.

It was twenty to five.

'Thank you,' she managed to say again, since they were all still staring at her; though Peg had turned away from Rosaleen Shaw and was watching from half-closed eyes, like a child at the circus. 'Please carry on. Miss Shaw - ' this was needed - 'thank you for covering.'

They moved back slowly, reluctantly to their places. Rosaleen Shaw waited beside the table. Narcisa took down her apron from its hook. Her movements seemed all to have been slowed down. She could see Peg emptying the teapots, swilling the tea-leaves into the sink-tidy and then shaking them out into the bin. The acrid smell of tannin filled the kitchen.

'I was beginning to think something awful had happened.' There was enjoyment in the woman's voice, scarcely disguised. 'Like I said to Dr Whitchurch, Mrs Humphreys is always so punctual.'

'You have reported me to Dr Whitchurch?' It came out too quickly; she couldn't stop herself.

'Not *reported*, Cook, no, I wouldn't do that. I was concerned.' She was still angling for an explanation.

But I have to get away from her, Narcisa thought. She drew in a long breath. 'Very well. Thank you, Miss Shaw. Now we will continue as usual.'

She sat at the table to plan the tasks for supper. She had missed tea duty. She had sat in the library under the great plain clock for how long? three hours? and never thought of the time. As if I were used to having hours to myself, she thought, and that was almost the worst part. As if I had always been someone who didn't work. Was it the same as the other day, losing time? But no, she had been reading all the time, she could remember. Then she must simply have forgotten. To forget to come on duty: what would she think if June had done that, or Peg? She watched them working, dragging the pig-bin between them out to the yard, talking under their breath. June glanced over towards her but she couldn't tell if the look meant reproach or pity or something else.

And Shaw of course had gone straight to Dr Whitchurch. She made herself concentrate on the evening meal: the meat to put through the mincer, onions to chop, and what was the vegetable? Leeks; so make sure they know how to clean them. Miss Shaw could supervise two of the patients. She listed the tasks, in large clear handwriting. *As if I won't be here by this evening.*

It was possible. At any minute, a patient could knock at the door and say, 'Dr Whitchurch wants to see you, Cook.' She sat still for a moment. There was no sound outside.

She put the pen down. She had never been in trouble; she had made sure, had made herself cautious and conscientious. It was like being a patient: you stayed quiet, you did what you had to do invisibly. You didn't attract the attention of people who had the power to hurt or humiliate. Just one slip, she thought, her eyes brimming: once in almost twelve years.

But it wasn't once. There was Dr Bosanquet. 'As your employer I am entitled to expect complete honesty, Mrs Humphreys.' She had become a problem; he would be pleased to be rid of her.

She stood up; the chair scraped on the stone floor; people looked round. 'Now,' she said, making her voice firm. 'June, water on for the steamed puddings, please. Peg, bring another sack of potatoes; take someone with you. Betty.. ' The reactions might have been resentment or relief. She went on, standing still in the middle of the kitchen, her kitchen with its layered smells, its constant steam of boiling and washing-up, its vast mutated fish-fryers and pans, and made some order, some kind of authority, though the unknown patient with the message for her might that moment be closing the door of the Deputy Medical Superintendent's office, and setting off through the asylum, full of his errand.

Part 7 - 1947

It was good, after the war, to have routines. That's what Walter Skelton thought, hefting his sack of letters out of the sorting office, getting out his bike. After Japan. He didn't talk about that. Now he could work again he was glad of it, the weight of the sack every morning on his bike, the effort of getting started up the slope. 'You know they've given you the loonies' round?' someone said, his first day back at work; but he liked it. The loonies' round meant out in the country lanes, the friendly gate-porters, sometimes a chat. Once or twice he let the nurses tease him, and stood, smiling, embarrassed, remembering life before. It was rare that he came across a patient. There but for the grace, he thought on many mornings. After Japan, that's how some of them had gone.

Strange chap, Des Wyburn thought, watching from the porch as Walter rode off up the drive. Something odd about him: too anxious to please. He tossed the bundle of letters between his hands. It wasn't his job to take in the post; that miserable woman, the Assistant Clerk, she was meant to log all the letters in. Still, since he'd been passing. There were lightbulbs needed, in old Bosanquet's office, and down the hall outside the store cupboards. 'Here you are, my dear,' he said to Miss What's-her-name, as she hurried towards him in her horrible green skirt. 'Save you the trouble.'

It was an important job they'd given him. Not difficult, of course, but responsible. John Arthurson had been a delivery boy, for almost a year before his nerves got bad, and that had been harder, finding the addresses, and then some people when you did find them.. Not like that here. But it showed the doctors had got faith in him. Probably they'd see how he was doing, if he could take the responsibility, and if he did all right they'd let him home. It was like that these days, they didn't keep you in.

Two fat letters for Matron. He knocked on doors and mainly, at this time, ten or just gone, they were in their offices. 'Morning, Matron,' he said respectfully, and put the brown envelopes on the desk beside her. One for Mrs Da Costa, who ran the laundry. Funny name, but she didn't look that foreign. Perhaps she'd married a soldier in the war. A whole bunch together for Dr Bosanquet, fastened by Miss Carrington with a rubber band. He quite wanted to look but it wasn't professional.

And there was Cook, just coming from the kitchen. He thought she looked worried. 'No bills today, Mrs H,' he said cheerfully, and remembered he'd said the same thing the day before. 'Very well,' she said in that odd way of hers, and didn't go into her office after all. 'Thank you, John.' She reminded him of his Auntie, who'd brought him up. Probably like Auntie she worked too hard.

Part 7 - 1947

Dr Whitchurch was sitting two or three yards from her, in a battered leather wing-chair in his office. His physical presence took all of her attention: not only the sturdy shoulders and large hands, but the sense of himself, how energetic and at ease he was. He had pushed up his shirt-cuffs; his wrists were strong, with a matting of dark hair. His thighs in the good grey suit looked muscular, like a runner's. She felt herself sit straighter in her chair.

He had been speaking; she hadn't been listening. A broad stretch of sunlight lay across her lap, and the Persian rug, which he must have brought in to cheer up his office, and the left arm of his expensive suit. She looked briefly into his face. He was waiting for her to give him an answer. He said, and it must have been a repetition, 'All I need from you is a simple explanation.'

He is a young man, she thought. He sees a middle-aged woman with greying hair. The realisation made her suddenly tired. Concentrate, she told herself, concentrate. If you say the wrong thing he is going to sack you.

'Dr Whitchurch.' She looked away from him, at the back of the leather photograph frame on his desk. 'I am sorry, I do not have an explanation.'

'Mrs Humphreys, please. I am asking you why you failed to report for work. You must understand - '

She wanted urgently to stop talking, to give up on speech as she had thirty years before, to let him fire her and not to have to argue. He would stand up, angry, righteous, energised, and shout at her, and she would cower in her chair, and go to her room, weeping.

She was filled with shame. Reluctantly, defeated, she found some words.

'Well.' He leaned forward; she must be whispering. 'What I can tell you. I went to Epsom, to the library.'

Do I have to explain? There was a way she could tell it to silence him, her family missing in a war-damaged country; but she couldn't do that. 'I needed to look for some information.'

'And.. ?'

'And that is all.' She allowed herself one excuse. 'Reading in English, it is difficult for me. Slow.'

It was not good enough, she could tell that. In any case he had probably decided before she came in. I can't go back to the kitchen, she thought, agonised. To be humiliated in front of all of them. Shaw, and June, and the patient Betty Dunlop. I will ask if I can leave straight away this morning. She wondered again if what had happened was the same as in the kitchen, when she'd lost several hours out of the day; but hadn't she been reading the whole time?

He had stood up and walked over to the window. Freed from his gaze, she looked around the room. A painting hung over the mantelpiece, a beach scene in bright colours. He must have brought it in himself, she thought. Why did I never think of buying a picture?

He turned, silhouetted against the long window. He is torturing me, she thought, making me wait. Or perhaps he must get his courage up to do it.

'Ms Humphreys. You are telling me you were reading and forgot the time?'

She bent her head.

'Miss Shaw was very perturbed.'

'Yes, she has told me.'

He muttered something, and came back to his chair. She saw him settle his shoulders against the cushion.

'Well, Mrs Humphreys, I do not think..' He seemed to change his mind. 'You will understand that this is very irregular. It could have had very serious consequences.'

She managed to say, 'I have worked here nearly twelve years. I have never - '

He interrupted. 'Precisely. I do not need to tell you, Mrs Humphreys, if you were an inexperienced member of staff.. However, in view of your good, your excellent service..'

She felt herself droop with amazement and relief. 'You are not.. ? You do not want me to leave?'

'Leave? Good Lord, no.' But he had been thinking of it, she was certain; he had almost made up his mind. 'Shall we just call it an unfortunate mistake? I am sure you will never let it happen again.'

She shook her head.

'Well, there we are. In fact I had hoped to speak to you, Mrs Humphreys. Not about that, of course; another matter.'

She tried to imagine what he was interested in.

'You know, I favour the modern approaches. We have scientific ways to assist patients, that our predecessors couldn't have dreamed of. I hope to be able to make some changes here. With Dr Bosanquet's approval, of course.'

The *new approach* again. Still she must be careful. 'I would like also. The meals to be better, more appetising.'

'Exactly,' he said, though he looked taken aback. 'Mrs Humphreys, forgive me, but I am very interested. Dr Bosanquet has told me, in confidence of course..'

She sat back, dizzy, and closed her eyes. There was a smell of furniture polish and something that might be his shaving-soap, lavender. So it was not the lateness but her history.

There was a flash across her closed eyelids, Madame Taté the French interpreter, beside her bed when Violeta was just born, carefully smoothing down her blue kid gloves.

If Violeta had never written to her.

He had stopped talking. I am so tired, she thought. I do not want to go through this any more.

After a while she said, 'Yes, it is true. I did not think it was necessary to tell them. When I started work here, it was already eighteen years.'

He looked puzzled. He has dark blue eyes, she thought. I do not think I have ever seen that colour.

'No, Mrs Humphreys, I merely thought.. I would be interested to discuss with you.. The history of our asylums is fascinating.'

With a great effort, an old woman pushing herself up with the strength of her fore-arms, she got to her feet. He looked up at her, bewildered, for a moment, then stood. 'Mrs Humphreys, please. I did not want to offend you.'

'No,' she said. 'I must go back to the kitchen. Excuse me. The lunch.'

He held out his hand. 'I do beg your pardon. I understand you may not want to discuss it.' He shook his head slightly. 'Well, never mind. I hope we will work productively together.'

She walked back through the building. A woman patient in too-large uniform ran out from a ward onto the corridor, growling in her throat like an angry dog. She stopped a few yards from Narcisa, where the curve of the corridor hid her from the ward door. After a moment she caught Narcisa's eye. 'Look at this,' she said, and pulled up her skirt, to show a purple bruise across her thigh. Then she let the cloth fall, and ran on again, though soon, it was clear, she would reach the locked door to the men's section, and have to turn back.

She came out of the station and looked around. The building was at the top of a slope, above the street. Opposite her were the upstairs windows of small shops, and a pub. A woman with a high black pram pushed past. A small boy rode a bicycle too large for him furiously up the steep slope, leaning forwards, and freewheeled down the other side, waving both hands.

She turned back to the station and looked for a map. A kind of panic was rising up inside her. Nothing out there was familiar to her, nothing; as if the name, Richmond, had been detached and stuck on arbitrarily to another town.

Of course, she thought, facing the framed street-map: I was always on foot, coming over from Mrs Pilgrim's. I never would have come as far as this. The agency was no more than five minutes' walk. She set out again, down the slope and to the left, past low-ceilinged shops with little in the windows, a grocer's, a newsagent's, one with a stack of faded knitting-wool and patterns.

On impulse she turned off the main street towards the river. There was a green; she thought she remembered that, with narrow old houses round the edges. On one cottage the lilac was in flower, pale mauve, as high as the front wall, a few great flower-heads drooping across a window. She stopped to look; it was so extravagant and unruly. A face appeared at the upstairs window, pale, half-hidden by the flowers, and gazed down at her.

She walked on, along the side of the green, and down a lane between high mossy walls. There was the river smell, like damp vegetation, sweetish, and the cooler air off the water. A man pushed a cart towards her, the high wheels clanking loudly over the cobbles. At the end of the lane was that shimmering light she remembered, and trees on the far bank; and now as she walked more quickly the blue-brown water.

On the towpath she stood and stared, suddenly calm. The tide was in, the water within a foot of the embankment edge. The sky, a high, light blue with shreds of cloud, was reflected and broken up on the riffled surface. A boat came slowly up beneath the bridge, a man in a dark hat standing amongst crates.

She walked along, beside a high wall with green plants spilling down the old brickwork. The feeling of those weeks came back to her slowly, when she had only just left the asylum; her nervousness and the gradual exploration, first down to the river nearby at St Margaret's, then further, into Twickenham and here. Once she had come with Mrs Pilgrim to a department store. She remembered a drawer with bright scarves, neatly folded.

She strolled on. The air was warm, with that lift off the water every now and then. I wonder what happened to Mrs Pilgrim, she thought. Did she marry again? Now she would be, what? sixty at least: still neat, quiet, the thin face with the shadows under the eyes: a more lined version of the same young widow. What would she feel now about her husband, killed in France in the first war, forty years back? I could go and visit her, Narcisa thought. I could walk there now, go and knock on the door.

Instead she sat on a bench and watched four mallards weaving to and fro from the bank. The deep green of the males' heads glowed in the sun. I should prepare for this interview, she thought. I am an experienced hospital Cook, now considering the other possibilities open to me. I was also a housekeeper for twelve years. Though I don't have references from Miss Grey and Miss Ainsworth. Would they still be alive? It was possible.

She stood and brushed the back of her coat, and walked back through the streets to the town centre, an odd sense of lightness threatening to subvert her.

*

The agency was in an upstairs office, above a cobbler's shop just off the High Street. I could bring my shoes here, she thought as she rang the bell. There was a long pause; then shoes clattering on stairs, and a thin woman in a mauve tweed suit stood in the doorway.

'This is the Petersham Agency?'

Narcisa followed her up a steep flight of stairs. The lilac-coloured skirt swung improbably. It was good cloth, Narcisa thought: it hung well. The woman's shoes, too, were elegant, black court shoes, an attractive cut to the heel.

Face to face the woman looked like Jessie Pilgrim: the same wavy brown hair tied back in a bun, the same thin features. Narcisa caught her breath. It can't be, she reminded herself; Mrs Pilgrim is in her sixties now, remember. She half wanted to ask. Could it be the daughter?

She made herself speak. 'I am working as a Cook in a hospital. Now I think I would like a change.' It sounded more frivolous than what she'd planned. 'I am very hard-working, very conscientious,' she said, aware of stumbling over the sibilants. 'I have also worked as a housekeeper.'

The woman – Miss Flowers, she had introduced herself – took notes, and looked thoughtfully at Narcisa. Well, she is taking me seriously, she thought.

'Mrs Humphreys, may I ask your age?'

'I am fifty-five. Nearly fifty-six.'

Miss Flowers wrote. 'Some of our clients prefer the mature person. But tell me, do you have plans for retirement? At what age, I mean?'

'I have never thought about it.' She felt ashamed.

Miss Flowers looked up at her speculatively. On the desk beside her was a green glass vase, with purple tulips bending extravagantly out. 'It is only that an employer would not like to take on a person for only four years. Of course, things may happen; you would not be compelled to stay longer. But someone available for only four years, that might be a problem.'

'I suppose,' Narcisa said after a pause, 'I will retire when I do not want to work. Or am not capable. But that is not yet.'

The woman smiled. 'That is rather how I see it. One needs some interest; something to make demands on one. Now, another question. Do you wish to find another residential position?'

'Residential?'

'Living in. As I imagine you do at the hospital.'

Narcisa drew in a long slow breath, considering. 'There is suitable work that is not living in?'

'Certainly. A number of ladies now prefer to have cooks on a day basis. Or if you prefer not to be in a private home, there are schools, gentlemen's clubs even. Are you willing to travel?'

'I will find rooms near to where I work. Yes, if it is possible, I would like not to live in.'

'Perfectly possible.' She wrote and sat back. 'I must say,

Mrs Humphreys, I admire your drive. It is a major step to change jobs, and even more if it means finding a new home. May I ask, is there some reason for this change?'

Ah, she is not stupid, Narcisa thought. After a while she said, 'No reason concerning my work, no. I believe that the hospital has found me satisfactory. Perhaps there are other reasons; it is hard to say.'

'I quite understand. Now, Holywell Hospital. I have not heard of it. Perhaps..?'

'It is an asylum. A mental hospital, that is what they call it now.' She watched Miss Flowers steadily writing something. 'This is a problem?'

'Not a problem, no. We will have to be a little careful, that's all. Unfortunately some people can be a little ignorant; I am sure you have seen this? But really, cooking is cooking, after all.'

Very well, Narcisa thought: let her be careful. She felt a peculiar confidence in this woman. She was honest; she would do her best for her. Perhaps she could telephone someone straight away, set up an interview that afternoon. No, I must be careful too, she told herself.

Miss Flowers was watching her with calm blue eyes. Narcisa picked up her handbag.

'Thank you. You have been very helpful.' But that was too easy; she wanted to say more. 'I was not sure that anyone will employ me, and you are saying yes, they may. Is that right?'

Miss Flowers nodded.

'Now I want to think about all this. To decide..' But what did she have to decide? '..if I will move, what kind of place, all this.'

If Miss Flowers was disappointed, she didn't show it.

'I will come back here in perhaps one week?'

'That is very sensible, Mrs Humphreys.' She waited till Narcisa had stood, before doing the same. 'Here is my card. You can telephone; do you have the use of a phone? Or write to me, when you are ready. Or of course come in again, if you would like to discuss anything further. I will look forward to it.'

It seemed as if she might mean it. Out on the High Street, Narcisa found a draper's shop, and used the rest of her clothing coupons to buy cloth, a dress-length of lavender poplin, with polka-dots.

*

She was up early, energetic, and went down at quarter to six to unlock the kitchen. The trolleys were laid ready, the teapots lined up. A pale light came in at the high windows, and made the stacked white crockery glow faintly. She hesitated a moment, then reached for the light-switch.She was filling the kettles when June Ragless came in.

'It's all right, June. It is just that I came down early.' She stood aside for the girl to take over; but she was standing awkwardly beside the table.

'Actually, Cook, can I have a word? I wanted to talk before the others come down.'

Miss Fleming: had the domestics been gossiping again? There was something about June's face; she might have been crying.

'You would like to go to the office to talk?'

She looked at the clock. 'It's all right, Cook. Miss Shaw won't be down just yet, will she?'

And Peg knows, of course. Though if it were that, wouldn't Peg have come too? She watched June sit opposite her at the scrubbed table, smoothing down her skirt with both hands.

'Very well, June. Tell me.'

'It's Donald. My fiancé. We're going to get married.'

So that was it. But the tone of voice was wrong. 'Congratulations. You must be very happy.'

'Oh, I am.' The smile came and went, quickly. 'I mean, I'm really lucky. He's ever so kind and considerate. And he says his mum can't wait to have a daughter. She's really nice, his mum.'

'So you will live with them? In the North?'

'Preston, yes. Well, we'll have to at first. Live with his mum and dad, I mean. But he's got a good job, we'll be able to get a house.'

So June is leaving too. 'Well,' she said, 'you will be missed here. You are very good at your work, I hope you know that?'

'Oh, thank you, Cook.' She was very pretty, June Ragless, with her wide-apart blue eyes and curly hair. Still there was something puffy about her face.

There was a pause, June looking at the dresser.

'To be honest, Cook, that's the thing I mind. Moving up North. My mum's down here, in Tulse Hill, and my sisters. There's four of us, I'm the youngest. I even, well I wondered if I should. Get married, I mean.'

She felt something heavy inside, that had to settle. Then she said, 'It is a big decision.'

'It is, isn't it? I mean, I do love him. But it's not just my mum, it's here too. I'm not just saying it, I love my job. One day I'd like to be in charge of a kitchen.'

The weight of the girl's gaze was too much for her. 'You will be able to find a job like this in Preston?'

June shifted; there was a look of disappointment. 'They won't let you, not if you're married, will they? And in any case, Donald wouldn't let me. You know how it is, he says, You won't have to work. I say I really like working but he, I suppose he doesn't believe me or something.' She paused. 'I don't know, Cook, I suppose it is the right thing?'

She sat still for a moment. 'I think it is very difficult. But if you love Donald.. And you will want to have children, yes?'

June was kicking at the table leg, looking down. Narcisa looked around her. The kettle she had been filling was still on the draining-board. One of the others was starting to steam. She stopped herself getting up to turn the gas off.

'There's something else. Maybe you know. It's Peg. Oh lord, I hope you're going to understand. It's just that, well, I've always hated sleeping on my own. Me and my sisters, we always shared. Well, that's no excuse.'

There was something from her days as a patient that tensed inside her; but she chose to ignore it. 'June, there are many girls here who do the same.'

'I know.' She looked up, her face suddenly shadowed. 'Only Peg, I mean poor Peg, she can't stand it. About Donald. She wants - well, she wants me to stay here. She says we could go on like we are, and I could keep working, well, both of us. And Donald doesn't know, he'd kill me.'

She was watching Narcisa's face, intent, hopeful. Narcisa said, 'June, I am not the person to ask advice. I have made decisions' - but it's only one, she thought - 'that I have regretted very much.'

The girl looked down at her hands. She seemed to be considering whether to speak. Come on, Narcisa told herself, give her something.

'But I think you have already decided, no? You have arranged the wedding?'

'Not the day yet. But it's going to be June. June wedding for June, that's what he says. I just don't know. Cook, do you think I've been really selfish?'

She shook her head, smiling. 'Perhaps you have been very'

- she searched for the word - 'very friendly and open. This is not a mistake.'

There were noises outside in the corridor. June got to her feet. 'Cook, I don't have to give you notice straight away, do I?'

'Only one week. But thank you for telling me now.' Though who knows which of us will leave first, she thought.

The door creaked behind them. 'Good morning. You two having a nice little chat?'

'Don't tell,' June mouthed, as Rosaleen Shaw turned to take down her apron.

Part 7 - 1947

Anthony Shearer was at the drawing-board, amending the plans for rebuilding a bombed-out school. The client, surveyor for a London borough, was difficult; or perhaps it was the committee he had to report to. This was the third time the plans had been returned. And what were the children doing meanwhile, he wondered. Did they double them up with the school down the road? If they'd managed like that for the past four years, was there any reason to go ahead with rebuilding?

The telephone rang in the outside office. That could be the client, to say the whole job has been cancelled, he thought, still working. He loved the drawing; he always had, since college. The fine pencils, the setsquares and rulers, the crisp paper, filled his mind with clarity and precision. And designing an object on paper: roofs and load-bearing walls and drains, even; it still seemed magical, a kind of language for telling what you saw in your mind to another person. He stood back to consider the pitch of the school roof.

A knock on the door. Miss Burns, his secretary. As usual, she blushed at having to interrupt him.

'You're wanted on the telephone, Mr Shearer.'

For some reason she never announced the name until he asked.

'A Mrs Humphreys.' Miss Burns stood holding onto the door-handle, like a gawky schoolgirl who always felt in the wrong. 'I'm afraid she wouldn't say what it concerns.'

'That's fine, thank you.' He put down the setsquare and went slowly to his desk, aware of trembling.

'Narcisa. How nice of you to ring. Good morning.' It was the first time she had ever phoned him.

'Am I interrupting?' There was that slight roughness, the accent he mostly forgot when he was with her.

'I'm delighted to be interrupted. How are you?'

The break in her voice was almost a laugh. 'I am feeling very good. For some reason.'

'Well, that's good.' He realised he'd been assuming some problem. 'Keeping that deputy of yours in line?'

'Deputy - oh, you mean Miss Shaw.' One of those pauses where she considered her answer. 'I think perhaps she is keeping me in line. I will tell you, not now. But it does not matter. Or perhaps' - the half-laugh again - 'it does matter and I do not care.'

'That's good,' he said again, concerned for her.

'Anthony, you are working, we will not talk for long. I telephoned just - well, for no reason.' He could hear her awkwardness; as if it were a burden for him to speak to her. 'Perhaps you are busy. I am off duty tomorrow evening. If you are free, I could come to London, or..'

He felt happiness knock him over like a breaker. 'Wait a minute.' With his left hand, he opened his diary, knowing already. 'How nice of you to ask. No, that's fine, there's nothing at all.' Only Mina, he thought: I will have to think what to tell her. 'Are you sure you can come up to town? Is that what you'd like?'

'Ah, Anthony, I want to be anywhere that is not here. Yes, I will get the train; you know I can come to Waterloo or Victoria.'

'Come to Victoria,' he said. 'I'll meet you.' He could see her already, walking along the platform. 'Now what would you like to do? There is the whole of London waiting to entertain you: concerts, theatre, a film..'

'Or else..' she said, and he felt his whole body quicken.

*

His meeting finished early, at half past four. He came out of the client's office, in Hanover Square, and started towards Regent Street and the buses; then changed his mind, and set off to walk to Victoria to meet her. The past few days had been suddenly mild; the trees were in leaf, people were sauntering. He unbuttoned his coat and strode down the back streets, past St George's, which made him think of Handel, on a zigzag route by Savile Row and the Burlington Arcade, towards Piccadilly.

It was one of his pleasures, knowing the streets of London. He had grown up in Mill Hill, which was too far out, but came in as a boy whenever he could, the interminable bus ride down Edgware Road, and explored whatever he could afford to enter. A silly thing to be proud of, he thought now: like a boy scout waiting to be asked directions. But the bomb damage had felt personal to him. He had come back from Italy, with a minor injury and a loathing of all armies, and found he couldn't remember what there had been, in the places turned to fireweed and dark craters.

He walked briskly through the arcade, though the chess shop normally drew him at least to its window. A few couples, arm in arm, were wandering, pointing out antique rings or hand-made shoes. He tried to imagine bringing

Narcisa here. It would be unfair; to enjoy looking, you had to have the money to imagine making some extravagant purchase. Though of course, she may have money, he said to himself, and wondered for the first time what she did with the pitiful amount they no doubt paid her.

He crossed Piccadilly, skirting the front of a bus that was slowed in the traffic. The driver hooted and called out of the window. Still, he would like to show her London. He supposed she must have spent some time in town; but there would be places he knew to take her to. 'Or else..' she had said. He would have to book a room. He would go into the Goring on his way. No luggage; but he thought they'd remember him. There were places nearer the station you could go, and rent a room by the hour; but then they would feel tainted. Or he would at least; hard to know with her.

In St James' Park he finally stopped walking. There was plenty of time: it was still not five, and he'd said he'd meet her at six, at the barrier. He sat on a bench by the lake, and watched the birds. Who was it that had brought the flamingos here? Ridiculous, out of place, the powder-puff pink that he'd heard had to be kept up by feeding them shrimps. Oh, don't be so solemn, he told himself, and stretched.

He had wept, the last time making love with Narcisa. He had found himself full of whatever it was, some tension, some anger that had made him hold her down and fuck her relentlessly; and then he'd wept. She had shown no surprise, nor indignation. He'd thought it through several times in the days between. She aroused something in him, he couldn't say what it was, but something more than Mina ever had, a person he didn't quite recognise. And probably that was a good thing, he thought; no doubt he'd become middle-aged and complacent. Only..

He watched a family standing at the edge, a small boy held

back by reins throwing scraps of bread in the direction of the water, an older girl laughing. It was all very well to want to open up; easy to say, he thought, feeling querulous: but what about Mina? Their arrangement, her sophisticated approach, was that he told her nothing about Narcisa; she knew, but didn't want to be made aware. He wondered again if she had a lover, and if he'd be as generous with her. Possibly not. All that was fine, so long as he stayed calm: some tenderness, human concern, and sexual pleasure: nothing that would disrupt his life at home.

It may be all right, he thought, as the family moved on, the little boy waving goodbye to a tufted duck. But that was dishonest; he knew it wasn't all right. He had talked last time about her returning to Prizren; and maybe that had been part of his outburst, the dread that had fallen on him as he spoke, that she would get lost in the new communist state that Yugoslavia seemed about to become. Well, he told himself ironically, you always did claim to be a socialist. Narcisa and I, building socialism in one country.

He stood up, impatient, and crossed the bridge, then walked along parallel to Birdcage Walk, on the new green grass, with the planetree leaves above him opening. Buckingham Palace stood squat and ugly in front of him. Poor aim, Adolf, he said under his breath. He reached the station just after half past five. He bought an evening paper, to keep his thoughts under control while he waited, and stood at the barrier, amongst the crowds of people hurrying home on the suburban trains.

*

In the end they went to a film, in Leicester Square. 'I would buy you sweets, if it weren't for rationing,' he said; but she shrugged it aside, and watched, sitting quite still, as

Humphrey Bogart survived impossible dangers. Once or twice she leant over to him with a question, and he was amused, translating the deadpan slang in a whisper into respectable English. She seemed completely absorbed, tense with the drama; like his younger son, who still flinched when the guns were drawn, though he laughed later.

He had planned to take her out to dinner, but it appeared she had other ideas. 'I have never eaten fish and chips,' she said, pronouncing the words with delicate precision. 'The girls I work with, when they go into Epsom, they always say they have had fish and chips. Unless' – she looked up at him, being careful – 'it is not something that people like you eat?'

He laughed, and led her up to Tottenham Court Road, and took pleasure in explaining the more arcane dishes. In the fug of chip fat and cigarette smoke, the man behind the counter cheerfully pointed to saveloys and roe. 'Rock is rock salmon?' she asked, and was proud to be right. 'I order this sometimes.'

They settled for haddock and chips, on his recommendation. He sprinkled vinegar on his chips and let her taste. She was in a mood he'd never seen before, reckless, exploratory, saying what she thought, and laughing suddenly. 'You mean you don't serve them fish and chips?' he asked, and she threw out both hands in an unfamiliar gesture. 'Fish yes, potatoes yes, but Anthony, there are two thousand people, how can it be the same? It is hardly food.' He felt a danger behind her honesty: as if she were jettisoning the way she had lived, and might be left with nothing at the end. So that's two of us, he thought briefly. But it was too much fun, sitting opposite her, amongst the working men in overalls hunched over their suppers.

'Well,' she said, her dark eyes glittering, her mouth shiny with fat, at the end of the meal. 'This week I have been very clever. Very active.'

'Yugoslavia?' he asked, apprehensive.

'Yugoslavia? Well, I will tell you about that. I have been to the library. But no, something else. I have been to an employment agency. And it seems' - she leaned back in her chair and smiled - 'it seems there may be people who will employ me. Ladies who want a cook to come in the morning and go away at night. Or what did she say? Gentlemen's clubs.'

'So you would have a place of your own? To live in?'

'Precisely.' She leaned towards him, across the table. Her sleeve brushed the side of her empty plate. 'I thought it is time I live like other people. Rooms, or a house, I do not know. I can finish work and leave it, and go and do whatever I like at home. Have a cup of coffee at two in the morning; imagine.'

He imagined the rigour of her life for all these years, and took her hand. 'Here, watch it, you two,' an old man called from the back of the shop, and roared with laughter.

'And have visitors?'

'Of course.' He wondered if she'd thought about it. 'You can stay with me and nobody will be watching. At least,' she added, 'if I have a house, or a flat. With rooms I don't know. So it will be a house!'

He leaned over and kissed her on the mouth.

Over white cups of milky coffee, he asked again, not wanting to but compelled, 'So you're not planning to go back home?'

'Really, I do not know what I am planning. To stay, to go - the asylum, a private house - nothing. Perhaps even I will stop work, and sit at home playing the piano.' He could see something wistful in the way she smiled. 'I went to the library and read some books, and newspapers, there is much in the newspapers. But really it does not help me at all. And then..'

She drew back into some private train of thought. 'Well,' she said, 'simply I do not know how I can write to them. What I can say, I mean. So much has happened, probably they cannot understand.'

Can I? he wondered, and made himself think from her point of view. 'But they are your family; they love you, don't they? I would think they would be delighted - overjoyed - if they have not heard from you for so long.'

'I don't know. Perhaps you are right.' Some of her earlier gaiety returned. 'Oh, I think it would be easier simply to go, to get on a train and whatever there is, a bus, a taxi, anything, a cart; and arrive and say Here I am. To whoever is there. Writing a letter, I don't think I can do it.'

'Narcisa,' he said, and traced the lines of her palm with his middle finger. 'I don't want you to go back.' He held her gaze. 'I know this is not what matters most - I mean I know you must decide what is best. You have all these choices. But I don't want you to go away.'

She took it calmly, her hand relaxed in his. Oh God, he thought, I have made a terrible mistake. She doesn't need any more claims on her. There was a long pause. He saw behind her head the man lifting a metal basket of chips, and setting them to drain on the edge of the fryer.

She laughed quietly. 'This week I told someone I have never made decisions. A girl - well, I will tell you some time, perhaps.' She smiled up at him, so he wondered what was coming. 'Anthony, thank you. It is a long time since anyone said that.' She stood, and leaned over to kiss him on the forehead. 'Now I would like to go to this hotel. We will be smelling of fish and chips and vinegar, perhaps they will refuse to let us in?'

He paid at the counter and put his arm round her as they came out onto the street. A taxi was passing and he whistled for it, four fingers in his mouth like a small boy. Inside he drew down the blind and kissed her, and spent the rest of the journey recounting in a whisper what he would like to do in the hotel room.

*

The next day, amongst the pile of bills and letters from suppliers, there was a blue envelope with the now-familiar careful writing. She took it into her office and locked the door.

Dear Mrs Humphreys,

Mrs Humphreys! she thought, and felt her eyes smarting,

Thank you for your letter of 27th March. If it is suitable for you, I will come to Holywell Hospital on Sunday 15th at 2.0pm to meet you. Please let me know if this is not possible for you. I am working Monday to Saturday, but I could come at another time on that day, or meet you somewhere else if you would prefer.

I look forward to hearing from you.
Yours sincerely
Violeta [Humphreys]

*There was no other good enough
To pay the price of sin*

The English voices rose together, trailing behind the thumped piano, out of tune. The chaplain seemed to be mouthing the words. From time to time a baritone made itself heard, a rich full voice, singing a little fast.

It was a terrible tune, Narcisa thought; whining, insistent. There seemed to be an endless number of verses. She could see Matron, in the first pew, her hymn-book held out at the level of her bust, with Dr Bosanquet and his wife beside her. June and Peg were by the wall, standing close. There was Colin, the maintenance man; and the two male nurses she'd met at Victoria station; and Esme, in a row of tired-looking patients, swaying to and fro slowly as she sang.

It had been a stupid idea, to come to chapel. They like it, she thought; it makes them feel at home. But they had no choice: they were required to attend. Being a foreigner, she was exempt. Or she assumed that was what they thought; at any rate, she had hardly ever come here, and no-one had ever told her that she should. It was only that today was Palm Sunday. Rosaleen Shaw had made a point of it: 'Such a lovely custom, I always think. I expect we'll all be going to church together.'

Something had come back, not then but afterwards: some memory of Easter in her childhood, the midnight service with the whole church darkened, the statues covered; then the explosion of bells and singing just at midnight, candles that were lit one from the other. Even her father had come to the Easter vigil, and stood on the left-hand side of the church with the other men. Had she really thought it would be like that?

The hymn had stopped; the congregation, packed rows of staff and patients, sat back down with a kind of sighing rustle. There was a faint smell of unwashed clothes and dust. The chaplain moved over to the brass lectern; a thin man with an oddly bouncing walk. Someone at the back muffled a sneeze.

In just a week her daughter was coming to see her. Narcisa sat still, the prayer-book closed between her hands, the worn red cloth gritty against her palms. Had Violeta realised it was Easter?

She would come to the main door, all the way up the drive, up the steps and ring. Who would go to answer? If no-one was passing it could take some time. Would she try again? Perhaps I should wait in the entrance hall, Narcisa thought. At least then not everyone will know. She looked down, ashamed, and traced the black lettering - *Book of Common Prayer* - with a gloved finger. It's true, she thought. I don't want them all to know it's my long-lost daughter.

The chaplain's deep, rather mournful voice broke off its chanting. Narcisa looked up. A woman had pushed her way out of Esme's pew, and was standing in a drab blue dress out in the aisle. She looked around her and began to scream, a wordless yelp that made Narcisa shiver.

A male nurse came quickly from the back. 'No!' the woman yelled, and kept on, rhythmically, 'No! No!' She ran flat-footed up to the front, and turned.

The chaplain stepped hastily back from the lectern.

The woman's plump fingers were at the neck of her dress. 'There!' she yelled and wrenched it open in one movement, down to the hem. A button rattled down the marble steps. 'There!' she shouted again, triumphant, struggling her arms out of the sleeves. The dress fell in a blue semi-circle around her feet. She stood, a little overweight, her fair hair rumpled, in a dingy white petticoat, looking out at the congregation.

The male nurse reached the front and hesitated. The woman was bending forward, both hands on the hem of her slip, her face flushed. She had the shoulders of a farmer's wife. A man's voice from the back muttered, 'Get on with it!' and stopped abruptly. The Matron turned round to the church and called out something. A female nurse shuffled out of her pew, and walked purposefully towards the woman, who straightened up and pulled the petticoat over her head, then waved it in one hand, cackling with laughter.

How sad her flesh looks, Narcisa thought. The arms were pale and shuddered slightly. The skin seemed slack. Then she saw the large bruise high on the woman's thigh, and recognised her. The bruise had that look of rotting vegetables. This was the woman from the corridor, the day Dr Whitchurch had sent for her.

The female nurse took off her navy cape and went to put it round the woman's shoulders, calling her name: Irene, come on Irene. The man moved forward at the same moment. Irene, in white cotton vest and shapeless knickers, darted away. She waved her arms above her head, laughing. Someone in front of Narcisa did the same, and was slapped by a nurse. 'Quickly!' Matron called out, and clapped her hands. Dr Whitchurch came striding from nowhere, holding up a hypodermic. Irene tried to knock it out of his hand, but he dodged to one side. Narcisa saw the white flesh of the woman's thigh dimple as the needle went in deep. The crowing voice turned to a yelp of pain and slid down the scale, like a gramophone needle slipping.

Once the little group had gone, Irene drooping on the arms of the two nurses, the chatter broke out. 'My friends,' the chaplain began, and stopped at once. 'Nurses!' Matron called sharply, and a general hushing and settling down began. A young woman sobbed loudly and was led away, a nurse gripping her by the upper arm. Dr Bosanquet stood by the chaplain and cleared his throat. 'If you please,' he said.

The chaplain took his place back at the lectern. There was silence.

They are going to pretend it didn't happen, Narcisa thought. 'Excuse me,' she said, standing, and pushed roughly past two of the laundry staff to reach the aisle, then turned and walked swiftly towards the door, hearing her heels beat on the tiles, till she could lift the latch and get outside, into the sunshine of a spring morning.

*

She walked quickly away from the main buildings, past the dark brick house where Dr Bosanquet lived, and out through the ornate gate by the west lodge. The porter looked up from his book and nodded. The force of what had been anger kept her moving; now she couldn't have said what she was feeling, except for physical energy, restlessness. After the chapel, the breeze was tantalising, cooling her neck, lifting the weight of her hair. The chestnut trees were coming into leaf. She noticed with some other part of herself the leaves not yet unfolded, like paper hats; a bird chirruping high up out of sight; a squirrel that stopped a few yards in front of her, squarely on all fours, testing the scent of something, its tail bent in a deep curve over its back.

The road branched after the farm buildings. She took the narrower fork and headed uphill, feeling the effort of movement in her thighs. There was a smell of slurry from the fields, sickly, but she held her breath and passed it. Her petticoat was sticking to her back; her collar was damp. A tractor came slowly down the lane towards her; the space between the high hedges was all taken up by its noise, the insistent rumbling. As it passed her the man ducked his head in greeting. Behind him two children, a boy and a girl, stood against the high wheels, staring ahead.

At the top of the hill she stopped to get her breath. A five-bar gate made a break in the hedgerow. She stepped carefully over the muddy wheel-tracks, and stood looking out over the fields. In front of her the new crop - wheat, she supposed, - was two or three inches high, and brilliant green. The hedge down on the left was flowering white. She leaned both arms along the top of the gate, and rocked it to and fro on its hinges. The sun spread warmth over her neck and shoulders.

So what was so terrible? It was nothing new. A woman had gone manic, as they said; the nurses hadn't managed to calm her down; Dr Whitchurch had given her an injection. In the chapel: that made it more shocking, no doubt, even for an unbeliever, even in that ugly unreligious building, with its low barrel-vaulted roof and smell of polish.

She rubbed her chin gently along her arm, pushing the sleeve back, feeling the fine hairs. It was because she had recognised the woman. No: because she had recognised the bruise. That plump, unvitalised thigh with its poignancy, its scant recollection of energy and desire; and the yellowing mark, whatever that demonstrated.

Narcisa looked out over the sloping fields. Farther down, a hawthorn was in flower, a bouquet of red in the middle of the field, the tractor-marks still on the bare soil, skirting the base of the tree in careful curves. Was it the bruise, then? It is hardly news that nurses hit patients, she thought. She felt herself shake; the lichened wood of the gate dug into her hands. A place on her calf twitched in recognition.

A line of cloud swelled up on the horizon. She watched it develop, expanding like dough rising. The sky above it seemed paler, faded fabric. She stood straight and turned towards the lane. The image of the woman Irene returned: leaning forward, her tow-coloured hair hiding her face, both hands on the hem of the dingy white petticoat, before she lifted it up above her head. The chapel had been quiet. At least the woman had captured their attention.

She walked slowly back, picking her way across the deep tractor-marks. She felt light-headed. I am no longer a professional, she thought, and wondered what she meant. I don't know whether I can go on with this. Then from the gate she saw the congregation leaving the chapel, the patients in two lines, male and female, the staff not on duty lingering in the sunshine. Dr Bosanquet waited for Dr Whitchurch, and put a hand on his shoulder as they walked. I don't know, Narcisa thought again, with dread, and hurried on to unlock the kitchen.

*

She was waking up thinking of Violeta. Each morning she had the sense of having dreamed, a remnant of bewilderment or dread, with no recollection of what the dream contained; and then as she woke fully, the sky behind her half-drawn curtains lightening, she knew again what it was she had to fear.

What is the worst that can happen? she asked herself more than once, when the queasy feeling came back to her, in the kitchen or in her office, or at night when she came back late to the same sparse bedroom, contriving to have no time to sit on her own. But the question each time slipped away from her, as though it had been asked in the wrong language. She was harsh with herself, saying again that she should be glad, that other women would welcome being found. She felt how time had made her coarse and unfeeling. It was possible, she told herself several times, that this encounter would free her from all that, redeem her in some way she couldn't yet imagine. It seemed to her sometimes that that was what she wanted, to be forced out of the calm of her routines, into something else, that she might have known once, some state of eagerness and intense feeling. But that change surely had already happened. The patterns of work had stopped being sustaining; she was unpredictable even to herself. Perhaps I envied the woman in the chapel, she thought, and shivered. That after all was the worst fear.

She worked with fierce energy all the week. She decided on a spring clean of the kitchen, and organised the staff and the working patients to empty the cupboards and wash the stacks of china. She herself climbed on borrowed stepladders to lift down jugs and tureens not used in years, and reached right to the back to scour the shelves. All of them, Rosaleen Shaw, Peg, June and the other kitchen assistants, the extra patients she had had drafted in, saw the reckless force of her mood and buckled down, speaking little when she was there, pausing briefly to wipe sweat off face or hands. Narcisa inspected, giving less praise than usual, nodding when the work was done as she wished, as if this were only to be expected; and when it was not good enough, if she found a shelf with grime left in the corners, or a plate was broken, simply pointing so that the woman saw, and blushed, reprimanded only by herself. Once she caught sight of the Assistant Cook, raising her eyebrows to the sly Betty Dunlop. So let them, Narcisa thought, and pointed out - they had all stopped to prepare the hospital tea - that the larder still needed doing, the heavy crocks of beans and salt and sugar moved out so that they could wash down the stone floor.

She was due for an afternoon off on the Wednesday; but the day before, Rosaleen Shaw came up, simpering with some erotic secret, and asked if she could have Wednesday instead of Friday - 'family problems.' Narcisa agreed at once, without questioning, and saw the woman's face, half disappointed. She thought at first that she would simply work on. Then later, in the bath on Tuesday night, looking sleepily at her large strong hands, pudgy and pale in the bathwater's refraction, she remembered Anthony. Her body tensed in the water, anticipating.

The next morning she left the women at work, and went to her office to phone him. It occurred to her briefly that someone might listen in, the hospital telephonist perhaps. She asked stiffly for the London number, and waited. The same diffident woman in his office answered, and seemed to know her name. In a few moments he was there: 'Good morning, Narcisa.' He was apologetic; there was a client with him, in the other room.

She found the words awkward in her mouth; it was too much, what she was asking, he would be repelled. Still she made herself say it. 'Anthony, on Friday I will have the afternoon off. I would like to see you.'

She waited nervously while he found his diary. 'It's Good Friday,' he said. 'Bank holiday. Of course you don't get bank holidays off, do you? My boys are home.'

'Your boys?' It was a moment before she understood. Then at once she wanted to end the call. 'Never mind,' she said. 'Of course. It does not matter.'

'I am sorry,' he said. 'I wish I could. How nice of you to have had the idea. Another time.' He felt bad, she could tell, for reminding her. 'Anthony, it is fine,' she said to stop him. 'You are right, I will telephone you again.'

Well, there is plenty of work for me here, she thought as she put the receiver down. The fish-fryers were still to be drained and cleaned. She would work on Friday; it would be better than being alone. In any case, she said to herself as she locked the office, and nodded to Miss Fleming who was passing, gaunt and severe as ever, a domestic in overalls trailing along behind her; in any case, I haven't told him about Violeta, and by Friday maybe I couldn't keep quiet any longer. She thought of him at home with his two sons, playing cricket perhaps - was that what they would do? Outside, in any event, one of the boys starting to look like him, perhaps one boisterous and the other quiet. And he will see himself in the quiet one; he will remember how he was at that age. So the younger, the noisy one will be easier for him. She hesitated before going into the kitchen, and went instead to look out at the weather. They seemed at that moment like a foreign tribe, whose ways of living together were remote and charming.

Part 8

1917 - 1934

1917

It was that silence you have at night with heavy snow, the trees sedated, the birds awed and in hiding. Inside in the ward someone muttered rapidly in her sleep.

The baby was lying spread-eagled in her cot, under the blanket Narcisa had knitted for her. It had been badly washed and the wool was matted.

At her desk by the door, the night attendant had fallen asleep, head on her arms.

Narcisa got out of bed as quietly as she could. The floorboards were hard and cold under her feet. She lifted her daughter up and hugged her close. The baby turned her head towards Narcisa's breast.

She walked barefoot down the middle of the ward. One bed and then another on each side showed itself shadowy against the dark.

At the wide bay window she stepped behind the curtain. It fell back, dark blue and dusty, sealing the two of them in to the sudden snow-light.

The baby stirred. Narcisa bent and kissed the top of the head, the black hair. She felt her wake up and began to croon.

The lawn was dazzling, like bleached damask. The rose-bushes were outlined in white, in elaborate detail, every rosehip and dried leaf weighted down with snow. To the right, the villa was like a gingerbread house, snow on the eaves and over each of the windows. The planetrees down by the fence were black and white cut-outs.

In the morning some woman would come down the lane on a cart, between handfuls of snow falling off the branches, in through the gates and up to the front door; then a little later go back the way she had come, the horse cutting out a new set of prints in the snow, Narcisa's daughter wrapped in a shawl in her arms.

She rocked where she stood. The curtain moved heavily against her shoulders.

The Matron had come to tell her in the evening. The baby was crying and she was walking up and down. The Matron raised her voice over the wailing. Already she couldn't remember what she'd been told, only her own voice screaming 'No! No!' and two attendants running into the room.

'Better,' the Matron kept saying firmly. 'Better for her.'

She had run away down the ward and crouched on the bed, holding the baby tightly. The people followed.

'Madame Taté.' She begged for the interpreter, but the Matron had shaken her head, smiling.

Wrapped in the curtain she rocked the child in her arms. If Violeta cried, they would be taken back and scolded; but she lay still, as if reflecting on her choices. If Narcisa cried, the baby would start as well.

She remembered how in the week after the birth she had wanted to smother the child to save herself.

An owl called softly out there in the grounds.

She could hold the curtain lightly over the baby's face. She lifted a thick blue fold in one hand. The fabric was faded in long streaks, and worn.

Better to choose to take her away herself, to do it tenderly so she knew Narcisa loved her, than let her be handled by some unknown woman. She had been baptised: she would not go to limbo.

She rocked with the child.

Outside the window nothing was going to change. The lawn would lie untrodden, the rose-bushes stay painted in lead-white. She made herself stare out at the glaring snow, until she was no longer capable of thinking, and stayed there drugged with light for a long time.

It seemed her daughter was murmuring in her ear. She would escape; she would grow up, out in the world, and run on a snow-laid lawn in leather boots. She could see the girl running from her, across the grounds.

She wrung the folds of curtain in her left hand.

Snow began delicately to fall again. The stems of the rose-bush seemed laden already, but the sky dropped more and more flakes onto it, and instead of toppling the lines of snow grew higher, a kind of protection.

*

The curtain flapped up. 'Humphreys!' somebody said, and shook her shoulder.

She was very cold; but the baby was still breathing. She got to her feet. The white light from the garden poured into the ward. The women standing at the ends of their beds seemed to have been painted in cruel greys.

She remembered.

The attendant hustled her back into the room, scolding.

She would not leave the baby for a moment. She put her down only when she had to, pulling the uniform dress over her head, or splashing her face. The attendant, a young woman with smallpox scars, watched nervously. Narcisa wondered if this girl might help her.

The other women went off to their duties. She folded all the baby-clothes she had made, and piled them at the foot of the cradle, under the blanket. Then she walked again, holding the child, to the window.

Out of sight, to the left, she heard a man's voice call out, and the creak of hinges; then the half-muffled steps of a horse.

Narcisa opened her dress and fed her daughter. She shook her head hard so her hair fell around the child, who sucked steadily, with little satisfied sounds. She felt already the bereavement of her nipples.

'Mrs Humphreys.' It was the Matron's voice.

She didn't turn.

'Mrs Humphreys.' Shoes clattered towards her.

She took the child from her breast. Violeta wailed. Narcisa held her and did her dress up quickly.

'Come on, Mrs Humphreys.'

She kicked hard at the window, hoping to break it. She pulled the curtain behind her again, but it was yanked back. The child cried desperately and she held her tight. She ran along the bay window, to an empty bed, and pushed it hard towards them, then stood with her crying child behind the bed-head. There were voices and movement, and the Matron in her navy-blue uniform. She shoved over a bedside cabinet with her foot, and moved behind the next bed, and began to throw things, a Bible, a comb, a glass, which broke on the floor.

She saw a nurse lifting a hypodermic. 'No!' she shouted and got down to the floor. Under the bed she tried to soothe her daughter, rocking.

The shoes and long skirts were standing all around them.

The whole cramped space was shuddering with her weeping. The baby cried with her, rigid with fear in her arms.

They rocked together, warm, for the last time, as if while they went on crying nothing could happen.

Slowly the bed was pushed out from above them. She bent her head and sheltered the child with her hair.

There is cold around her face, and sometimes, when she looks beyond the woman, a mushy snowflake settles against her skin. The woman is wearing a dark brown cloak; the cloth is harsh and smells musty. Violeta is lying along the woman's arm, held down - or held secure - by a broad hand in a brown woollen glove.

Beneath the woman and Violeta the cart jostles. It has two counterpointed rhythms, the regular bobbing over its axles, and the jolts and shakings as it trolls along the lane. Both are bewildering to Violeta, who has scarcely before been in the open air, and then only in her mother's arms. Her mother's arms are smaller, thinner, more insistent than this woman's; they mind, they want her to be there, they hold her urgently at times. Her mother's clothes smell of laundry soap and skin, which is like vanilla.

There were great white spaces of hunger and isolation but still, when she waited long enough, her mother.

*

Field is away from work again. Rhoda Woodruff says Field sent her little sister with a letter; but the sister, a poor timid little thing with stringy hair, didn't dare ring at the door, and gave the letter to Rhoda to bring in. 'My sister is very ill,' the girl said. 'Out too late with her fancy-man, more like,' says Rhoda. 'Unless it's the morning sickness got her already.' The women disperse to their tasks around the building, more than one of them thankful the morning sickness hasn't yet got her; or half-wishing it had, so that like Ellen Field she could stay in bed, while the others did her scrubbing and scouring for her.

Field is the one who doesn't mind the infants. 'Must have given her the idea,' Rhoda mutters to Nancy O'Brien, under the eye of the receiving officer. 'I mean, if you're going to wipe bottoms.' Rhoda is engaged to be married to fat little Wilfred Parsons, the postman, and intends to remain pure till her wedding day. 'And after,' Nancy said to Ellen Field one evening. Knowing she will be transported out of employment makes Rhoda Woodruff superior at times.

The latest one is being bad, as usual. Rhoda holds the baby to her shoulder with one hand, and with the other tugs away at the soaked sheet. The latest baby only wails the louder. 'Bad-tempered little thing,' says Rhoda, and hands the child to Nancy while finding a clean sheet. This one has been turned sides-to-middle, and the seam will rub. 'Still, that kind of parents, what can you expect?'

Nancy, who claims her father died at Mafeking, puts the baby back quickly, and moves on. For at least half an hour, the imprint stays with her as she cleans up the children's room: the sturdy body squirming against her chest, warm and determined.

For Violeta the morning is patterned like this: the acid smell and the cold wet sheet; abrupt clutching; two successive kinds of overall cloth, the second smelling faintly of lavender; and then the cot again, the dark green paint on the walls and the grimy white ceiling. She lies still. The back of her head, the scant flesh on her back and her upper arms, hold a long way down inside them the recollection that there was something more.

1921

Her ear hurts where Mrs McIver slapped it.

'And stop that snivelling!'

She wants to stop crying but she can't quite. Her nose is running.

'You know there's no clean clothes left on a Friday! You'll just have to go round in your under-things. Then they'll all know what a wicked girl you've been.'

It's true. They will all know, and the boys will shout *Violet's a baby, Violet's a baby,* like last time.

'Now get out of here. You know quite well I'm poorly. Go and tell Ailsa to give you some work.'

She goes down the stairs slowly, one step at a time, one hand on the banisters, the other one still pressed to her ear, for comfort.

They are laying the table. Her job is the knives and forks. She's late.

Ailsa is in the kitchen, making the porridge, a big white apron tied round her middle. The steam is making her round white face wet and hot.

Violeta stands just inside the door. She doesn't want Ailsa to know that she's been wicked.

'Violet Humphreys, why haven't you got a frock on?'

She tries not to cry again, but can't manage. The other girls in the kitchen start laughing at her.

'Shut your mouths, all of you; get on with your work!'

The girls are quiet but they are still watching her. She says: 'In the yard a boy hit me,' - she won't say it was Arnie - 'so I hit him back and I tore my frock and it was all dirty. And there aren't any clean frocks, Mrs McIver says.' She lets the words stop. She can't bear to tell the rest of it. Her legs are cold, and her arms.

'Well,' says Ailsa, so maybe it's all right. 'We can't have you running round in your smalls, can we?' The little girls giggle, and this time Ailsa lets them. 'We'll see what we can find. Edie, come here and stir the porridge, and make sure it doesn't burn, or you'll be for it. Come *on,* Vi, if you're coming' - and she's out of the door.

When they are safely out of sight, on the stairs, Ailsa holds out her sticky hand, and Violeta takes it.

*

The Board is coming.

'What's the Board?' she asks Ailsa, who takes no notice. The house has to be tidy, because of the Board.

'They're people all made out of wood,' Arnie Smith said, before he punched her. They were in the yard, the big girls out of hearing. 'And they walk like this,' - he did a scarecrow lurch – 'and they're all flat like floorboards. And they say: *Has he been a good boy, Mrs McIver?'* They all laughed at Arnie's floorboard voice; but Violeta thought Mrs McIver would come, and was scared.

She is carrying the kindling.

The front parlour is cold, and dark, with shadows. It smells of dust. Ailsa goes over and pulls back the long blue curtains. Little blobs of red glow on the parlour wall, between the pictures. She puts down her kindling, then goes over to touch one. The red jumps on her hand. Then she moves her hand to the side, and it jumps back.

'Silly,' says Ailsa: 'it's the stained glass.' She points high up to the top of the bay window. There are coloured pictures, red, yellow and brown. She can see an apple and a big yellow flower.

'It needs a good dust in here,' Ailsa says. 'Never mind, I'll lay the fire first.'

Violeta helps her, handing pieces of kindling. Some of them make little trees, with branches; one even has an old brown leaf. She would like to keep it, but it has to go and be burned.

'I can dust,' she offers.

'You're not big enough.' Ailsa finishes stacking the bits of coal. 'Mrs McIver said I was to light this now, and get the room warm before they get here.' She puts a match to the paper, and they watch it flare. Violeta holds out both hands; the palms get hot quickly, even though the rest of her is still cold. She hugs herself, spreading the heat through her arms.

'Now you be careful, you know you're ever so clumsy.' Ailsa picks up the coal-scuttle. 'I'm going to get the feather-duster. You sit quiet, eh?'

The twigs are being wrapped round by the flames. The one with the little leaf is sticking out. She squats down to watch. The leaf catches, and almost at once goes black and crumbles.

'Now you be careful, Violet,' she sings to herself. 'Now you be careful.' She stands up and goes to look for the red patch. Instead she finds a yellow one, further up. She can't reach. She stands on tip-toe, and the end of her middle finger goes bright yellow. She can't keep it.

Now the flames are all round the heap of coal. Some of them are coming up in between. The fireplace smells like the coal-hole under the steps.

I'm meant to be sitting quiet. She squats down right beside the wooden fender. Here I am, Ailsa, I'm sitting quiet. A long flame wavers up at the dark chimney.

Her ear is hurting again. She puts her hand over it. Then, testing, she reaches the hand out towards the fire, gets it hot, and puts it back tight over her ear. That's nice.

Only it gets cold too soon.

She is doing the same thing again when a flame jumps up, and she is scared and falls forward, and then the hurt, all the way up her arm, and her hair burning right next to her face, and it smells awful, and she is screaming, she mustn't scream but she does, and Ailsa is running into the parlour shouting, 'Oh my god Violet oh you stupid girl oh what are they going to say?' and pulling her.

*

She is in the dark. Her arm hurts right inside, all the way up.

'The devil's got into you today, Violet Humphreys.' That's why she's been send to bed without her dinner.

'What can you expect?' she heard Mrs McIver say to Ailsa. Has Mrs McIver always known she's wicked?

She wriggles further down under the blanket. Her feet are cold.

Ailsa said: 'I don't love you any more.'

She cries again; it keeps making her cry. Only she's tired. She aches with having cried too much. Maybe that's why they tell you not to. What will she do if Ailsa doesn't love her?

The boys will all punch her and pull her hair. I'll fight them back. Fighting's wicked too.

Ailsa doesn't love her because she cried too much when she fell in the fire, and Mrs McIver came down, with the doctor. And Ailsa was doing something to her arm, and the doctor said, 'No, no, you ignorant girl.'

Then she was sitting on the kitchen table, only it was all right because the doctor had put her there, and he was wrapping a big bandage round her arm. And he said, 'You're a brave girl,' and patted her head. The doctor was very tall and thin, with a brown coat. It was nice when he wrapped the bandage round and round, and played peep-bo with it, like you do with babies.

But she wasn't brave, she was wicked. When the doctor had gone, Mrs McIver said 'Well, Ailsa Jordan, you'd better explain.' Ailsa said, 'She came out of the room with me but she sneaked back in.' Violeta didn't tell, but Mrs McIver sent Ailsa upstairs anyway for a beating.

The curtains are drawn. There is a little scratching sound under the bed. She watches the mouse come out into the space between her bed and Edie's, and pause, twitching its front feet, and then run quickly in the dark towards the light at the bottom of the bedroom door, and squeeze under.

1924

'A great pleasure to have met you,' Mrs McIver said, standing at the door. She had put on her best dress, the yellow-and-brown one, and Violeta could see that her shoes were hurting. 'And we are all very pleased about your decision. Aren't we, Violet? I'm sure you won't regret it. Say goodbye to Mr and Mrs Caulker, Violet. We'll see you on Saturday. Goodbye.'

Violeta watched them walk down the front path. Mr Caulker's sleeve brushed against the rosebush, but he didn't seem to notice. Mrs Caulker turned to latch the gate. She's got a stupid face, Violeta thought, all fat and line-y. She looks as if she's going to cry all the time. Mrs Caulker waved, then took her husband's arm.

'Well,' said Mrs McIver, closing the door, 'you're a lucky little girl. You'll have to work hard and be a credit to them.'

She didn't feel lucky. When they were washing up, Edie asked, drying the saucers: 'Here, are you going to be boarded out then?' Edie had been boarded out, but after six months she had come back.

Violeta nodded.

'They're a bit *old,* aren't they?'

Violeta went on to the cups. She still had to stand on a stool for washing up, and lean forward into the big white sink.

There was a black, branching crack next to the tap, which made her feel peculiar every time she looked. Washing-up water splashed up on her apron. Edie was right, that was what they were, old.

'And she's got that weird hair, all grey and yellow,' Edie went on. The other girls sniggered, watching Violeta.

'I don't care,' Violeta said, 'I'm not going.' She lined the cups up on the rack, handles all facing inward so they didn't get broken.

'You'll have to.'

'No I won't.'

'Yes you will,' said Margery, who was ten. 'If they come and choose you, you've got to go. And you've got to stay there till you're fourteen, then you come back, like Ailsa did, and Dot. Unless you're bad, like Edie, and get sent back.'

'I wasn't bad,' yelled Edie, waving a plate close up to Margery's face, so she stepped back, squealing. Dot opened the scullery door: 'Bleeding hell, you're slow! Get on with it, will you!'

Ailsa's name made Violeta want to cry, suddenly. She rubbed hard at a bit of crust burnt onto the pie-dish. Ailsa had gone into service in Horsham. She'd sent a postcard with a picture of a horse and cart; but it was to all of them, not just to her, and Mrs McIver had kept it in her room.

If Ailsa was here she wouldn't let me be boarded out with them.

'Edie,' she asked, when they were getting ready for bed. 'You know when you were boarded out?'

Edie was tugging a tangle out of her hair.

'Well, were they' - she couldn't find the right question – 'were they not old and everything?'

Edie got into bed and closed her eyes. After a while she said, 'She had lovely hair. All blonde, and wavy.'

It's not fair, Violeta thought in the dark. She was near to sleep. It's not fair. Maybe her mother would come and take her away in time. Her mum was beautiful, with long black hair, and one day she was going to come and take her away. Ailsa had laughed when she'd told her, once when she'd been beaten for telling lies. She didn't want to remember what else Ailsa had said. It wasn't true.

*

In the end Mrs McIver took her there, on a bus. 'Go upstairs, go on,' she said to Violeta, and they sat at the front, looking down at people's hats. She could tell this was meant to be a treat, but she felt strange, and was almost glad when they had to get off.

The house had a tall hedge in front, and a lot of windows. She wondered if she'd have to clean them all on her own. She hung back at the gate; but Mrs McIver was already ringing the doorbell, and someone in an apron was answering.

'But Mrs McIver,' the woman said, 'doesn't she have a bag? Or are you having it sent on later?'

I've done something wrong already, Violeta thought.

'No, nothing like that,' Mrs McIver said cheerfully. 'She's just as she is, all ready for you to care for her. Oh, there is this,' and she opened her black handbag. 'The birth certificate, you know.' She handed a big letter to Mr Caulker.

They were sitting in the front parlour, with the fire lit, even though it was still morning. It was like the parlour at the home, she thought, with lots of dark pictures, though the curtains were red instead of blue. She swung her legs against the front of the sofa, till Mrs McIver tapped her knee, not looking at her.

'Violeta Humphreys, eh?' Mr Caulker said, behind the big piece of paper. He said it oddly, Vee- instead of Vi-.

'Shouldn't there be two Ts? Still, I suppose the registrar knew what he was doing.' He put the paper back in the envelope.

'We prefer to call her Violet,' Mrs McIver said 'Of course you may want to..? I know some people rather choose their own name. You know, to make it, well, a new start.'

'But her clothes, Mrs McIver,' the woman said.

'Oh I am sorry, Mrs Caulker, I should have told you. You don't know our system, of course, why should you?' Violeta stopped listening. The carpet had a very difficult pattern, not flowers like at the home but bits of colours, like boxes inside each other. She pretended to play hopscotch, like in the playground, from one dark red bit to the next and then the next. She wondered if she would go to a new school.

'Well then,' Mrs Caulker was saying, 'I can see I'll have to call in the dressmaker. That will be fun, won't it, Violet? New dresses?'

'Oh, I don't think that..' Mrs McIver said; but then she seemed to change her mind, and sat back on the sofa. She took a handkerchief out of her bag, and blew her nose, not as loudly as usual. 'You do get attached,' she said to Mrs Caulker.

They all stood up, then Mrs McIver squatted down and hugged Violeta. Violeta felt shocked, and then hugged back, hard, feeling sad. Even Mrs McIver was leaving her.

'Now be a good girl,' Mrs McIver said, standing up and smoothing her skirt. 'And help Mr and Mrs Caulker and do what they say, and be a credit to all of us. And no more fighting,' she bent down to whisper; but Violeta was sure they had heard. She began to cry.

'No tears now!' said Mrs McIver. 'I'd better be off.'

By the time they'd come back from seeing Mrs McIver out, Violeta had wiped her nose on the hem of her dress, and was standing on a dark red bit of carpet, facing the door.

*

'I want Ailsa! she screams, waking night after night in her new bed, in the big room all on her own, with ripples behind the long brown velvet curtains. 'Ailsa! I want Ailsa!'

'Who is Ailsa?' Mrs Caulker asks. She stands in the doorway in her dressing-gown, her yellow and grey hair undone like a witch's. On the fifth night she comes in, and sits on the counterpane. She holds out her hand gingerly, and Violeta, sobbing, clutches the fingers.

'Your Ailsa is not at the workhouse home any more,' Mrs Caulker says. 'She's gone out to work, hasn't she? In service. You know that, Violet.'

She does, but hearing it said makes it all the worse.

'Ailsa has other duties now, to her new employers. And you're here with us now, aren't you? So you must put all of that behind you.'

She lets go Mrs Caulker's fingers, and flings herself onto her side, her eyes tight shut. She is crying so hard it makes her hurt all over.

'Your job is to learn to be a good girl,' the voice goes on. 'Violet, are you listening? God doesn't want us to be too fond of people. So we have to be brave and say goodbye to them.'

She lies, exhausted, while Mrs Caulker prays: 'Please God, help Violet overcome her misfortunes and temptations, which you have created to test her, and let her become your worthy servant. Amen.'

When Mrs Caulker has gone, Violeta's mother comes out of the curtains, and lifts her.

1930

'Please Vi,' says the child.

It is cold in the big bedroom, and still dark outside. The children are not dressing fast enough. Their fingers fumble with sleeves and socks in the cold. 'Come on, you won't get any breakfast,' Violeta says.

There are too many beds. Violeta would walk round the room to chivvy them on, but the children dressing take up all the space. Sometimes it gives her a cold leery feeling: that they won't stay still, that one of them is missing, that they will stop taking notice of what she tells them. 'You've done it all wrong,' she says, and roughly pulls open the child's shirt buttons to start again. 'Look, you've got to get the bottom one right.' The child whimpers. When she's finished he tries to put his arms round her neck, but she won't let him.

It's the way they press against you. You keep on feeling it even when you've stopped them.

Rain starts beating against the bedroom window. She looks out. Over towards the town the sky is queasy yellow. 'Two more minutes,' she says. 'it's getting light.'

The children file into the dining-room on time. It smells of cold anthracite, and porridge. The bigger girls, already up for an hour, serve out breakfast. When Mrs Hopkins comes in they are all sitting down.

'For what we are about to receive may the Lord make us truly thankful amen.' Violeta can tell from her voice Mrs Hopkins is tired this morning. There is the sound of the rain, the children hurriedly slopping porridge, the damp air. Violeta's vest sticks to her back. 'Use your hanky,' she says under her breath to Ruby Shorter.

'No problems last night, Violet?' The housemother speaks too loudly. A boy starts to snigger, and is kicked. Billy Sherwood, who couldn't do up his shirt, tries not to sniff.

Violeta sees him again, skinny and shivering, at half past three when she ripped off his soaked sheet.

'No, Mrs Hopkins.'

Later, when they're counting the coal sacks in, standing inside the back door out of the rain, Mrs Hopkins says, 'You're doing quite well, Violet, I'm pleased with you.'

The coalman overhears and winks at her. 'Eleven,' she says, looking down at the coal merchant's book. 'Thank you, Mrs Hopkins.'

I won't do it. I'm not going to cry again. I wish she wouldn't. Stupid old cow. Lazy old cow. She couldn't get by without me. Why did the coalman do that? I don't care what she thinks. I wish she wouldn't.

Rain drips from the lintel above them, from the tiled slanted roof of the coal-bunker, and the ivy-leaves on the tall side fence. Rain mixes with coal-dust and makes black mud on the path. The coal smells acrid. The coalman returns up the path, stooped under a sack, the sacking getting dark with wet. There is the rushing sound as he empties it onto the pile. A gust blows rain in her face.

She stands up straight, and turns a little away from the housemother. When the coalman comes back with the folded bag, she stares at him.

*

She had almost forgotten about the beatings.

How could she have? she thought when she came back. But it wasn't the same; Mrs McIver had gone, sacked someone said, though they didn't seem to know why. Anyway, here instead was Mrs Rosita Hopkins: fat, sentimental; clutching the little children, the boys especially, at one minute, so they clung to her, bewildered with touch, and hopeful; then the next slapping, or ordering Violeta to beat them. 'It's the drink, can't you tell?' said Louie, who was leaving, going into service in a house in Staines. Violeta couldn't tell; the Caulkers were teetotal. She'd only seen men, lolling on the bench outside the Red Lion, calling out and she didn't know how to respond to them. Still she took heed of Louie, and soon picked up the signs, hushing the children and hiding their misdeeds, less out of any kindness than self-protection.

The worst was the beatings.

Not that she hadn't been beaten at the Caulkers'. When she was little there was Uncle William, solemnly counting out the strokes of the cane; making her stay down in his cold study to pray with him afterwards. There was the cold fear, the pain that she wanted to run away and cover; the understanding that God too would have beaten her, if only he'd been on earth again; and then Aunt Beatrice, sad, coming heavily up the stairs. Nothing could be so bad, she remembered thinking, crying silently for Ailsa, who never came, or her mother who they said was dead but mustn't be, mustn't. Then when she was, what, eleven? and had done something, told a lie no doubt and been found out for it, she remembered standing in the drawing room, sullen, head down; and Uncle William stood up, and Aunt Beatrice said, 'William, perhaps, I think, no.' They both had looked at her, horrified, she thought, so she stood there and went hot, full of shame, too tall in her school smock. Aunt Beatrice was going to take over the beatings. They went up to Violeta's bedroom, but Aunt couldn't do it. 'I can't bring myself to,' she almost apologised, and made Violeta kneel beside her. From then on they kept to telling her off and praying. It was as if God too couldn't bring himself; without the pain she began to imagine him greying, as they both were, not knowing quite what he should do with her. Which was what Aunt Beatrice said, round-shouldered in her armchair: 'Violet, I don't know what to do with you.' She was a disappointment, she understood: whatever she did (and she'd never quite stopped trying) she was not the child they'd wanted to take in.

Perhaps I got soft, she thought, those last three years. Mrs Hopkins' beatings were a different thing. In some ways better; there was no questioning, no *How could you, Violet?* or *You've upset your Aunt again.* Mrs Hopkins would stay unreachable in her room, so that Violeta had to deal with everything, the boys tormenting a pigeon, the food, the cleaning; and then sweep downstairs, her thin brown hair flying up from its bun, throw open the door to wherever they were working; and look for something, look around for some mistake, then grab her arm and steer her out of the room. Perhaps what was so bad was being beaten by a woman. Ailsa and Mrs McIver had beaten her, but she was so little then, it was quite different. Mrs Hopkins' fat little hands grasped onto her, her beery breath made her gag, she leaned close, the belt flailed in the narrow space between them, there were the smell of sweat, the pain going deeper and deeper, the cold air on her skin. Each time she swore she wouldn't cry. She would start off saying in her head *Stupid old cow, bloody drunken tart,* as if the bad words might protect her; but each time she was defeated, could only pull away as soon as possible, while

Mrs Hopkins gasped and looked triumphant; pull her clothes back right and run up to the bedroom, and push the cabinet up against the door. What would the Caulkers say? she wondered once; but there was no help there. They might disapprove of drink and anger, but they too would be certain she had done wrong, and that beating - *chastisement* - was the way to alter her. Only she knew that she couldn't change.

*

'Get on with it, then,' she said to Harry Silver: who was standing at the foot of the step-ladder, the bucket full of hot water in his hand. 'I ain't got all day,' and she lifted her hand to slap him.

He still didn't move. 'Go on,' she shouted, 'What the heck's wrong with you?' The windows all had to be cleaned today; and it got dark by six, they'd never make it. The others at least seemed to be doing something, four other boys, all of them due to be boarded out, in the country, on farms, where they'd be useful. 'You ain't left yet,' she told Harry. 'Now earn your keep.'

He was queasy, she guessed: had no head for heights. But what good was that when he'd be working soon? Eddie Jukes had come down for some more hot water, and was standing watching. 'And you mind your own business,' she snapped at him.

He was out of her reach before he started chanting; just loud enough that the others boys would hear.

'Violet's a loony, born in the loony-bin. Violet's a...' but by then she had run, fast as she could, and caught him, knocking the bucket out of his hand, hitting both sides of his head at once, but it felt hard, hard, his cropped red hair, the tough flaps of his ears against the flat of her hands, so she had to go on trying to beat him down, till he cowered, whining, covering his head as best he could with his arms.

She made herself stop.

'Upstairs and no dinner for you, and I'll tell Mrs Hopkins.' Though of course she wouldn't; he would know she wouldn't. She turned back, but Harry was half-way up the ladder, his bucket shaking and slopping out hot water.

*

It was true, she thought that evening, sitting darning with Mrs Hopkins and two of the bigger girls. Uncle William had given her the birth certificate to bring back, but she'd opened the envelope the first night and read it. *Name, if any:* what on earth did that mean? But her name was written, just like that: *Violeta*, and *Girl* in the next box. Then *Name and surname of father*, but nothing there. No father; I didn't ever have one.

The next part told her something she hadn't known. *Narcisa:* her mother was called Narcisa. A weird name; she wasn't sure how to say it. Then again, she'd always known her mother was foreign; it was why she was Violeta, not Violet. Vee-oleta, she tried saying to herself, the way Uncle William had the first time. Perhaps that was how you said it if you were foreign. My name is Veeoleta Humphreys. She liked that. No point in trying to get anyone to call her that, not here at the home anyway. Veeoleta, she said, sitting on the bed. Nar-cisa.

Back to the certificate. The first box said: *Third July 1916 Holywell Asylum*.

Did it mean her mother was a lunatic?

It was what Ailsa had said to her, years ago. Ailsa had been fed up, and made her cry: 'Your mum ain't coming, she's in the loony-bin.' 'She ain't, she ain't,' Violeta had screamed, and hit Ailsa with her fists; and Ailsa had been embarrassed almost, and stopped arguing.

She sat hunched over her darning, working fast, while Mrs Hopkins read them some daft story. The Caulkers said her mother had gone to heaven. 'Jesus has forgiven her,' they said.

She had lost her temper with Eddie; almost gone mad. What if I've got the madness from my mother?

She picked up another grey sock. It was darned already, but the heel had gone again, right next to the old darn. Was it bad enough to throw out? She'd have to ask. She put it aside, and took another one. 'The castle was tall and dark and said to be haunted,' Mrs Hopkins read.

Was what the Caulkers found wrong with her really madness?

Her mother was bad because she'd had Violeta. The Caulkers thought that. They didn't have children; probably they thought it was a sin even if you were married to sleep together. But everyone did it, that was what she'd learned, at school where the girls and boys all laughed at her, because she didn't know why Bessie Garner was fat in the face, and sluggish; and then Bessie had marched down Market Street proudly, pushing her pram. Though someone, she'd heard, had turned and spat at her.

I wonder if I could try and find my mother. At least then I'd know.

I wonder what she looks like. Why did I always think she had long black hair?

She waited till Mrs Hopkins paused for breath, then made an excuse and put down her darning. The paper where she'd copied out the certificate was still folded safely inside her prayer-book.

Narcisa Humphreys, formerly Gashi, of 102 Camberwell Road, SE.

She put the paper back and ran downstairs.

*

Dear Miss Humphreys
I have taken the liberty of opening your letter of 12th January. I regret that this reply will be disappointing to you. My former wife, to whom you addressed the letter, has not lived in this house for many years. I am therefore unable to provide you with information.
I do not know how much you have been told about the circumstances of your birth. Please believe in my sincerity when I suggest that you would be better served abandoning this plan. I am sure that those people who cared for you in your childhood, as your mother was unfortunately unable to do, deserve your continuing affection and respect.
You are clearly a person of intelligence, and I am sure you will lead a useful and fulfilling life, once you are able to give up this distressing search.
Believe me,
Yours sincerely
Edwin Humphreys

PS. My wife is at present expecting our second child. In view of her fragile health, I am sure you will understand when I ask you not to contact me any further.

The paper was white, and thick, with a wavy edge she thought at first was torn. The handwriting was very even and elegant, the signature almost as neat as the rest. He must, she thought, be a very calm person.

It was the most important letter she'd ever had. She folded it back into the envelope. Her hands torqued the paper a little, as if wanting to tear it up. But that was not right; she might need to look at it some time.

It had taken her three readings to understand it. *My wife is expecting:* she thought at first that he meant her mother. But that didn't make sense; he must have married again. So she's dead, she thought, and heard herself whimper. But if he knew she was dead, surely he'd say so.

Please believe in my sincerity. Why should I? *Damn,* she said under her breath, *damn and blast him.* Who was he to tell her to give up looking? And what did he know about the home, or the Caulkers? Another one telling her she should be grateful. When I get out of here, no-one is going to tell me what to do, ever again. But that was stupid; she would go into service. Well, apart from working. She sat on the bed and stared out of the window. The snow was thick all the way along the branches, and down on the square beds of the kitchen-garden. When I'm sixteen. Another year and a half here in the home. She slumped forward a little, over the letter.

He was very polite. *You are clearly a person of intelligence.* No-one had ever said anything like that to her. Was that how fathers wrote to their daughters? So there, she said in her mind to Miss Mortimer at the school. I am clearly a person of intelligence, only you didn't know it.

He's not my father. I'm illegitimate, then. But that was not a surprise; she'd always known. Only she'd hoped, writing to her mother: her mother and her father living together, a mistake his name wasn't on the birth certificate. 'Violeta!' they'd say. 'We've been trying so hard to find you!'

The snow had started slowly all over again, big floppy flakes idling towards the ground, the sky close and brownish like old bed-linen. No chance of getting the washing done today. And the shoe-mender hadn't come; the children's boots were letting in water. Better do them over again with dubbin. She stood up and went downstairs, yelling, 'Harry! Edward!'

1933

It was a tall house, sooty brick like all of the street and dark inside, with a narrow staircase and high-ceilinged rooms. In the drawing-room, which was the ground floor front, Mrs Willmore kept the old shutters half-closed: 'To keep it cool for our guests. Violet,' she said. None of the guests was in the drawing-room, though Violeta supposed they must come in, after breakfast perhaps, and sit and talk to each other in the gloom. Between the wings of the wooden shutters the net curtain was grey, with a mend near the top as if it had got caught.

'And this is the dining-room,' Mrs Willmore said, weaving out to the hall and in at the next door down. She was tall and seemed to sway, like a large tree. There were four square deal tables, tops ringed and scarred. 'It looks very nice when it's all laid, you'll see. With the damask.' She looked down sharply at Violeta. 'I hope they taught you how to lay a table. Well, never mind, I'll show you. I'm very particular about my tables.'

They went back to the hall and up the stairs. The oilcloth was dark red, and worn in places, so the backing showed, looking like rush matting.

There was the sound of a lavatory flushing, then a man came out of the back room, doing up his belt. He looked at them and hurried along the landing. 'Good morning, Mr McAllester,' Mrs Willmore called. 'This is young Violet, the new help.'

Mr McAllester turned reluctantly towards them. He was old, Violeta saw, with a fat discoloured moustache and a double chin. He looked briefly at her, and said to Mrs Willmore, 'Well, better luck this time, eh?' then laughed wheezily and went into his room.

'A very nice gentleman,' Mrs Willmore said. 'Travels in glass. Been coming here for years, faithful as anything. This is the bathroom,' she added, opening the door. There were gulping noises as the cistern filled. 'Now I'm sure I don't need to tell you, I want it spotless. Never mind how you find it. People judge a guest-house by the state of the bathroom, believe you me.' She peered down into the bowl at a yellowish smear.

It was ten o'clock before Violeta got to bed, by the time she'd cleared up after supper and done the stove, which seemed to have been left unscrubbed for a long time. 'I expect you'll want to get that done,' Mrs Willmore had said; and then, because Violeta had stood still, 'Oh for goodness' sake, girl, it needs cleaning.' So she had scoured it, piece by piece, boiling up more water when the tap ran cold, scraping off something black and hard around the burners. It was good to have something she knew how to do. Mrs Willmore wandered away while she was working, and someone, she supposed it was Mr Willmore, stood in the doorway and watched her for a while, and said, 'Great stuff, good girl,' when she looked up. At the end her hands smelled of Vim and were red and sore. She looked round for some lard to rub on them, the way Dot had taught her; but by then Mrs Willmore had come back in.

In her attic Violeta sat on the bed and looked around. A little rug at her feet, with faded flowers. The curtain was flowered too, blue and yellow. The bedspread was pink, one of those swirly patterns. There was a washbasin and the bed, and a narrow green-painted wardrobe in the corner. The room smelled slightly of someone else, cologne and sweaty clothes. The window looked out over the back gardens. In the dark she could see the shape of a tree, swaying, and windows, the glow of light through coloured curtains. One was on a level with hers, another attic. Maybe there's another girl in service there, she thought, and stood looking out, until the light went off.

She sat down and began to unlace her shoes. Now I'm grown-up. This is my first ever night being independent. Now I can do what I like, when I'm not working. She kicked off her shoes, then stood up again and opened the sash window. The air was still warm on her face and hands. A little breeze lifted a lock of her hair. A white cat leapt down from a shed roof and stalked the length of a garden wall. I could sleep with the window open if I wanted. But if Mrs Willmore found out, she might complain.

She felt a kind of lightness, something lifting through her like air into a balloon. This is it, this is what I've been waiting for. That was what she'd been doing, the three years back at the home, and even before, boarded out with the Caulkers: waiting to get out. The work was hard, but that was the least of it. You worked so that people would leave you alone. Out there, maybe in that other attic, there were girls like her; or rather not like her, girls who'd had normal homes and proper families, but girls she could make friends with and learn things from, whatever it was you learned if you'd lived like that. Clothes, for instance, and make-up, and going out. She wouldn't ever tell them about the home, or the rest of it either. She would make something up.

*

The post office was in a little corner shop, beyond the groceries. When it was her turn, she leaned forward and spoke under her breath: 'I want an account.' It sounded all wrong; she looked down at her hands, away from the woman with steel glasses behind the counter.

'An account, what? To put your wages in?'

She nodded.

The woman got down from her high stool, stretched, and went to a metal cupboard at the back. She was short and plump, and walked with a list to one side.

'Fill this in.' She pointed to an inkwell and pen at the end of the counter. 'Then bring it back to me. All right?'

Violeta hesitated, looking at the printed paper.

'Maybe she can't read and write, poor thing.' It was an old, toneless voice from the queue behind her. She spun round. An old man and two thin women were watching her. 'Course I - ' She made herself stop, and moved over to the inkwell.

The form wasn't so bad when she concentrated. The pen-nib was splayed and scratched on the heavy paper, but she managed to write clearly, without blots. Name: *Miss Violeta Humphreys*. Address: *Avalon:* but what was the number? *226 Clapham Road, London SW*. Date of birth: *9th July 1916*.

She waited, form in her hand, till the queue had been dealt with. 'You should have come back to me straight off,' the woman said; but she smiled, and read over the form, nodding. Then she lurched off to the green cupboard again, and came back with a little blue-covered booklet. 'Now you guard this with your life,' she said sternly. 'Is it a hotel you're working in?'

'Boarding-house.'

'Right. Well, I'd advise you, keep it out of the way, in the drawer with your smalls, maybe, and tuck it right at the back. You understand? Anyone who gets hold of this can get hold of your money. I know you think they're all nice respectable people, but you'd be surprised. Especially when you've got guests coming and going, you can't tell. You get me? Now, what's this? Violet A. Humphreys?'

'Violeta.' She spelled it. 'That's my name, Violeta. It's foreign.'

The woman copied it into the blue book. 'All right, Miss Violeta, and how much do you want to put in here?'

She reached in her pocket for her pay packet. 'All this.'

'Come one,' said a man who'd appeared behind her. 'What you got there, the crown jewels or something?'

'I'll be with you in a minute, Len,' the woman said. 'You just be patient while I help this young lady. Now, it's up to you, but don't you want to keep some spending money?'

She looked away, flushing, feeling caught out.

'You're going to need your bus fares, aren't you? Tell you what, how much have you got in there?'

'Nine and six.'

'Nine and six. Well, for this week, why don't you pay in eight bob, and keep one and six for yourself, and see how it goes?'

Violeta opened the brown envelope, and took out two threepenny bits and a shilling, then pushed the rest across the counter. The man behind her sighed loudly. The woman wrote *Eight shillings* in the book, and handed it over.

'It's these Poor Law girls,' she said when Violeta had gone. 'Makes me so angry, they send them out all gormless. Do you know what they're paying her? Nine and six a week.'

'Look at it this way,' the man called Len said. 'She won't hardly have got expensive tastes in there. Now come on, Mary, let me have some stamps, eh? Or do you want to keep me all day here chatting?'

*

It gleamed from the plug-hole of the washbasin.

Violeta had got as far as the end bedroom. The sheets as she peeled them off were still sticky. She folded the wet part in so as not to touch it. A hairgrip fell from the pillow onto the rug. *Dirty bugger,* she thought; what the other women said when a room let as single gave away its secrets. Tall, a bit tubby, the gentleman from this room, with a port-wine stain high up behind his ear. *Must have had to pay for it.* She felt grown-up thinking this, as she pushed the Bissell roughly under the bed, and into the corners.

Just across the corridor, in the bathroom, she didn't see the ring for some time. She stood the cork bathmat against the wall, and got down on her hands and knees to scrub the bath. It was what she hated most, the dirt from other people's bodies, mixed with the harsh green soap to a thick scum that she felt on her fingers before she started cleaning. Even back in the home it had made her feel sick. She held her breath and scoured, as hard as she could, plenty of Vim sprinkled along the tide-mark, the dry bleachy smell masking the rest. Expertly she ran a finger round the drain, picked up the dark matted hairs between two fingers and leaned across to dump them in the toilet.

When she stood, the gold was the brightest thing in the room, in the grey light through the net-curtained window. She plucked the ring from the basin hastily; she could have turned on the tap and swilled it down. Though perhaps it wouldn't have gone through the plug-hole grating.

She dabbed it with a towel, on the palm of her hand. A wedding-ring, quite wide, but small, a woman's. She bent forward to feel the flat surface against her lips. It was still cool from the basin, and very sleek. As she straightened, something glinted inside the circle.

Rita 10 Oct 1928.

The copperplate script, showing white on the reddish-gold, seemed extraordinarily fine and precious to her. There was also the second of disappointment, as though it could have been her own name in there, on the private surface right against the skin. *Don't be stupid,* she told herself, and then was shocked. How could this woman Rita be on the game, when her husband had had her name engraved in here?

Very carefully, Violeta tried the ring, on her right hand. For a moment she thought it would be too small; but no, it fitted. A few flakes of Vim were stuck to the knuckle above it. Her hand had become another kind of hand, the competent hand of a brisk grown woman, muttering *Dirty bugger* about the guests, and laughing that brief guttural laugh they had.

A door shut. Someone ran heavily down the stairs.

She took the ring off, delicately, and paused. Then she slipped it under her uniform, into her bra.

All day as she changed the sheets, dusted and scoured, the white cotton bra pressed the wedding-ring against the side of her small left breast. The metal was warmed by her flesh and settled, so that when she undressed at night she had a brand, a perfect circle, red on her fawn skin. Awkwardly, she stood before the mirror, and pulled the breast to one side to see the mark.

1934

When there was enough steam to warm the room, she took off her dressing-gown and nightie, and clambered in over the side of the bath. The Ascot grunted and throbbed above the taps. There was only just enough water to lie down in; it lapped over her hip-bones and left her stomach and breasts bobbing. She slid further down, her head pushed awkwardly forward, the bath-cap threatening to come off her heavy hair. The thing was to get as much warmth inside you, right through the flesh and deep into the bones, before the water started to cool down and sitting up to wash became a torture.

She stretched out her hand and looked at the wedding-ring. The steam had misted up the broad surface. The gold made her hand look pale, almost elegant. She rubbed at the callus on her index finger. If she buffed her nails…

The black-haired man had asked, 'You're not married, are you?' Brian. On the grass beside her, playing with her hand. Quiet, the little clearing on the Heath, brambles and some kind of undergrowth all around, cool air amazing on her exposed thighs. (She flapped more water over her breasts to warm them). Her sallow hand spread flat against his chest. His skin white like china.

'Course I'm not married. It's the wrong hand, anyway.'

Wanting to lean forward and kiss his chest, right in the centre where it was flat and lean; but she couldn't.

'What's the ring for, then?'

She brought it up into view. Surprised herself, touching the gold to her lips. 'It was my mum's. She gave it me.' Lying back, his arm under her neck. A branch dipping up and down above her. His hand stroking her arm over and over.

'How come? Had your dad left her, or something?'

Why did he want to spoilt it all with questions? 'It's too complicated.' A bird hovering, a thin rag of cloud behind it. She closed her eyes. 'She's dead now. I don't want to talk about it.' Pushing herself up and on top of him, biting his ear, daring her hand on his cock, till he held her hard.

She sat up and reached for the soap. The water sucked back around her shins. She must have left her flannel in her room. She soaped herself quickly, the lather cooling, chilling each piece of skin. Leaned forward to wash between her toes. The water clouded up and as usual she didn't want to lie down in it again. She splashed with her hands to get rid of the soap. Washing her fanny, she thought again of the man, Brian, in the summer on Hampstead Heath. When he'd finished he'd run his finger up and down between her legs, and found the place where he could make her gasp, till she couldn't stand it and pulled at his wrist to stop. 'What's the matter?' he sounded hurt. 'Don't you want to?'

She got out of the bath and wrapped the thin towel around her. The plug came out with a squelch and the water spiralled away, the soap-scum thinning out and disappearing. The towel wasn't big enough; she started with it like a cloak over her shoulders, then moved it down to tie across her breasts. There was still just enough warmth for standing around, till the water had all gone down and she could sprinkle Vim on the tide-mark and scour the enamel clean. The powder caked under her ring; it started to rub. She held her finger under the cold tap, till the Vim ran off, then rubbed hard with the towel to warm it up again.

Part 9

1947

Part 9 - 1947

The entrance hall needed some work, she noticed. A number of the black and white floor tiles were chipped; one was missing, replaced by a square of plywood. There was a long crack in the wall beside the door, beginning just below the picture rail, beside a dark print of a landscape painting; it ended, branching once, a yard off the floor. The transom above the left-hand window had suffered, the pattern of pale green and amber glass patched over with cardboard. And it's none too clean, she thought, looking around. The floor was smeared; there was a footprint over by the door, the heavy treads of a man's boot drawn in dark mud, and cobwebs in the far corner beneath the cornice.

She had come down early, in the yellow dress and jacket she'd made the summer before and hardly worn. It had suddenly seemed important to look good: to feel she was looking good, a middle-aged woman but smart, taking care. It must be months since she had thought like this. Even with Anthony: she remembered once getting changed and thinking: Oh, he can put up with it, as if her appearance were a punishment for him. The dress and jacket had been in the bottom of the chest of drawers, folded in paper. Fortunately they hadn't creased too much. She stroked down the skirt. It was a good colour.

Her hand was shaking. She looked at the clock: just gone half past one.

I can't wait here for half an hour, she thought. Anyway, it's not nice for Violeta. The high-backed chair was quite uncomfortable, and too tall; her toes just reached the ground. She stood and went over to the window. The tiles felt slightly sticky as she walked. It is Easter Day, she thought, someone will come. Dr Bosanquet might have visitors, or Dr Whitchurch. She dreaded the thought of having to answer questions. I'll wait out of doors.

She shook herself free and opened the heavy door. She had left the asylum, in spring it must have been, hotter than this, the sun suddenly striking the side of her face. But I have been back here eleven years, she thought.

She walked slowly down the drive to the main gate. The yellow roses - from the buds they seemed still to be yellow - were not yet out, the bushes neatly pruned, with small new dark-green leaves and a few buds. The white cat that lived in the maintenance sheds stalked across the gravel in front of her. At the flower-bed it turned to stare with light-blue eyes. 'Puss,' she called softly, and held out her hand. It looked intently for a minute, then went on at its deliberate pace towards the trees.

Then there was nothing for it but to wait. She stopped short of the lodge, not wanting to have to chat to the gate porter. There was nowhere to sit. She remembered from years back, when she'd first started, a decision to buy deckchairs for the use of the patients: invalids and the elderly, that was it, the chairs were strictly rationed. No doubt they would be lying unused still somewhere. She checked her watch. There was still plenty of time.

She found them in one of the potting sheds, a dozen deckchairs stacked against the wall, the striped canvas muted in the greenish light. The first one she opened had dark mould over the seat. She put it aside. The next seemed cleaner, and she dragged it outside.

Where shall I sit? she wondered, and looked round. She chose a place a few yards from the drive, halfway between the fence and the back of the chapel, where she thought people were unlikely to pass. The deckchair opened stiffly, with a creak. The wood was grey, the canvas striped blue and a dingy white.

She had another idea. Most of the other deckchairs were mildewed or broken; but finally she found one that seemed safe enough, and lugged it back to her place on the lawn. It was very public; would that matter to Violeta? She didn't want to be alone with her daughter in some closed room. They could sit here facing each other, turned away from the comings and goings, not interrupted but not isolated.

She sat in the blue and white chair, facing the gate, the sun warming her face, the sweat drying. The white cat circled back to her right, as if assessing, and then veered off. This is it, she thought. It's too late to run away. She lay back on the cradling canvas and kept watch.

*

She felt it like a lurch; as if all the parts of her that had been disturbed in the last months, overlapping, piled up like rubble on a bomb-site, had fallen into place again, but a new place, a new arrangement, and how was she going to live in this new body? She flexed her shoulders, standing already to face it.

A woman had emerged from beside the lodge, a young woman with dark bobbed hair, in a green coat. She was walking up the drive, quite hesitant, or perhaps her shoes were unsteady on the gravel. It was the coat, though, that Narcisa saw: apple-green, flaring out from the waist, probably new, the cloth a little shiny.

She moved quickly across the grass to intercept. She felt too light, the inside of her body empty as a balloon. At the same time there was something new, in the few seconds of watching unobserved: a kind of fear or compassion for her daughter, treading carefully up the drive in her cheap coat. If she had stopped it might have made her weep.

She reached the edge of the drive and paused a moment. The face was narrow, and taut with apprehension. Thick eyebrows, very dark, and deep-set eyes, with shadows on either side of the nose: a tired face. Wide mouth, unexpected, with crimson lipstick. A person; she could not have said what kind of person, only that she, Narcisa, would have to make it easier, would have to be kind, not least because she was older.

'You are Violeta?' She had no doubt, but still, she had to say it.

There was a closed expression, unfathomable, thinking. Then the young woman said: 'I'm sorry. Are you.. ?'

'Your mother.' Impossible that she had said it. 'But please,' she hurried on, 'my name is Narcisa. Of course, you know that.'

They stood facing each other in the drive. Violeta was almost the same height, an inch taller perhaps, and very slim. 'I didn't know how to say it.'

'Narcisa.' She pronounced it slowly, and waited, smiling. She thought Violeta would perhaps repeat it, but instead she nodded, as if hearing it again. Then she said, 'I didn't know how you said my name either. But you said Vee, didn't you, Vee-oleta. My uncle - he wasn't really an uncle, I was boarded with them - he said it like that.'

'Why, how did other people say it?'

She gave a little shrug, dismissing them. 'Vi, mostly. I've always been called Vi, or Violet if they had to. I thought it was like Violet with an a, till I was boarded out, and he said it.'

The voice was deep, with an accent like Clara's, but disconcertingly flat and inexpressive. Already there were too many things to ask. 'Come,' Narcisa said. 'I have found two chairs, very old but I think we are not too heavy. I thought it is better if we stay outside. Unless you are cold?'

They sat down. I should have brought out some cake, Narcisa thought. 'But you have come a long way. Would you like some tea? I can go in and make it, it will not take long.'

Violeta shook her head. 'No, I'm all right, thanks.' Of course, she wouldn't want to be left alone. There was a pause. Violeta, facing the buildings, was looking round, taking in the flower-beds and the chestnut trees, the water-tower, the half-hidden wards and residential blocks. After a while she said with a little laugh, 'It's quite nice, really, isn't it? I thought it would be, you know, grim.'

'Were you afraid?' But that was too abrupt; it would sound condescending.

'I was a bit nervous.' There was the laugh again, a chuckle that didn't expect to be overheard. 'I mean, what they tell you.' She glanced across at Narcisa and flushed slightly. 'But I reckoned, if you were working here, it couldn't be that bad, could it. And anyway..'

She wanted to meet me enough to make it worth it. Narcisa sat very still. Violeta was looking down at her hands, competent hands, callused like her own, the nails bitten.

Narcisa made herself speak. 'Can you tell me the reason why you tried to find me?'

'You're my mum, aren't you?' This was a different look, the dark eyes hooded.

So simple. Not for revenge, or vindication. 'I am sorry,' she said. 'I did not want to offend you. Of course, I can see: you want to find out who your mother is.' I mustn't spoil this, she thought, I must get this right. 'There is some special reason that you do it now?'

'I didn't know what to do before. I mean, how to find out where you lived.' She considered. 'I did try once. When I was about fifteen. I wrote to the address on my birth certificate. Camberwell.'

'You wrote to me there?'

'I got an answer, too. From Mr Humphreys.' Again the quick cautious assessing glance. 'He was very polite. But he said you hadn't lived there for a long time, and I should get on with my life.'

Edwin, she thought. Yes, that's what he would think. She breathed out slowly. 'It was very brave of you, when you were only fifteen.' She wanted to say: It must have been important, but couldn't, it was too boastful or too honest.

They sat silent. A blackbird flew down to the grass by Narcisa's feet, and pecked vigorously for a while with its yellow beak; then gave up and strutted away towards the flower-beds.

Violeta said, 'Can I ask you something?'

'I thought you would want to ask me many things.'

'How come you work here?' She corrected herself. 'I mean, I was really shocked when you wrote and said. I thought someone might tell me where you went when you left, or maybe' - she hesitated - 'maybe you'd still be in here. Well, you know, you do hear about people who've never got out. But working.. Did you just come out and get straight into a job here?'

She smiled. 'No, not as bad as that. But I have worked here a long time now, eleven, nearly twelve years.' She paused: yes, go on, tell her the story. 'I was working not far away, as a housekeeper, and suddenly I thought I can't do this any more, so I ran away.'

'You ran away? What, with a man or something?'

'Not with a man, no; all on my own. I went somewhere I had never been before, out in the country, and I stayed there for, I don't know, several weeks. Perhaps two months. I was very happy.' She looked up and found some kind of recognition, or amazement perhaps, on her daughter's face, the crimson mouth half-open. 'Then I thought, well I cannot stay the rest of my life in a room in a pub. Though now I think.. But I needed to do something, and I did not know who would employ me. Of course I could not get a reference. So I wrote to the asylum, and they took me on.

'And you,' she changed the focus, feeling awkward. 'I do not know anything about you. You are working?'

'I've always worked, since I was sixteen. Well, before that really. I used to be in service, in boarding-houses, I was a chambermaid. Maid-of-all-work, more like. Then when the war came, I got a job in a shop, a tobacconist's, right in the West End. And I'm still there.'

A shop assistant. Perhaps that was a good thing, independent? She could see her, that tense smile, behind a counter. 'You like it?'

'It's work. Yes, tell the truth, it's not bad. Better than cleaning up after people, I'll tell you.'

'And friends, you have friends there, where you work?' She wanted this, for there to be good people, women she would go out with, whatever they did, the cinema, dancing, friends she could confide in. Violeta in the deckchair opposite was so slight, her coat open on a thin gingham dress.

'Not at work. There's just me and the boss, Mr Van Wit he's called, he's Dutch. I'll tell you,' she said, in a rush of confiding, 'I'd rather work with a man than a woman, any day. Even the ones that get up to something, you can handle them.' She started to snigger and suppressed it quickly. 'But women, they don't make allowances. He's all right, Mr Van Wit, he's really old and he's ever so polite, it's Miss Humphreys, would you mind? We get on all right, him and me. He says I'm the first woman he's taken on, and I've convinced him.'

Narcisa sat back, wondering what to say. Violeta seemed to know so much - too much, she thought, and had to remind herself that the thin young woman with shadows under her eyes was thirty. And probably she was right about men and women. It was true, she expected hard work from her staff; perhaps a male cook would have been kinder to them.

'But friends?' she asked. 'You have friends, outside work?'

'Yes, of course.'

The question must have seemed strange, too personal. She apologised. 'I do not want to intrude. But you see, I want to know if you are happy.' She smiled sadly. 'Perhaps you will think it is too late.'

That was it, she had said it. She waited for the answer. I have no justification, she told herself. I could have tried to find her at any time: in Pimlico, at Miss Ainsworth and Miss Grey's, here even. It would have made my life difficult, that is all. The failure of courage was very clear to her. She rested her head back and closed her eyes. The afternoon sun was still warm on her eyelids.

But Violeta was speaking. 'To tell you the truth, the girls I used to know have all got married, the ones I worked with, I mean. I do go and visit. I'm godmother to one of the little boys, Duncan he's called. They live in Putney.'

'And you?' she asked gently. 'You have not got married?'

'Nobody's asked me.' Again the hoarse laugh. 'Actually that's not true, a boy did, years ago, but he was hopeless, I'd have gone mad. Well, you know what I mean.' She smiled, the wide red mouth suddenly sad. 'I don't think I'm cut out for married life. Maybe it's growing up in a home, and all that. Not that I tell them, but I reckon it shows.'

Narcisa was struggling to understand. 'You think it is because of where you grew up?'

'I keep forgetting, you don't know about it, do you?' She paused and watched two nurses on bicycles ride up the side path towards the cycle shed, laughing. 'You know, when I was little, I used to think you knew, and you'd come and get me.'

Narcisa felt tears brimming in her eyes. We could just sit here all afternoon and weep, the two of us, she thought. She made herself stay still. One tear ran down the side of her nose. As long as Violeta hadn't seen it.

'Please,' she said at last, when she could speak. 'Please tell me. I know only that they took you away from me, when you were six months old. They said it was to the workhouse.'

'They took me away? You didn't want them to?'

She shook her head.

Violeta sat for a moment. 'Well,' she said. 'It was the workhouse children's home, not the actual workhouse. I was there till I was eight. Then I was boarded out with these people, husband and wife, they were very religious. I told you, he was the one who knew about my name. That was till I was fourteen. Then it was back to the home. You know, the big girls, they get you looking after the little ones, it's supposed to teach you about housework and stuff like that, but it's cheap labour.' The voice was flat again, as if she were telling someone else's story.

Narcisa got up awkwardly from the deckchair. 'Come,' she said. 'I would like to go out of here. If you agree? To go for a walk, down the lane?'

'Well, if you like.' She stood up, obedient. 'Do we need to put these away somewhere?'

Child of an institution, Narcisa thought. 'It is fine,' she said. 'I will do it afterwards. Perhaps someone else will like to sit here.'

*

In the lane she wanted to take Violeta's arm. But there was something about the young woman, some awkwardness that made it feel a risk. Instead she pointed out the farm buildings, the milking-parlour and the smithy, the farmworkers' cottages. It was easier to talk about the asylum system, the self-sufficiency in vegetables and milk, the patients' labour that made it possible. At the same time, she felt she had interrupted.

At the junction she said, 'This road is a little rough - dry, I think, but perhaps not good for your shoes?'

'It doesn't matter.' But Narcisa could see they were city shoes, with two-inch heels, not suited for country walking. 'Can we go up there, up that hill?'

It was the way Narcisa had taken, the week before. When I walked out of chapel, she thought, surprised at herself. They went slowly, Violeta picking her way. At the top she seemed a little out of breath. They paused by the five-bar gate, where the mud had dried into deep wheel-track furrows.

Narcisa pushed the hair back from her face. 'Listen,' she said, having just then decided. 'I was a patient here, you know that. For five years. You were born after I tried to escape. I got out through the fence, close to that gate, and onto the lane. When they caught me I had walked along that way' - she pointed down at the road - 'as far as the railway station.' She stopped and looked intently at Violeta, needing to make the story clear to her. 'Your father, he was the man who helped me escape. His name was Francis; he was a gardener here. I cannot explain, how I came to know him; but he understood that I must get out. That was all. And because he was so good' - she could picture him now, his brown curly hair and open face - 'because he was kind, you see, and I, oh I was so excited to be out at last, I thought it would all be fine now I was not a patient - well, we made love together, in a field, under a tree.' She could see the field from here, but something kept her from pointing it out.

Violeta stepped over the ruts to lean on the gate. After a little while she said, 'Francis.' Then she turned back to face Narcisa. 'Do I look like him?'

Such longing, in the voice that she'd thought flat. She stepped forward and took the narrow face between her hands. Violeta was trembling. Narcisa looked steadily, till her daughter turned away. 'Your mouth,' she said in the end. 'He also had a wide mouth, I had forgotten. And perhaps your hair. Though my sister too had brown hair, not black like mine.' She let her hands drop.

'It was just once? Before they brought you back?'

She nodded. 'I do not even know his surname. I am sorry. Though perhaps now I can find from the registry, if you would like. Of course you would like to know, it is your father.'

They began to walk back down the hill, towards the asylum. A brown and white cow looked up from the grass, and watched them, chewing.

Well, I have said it, Narcisa thought. I can do nothing about what she thinks.

As they came down to the junction, Violeta asked, 'You weren't in love with him, then?'

'I am afraid not. It was a big scandal here, of course. For the first time they brought an interpreter. But I - well, I will not make excuses.'

'It's not that. I mean, people do, don't they? People

pretend it's only when you're married, but everyone knows it's not really like that. It's just' - she was searching for words, looking down at the ground, walking slowly - 'I suppose I sort of hoped you were in love.'

'Perhaps for that moment. But that is not what you mean, is it?' She wondered what might make it better. 'He took a big risk, helping me. He could have been fired. Perhaps he was; after I escaped, they would not let me out of doors, so I did not see him again, I do not know. But he was a kind man, very' - she looked for the right word - 'very warm. You should know that.'

They walked back in silence. At the gate Violeta said, 'I'd better go and get the train.'

They stood awkwardly, out of sight of the lodge. Narcisa felt shocked. But she will have had enough, she told herself. So much drama.

'You will come back and visit me again?'

That guarded look in the dark eyes again. 'If you want.'

It seemed there might have been another question; there was a pause, Violeta looking down. In the end she buttoned up her coat. 'Well, thank you.'

'I should say thank you. You have been very kind to me, considering.'

Puzzled.

'Never mind. I am glad that you came.' She leaned forward and took the young woman's head once again in her hands. The hair was soft and springy against her palms, and smelled of soap. She kissed the forehead. 'You see,' she said. 'I am a foreigner. That is how we say goodbye.' Not true; there would be tears and hugs, she thought.

She watched the slim figure walking away, beside the high fence, hands in the pockets of her new green coat, which swayed slightly.

Part 9 - 1947

The asylum was peaceful. From the top of the water-tower, ungainly amongst the spreading grey-brick buildings, a watcher, Colin Allen if he'd been there, leaning over to inspect the pointing, would have seen green: the chestnut and plane-trees shimmering in new leaf, the lawns as if perfected by months of snow. Beyond the fence, the Guernseys munched steadily in their field, pigs rooted in the mud of their narrow yard, potato-plants showed short and dark in rows. The chapel seemed squatter than ever, its barrel-roof pale in the bright sunlight. The doors were shut, the morning service over. Kitty Bosanquet had done her best with the piano, while the voices rose with some enthusiasm, as if the wild idea of resurrection, expounded with awkward zeal by the new chaplain, might after all have something to do with them. During the last hymn Dr Bosanquet had worried: religious devotion could be too stimulating, he'd seen it before in certain manic-depressives; but Kitty played some Mozart at the end, and the pews emptied out in the usual shuffling silence.

Every half-hour a trail of visitors came, remembering the way from the railway-station. If Colin had been on the tower he would have seen; but Colin had left his assistant Banks in charge, and was dozing in the sun in his daughter's garden, while her youngest decanted earth into his turn-ups. One or two or a family at a time, the relatives paused at the lodge, then walked rather jerkily up the drive, looking round at the roses - *Say what you like, they do keep it nice* - and wistfully at the sun on the shaved grass, before tackling the steps to the front door. The building absorbed them out of sight as they came; then there was a pause, the grounds all but empty, until the next train had arrived from London, and another scattering trudged along the lane, steeling themselves and practising what to say, before turning in at the gate to face the porter.

At two o'clock the shift of nurses changed. By ten to, those on lates had come back in, by bike or on foot, one or two of them lingering out of sight of the lodge, for kisses to print the languid morning on their flesh. A group of men hurried in, in cricket whites, the match disrupted by the working rota, with the score so close they were still arguing, laughing out loud and slapping each other's shoulder. Then after handover the early shift emerged, on gravel paths that met half-way down the drive, off-duty voices starting already to shout, and shushed again as they passed the visitors. One girl veered off from the group, seeing her boyfriend step up to the gates; another looked at her watch and began to run, her friends calling after her till she disappeared.

It was Easter Sunday and the sun was shining. From the top of the water-tower it was all sky, and open country on three sides of the grounds, with the town's last houses hidden behind the trees. The invisible watcher, a long-stay patient perhaps, whatever remained of his will pushing him up, out of the damp ward into a place alone, where the wind would ruffle his hair and chill his earlobes - the watcher had chosen the unimpeded view. He had missed the slow walking-party of patients, a double crocodile marshalled by two male nurses, heading out towards the closed pubs of the town. Or perhaps that had happened thirty years ago. The present patients, a thousand or more of them, were invisible so far this afternoon. Even the men who worked outside in the week, weeding paths or bringing in cattle or lifting greens; even they were confined by leisure to the wards, and sat too large in their chairs, with dangling hands. When visitors came, lifting cakes out of wicker baskets, the patients watched in thwarted expectation, the objects almost unknown as they came to light, the smell of a sponge cake, made from precious rations, vanilla and sugar and a hint of lemon, bewildering as a sudden burst of music. So the patients roused themselves to give back thanks, the least they could do, and looked round, hesitant, hoping a nurse would bustle up and issue orders - slice the cake, take it back - anything might have done to disturb the calm, the little circle of placating faces, and the terror of what accepting the gift might bring.

Then it was Easter Monday: Bank Holiday. In New Cross, Clara Wooldridge got out of bed without waking Stan, and stretched up to the ceiling. It wasn't often Stan got to lie in. She would bring him a cup of tea a bit later. She went downstairs barefoot in her dressing-gown. It was cold in the kitchen: the boiler must have gone out. She levered the round lid off and peered in, then raked down at the coals with the long poker. It had just burned low; it should take again. She lifted the tall grey hod and poured the anthracite in, with a sound like shingle.

When the kettle was on, she searched for her cigarettes, and stood at the back door, smoking, looking out at the garden. It was about time she sowed some lettuce. What with the winter going on so long, and floods they'd had in some parts, though not here, she hadn't been thinking much about the garden. Lettuce, and beans; and sprouts she might try this year.

She ground out her cigarette on the wall, and took the stub inside to throw on the boiler. Dennis and Rose, her elder son and his wife, were coming for lunch. He'd always liked liver; she was doing liver and bacon. And maybe she and Stan would go out first, for a walk, Telegraph Hill perhaps. It was a long time since they'd gone for a walk together.

She left the back door open to get the sun, and filled the kettle. Dennis might like to take them out for a drive. Or Stan; but Dennis reckoned his car was better.

She made up a tray, teapot, milk and sugar, and the best cups, two that she'd bought in the market on Lower Marsh. At the last minute she looked outside again. There was nothing in flower; she'd never been keen on flowers. She fetched the kitchen scissors and cut a branch of rosemary, and put it on the tray in a cracked glass. Daft, I am, she thought, going up the stairs.

*

Howard Rathfelders asked, 'Shall I take the monster off your hands?'

His sister was ironing sheets in the big light kitchen. 'I don't know why you don't get someone in to do that,' he grumbled, without conviction. 'For heaven's sake,' Lilian said, 'of course you know. Yes, take him out for a long walk or something. Anything. Susie can stay here with me and do colouring.'

He called his nephew, and began the lengthy preparation for going out. 'Hold still,' he said, buttoning Bobbie's coat awkwardly with his one hand. Bobbie wanted his red striped scarf and gloves. 'Let him,' Lilian said. 'If he's too hot he'll just get rid of them. Onto you, of course.'

Outside he felt the damp of the old house, Lilian's anxiety and his own depression, the children's restlessness, fall away from him. Along the street there were cherry-trees in flower. He reached up for a blossom and handed it to Bobbie in his push-chair. 'Flower,' said Bobbie, and crushed it against his face.

'Where shall we go?' Howard asked. 'Which would you rather, the gardens or the river?' He was feeling a hankering for the wide towpath, the cool air off the water and that light. But Bobbie would have to stay in the chair, or hold his hand. 'Palm-tree, palm-tree!' Bobbie cried out. It was his latest word, rehearsed by Howard.

It was awkward getting the push-chair through the gate. Kew Gardens, open to everyone with two hands. The man at the booth inside watched impassively, as Howard used his duff arm to push the turnstile, and lifted the pushchair, emptied of Bobbie, with his one hand. Bobbie ran forward onto the wide path. Howard cursed under his breath, but paid the tuppence entrance fee calmly, and caught up.

Flowers were coming out, and new leaves. He'd never learnt the names for plants and trees. He kept an eye as Bobbie explored borders, picking up stones and acorns and, once, a woodlouse. His mind drifted. Miss Carrington's choir had been singing the day before. He wondered now if she'd been trying to invite him. 'It's at Kew Church,' she'd said. 'The one on the green.' Did she know he lived in Kew? He couldn't remember. 'I hope it goes well,' he had said, and she had blushed, perhaps remembering too late he was Jewish. Though before the war that wouldn't have stopped him going.

It was good to have a long weekend for once. In three weeks Lilian's husband was due back. He supposed he'd have to look for other lodgings; they wouldn't want him around once Gibb was home. Ham Common might be all right; near enough to see them all, take Bobbie and Susie out every now and then; but less suburban. Perhaps after lunch he'd go and look around.

'Palm-tree!' said Bobbie, tugging at the pushchair. 'Quite right, old son,' Howard said, and pointed out the palm-house ahead of them. Bobbie ran on, small and round, the striped scarf beginning to slip off his neck, the gloves, Howard saw, possibly lost already, his fair hair flopping up and down as he went.

*

June came back from the toilets and got into bed again. She was queasy still; she wasn't sure she'd finished being sick. That was the worst of it, creeping down first thing, hoping no-one heard her. At least today she had the morning off. She pulled the bedclothes round her, shivering. Peg might come in and cheer her up. But Peg was on duty; she'd be down there already, they'd be clearing the breakfast things. She pushed aside the image of smeared plates, gagging.

She did want to see Donald, really she did. By ten o'clock, nine if she was lucky, her stomach would have calmed down and she'd be fine; and then she'd want to make the most of him, before he went off for his train, around teatime. He'd wanted to meet first thing and she'd said no. She couldn't bear to have him see her like this; and if he knew anything he wouldn't want to either. But it was more than that. He was so pleased, like she'd known he would be. It had never occurred to him that she wasn't too. 'Just wait till you're over the morning-sickness,' he said. He was just thinking about the wedding. He'd joked, 'Better be soon, before you're showing.'

And Peg: she was losing Peg already. On Friday night she'd schemed to introduce them, getting Donald to come at meet her at the White Hart, and dragging Peg down there for a drink. Donald had been put out but polite, and Peg had been awful, sulking like a baby. Even before that Peg had been getting strange, making excuses not to come to June's room, contriving to work with the patients instead of her. She wants me to ditch Donald and live with her. And bring up the baby, just the two of us. She imagined a cottage like the one in Penge, right near the station, where her cousin lived; Peg hanging out nappies on the line, while a plump little girl played around her feet, and she, June, watched them from the kitchen.

Was that what she wanted? Domestic life with Peg? She turned on her side, and laid one hot hand on her belly for comfort. How do I know? she asked peevishly, the way as a child she'd answered back to her mother. She should go home and let her mum go on at her. *You should have thought of that before you let him*, that's what her mum would say. Then after three or four days she'd sit there at breakfast, and pour the tea and say, 'I'll tell you what,' and there it would be, the best way out of it.

*

On Parliament Hill the kites were already up. They walked from South End Green, the two boys first, racing each other up the steep slope, turning to jeer at their parents for being slow. 'You watch it!' Mina called out and ran, and caught up with Michael close to the top. She stood with her arms around him, both looking up at a blue kite with a long tail, wheeling high above the railway line.

Anthony followed slowly. All weekend he'd been filled with love for Michael and Christopher, both leggier since they were last at home, graceful and funny and full of enthusiasms. At the same time there was something painful there, a slight awkwardness as though this were not their home, as though they were visiting an indulgent aunt and uncle. 'We should take them away from that place,' he'd said to Mina, in bed on Friday night. 'We should bring them home. They could be day boys at Westminster, or Highgate.' She had smiled at him, not thinking he could mean it.

Probably she was right, boarding was what they needed. He handed the folded kite to Christopher: 'Your go first.'

They found a place, on the slope facing the city. Michael took the kite and walked backwards away from his younger brother, who held the strings anxiously out in front of him. The first time the kite drifted up a few yards and fluttered down. Michael jeered. The second time they were all holding their breath, willing it up. It wobbled, hesitated. 'Pull, Chris!' Anthony said, standing close to him, and the boy pulled back, hard, and the kite lifted and went on lifting, up over their heads. 'Well done!' Mina called out, clapping her hands.

But why was he suddenly thinking about Narcisa? He had sworn not to while the boys were home. He had been getting obsessed with her, he knew that. And Mina knew, he was sure, though she'd said nothing. But here was this image, Narcisa with a kite, himself standing behind her to guide her hands, her black hair pressing back against his throat.

Ah, it's impossible, he thought. You start by having a pleasant little affair, and you really believe it won't harm your marriage. And then look what happens. Because she's a real person, with a life, a difficult life too in Narcisa's case, you get interested, you care about her, who wouldn't?

He was being less than honest with himself. The first time, in his room at the George, he had seen he wouldn't be casual about Narcisa. They had made love and then he'd got her to come again, her arms thrown back, gripping the wooden headboard. She had made some cry that sounded like despair, a gasping moan that he felt he'd forced from her, and he'd known, that moment, leaning on his elbow. She was strange and intense, for all that sturdiness, foreign in ways he didn't understand. Perhaps I was looking for difficulty, he thought, and blamed himself for not giving in to passion.

Christopher brought the kite down with Mina's help, reeling it in, while Michael danced on the spot, wanting his turn. It was all very well; but he couldn't take risks with the children. Christopher turned towards him. 'That was brilliant!' The first time this holiday the boy had looked so happy. 'Come on now, Titch, let's have it,' Michael called. Soon the yellow kite was up there again, floating in some impossibly pure space.

*

Her landlady's grandfather clock had just struck nine. Violeta, sitting hunched up on the bed, worked out again how long it would take to Hyde Park. Ten minutes' walk to the tube station, then two minutes a stop; how many was it? She should know by now, she'd been living here nearly a year. Turnpike Lane, Manor House, Finsbury Park, Arsenal; she counted on her fingers, but after Kings Cross she couldn't remember. Say half an hour: a bit more, thirty-five minutes, plus the ten to the station, that made it quarter to. But she still had to get ready; her blouse needed ironing.

Her friend Tilly would have given up by the time she got there. She tucked her feet under the coverlet for warmth. I'm ever so sorry, Till, I overslept: that's what she'd say, tomorrow when she saw her. It was stupid anyway, arranging to meet at ten o'clock on a Bank Holiday. Tilly would hang around and be cross for a bit, but then she'd go off, and probably meet someone by the Round Pond, some man no doubt, she was always meeting people and getting to know them.

I just don't feel like it, she told herself. She'd had breakfast as usual with the other lodgers, and come straight back, intending to go out; and instead she'd sat here for all this time, half an hour or more, in the corner on the bed, unable to make up her mind to do anything.

I ought to be really happy, she thought. But her mind wouldn't stay on the day before; it kept veering off; Mr Van Wit's arthritis, the bony bald head of the upstairs lodger. This is really important, Vi, she scolded. I was really stupid. I didn't ask her anything I meant to. And what on earth made me come away so soon? I could have gone back with her and had some tea.

On the train coming home she'd realised the problem; the picture she'd always had in her mind of her mother, a beautiful young woman with long black hair. Younger than she herself was now, even. And the woman who'd stood there, blocking her way, by the drive, was small and ordinary, going a bit grey. She hadn't even sounded that foreign.

Still, nobody's mother was really glamorous, not when you were thirty and they were old. Tilly had said: I don't know why you bother. But Tilly's mum was just a daft old woman, as far as Violeta could tell, embarrassing. It could have been worse; her mother might have been like Tilly's, drinking too much and always short of money. She could have disowned her.

I don't know what you're moaning about, she told herself. You can always ask her the rest another time.

She rubbed her forehead where her mother had kissed her - embarrassing, that had been, she could still feel it - and got off the bed. Her library book was on the floor by the armchair. She opened it where she'd turned down the corner, and sat for the rest of the morning in the bad light, the curtain still half-drawn, amazed, absorbed, as the heroine escaped from the mountain palace, and set off on a stolen white horse through the forest, galloping down to save her lost lover in the city beside the sea, before they could catch him.

I have no gold left, not even my wedding ring, wrenched off my hand one day in the locked ward, by a nurse who wore it not many weeks later, and laughed as the others gave their congratulations.

A man stands up to his thighs in running water, and swivels a shallow dish in both hands. It is patient work, of the kind they give to women, since we are supposed not to become impatient. The sun shines down on the crown of his leather hat, and on his hands which are wet and will quickly burn. A few specks of gold for forty minutes' standing; then he leans down and scoops up mud again, and swills the water over the dipping rim, so the dirt drifts out, leaving a few more grains.

Alluvial gold like this is the simpler kind. The man may fall ill with sunstroke, or with hunger; he may go mad, looking for specks of light in the mud of a half-dried river; but he needs only himself and his shallow pan, and a means of returning to some kind of a town, where another man will look disparagingly at the scraps, and pay him less than he knows he has earned for them.

The second way involves machines and other men's labour. Reef gold is hidden, inside lodes of quartz, which may be sparkling, or milky, or rose-pink, or green; or in slate, mica schist, granite, porphyry. To release the gold, the beautiful rock must be mined, then crushed in some kind of mechanical mortar. The fine rubble is mixed with mercury, to which the gold clings, and the amalgam poured over a blanket table, the heavy particles sticking amongst the hairs. The mercury then can be driven off as vapour. A muscular process, requiring all kinds of force. At the end there are still no more than tiny morsels, and thousands of morsels must be melted down before you have a bar of gold that can be traded. Someone is turning the handle of a machine, sweating. Someone loses his sight over the blanket tables. Mercury causes a terrible poisoning. The poorest men, who barely profit from it, spend their own force in this work of decimation, before a man can stand in a room with filigree-tongs, and distort the metal into a gift for a woman.

I can see a chain made of twisted links, held up in the cool light of a Balkan workshop; how the air around it glowed with the light off its facets; and I held out my arm and my father laid the chain sleek and light against my wrist for my wedding.

On Tuesday morning Narcisa was shivering, eyes dry and prickling, her nose blocked. Without energy, she went down to the kitchen and opened up. The staff seemed excited, chatting about the weekend; the patients eavesdropped, silent, with dull eyes.

When Narcisa had sneezed for the third time, turning away, handkerchief to her face, Rosaleen Shaw came up to her at the sink.

'Excuse me, Cook, but don't you think you ought to go off sick?'

Narcisa looked at her, half comprehending.

'I mean, I don't want to be rude, but it's not hygienic. You know when Peg had a cold, you made her go off.'

She was never ill, had forgotten how it was. 'Thank you,' she said, and felt the weakness rise from the soles of her feet, so she had to lean on the sink with both hands. 'You are right, I will go to bed.' Then, as the woman was clearly waiting for something, 'Please, take over today. I am very grateful.'

She slept for two or three hours then woke, coughing, and had to sit up again. It was cold in her room. The rest of the block was silent. Outside she could hear the lawn-mower.

After a while she got out of bed, and found an old shawl to

put round her shoulders. It seemed as if something had decided for her. She took out her writing things, the pad with the line-guide, envelopes, ink-bottle, dipping-pen, and cleared a space to work at the dressing-table.

Dear Dr Bosanquet

Was that right, or should it be Dear Sir? She remembered his fleshy hands on the blue letter. What did it matter?

This is to give you notice that I will leave my employment in one month, on 14th May.

She stopped to blow her nose. Was there anything else to say to him? She thought for a moment, then added:

Miss Shaw, the Assistant Cook, is very capable, and can take over if this is required.

She wrote *Yours sincerely*, and signed her name. What did people say when they gave notice? *It has been a pleasure:* but that wasn't true.

He would think it was because he'd found out about her past. He would be relieved: a problem taken away.

She wrote his name on the envelope and sealed it, then sat back. So simple: as if she had planned it all along. Perhaps I am feverish, she thought, but didn't believe it.

She was shivering; she stood up and ran the hot tap, and held her wrists in the warm flow one at a time. Then she took her handbag from the wardrobe, and found the card for the employment agency.

Dear Miss Flowers

With reference to our meeting - but she didn't know what the date had been - *recently, I would now like you to look for employment for me. I have given notice and will leave this address on 14th May.*

She will think I am foolish, without a job to go to.

I should like a non-residential position, in a school or something similar, not a private house. I prefer London but this is not essential.

Was that demanding too much? It was what she wanted. She could manage for a few weeks, if it came to that.

If there is nothing before I leave the hospital, I will find lodgings and will send you my address.

She sneezed again, twice, and went back to sit on the bed, the pillow propped up, the counterpane over her. It was very faded, the pink paisley blurred almost to cream, the cotton soft. She stroked it with something like affection.

Would she miss this place? People did, she supposed. She couldn't remember missing anywhere, not since she'd left Prizren and come to England. She thought of the evening at Victoria, the two cheerful male nurses and between them the haggard young man they were bringing back.

She pushed the covers aside and returned to her task.

My dear Clara

This is to tell you that I am leaving Holywell. You will say, At last!

She smiled, seeing her friend, in her red coat with the fur collar, at the kitchen table.

I will write to you when I have found lodgings, I hope in London.

Should she tell Clara about meeting Violeta? But it was too much to manage writing down.

I look forward very much to see you again. It was very good that you came before to see me.

For minutes she searched for Clara's address, suppressing panic. Finally she opened the leather box she kept her bank book in, and there it was, on a torn slip of paper.

Perhaps I will live near her, she thought, but doubted.

*

In the morning she got ready for work again. Her cold was retreating; the sneezing had stopped, and the constant shivering. Her nose was blocked; that was what had woken her. It was quarter to five but she got up anyway, and washed all over, quickly, at the basin. As she dressed she looked down at the three letters, a neat pile at the edge of the dressing-table. No, she had no doubts about what she'd written. Her head felt weighted, her body empty and clear, as though she'd been fasting.

She opened up the kitchen at half past five. In the pale-grey light the metal fryers and the white sinks gleamed. The spring-clean had paid off; the place looked neat and professional again. She checked the day's menu, pinned to the back of the door. Sausage and mash for lunch: straightforward. There was something Mrs Olby, the old cook, had called it, some odd English joke from the first war. *Two tired Zeppelins sitting on a cloud.* She wondered how many of these patients remembered.

She sat at the table to think about the day. There was June, presumably going ahead with the wedding. She must have seen her young man, over the weekend. And Peg, rejected Peg with the round shoulders. Would it be difficult for them to work together? They came to work in the kitchens, these young women; you taught them the routines, cooking and cleaning; but all the time their lives were continuing, they quarrelled with their parents or fell in love. She imagined June and Peg in bed together, giggling at first then reaching out a hand. And I knew nothing; I had no idea.

She stood up, and walked the length of the quiet kitchen. It smelled of scouring-powder and hot lard. Soon the staff would find out she was leaving. Probably she would have to announce it to them, call them together first thing in the morning. But not today, she thought, suddenly nervous. Not until Dr Bosanquet has had my notice.

There were the three letters that she'd written, on the desk in her office now, two waiting for stamps, the third for collection by the post-room man, for internal delivery halfway through the morning. There was a fourth she still wanted to write, to Alma; or rather that she'd wanted to write but been afraid. She thought back to the conversation with Anthony, amongst the sweetish smells of the fish-and-chips shop. He had said he didn't want her to go to Prizren. The hair had fallen across his forehead; he had leant across the table and kissed her.

Did it matter what he wanted? He seemed at this moment very kind but distant, as if she were already travelling home. No doubt she had been selfish towards him. But he's married, she protested to herself; he's not planning to leave his wife and children. She didn't even remember his wife's name. And she was no deceived mistress either. It was simply an affair between grown people, each with their separate life and their odd secrets. She had said nothing to him about Violeta; probably now she never would.

She looked at the clock: a quarter of an hour left till the staff came in. She leaned back against the shelf of a tall dresser, and looked at the young cook in the picture tiles, kneading improbable dough on a small table.

She would write to Alma. She thought of the old lady on the train, whose sister met her every week at Wimbledon station. Would Alma be an old lady by now? If I am fifty-five, she's sixty-two. She tried to picture her sister with white hair, plump and stately, no doubt a grandmother.

What can I tell her? she wondered, desolate. Her sister thought she had gone mad; if anything, if she ever thought of her now, it would be as that, a long-stay patient in a foreign asylum.

There was a sound out in the corridor. Narcisa went quickly back to the long table, and blew her nose, still blocked with the cold, and stood very upright as Rosaleen Shaw entered.

*

The day seemed filled with small acute perceptions: Betty Dunlop stalled in the middle of the kitchen, one hand on the dresser, looking down at the floor; Rosaleen Shaw lifting her broad plain face into a moment's sunlight from the window; Peg peeling potatoes and watching June. Perhaps it is because of my cold, Narcisa thought. Again the kitchen seemed noisy with people's lives.

She was busy today and competent. Among the glances there was one from June, that might have been finding some reassurance. At the same time, as if freeing her to work, the thought of Alma stayed with her all day long. And as if to please her, everything ran smoothly; water was boiled and poured safely into teapots, bread and butter piled itself high on plates, cabbage was drained and dished up without incident.

After lunch she went to her office to do the books. Hartley the butcher had given no more problems. No doubt, as soon as she left, Rosaleen Shaw and he would reach some black-market arrangement. Let them, she thought, as she filled in the week's order.

She was half-expecting to be called to Dr Bosanquet's office. Perhaps he is on leave today, she thought, relieved but equally wanting it to be over. Perhaps he has an emergency to deal with.

She added last week's accounts and wrote in the total. Behind her on the shelf was a row of ledgers, just like this, with flaking leather spines. Every week, since she took over from Mrs Olby, she had sat at this desk or at the kitchen table, and added the vast sums the asylum spent on cooking. And now no doubt she would do the same elsewhere: in the office of a school, or a gentlemen's club. And then I will close the ledger and go home.

The thought of leaving brought her back to Alma. She sat back in her chair and stretched her arms high over her head. *The point is that I don't know if I was mad. I don't know what to tell her. Once I was in here, yes; but not before.* It came to her, the smell of the bedroom in Camberwell, mothballs, that terrible dead smell, that her perfume never seemed to cover.

How strong the memory was, after all this time. But what had kept her there, a fit young woman, in bed day after day? She could see Edwin coming in from work, perplexed, withdrawing. His elegant mother with her disapproval.

Was I mad? she wondered. What had gone was how she had felt in those long days. Despairing, she supposed: but was it true?

She stood up from her desk and stood in the wide beam of pearly sunlight through her office window.

I had no-one to talk to. Only Edwin, in French, when he was at home. But being lonely isn't being mad.

This was the thing Violeta hadn't asked. Surely it was what she would want to know: *Why were you in the asylum in the first place?* Perhaps she was too embarrassed to say it. Though she'd asked other questions. Perhaps she took it for granted, if you were in the asylum you were mad. And it's true, Narcisa thought, standing still, leaning back lightly against the book-shelves, the heel of her hands resting on the wood. *I was mad some of the time while I was a patient.*

Then for some reason there was another picture, her handsome father leading her by the hand, down through the house and into the secret place, the workshop she'd never yet been allowed to enter. There were smells of sawdust and leather and machines.

At the door he turned to speak to Narcisa's aunt. 'She'll be safe with me. It may even distract her.'

She was sitting on the high stool, her heels only just reaching the top rung, the tears drying slowly, stiff, across her face. He looked over to see how she was, but explained nothing. His long fingers manipulated metal.

And I was distracted, he was right, she thought. It must have been after her mother's death. There was a word they had used to say how she'd been: inconsolable.

I don't know, she said in her mind to Violeta, to Alma. I don't know whether I was mad or not. Edwin didn't know what to do with me.

I should have gone home. I should have gone back to watch my father in his workshop. There were voices outside in the corridor. She rubbed her hands hard over her face. I was not a child, to distract with goldsmithing.

She put away the account books, and locked the office. Well, I have never known, she told herself. I have never been able to recall that time. I have managed so far, no doubt I will again.

Epilogue

1919

Epilogue

I was wearing a saxe-blue dress and a navy coat.

The clothes felt strange; I didn't know how my body might move in them. I walked and fabric flowed around my legs, in wide folds. The bodice seemed to pull my shoulders straight, to make me keep my arms close to my sides.

I dressed with a big group of the women watching. Two or three rubbed the cloth between their fingers; Bet from the ironing-room was looking scornful. They stood around me in their asylum dresses, washed-out blue cotton, soft with wear, with patches under the arms or at the hem; too tight over one woman's weighty breasts, too short on another and showing her white stockings. It was only being in my own clothing - a dress and underthings I'd been measured for, standing still with my arms stretched out, while a grey-haired woman touched me with a tape-measure - that I could see what had happened to all of them. They were subdued by the shapeless shared clothing, all of them, even the savage ones who shouted at nobody and soiled themselves. It was as if they had no bodies, or only lumps of flesh that could walk around and work. I took a few steps down the ward in my dress, and began to remember how it had been, to feel a kind of pulse that rose up through me and spread right to my fingers. Then I was frightened and quelled myself again.

The young attendant Clarkson came to escort me. She was trying not to grin at the special task. 'Humphreys,' she said. 'The gentleman has come to collect you.' Somebody made a deep throaty comment; the others sniggered and watched for me to react. Clarkson looked away, not to be seen to smile.

The old woman called Ann stood up slowly, and came towards me, leaning on the bedframes. She stood close in front of me; I could smell her rank hair, white and yellow like the moustache of a man who smokes. 'Good luck,' she said clearly, to be understood. Then she leaned closer; I saw that it gave her some pain. 'Tell them, don't forget, will you? Tell them.'

'Get a move on, Humphreys,' the attendant said. 'Can't keep the gentleman waiting, now, can we?'

I said goodbye to two or three of the women; Liza and Tris from the beds either side, the young girl Cissie who I had kept an eye on. Cissie started crying. 'Goodbye,' I said again, to all of them, and turned to follow Clarkson. 'Goodbye, Nora,' I heard somebody call. Then there were voices saying Goodbye, good luck, look after yourself, fading behind me as I left the ward. I wondered if it was kindness or only envy.

We walked down corridors I had never seen. Clarkson slowed down so as to chat to me. 'He's very young,' she said, 'the gentleman. Do you understand me, Humphreys? He's not bad-looking. Maybe you could - you know?'

She was used to my silences, and not deterred. 'What an adventure, eh?' she said. 'Aren't you excited? Time to have a normal life again. Your husband will be home tonight, I suppose?'

I stared. ' Well, I didn't know,' the attendant said. 'Well, never mind. You won't know yourself once you're out of here.'

She opened a door and we came to the entrance hall. The

floor was polished; a dark green carpet led to the front door. Beside the umbrella stand was a small black trunk. 'That's your things,' Clarkson said. 'You know, the rest of the clothes they got made for you: things like that. I'll just go and get him.'

She came back with a thick-set young man who looked nervous. 'Mrs Humphreys?' he asked, and held out his hand. His handshake was brief and firm, a man's touch, strange. 'My name is Noones; from your husband's solicitors.' He spoke carefully, watching to see if I understood. 'Where are your bags?' he asked. 'I'll have them put in the cab.'

'There's just the one trunk,' Clarkson said, and pointed. 'People don't have much in here. It's not a hotel.'

He opened the door and called. A burly man in heavy boots came in, looking down as if ashamed, and lifted the trunk on his shoulder. A bar of sunlight lay across the floor, and brightened the leaf-pattern in the carpet.

'Well, ta-ta, Humphreys,' the attendant said. I was astonished to see that she looked moved. 'Don't forget us.'

'I am ready. We go?' I said to Mr Noones. He opened the door and I walked on my own, across the porch with its pillars and down the two steps. The sun was suddenly hot on the side of my face. A grey horse stood in its traces before the cab, its nose in a hessian bag. The man in the brown boots held the cab door open.

Acknowledgments

The 'jeweller's skin' is the leather apron tacked to the goldsmith's bench to catch the leftover fragments of gold. This and other details of goldsmithing and gold mining emerged from the fairy-tale stacks of the London Library.

The idea for Narcisa's story came from research I did in 1996 in the London Metropolitan Archives for a history of Horton Hospital in Epsom; the book was published that year as *Asylum, Hospital, Haven* by Riverside Mental Health Trust. Ten years later, I went to the Family Records Centre (now, alas, closed) to follow up the story that obsessed me, and wrote it up in a piece for Iain Sinclair's *London, City of Disappearances* (London, Hamish Hamilton, 2006), called 'Stalking the Tiger'. The essay includes an extract from this novel. I have borrowed a few historical and topographical details from Horton, but otherwise Holywell and its staff and patients are entirely fictional.

I owe very many thanks for advice, support and encouragement to my tutor on the Sheffield Hallam MA in Writing, Lynne Alexander; to the inspiring, exasperating, late and much lamented Archie Markham, also at Hallam; to my fellow students Bryony Doran, Julia South, Emily Brett and Lily Dunn; to other friends who read and commented, Caroline Maldonado, Mimi Sanderson, Barbara Stow and Bill Allerton; to Hana Islami and Indira Kartallozi for reassurance about Narcisa's origins in Prizren and to everyone who lent or rented me a space to write in, put up with my agonisings and refused to accept my defeatism.

Ruth Valentine

Milton Keynes UK
Ingram Content Group UK Ltd.
UKHW020836250224
438379UK00015B/1654